W9-CAV-653

ALSO BY GARSON KANIN

PLAYS
Born Yesterday • The Smile of the World • The Rat Race
The Live Wire • Come On Strong

Musicals
Fledermaus • Do Re Mi

Adaptations
The Amazing Adele • The Good Soup • A Gift of Time
Dreyfus in Rehearsal

NOVELS
Blow Up a Storm • Where It's At • The Rat Race
A Thousand Summers • Do Re Mi • One Hell of an Actor

SHORT FICTION
Cast of Characters

FILMS
With Ruth Gordon
A Double Life • Adam's Rib • Pat and Mike • The Marrying Kind

In Collaboration
From This Day Forward • The More the Merrier • The True Glory

Original Stories
High Time • The Right Approach • The Girl Can't Help It

Original Screenplays
It Should Happen to You • Where It's At • Some Kind of a Nut

NONFICTION
Remembering Mr. Maugham • Felix Frankfurter: A Tribute
Tracy and Hepburn • Hollywood • It Takes a Long Time to Become Young

MOVIOLA

Garson Kanin

SIMON AND SCHUSTER

NEW YORK

Copyright © 1979 by TFT Corporation
All rights reserved
including the right of reproduction
in whole or in part in any form
Published by Simon and Schuster
A Division of Gulf & Western Corporation
Simon & Schuster Building
Rockefeller Center
1230 Avenue of the Americas
New York, New York 10020
Moviola® is a registered trademark of the Magnasync/Moviola Corporation.
Designed by Irving Perkins
Manufactured in the United States of America
Printed and bound by Fairfield Graphics, Inc.
1 2 3 4 5 6 7 8 9 10

Library of Congress Cataloging in Publication Data

Kanin, Garson, Date.
Moviola.

I. Title.
PZ3.K137Mo   [PS3521.A45]   813'.5'4   79-17631
ISBN 0-671-24822-7

To me, a Moviola—that's that machine we have in the movie business—is a wonderful thing—maybe the *most* wonderful. If you use it right, you can make time go backwards and forwards, faster or slower; you can stop time and stay on one second; you can cut out the parts you don't like, and the parts you *do* like you can have over and over. In some ways, it's even better than life. Even better than *my* life—you know I'm ninety goddam *two?*— and *my* life's been unbelievable, sensational, like some kind of a crazy miracle. I love pictures—moving pictures—and I always loved the picture people—even the ones I hated. My whole life practically I've been in the picture game—my whole life is like a picture—the only trouble is, I would never make it—you know why? Because they wouldn't believe it. That's why. That's why not. Nobody. And I'm ninety goddam *two!* You believe it? *I* don't!

B.J. FARBER

PART I

GOLD IN THE STREETS

I

My MISSION had been made clear to me by the terrifying Man in Charge as I sat in his office on the 101st floor of the World Trade Center in New York. He is a dark, stocky, muscular middle-aged man. One would guess quickly from his behavior that he is a supremely well organized and efficient creature. One would be right. He is Hareem Adani. Syrian? Saudi? Iranian? He does not say. He is president and controlling stockholder of Omni Universal, after Transamerica Corporation and Gulf & Western, the most affluent conglomerate in the United States.

Standing there, shoeless and in his shirtsleeves, he said, "So I want you go on out there and I want you to buy his goddam company for me. I need it. Unnerstan'? I want you go on out there and doncomeback till you got it sewed up. Unnerstan'?"

(He speaks English fluently—perhaps too fluently. He tends to make one word out of several: "Comeon*up*here"; "*make*adeal"; "squeezetheir*balls*"; "get*a*proxies." Ignorance? Convenience? In any case, it is necessary to listen to him carefully, deciphering. I wonder if he does it in the other nine languages he speaks.)

In the pause that followed, I said, automatically, "Yes, sir"—

11

and knew at once I had blundered. He stopped his nervous, caged-lionlike pacing, took a step toward me, pointed a finger as though it were a pistol, and asked, "How many times I told you don'ever say 'sir' to me?"

"Several."

"So, God damn it, why you keep it up?"

"Sorry."

"Don' be sorry. Just don' do it!"

"All right."

"Number one, I'm not so old, you're not so young. Number two, when I hear it—that 'sir' shit—I feel like I'm back in some army, and one feeling I don' like to feel, that's it."

"Sure."

"Guy makes your kind money around here don' make it for stupid . . . also I got no time for training pissheads—saps my strength. I tell you something one time—or anybody—that's enough, unnerstan'?"

"Yes," I said.

He lit a cigar with care and ceremony, expertise and respect. One gathered from the way he did it that he owned the plantation where the leaves had been grown, the factory where the cigar had been made, and the plane that had brought it into the United States. He began pacing again. When he spoke, I could scarcely believe my ears. He was repeating, virtually word for word, what he had told me the day before about his plans to take over Farber Films.

A speech formed itself in my mind: *Hey, you little Arab asshole—you're telling me exactly what you told me yesterday. A guy makes your kind of money around here don' make it for stupid!* I did *not* say it, but thinking it relieved my tension considerably.

One of the prerequisites required in working for Hareem Adani is built-in impassiveness. He bullies, insults, threatens, and terrorizes everyone in his vast army of underlings, who take it because it pays well.

I had been with him for five and a half years. Before that, Columbia University School of Journalism. I used to dream of covering China (Pulitzer Prize); Richard Harding Davis (fiction, too); analyzing and predicting the details of the presidential campaign so brilliantly for *The New York Times* that I became the president's press secretary; and then and then. . . . Instead, I got a job

12

as a copy editor on *Rolling Stone*, moved to editing, reviewed records—very well, I suppose—which led to a lucrative job with Fantasy Records (vice-president in charge of promotion). Then Adani acquired our company. That is his principal business—acquiring other people's businesses.

"This little bastard thinks he's Napoleon," my boss had said, then added, "and *I* think so, too!"

On his first visit to our office, Adani pointed that same imperious finger at me and said, "Come*see*me tomorrow ten and a quarter."

I did so and waited in his outer office until 3:20 P.M., watching him go out to lunch and return.

When, finally, I was ushered into his awesome office, he stayed on the phone for over ten minutes before he hung up, looked at me, remembered who I was, and said, "Siddown!"

"No, thank you."

"What?"

"I resign. In fact, I resigned an hour ago. Here it is in writing."

I walked over to his desk, the size of a Ping-Pong table, and tossed my letter onto it.

"What's a matter?" he asked.

"I don't want to work for you."

"Why not?"

"Because you told me to be here at ten fifteen. I arrived at ten. You finally received me at three twenty."

"I'm busy! Anyhow, you got paid your time so woddahell?"

"Goodbye, Mr. Adani."

I started for the door, about a city block away.

"Hold it!" I heard him shout.

I stopped, wondering if I should turn back. No need. He was beside me, laughing and leading me back into the room. Stopping at a sunken conference area, he bade me sit. He poured coffee for both of us.

"We talk, yes?" he asked.

"Go ahead."

"What do you make?"

"Thirty-seven five."

"Wrong," he said.

I bristled. "Look it up," I said.

"You make one twenty-five—"

"What?!"

"—per annum. Starting this morning. This morning ten fifteen."

I was, all at once, damp—and my bladder was bursting.

"Where's the men's room?" I asked.

"Use mine," he said, expansively, and pointed to a door behind me.

I went in and found a series of cubicles: a gym with exercise machines, a massage table, a sauna, a barbershop, a small pool and Jacuzzi. It took me three minutes to find a urinal. I felt drunk as I peed. Afterward, I dashed cold water onto my face and returned. He was on the phone again, but hung up as soon as he saw me.

I sat down. He poured more coffee.

"I don't get it," I said.

"Me," he said, "I'm a hunch player, y'know? How I am. *Always.* I like tough. Like you. Maybe because I'm tough myself is why. You got to be because we got a tough world here, unnerstan'?"

"Yes, sir."

"Don't call me 'sir,' " he snapped. *"Never!"*

"Right."

"What's hard to find is tough, like I need. Ass-kissers, yes-guys, servants—dime a dozen. See, how *I* see . . . not enough to be tough . . . got to be more tough—*tougher.*"

Thus was I hired. My duties, at first, were vague and undefined. Once, when I complained about this condition, he looked at me with those x-ray eyes of his and said, "Good people don' ask such questions. They make up their *own* jobs."

He was right. I now occupy a spot which might accurately be called Left-hand Man. His *Right*-hand Man is a woman, Reba Resnick, who is tougher than I am and, in fact, tougher than *he* is. She has made herself, in her fourteen years with him, absolutely indispensable by conducting his business and personal affairs in a superconfidential way, squirreling away Dictaphone belts, transcripts of monitored telephone conversations, documents and canceled checks and triple-entry bookkeeping. All that goes on in that ivory tower of his is treated as a matter of the highest security, like that superclassification we joked about in the Navy: BURN BEFORE READING.

I am no challenge to her and she knows it. The reason: She is the one person in the world who knows that for the past three years, I have been balling Mrs. Adani.

A little over two years ago, Reba invited me to lunch. La Grenouille. A corner table. We spoke French. Business gossip, office strategy, personnel shifts we agreed upon.

Over stingers, she said, "Six weeks ago, he told me to find out if there was anything doing between you and Youknow. He said he thought he noticed some funny business at the Yamani party. First at the table, then the way you were dancing with her." (I had found the evening oppressive and had tried to relieve it by getting stoned, idiotically and dangerously.) Reba went on. "So he asked me to check it out. So I did."

I reached over, took a cigarette from her diamond-studded gold case, and lit it.

"What're you doing?" she asked. "*You* don't smoke."

"No, I don't," I said.

"So what do you want me to do about it?"

"What do you *think?*"

"Fine," she said, and handed me a red-bordered memo. All memos were color-coded. Red meant highly confidential and personal.

It read: "HA from RR. Re requested information on GB/SA situation. Three-week check on all movements both, also phone taps and mail intercepts, reveals absolutely no foundation suspicion. Does show close relationship SA with Arden hairdresser— meetings, meals, daily phone—but he definitely and unquestionably gay. Will continue to spot-check, however."

Her job is safe. I have gone as far as I can go in this particular company.

I returned to the present just as Adani (I have never heard *anyone* call him Hareem—not even his wife) was finishing his strategy review.

"I don't think you gonna have too much trouble. Now I know you invited to stay with him for the weekend, right? That was prettygood how I set that up, huh?"

"Perfect."

"But if you gotnodeal by Monday morning—I mean, except maybe a few short strokes, I don't care—then move out, see, and take a bungalow Beverly Hills Hotel. Youseewhy?"

I did, but I said, "No, why?"

"God damn, you're dumb. I wonder if I'm right sending you. You could blow the whole thing. By the way, if you do—don' come back."

"Don't worry."

"Don't tell me don't worry! I worry all the time. That's why *you* work for *me!*"

"You bet." (What the hell did that mean?)

"You shouldn't have too much trouble with the old fart. Jesus, he's maybe over one *hundred!* And, y'know, he's like from another *time.* He thinks *currency's* worth something! And remember *he* owns it, the company. No stockholders, no board, no nothing. Family, sure . . . but his wife . . . under the thumb, and the sons and the daughter . . . some don't speak to him . . . or to each other . . . fight fight all the time . . . can't wait for him to croak and start to cut the pie, so our information is, he like to sell out and fuck 'em all! Also, his company's been going down the toilet these last few years. But if no deal by Monday—and you move out—it's a sign, you know?—*gesture.* But staying out there, see? He can think you in action with somebody else—maybe U.A., maybe Paramount. I'll make Gordie leak some bullshit."

"Right," I said. "I'm all set."

He handed me a Gucci briefcase made of a silky leather I had never seen before.

"This got everything inside. More about his company than he knows himself. I've had this guy Jack Heller, his secretary, on my payroll almost one year. He Xeroxed the balls out of Farber's files —so the ammunition all here. You like the briefcase?"

"Gorgeous."

"Reba bought it—she told me good joke with it. She says it's made of elephant's penis."

I laughed dutifully.

"Not yet!" he yelled in irritation. "Not *yet!*"

"Oh."

"She says it's made of elephant's penis. You rub it and it turns into a two-suiter!"

He laughed uproariously. I joined him as uproariously as I could. It seemed an ideal time to leave.

For the flight to Los Angeles (TWA Flight #1; 12 noon, arriving LAX 2:34 P.M.), the company had bought me both 2A and 2B to ensure not only privacy but security.

16

With the exception of half an hour out to eat only the main course of the meal, I spent the whole time studying the contents of the elephant's penis.

Jack Heller had done a remarkably thorough job. By the time we landed, there was precious little I did not know about Benjamin J. Farber and his staggeringly impressive life in the movie business, and about his three wives and four mistresses, four sons and one daughter and seven grandchildren and three great-grandchildren, the remarkable, secret Pempy in his life, and two bankruptcies and Farber Films, which I was about to steal from him for Hareem Adani.

II

WE LANDED twenty minutes early, and I was already standing beside the unsettlingly erotic stewardess when the signal to open was banged on the exit door. She pulled the heavy equipment into place and stood aside, ready for the ritual farewells.

" 'bye!"

" 'bye now."

"Thank you."

" 'bye now."

"Have a nice day."

" 'bye now."

" 'bye."

"Have a good day."

" 'bye!"

I could not help glancing at the nameplate pinned onto the outline of a breast to remember. Who knows? I might run into it —her—again one day. It read "Tertu Lundquist," and Groucho's joke flashed through my jet-lagged mind: "What do you call the *other* one?"

"Goodbye," she said, with an automatic smile. "Have a nice day."

"Sorry," I said. She would know what I meant. She had tried to start a conversation when she bent over to pull down my shades prior to the movie showing and I had not picked up my cue. How could I? I was not even halfway through the mass of material. As she moved across me, had she deliberately featured those superlative knockers? Or was I imagining it? No, my radar in that field is still in excellent working order. Moreover, I had noticed, when she took the dinner order, the "TWAIP" beside my name (TWA Important Person). We would meet again. I was sure of it.

As I stepped through the door, my briefcase and flight bag and topcoat were suddenly taken from me by a tall, thin, handsome blond man wearing a morning coat and striped grey trousers.

"Good afternoon, Mr. Barrere," he said. "Welcome to L.A."

He walked off, leading the way, and I panicked. What the hell was going on here? Why did he snatch my briefcase first?

I caught up with him and grabbed the briefcase so roughly that he stopped, regarding me with a worried look.

"I'll take this one," I said.

"You already *have*," he said rather haughtily. British. Who *was* he?

"I'm Mathews," he said, as if answering my unspoken question. "One of Mr. Farber's valets. Perhaps I should have mentioned that straightaway. I'll be looking after you, sir." (Did he say "One of . . ."?)

"Thank you," I said. Then, hefting the briefcase, added, "Full of money, that's all." A porter joke. Lame.

"You can trust me, sir."

I almost said, "Don't call me 'sir,' " but held it. I recalled an oft-repeated precept of Adani's: "Don't trust nobody who says 'Trust me.' "

Had the trip begun badly? It was nothing, of course. The tiniest contretemps. Still, I have a quirky way of considering omens: If the elevator fails to stop, it's going to be a bad day; if the pencil point breaks, don't send the memo; if she looks up once more, it's a score.

My misgivings were put to rest at once by a pink scarf being waved, and below it, a saucy lace pillbox hat which sat on glistening white white hair—not grey, *white*—which crowned one of the most utterly lovely faces I have ever seen. More than beautiful—great beauty alone can be and often is forbidding. Willa Farber's face is beautiful *plus*—appealing, warm, inviting, and deliciously humorous. Had I ever before known anyone with black eyes?

And what about the way they went with her white white hair? I knew her at once from my exhaustive dopesheet. I waved back, dripping charm. And there was Jack Heller, Farber's secretary, standing beside her; and Otto, the chauffeur. How come the sheet had omitted Mathews? Was he an addition for the occasion? A plant? Watch that briefcase!

"How *very* nice to meet you!"

Mrs. Farber's hand was smooth and cool.

"This is Mr. Heller, Mr. Farber's associate—and Otto."

Otto saluted, and I thought I heard the click of heels. Jack's handshake was friendly but limp.

"May I have your baggage checks, please?" he asked.

I handed them over. He and Mathews disappeared. Otto led the way as Mrs. Farber and I started for the escalator.

"I promise not to ask about your flight," she said, "if you stay off the beautiful California weather."

"Done and done."

Riding down, she studied me, frowned.

"What's the trouble?" I asked.

"Trouble?"

"You look disappointed."

She laughed musically.

"I *meant* to look surprised," she said. "My acting must be rustier than I think."

"And what, may I ask, surprised you?"

"Your youth," she replied. "You're so very young."

"For *what?*"

The laugh again. "Well, it's such an enormous transaction—at least it seems so to us. Perhaps for Omni Universal it's like buying a magazine at a newsstand."

"That's it exactly," I said. "I'm an office boy they send out to pick up the latest."

"Oh, hush!" she said. "I know I'm saying all the wrong things. It's because I'm flustered."

"You're not flustered," I said. "You're beautiful."

"I'm not beautiful," she said. "I'm seventy-three."

"I'm forty-two."

"Oh, well, in that case, you *are* old enough."

At the foot of the escalator, Otto waited with a TWA passenger agent and an electrical cart.

"How are you, Mrs. Farber?"

"Fine, Carol. This is Mr. Barrere."

Carol offered her hand. As I took it, it occurred to me that she could help me find Tertu if . . .

She and Otto on the front seat, Willa and I riding backward. I was already thinking of her as "Willa." Why not?

"You *will* forgive my gaffe, won't you? I was expecting a portly tycoon, or at least, an *assistant* tycoon. So I'm afraid my dinner tonight will be a great flop."

"Why?"

"Well, the guests are . . . well, not exactly what you . . . Fred Astaire, the Jimmy Stewarts, Claudette Colbert, the Pecks, the Fondas—grand people, all—but we'll probably seem like old chromos to you."

"You're not only beautiful," I said, "you're also *crazy!* Those are all *idols* you're talking about. Good God! Do they exist? I thought they were only shadows."

"You mean to say you do go back that far?"

"I go back to Willa Love," I said.

Her head snapped toward me so suddenly that I heard a delicate little crick. I looked at her. She blushed.

"Willa Love," I continued. "With Wallace Reid. Rudolph Valentino. John Barrymore. Antonio Moreno. *Mediterranean Madness*—I saw it ten times."

"You astonish me," she said, looking at the handbag on her lap. "That one was made in nineteen twenty-five, twenty years before you were born." (A math wiz, too, I noted.)

"I'm a movie buff," I said. "The silents, especially. Look for me at the museums; Eastman House, Rochester; wherever."

I was astonishing myself somewhat. Still, if you are lucky enough to be a born liar, it all comes easily. The fact is, I had never heard of her before that very morning, and as for silent films, if I ever had seen one, I had forgotten it. However, my duty at that moment was to build character with these suckers.

We were alone in the back of the limo. Jack and Mathews would follow, I gathered, in that Cadillac station wagon I had noticed with the Farber Films logo on its door.

"Do you mind this air-conditioning?" she asked. "Would you prefer fresh air?"

"Whatever," I said.

Fresh, she decided, and touched the switches, dropping both

20

back windows. Otto turned off the system, and a cool breeze swept through the car.

"Ben *had* planned to come out and meet you himself, of course," she said, "but his hearing aid went on the blink this morning and he had to go off to get it into shape for tonight. He said, 'I don't want to go through this whole night saying, "What?" "What?" "What?" Also, I want to hear the *picture!*' "

She performed a loving little imitation of her husband as she spoke, which was revealing.

"Picture?" I asked.

"The new Fellini," she said. "I do hope you haven't seen it. If you have . . . we have some others." In answer to my bemused look, she said, "Oh, yes. We run a picture every night. It's hard to believe—even for me—but Ben's been in this business for over seventy years, and still gets excited when the main title goes on . . . and cranky if for some reason—traveling or social—we can't see a film."

"Secret of his success, I suppose."

"Not really."

"Oh? What is?"

"I'm not supposed to tell you."

We laughed together.

"I'll tell you what I *would* rather see than Fellini."

"Yes?"

"Willa Love in *Zuleika Dobson*."

"Oh, go along with you!" she said.

"*That* sounds more like *Peg o' My Heart*," I said. I was going great guns. "You do have prints of those wonders, I hope."

"Only of the Farber pictures," she said. "Ben takes care of those things as though they were children."

"From what I hear, *better* than children."

The color of life on the back seat changed.

"Yes," she mused. "Isn't it sad that our family feuds are so horribly publicized?"

Had I broached this disagreeable subject too soon? I tried to brush it away.

"Well, it's a price paid for public life, I guess."

We were silent for a time. I studied the demented freeway traffic and thought, *How pleasant always to have a conveyance at one's disposal in this peripatetic life, and a jehu to drive it.*

"Not mine," she said.

21

"I beg your pardon?"

"Not *my* children. They're no part of the situation. Our daughter, Leonora, lives in Italy. We see her twice a year . . . she comes here with the kids—there are four—and I go there . . . alone, lately—Ben used to *love* Italy." She was speaking so softly now— almost to herself—that I had to lean toward her to hear. "My son teaches at Stanford. He's an art historian—the best, I think. Ernst. Named for Ernst Lubitsch, his godfather. He and Ben were partners for a time, you know."

"Yes."

"I seem to be talking a good deal—"

"For a *silent* star, yes," I said.

She gave my shoulder a mock blow and laughed. "We all need someone to tell it to, don't you think? That would explain psychoanalysts and the confessional and diaries, I suppose."

"Well, in your case there's a lot to tell."

"Oh, yes."

"And in Mr. Farber's—even more. . . . My God, he's the history of Hollywood."

"Part of it, let's say."

"I mean, in terms of, say, politics it would be like meeting one of the Founding Fathers. Jefferson, Franklin, Adams . . ."

She laughed and said, "He's not much like them, I assure you. And he's not as blabby as I am. I say any old thing. He's far more circumspect, careful. A man from New York—nice man named Sam Vaughan. Do you know him?"

"A publisher, isn't he? Doubleday?"

"Exactly. Well, he came out here twice last year to get Ben to allow him to do a biography. Ben was flattered at first—but then said no, and in no uncertain terms."

"Why?"

"I'll tell you, in his words. At the end of the last meeting, Ben said, 'Mr. Vaughan, let me put it plain. If you do a book like this, you have to tell the truth. Otherwise, it's no good.' 'Yes,' said Mr. Vaughan. 'Well,' said Ben, 'that's it. I don't want to tell the truth!' "

"I'm going to like him," I said.

"I'm sure of it."

We had reached the massive stone gates, driven through them and up the driveway toward the house. All at once, I was in Virginia, not California. The house was the largest Colonial ever.

22

"Here we are," she said.

At the house, I was amazed to see Jack and Mathews standing on the front steps, Mathews having changed to a beige alpaca jacket. Otto had driven over seventy all the way. How had they beat us there—having had to wait for the luggage and all that?

I asked Willa.

"Don't trouble your head about it," she said. "Just remember you're in Hollywood—the land of magic—where we specialize in the unbelievable. All sorts of mysterious things are going to happen to you in the course of the next few days."

III

IN THE splendid foyer, I thanked my hostess, kissed her hand, and followed Mathews up the grand circular staircase. He guided me through a glass-enclosed passage which led to a wing, separated from the main house, and finally into a guest suite. I gathered there were more than one—but there could hardly have been one more luxurious. A bedroom with an enormous bed; Contour chair and lamp; awninged, furnished terrace overlooking the gardens and pool; a sitting room; a small office; bath and dressing room the size of my New York apartment; and a tiny kitchenette. Flowers, fruit, newspapers, trade papers, magazines, six best-sellers, terry-cloth bathrobe—I was well and truly dazzled. I threw off my clothes, put on swimming trunks, and made my way down to the pool by the private staircase which led from the terrace. I dove in and swam furiously for half an hour, trying to release the stress I was already feeling. To my surprise, I succeeded. I went back upstairs and into the dressing room. The phone rang. I picked it up.

"Mr. Farber calling."

"Oh, sure."

"Welcome to California!" said a surprisingly well modulated voice. "You know why I couldn't be there to meet you, is that so?"

"Please," I said. "It doesn't matter. Mrs. Farber couldn't have been more kind."

"She's a fine girl," he said. "She likes you."

"Thank you. Wonderful being here."

"What do you think of this?" he asked. "Dinner is eight thirty; cocktails, seven forty-five. How's about you and me meet seven fifteen? For a chat—a little chat?"

(The first one sounded more like "shot," and I worried about beginning booze quite so early. When he repeated it, I realized what he meant.)

"Great," I said. "Perfect."

"I'll be in my study."

"I'll be there."

Naked, I wandered into the bedroom. The bed had been turned down. When? I looked at the digital clock on the bed table: 4:22. Now I understood. It had been turned down not for the night but for a nap. Why not? I got into bed and luxuriated for a minute between soft flowered sheets I had seen in that shop window on Fifty-seventh Street. Porthault's, that was it. He is ninety-two, I thought. Well, realistically, how much longer? When the inevitable occurs—why not? She is wonderfully attractive, and these days, they say . . . And even if not, it would be another kind of life—original, dramatic. Travel. Would I write? Could I? Or learn the movie business? I fell asleep. . . .

The phone rang insistently and awakened me. Where was I? No idea. Oh, yes.

I got the phone, and my voice was a husky croak as I said, "Yes?"

"What's doing?"

"Huh?"

"How's it going? God damn it!"

I was fully awake. The clock. 5:10. 8:10 in New York.

"So far so good."

"How is he? Friendly?"

"I haven't seen him yet."

"*What!!?*"

The blast pierced my ear.

"Take it easy, will you?"

"You been there three hours and—"

"Not quite."

"So what the hell you been doing?"

I got out of bed and stood up. "Well," I said, "I had a nice visit with *Mrs.* Farber—she used to be Willa Love, the silent movie

24

star; and I saw your friend, Jack Heller; and her chauffeur, Otto; and my valet, Mathews; Willa met the plane—wasn't that nice of her?—and I took a swim and a nap, and here we are."

"All right," he said. "Stop the shit. You know I got no sense-a-humor. What's been goin' on?"

"I'm meeting him at seven fifteen. Privately."

"O.K. Call me right after."

"I can't."

"What the hell you mean 'can't'? You bananas? I tell you *call* me!"

"I can't," I repeated firmly. "There's a dinner party. Black tie. Seven thirty. What do you want me to do—tell them I can't because I've got to give you the blow by blow?"

"All right, that's *enough!* You get out of there tomorrow first thing and back here. I'm comin' out there myself to handle. I see I made a mistake sending you."

"Fine. I'll tell him when I see him seven fifteen."

"No! Don't tell him nothin'. Say you got to leave suddenly. Then I'll come by surprise. Unnerstan'?"

"Yes, *sir,*" I said, and hung up.

I fumed around for a few minutes, went in and took a cold shower, came back and began to study the contents of the brief-case again.

The phone rang. I studied it and the problem before picking it up. When, finally, I did, it said, "How many times I told you don't call me 'sir'?"

"Hello?" I said.

"Hello! You get your ass back here!"

"Hello?"

"Tomorrow. I take over!"

"Hello?"

"Hello! You hear me?"

"Hello?" I shouted.

"God damn son-of-a-bitch!" he yelled, his voice breaking just before he hung up.

I picked up a luscious McIntosh apple, bit into it, and continued to bone up on the details of the deal.

IV

7:12. I look at myself in the full-length mirror, trying without success to find a flaw. I am resplendent in my new Brioni dinner jacket and Bill Blass accessories. I look like a man who is going far.

A knock at the door.

"Come!"

Mathews. "May I show you to Mr. Farber's study, sir?"

"Will you? Thank you."

I notice that he eyes the suddenly important briefcase as I pick it up. I mean to take it with me. Yes, there is a safe in the dressing room, but how can I be certain there is not another key to it in the hands of the management? Is that why I was asked to be a houseguest in the first place? For now, it stays with me. It will look peculiar. Let it.

I follow Mathews through what seems an endless maze of corridors and staircases, all beautifully, extravagantly appointed. The whole trip is made in mysterious soundlessness, since the piling of the carpeting is lawnlike. The circumstances make it seem like a silent movie in progress. I can almost hear a single piano trying to follow the action. Why do I feel I am on my way to my fate? We stop, finally, at a beautiful oak door, so highly polished that I can see my mirrored reflection over Mathews' back. I look marvelous, successful.

Mathews knocks twice, softly, opens the door and stands aside. I walk in, the door closes behind me, and there he is. B.J. Farber. The first surprise is his height. He is small, a head shorter than I am. Why did I expect to find a tall man? I am next aware of his smile—wide, true, perfect teeth. His impeccable dress makes me feel a sudden slob. He comes toward me, hand outstretched, and says, "Thank you for coming. I'm so glad you are here."

His handshake is overpowering. It takes my hand a minute to recover. Can it be? Can this smiling, perfectly postured powerhouse—without a wrinkle on his face—be ninety-two years of age? Is there a mistake somewhere?

"Mr. Farber," I say, "this is a great honor."

He regards me as though measuring my sincerity.

"No," he says. "No, it ain't. But I'll tell you—I'm glad you think so. I like young people to like me. The old ones? What the hell—they *got* to!"

He laughs—a characteristic two-note small explosion: Ha *ha!* The fourth or fifth time I hear it, I realize it spans an octave:

His speech is not as accented as I had thought it might be. It is, in fact, good except for a carelessness about dental *d*'s and *t*'s and glottal stops: givin*gup,* and Lon*gisland.* Somehow, the flaws lend charm to his expression.

"Let me get you a drink," he says, as he moves to a Chippendale cabinet. He touches a button, the cabinet opens to reveal a glittering, well-stocked small bar. "What's your pleasure?"

"I'll have whatever *you* have." (An old trick of ingratiation, taught to me by Mike Todd, one of the greatest operators of them all.)

"Oh?" says B.J. "I'm sorry to hear it."

"Why?"

"Because I drink the most expensive scotch on the market. Glenlivet."

I take a notebook from my pocket and make certain that he sees me enter Glenlivet, which I have been drinking for at least ten years.

He pours two drinks in the manner of an ancient religious ritual. Baccarat glasses, frosted bottles of Perrier, no ice.

As he performs, he says: "In here, I take care of myself—always —and my guests. No maids, no butlers. I'll tell you something funny. Long time ago—when my mother was still alive—she came out here to stay with me. And she had a whole wing, with a day maid and a night maid and a personal maid. Her own driver. Everything. But she used to go down to the kitchen four thirty, five in the morning and make her breakfast, and sometimes it caused a little trouble in the kitchen, and one time she was very unhappy, and I asked her what's the matter, and she said [here he affected an overcareful English speech]: 'Oh, Benny—I hope some day you'll be so rich you won't have to have any servants whatsoever!' Ha *ha!*"

He brought the drinks over, handed me one, raised his glass

and was all at once solemn as he said, "Let us drink to the conclusion of a transaction that no one will later regret!"

We touched rims and drank.

"Sit! Sit!" he said, motioning me to a large armchair. I did so. He took his place in a similar chair opposite me.

"Don't mind me how I drink slow. Whenever you want, help yourself."

"Oh, no. This'll be fine."

"I drink slow, because this is it. My one drink of the day. I used to drink a lot. Not too much—just a *lot*. I liked it. Now my doctor, a *good* doctor . . . you know how I know? He's got six patients in their nineties—five except me—and two over a hundred. Write down his name in your book—Doctor Hyman Engelberg—of course, by the time *you* need him, he'll be over a hundred *himself!* Ha *ha!*"

I wrote down the name, saying, "I may need him a lot sooner."

"Why, you're sick?"

"No, but not as well as I'd like to be."

"What's your sickness?" he asked. "Working for Hareem Adani?"

I looked up and found a new face: probing, suspicious, no longer smiling.

"God, no!" I said, going for an Oscar. "Mr. Adani is the finest man I've ever met and one of the most brilliant. And generous."

"Is that so? I understand he's a prick."

He sipped his drink slowly, relishing the flavor.

"All great men have their detractors," I said, then, taking the plunge, added, "I've heard a good many uncomplimentary things about *you.*"

"All true," he said. "All true. . . . One damn drink! And almost gone." He studied his glass. "Hy says, when it gets down there, don't think, It's half empty already; think, It's still half full. A regular philosopher. One drink and one cigarette—*that* I have after dinner with my coffee. She calls it coffee, my wife. It's some kind of decaffeinated dishwater. I drink it. I make out she's fooling me. Why not? She's doing it for me. If not for her, would I be here? No. She keeps me alive. She's kept me alive a long time—maybe too long."

"Don't say that. Look at Adolph Zukor."

"*You* look at him. I can't stand him. We didn't speak forty years.

But I went to his funeral all the same. A man lives to a hundred and two—that's something to respect. That one cigarette. It makes everybody mad. I don't know why. They think I'm crazy. Not true. I've done crazy things in my life, but I'm not crazy, or if I am, it's like—you remember Bert Williams? How he sang 'I May Be Crazy but I Ain't No Fool'—no, you're too young. Bert Williams. I wanted to put him in a picture. My partners raised the roof. At that time, no coloreds in the movies—in *Birth of a Nation,* even. Griffith had white actors black up to play the coloreds. Imagine it. How can people say we haven't come a long way? Have another drink. I see you're empty."

"No, no. This is fine."

"Go ahead. I like to watch you have it."

"All right," I said, "if you insist." I got up, went to the bar and poured a second drink, imitating his routine. As I did so, I spoke.

"You're misinformed about Mr. Adani," I said. "I don't deny he's sometimes tough in business—but it's a tough world. He's strong, sure, but he's honest and trustworthy—and all of us who work with him respect him."

Farber said, "I had a writer at the studio one time—charming fellow, fine artist, but a gambler. I think it ruined him—Bill Saroyan—but I liked him. So original and funny. And one time he was here at the house . . . we had a party. And a bunch of them were here—the Goldwyns, and the Schencks, and Mayer—and it was a time when all kinds of mergers were in the air and everybody was figuring to screw everybody else, and after dinner, Willa arranged a little entertainment—it was fine. Heifetz played and Gershwin and then Saroyan got up and he sang a song he'd made up—the name of it was 'All I Want Is All There Is and Then Some'—and they were all embarrassed, those fellows—not me— I laughed. I never wanted to be big or bigger—I only wanted to be good. Adani wants big *and* bigger. I think he wants all there is and then some—like in the song."

It was time to go to the mat with this guy.

"I'm afraid you don't understand the theory of the conglomerate or of diversification. There's a perfectly sound reason for Transamerica, for Gulf and Western."

"Sure, sure," he said. Did I detect uncertainty? Pile it on.

"The tax structure impels it. Mr. Adani feels a deep responsibility to his stockholders."

"*I got* no stockholders."

"Of course, Mr. Farber, that's what puts you into such an enviable position and that's what makes your company such a rarity."

"What's his offer?" he asked, too suddenly.

"Can we wait until tomorrow?"

"What's in that fancy briefcase?" he asked.

Christ, I'd forgotten all about it!

"Briefcase?" I muttered.

"Money, I hope. And plenty *of* it."

"Mr. Adani," I said, "is prepared—"

A knock at the door. A butler.

"Your guests are arriving, sir."

"Thank you, Chapman." To me: "Ready?"

"Yes, sir."

"All right, let's go. Did she tell you who's coming? She got a nice group for you. Even Doug and Mary, and they don't go out so much these days."

"Who?" I asked, startled.

He looked at me evenly and said, "Douglas Fairbanks and Mary Pickford. Don't tell me you never heard of *them!*"

"Of course I have."

"But you never *met* them."

"No, sir."

"Well, tonight you will. Come on."

On the way to the reception room, I was in a state of wild confusion. A joke? No. I had already come to know when he was being playful. A lapse? Would it happen again? Was it something I could discuss with Willa? Should I? I was distracted as we walked by the Picassos, Bonnards, a huge Manet, and one hall filled with Monet's lily paintings; a Toulouse-Lautrec, and a staggering Cézanne.

Willa's voice: "Fred—this is our friend, Guy Barrere. Fred Astaire."

"Hello!"

"How do you do?"

"Just arrived, Willa tells me."

"Yes, and it's—"

"Here's *your* partner," said Willa, presenting me with a creature who clearly made her home in the pages of *Vogue*. "She looks like an actress, doesn't she? Well, *surprise!* She's not. Guy Barrere, Melanie Hull. She's your fellow houseguest."

30

We were alone.

"Some fellow," I said.

"Willa says you're a financial wizard."

"Of other people's finances, yes, My own are in disarray."

"Still, I wonder if—"

"Claudette Colbert, Guy Barrere," said Willa, and left.

"French?" she asked. "It's a French name."

"Only on my mother and father's side. I'm afraid I was born in Ashtabula, Ohio."

"What's wrong with that?"

"Nothing, but I wish I could say Aix-en-Provence or Verona or somewhere glamorous."

"Out here," said a familiar low voice, speaking in slow cadence, "we think Ashtabula sounds pretty glamorous. Hi. I'm Jimmy Stewart."

"You certainly are," I said.

"You're with Hareem Adani, aren't you?"

"I am."

"We met him in Africa a couple of years ago. Hell of a nice fellow. And a wizard of a shot, too."

That news failed to thrill me.

Willa again, this time with another beauty—a willowy, extremely young creature whose eyeglasses somehow accentuated her loveliness.

"This is Ben's great-granddaughter," she said. "Beth Farber."

"Great is right," I said, taking her hand. "What do you do in the world, Beth—other than upset men?"

"I'm an agent."

"A *what?*"

"Yes. With my uncle's company. Our family's not religious, but we *do* believe in nepotism." She retrieved her hand.

The dinner itself had the shape of a dream. I sat on Willa's right. On my right, Mrs. Henry Fonda, who laughed a lot. Melanie sat directly opposite me, between Stewart and Fonda, and we exchanged eyes for an hour. The food was superb: a delicate cream of cucumber soup; tiny individual lobster soufflés; roast chicken with stuffing and gravy and mashed potatoes; a tray of nine fresh vegetables; salad, and a perfect Brie; crème brulée. White wine, red wine, Crystal champagne. I drank too much, but not enough; not enough, that is, to calm me down. I felt as though

31

I might never sleep again. Coffee and brandy were served in a room I had not yet seen. Afterward, I found Melanie on my arm as we trooped into still another exquisite casual room and sat in large soft armchairs—some single, some double—set in three rows, the last two raised. On long tables in front of the seats—mineral waters (Vichy, Perrier, Apollinaris); whiskey; brandy; cigarettes, cigars, candies, and mints. And bowls of popcorn. Was this life, I wondered—or nonsense? Melanie led me to one of the doubles. She kicked off her shoes and sat comfortably on her feet. She seemed at home and at ease.

Music. The lights dim to black. A whirr. In the darkness, a screen is lowered through the ceiling at the other end of the room. The picture begins. My dopesheet had told me that even though it is common practice to talk aloud during screenings on the so-called Bel-Air Circuit—to make jokes or cracks or answer questions on the screen—it was definitely *not* done at the Farbers'. B.J. did not permit it, and anyone who violated this rule not only was asked to leave but was probably not invited again. Melanie reached over and took my hand. As time went by, her hand became a sexual organ.

The half of my mind that was on the movie could discern it was a superior work, but the other half was on top, worrying about my fuzzy head, about Willa and her part in all this, and about what was with this number coming on at my side? Was she part of the deal? Or more, or less? God knows, we had often provided women for some of our more important visitors to New York, but the *Farbers*? It seemed unlikely—and yet . . .

My attention was taken suddenly by a shot of a naked woman sliding out of a bed.

B.J.'s voice: "Stop the picture, please, Shorty!"

The picture disappeared from the screen as the sound growled to a stop. B.J.'s voice: "Roll it back, Shorty." The lights came on. B.J. was standing in front of the screen, pale.

"Listen, my friends. Some of you know how for a long time I didn't allow such pictures, dirty pictures, on this screen in my house. But lately, there's so many—and Mrs. Farber says it's rude to ask people and then shut off the picture. So who wants, stay and enjoy yourself. And who not, you don't have to. Tell him start, Willa."

He stalked out of the room.

Willa touched a button and said, "Go ahead, Shorty." The lights dimmed more swiftly than before and the picture came on, repeating a minute we had already seen. I watched to see if anyone would leave. No one did. Good. I would. I disengaged my hand from Melanie's, leaned over, kissed her lightly, and said, "Excuse me."

"Come back," she whispered.

"Sure."

I found B.J. in the sitting room, playing solitaire. He looked up, surprised to see me.

"You don't like bare ass?" he asked. "What's the madder with you? Tits neither?"

"Not on the screen, especially," I said.

"Play gin?" he asked.

"I'd rather take a walk. Is that possible?"

He jumped up so fast and hard that he upended his chair. I made to pick it up.

"Leave it, leave it," he said. "We got people here pick things up. Let's go."

I followed him out through the French doors, across a wide terrace, down stone steps and into the spacious gardens.

"This way," he said, and led me onto one of the paths. "I never hardly meet a walker. Not out here. They don't believe in it. Running, yes. Everybody runs. I don't understand it. What are they running from? Where to? It's like they feel they're getting away from something or running *to* something. What's better than walking? I walk."

"So do I, whenever I can."

We went on in silence for a time, my instinct telling me to be still. Let him introduce a subject. He said nothing, but from time to time, pointed out something.

The gardens were beautiful, not overtended as so many out here are. These had the semblance of nature. I mentioned it.

"My son, Ernst," he said, "he's responsible. He has a beautyful eye, loves nature. This whole place is mostly his."

"Your eldest?" I asked.

"Youngest. The eldest I haven't spoken twenty years. He's a son-of-a-bitch—just like me."

"I don't believe that, Mr. Farber. You have a fine reputation."

"A lot *they* know!" he said. "I've done plenty bad things—but God damn it, never to my own father."

"I don't understand."

"Here. You want to hear the story of my life, you bedder sit down."

We moved into a stately little teahouse which stood near the end of the massive swimming pool. He sat into a large wicker chair, so did I. I could not help but think that this was a perfect atmosphere for confidence. The warm summer evening with just enough life in the air to remove the oppressiveness; a perfect star-filled sky; from afar, the sound of the film being run in the house—the sound waves carrying only the music, it seemed; crickets; frogs—both of us full of food, and I with drink, as well; two men in contact. I waited.

"That's it," he said. "That's why I'm so troubled right now. Why I can't make up my mind to sell out or not. You see?"

"No, I don't."

"My life we were saying, wasn't it? The story of my life. If I sell—the one who buys, buys what? A studio, equipment, the vaults with my pictures, two thousand three hundred and forty-four properties never made, goodwill, some personnel contracts (not so many anymore) and a backlot and a ranch. That's what they buy—but that's not what *I sell*."

"It isn't?"

"No! What I sell is my *life*—and it's the only life I'm ever going to have!" He had made himself angry. "What does a man dream? To leave something behind, a going concern. If I knew the right one, I would rather *give* it than sell it. Then I could feel I made something in life—something *permanent*. When you come—to-morrow—to the studio, I'll show you something. All up and down all the streets, you'll see little pieces of gold—right in the concrete or asphalt—coins, nuggets, bricks—all kinds. At first, it used to be real gold—I swear to you—then some got robbed, so now it's all from the prop department; they take care of the fake gold and keep it shiny and good. You know why it's there?"

"I've heard, but I'd like to hear it from you."

"All right. In nineteen hundred and oh one, I came here to America. My mother, my father, me, that's all. Two small sisters died already—an epidemic—typhoid. So we came, the three. Everybody will tell you . . . I've read a thousand times how terrible

34

it was there in steerage . . . how dirty and smelled and sickness and terrible. Could be, but not on the S.S. *Pennland*—not how I remember it. The people were optimistic. After all, they were going away from the bad and towards the good. The expression I heard the most—in Russian and Polish and Yiddish, in Lithuanian and Romanian and Italian—was 'Gold in the streets!' 'Gold in the streets!' And there was lots of singing, mandolins."

As he spoke, graphically and vividly, I could see it all—he was conjuring up the sights and sounds of another time—I saw it as though on a huge screen behind him.

V

HE RECALLED constant music and singing. He remembered kindness, people sharing food, utensils, blankets; caring for one another. He himself was ecstatic and terrified by turns. Gold in the streets! What would it be like? He was twelve years old. In a year, according to Hebraic law, he would be a man. He felt every inch a man *now*. His father, a poor sailor, was not taking the voyage well and spent most of his time lying too still, now and then coughing. A fellow passenger was a veterinarian and did his best to help. Benny did not like the frown on the vet's face every time he rose from his father's pallet. Everything was going to be perfect. Gold in the streets! Everything was going to be disastrous.

Eleven days and nights after sailing from Hamburg, the S.S. *Pennland* docked. The passengers disembarked and were herded into spacious cages on Ellis Island. Now it began. Two days of confusion and rumors and scares and exchange of information and misinformation and experiences. Pretty girls get let in easily if they agree to lovemaking with the inspectors. Men over sixty are sent back. Don't mention any operation ever. Pregnant women are held until after the birth, to make sure the baby is not a cretin. The eye examination is the worst; if they find trachoma, you are sent back—and they have been finding a lot. The men must line up and open their pants, and the medical examiner handles their privates, looking for clap or hernia. Say this. Don't say that. Tell them you have a job waiting. No, don't. There is a law against importing labor. Tell them. Don't tell them. Say. Don't say.

Papers. Forms. There are representatives of various immigrant assistance groups, principally HIAS (Hebrew Immigrant Aid Society), but they are hopelessly overworked.

A man approaches Ben's father.

"What's your name?"

The father looks stricken. An interpreter intervenes.

Finally a reply: "Haim Bestritsky."

"Over here."

Haim does as he is told and moves to a new queue. His wife and Ben follow. Half an hour later, another inspector.

"What's your name?"

Haim panics, looks about. No interpreter. What could the question be? He has already given his name. Occupation? Of course!

"Farber," he says in Yiddish, meaning "dyer."

"What?"

"Farber," Benny repeats.

"Shut up!" Then, to Haim, "First name?"

"Haim der Farber." (Haim the Dyer.)

"Jesus! They're *all* Haim. O.K., Haim Farber, over here. You and the kid." To the mother: "You wait here." He and his father move through a canvas curtain.

"Open your pants!" is the order. They do not understand, but do what everyone else in front of them is doing. The scene is never to leave his mind.

Another queue. Chest examinations. The doctor examining Haim's chest looks grim, and sends for a second doctor.

"Spit in this cup."

Haim does so, then sits with Benny. They worry about the mother, but for the present, there is nothing to be done. They are trapped. Hours pass. The doctors return with an inspector of importance. Not only his gold badge (the others were silver) but his bearing bespeaks authority. He takes a piece of blue chalk from his pocket and marks Haim's jacket with a set of hieroglyphics. The inspector leads Haim away. Benny follows, but is propelled away and pointed in the general direction of the place where he left his mother. Two more days. Their shipmates have all disappeared. Most of them are on the mainland—Gold in the

36

streets!—some are in the detention block. New arrivals stream in. Food is sparse and, in any case, inedible (not kosher). Benny and his mother subsist on handouts and tidbits bought from itinerant vendors at exorbitant prices. What must Tante Channah think? It had been arranged for her to meet the boat.

Finally, the dread verdict: Haim is to be sent back. He is not permitted to enter the United States. He has tuberculosis—around here it is called "The Jew Disease"—and thus is ineligible and undesirable.

A full day of tears, hysteria, commiseration, discussion. They will *all* go back. This idea is dismissed with patriarchal power by Haim. He will go, she will stay with Benny, he will return when he is cured. Hysteria from the mother. Haim and his wife will go, Benny will stay in the care of Tante Channah. Screams of terror from Benny. But, in the end, it is so ordered.

He lives with his Tante Channah, an embittered, childless widow. She gets him a job delivering shirtwaists out of The Triangle Shirtwaist Factory, where she works. He discovers the streets: the teeming, lively, wicked, exciting streets of the Lower East Side.

At sixteen, he sneaks a girl into his room by way of the fire escape. She turns out to be one of those noisy ones. Channah breaks in, beats the girl with a broomstick, beats him, and ends his residency.

He leaves New York and finds work in Newark. He tries to learn a trade: tinsmith, plumber, tailor—nothing works. He has no apparent aptitudes. He goes to work in a dry-goods store in Plainfield, New Jersey.

News from Europe. Haim is dead. The mother will come to America in a year.

When the boat arrives, he goes to New York to meet her. They hardly recognize one another. It has been no more than four years, but in the meantime, he has become a young man and she an old woman. He takes her out to dinner at Moscowitz and Lupowitz on Second Avenue, and to a performance of *Neptune's Daughter* at the New York Hippodrome. They spend the night with Tante Channah, and the next morning, they are off to Plainfield.

They found a small flat. A better life began. One night, over the splendid cholent, she said, "This is good, this flat, but I think we should buy a house. I saw such a house today—an agent took me—it is in the next town—Dunellen."

"Yes, I know," he said, knowing that the poor old woman had gone off her head. Be gentle with her.

"We can buy it for four thousand dollars cash."

"Good," he said, "but where are we going to get the four thousand?"

"I have it," she said.

"You have?"

"And more. Much more."

Ben had to go and lie down.

Later, the explanation. Her brother had been a diamond dealer, but since this was an area of occupation and activity barred to Jews, he had to operate clandestinely. When he heard she was leaving for the States, he asked her to deliver a supply of gems to a dealer in New York. It was dangerous, yes, but he would make it worth her while. A few weeks ago, she had sought out the dealer, and after the proper exchange of identification, he had given her a sealed envelope, making it clear that this was her share; her brother's would be paid to him by an intermediary in Amsterdam.

When she got home, she opened the envelope and found in it $40,000 in American currency. A fortune! Only then did she realize the enormity of the risk she had taken. What must the value of what she had carried been?

Ben came slowly to the realization that his mother was an extremely rich woman.

The house was bought, and soon afterward, in Dunellen, a dry-goods store opened. "B.J. Farber: Dry Goods and Notions."

Business was slow at first, but that was to be expected. What was not expected was that it would stay slow. Bessie made up the losses. Ben was now $9,000 in debt to her.

"You are working too hard," she said. "You will kill yourself. I'll come and help you." He vetoed this idea. Bessie's English was nonexistent. "Hire a helper," she said. "But a goy—I think they don't buy from you because a Jewish store. Take in a goy—you'll see."

She turned out to be right.

The HELP WANTED sign had been in the store no longer than one morning when a vision was wafted into the little store. Tall and slim and red-haired and alive—God, how alive!

"It's about the job," she said.

"You've got it."

She laughed. "What is it?"

"Everything. To do what I do."

"And what do *you* do?"

"I buy, I sell. Take stock, make signs, pay bills, go to the bank. I'm a merchant."

"What do you pay?"

"What do you want?"

"On my last job, I got sixteen dollars a week, nine to six, half-day Saturday."

"No," he said. "Here is nine to six, *all* day Saturday—in fact, alone, because I don't work Saturday—and Thursday till nine."

"Nine to nine?"

"Yes."

"That's a long day. I don't know—"

"All right," he said quickly. "So no night. I'll do the night myself."

"And how much?"

"Eighteen."

"Um."

"Eighteen-fifty."

"Can you make it twenty?"

"I'll make it nineteen."

"All right."

"Good."

"When do you want to start?"

"Now."

"Tomorrow morning?"

"Nine o'clock."

They shook hands. She turned and left. He stood stock-still, his gaze on the door through which she had left.

There had been girls, of course—and women and tramps and matchmaker candidates—but none had made this sort of powerful impression upon him.

The next morning, he learned her name: Alice Bohl. She was

sixteen, her father was a Plainfield policeman, she went to night college in Bound Brook, New Jersey, studying shorthand, typing, and bookkeeping.

She turned out to be perfect, all he had hoped for. Better still, she made a great hit with Bessie, who took to bringing lunch for them both daily. Thus was Alice introduced to chicken soup and matzo balls, potato kugel and blintzes and borscht. Fine times.

The time for inventory came and presented a problem. It took two. Alice was not free evenings. Bessie was hopeless at it. Sundays impossible.

"How's this?" asked Alice. "On Friday, I finish at nine-thirty. I could be back by ten, and we'd have eleven hours before the store opens."

"Work all night?" he asked.

"Sure. Then Saturday you can sleep."

"But what about you?"

"Nothing. I've done it many times—boning for an exam or," she giggled, "an all-night date."

"An all-night date!" he said. "And your father lets you?"

"He doesn't know."

"I'm going to tell him."

"I'll bet you would."

"No, I wouldn't."

"So. What about the inventory? This Friday?"

"No, next."

"Swell."

Bessie thought it entirely meshuga, but could suggest no reasonable alternative. When the Friday came, she provided two enormous hampers of food and thermoses full of strong coffee. Ben began alone at six, and was in pretty good shape by the time Alice arrived at 10:15. They worked together, efficiently and well, stopped for food at midnight. They spread blankets on the floor of the stockroom upstairs and ate picnic style. Then they continued to work feverishly. Coffee and cake at 2:30 A.M. To their utter astonishment, at 4:30 they had finished the inventory. They went back up to the stockroom.

"Let's call this breakfast." she said.

"All right with me."

"And do you mind if I rest a minute?"

"Absolutely no." He moved the hampers aside. She stretched

out. He left her, went down, and returned with pillows and a light quilt. She thanked him. He left again. An hour later, he went up to check, found her asleep, and was startled to see her dress and stockings and chemise and brassiere neatly placed on a crate. He went back down, trembling, and returned with a bathrobe and slippers. He placed them near her and heard her say, "Thank you."

"Are you awake?"

"Sort of." She stretched.

He started out.

"Where are you going?"

He stopped and so did his heartbeat for a moment. He came to her and knelt beside her. He leaned over and kissed her.

"Ten months, two weeks, three days, sixteen hours, and seven minutes," she said.

When he told Bessie, some weeks later, that he and Alice were going to be married, she said nothing, but stared at him for what seemed like an hour. During this time, he explained and begged and cajoled. He joked, grew angry, wept. Still, she remained relentlessly silent. She went slowly upstairs and into her room. He decided to leave her alone for a time.

When, finally, he went up to join her, he found her packing

"What're you doing?" he asked. "What the hell are you doing?"

Silence. It was as though she had been struck dumb. Indeed, he was not to hear the sound of her voice for nine years.

VI

"I HAD to let her go," said Ben. "What could I do? A few days later, I went to New York to find her. She was with Tante Channah. I walked in, I'll never forget it. There they were, the two of them, and some other relatives—men and women—and some friends. They were sitting on the floor with shoes off and tearing their clothes and praying. They were what they called 'sitting shiva.' You know what that is?"

"No, I don't," I said.

"It's the service for the dead. You hear? To them, I was *dead!* You've never been to your own funeral. I have. It's some experience, I can tell you! Disgusting."

"I should think so."

"So then we got married, me and Alice—in her house—by a Justice of the Peace. To tell you the truth, her family wasn't jumping up and down from happiness neither. And some of their friends wouldn't come—on account of me—but the family took it all right. The way it was arranged, we got married the Sunday before her father's vacation. So then when we went to Niagara Falls for the honeymoon, he watched the store for a week. He did such a fine business that week, I began to think maybe Bessie was right about what was the trouble there for me. When we came back—"

The butler appeared.

"Shorty says five minutes, sir."

"Thank you, Chapman." He turned to me. "To be continued," he said, smiling. "Like those two-reelers we used to make: Pearl White, *The Perils of Pauline;* Elmo C. Lincoln, *Elmo the Mighty; The Black Hand; The Purple Mask.* Junk but moneymakers."

We were walking back to the house.

"How about twelve noon tomorrow?" he asked. "At the studio."

"Perfect."

I did not entirely believe Adani would come out to take over. If he did, well . . .

"You want to know the truth? I enjoy talking about myself. The trouble is—around here—who wants to listen? You got the advantage you're a fresh ear—or the disadvantage, maybe?"

"Not at all. It's fascinating."

"Now," he said. "Yes. Remembering it. Doing it was *not* so fascinating."

We reached the house just as the party was emerging from the projection room. Drinks were being offered, comments on the film exchanged. I lost B.J., and a few minutes later realized he was no longer in the room.

Melanie approached me. "I missed you," she said. "It got pretty scary, and I had no one to cling to."

"We can cling later, if you like," I said.

"No way," she said, and moved away. A few minutes later, I saw her whispering and giggling with Willa and Beth. What the hell was going on? Obviously, I had misread a few signals.

The party broke up at 11:45, as though rehearsed. Odd, I thought. In Washington, they invariably end at 10:45. Tribal customs and rituals.

Mathews approached. "Will you wish to be called in the morning, sir?"

"No, thank you. I'll ring down."

"Breakfast?"

"I'll tell you then."

"Very good, sir."

Melanie again. In the foyer as we said our good nights to the departing guests.

"May I drive you home?" I asked.

"I don't have a home," she said, and went up the great staircase, undulating.

Willa and Beth and I wandered into an alcove off the library and sat at opposite ends of a large sofa.

"I wouldn't call that a flop," I said to Willa. "My God! It was memorable. How can I ever thank you?"

"No need," she said.

"You understand that I left the movie only because I'm so anxious to get whatever time I can with Mr. Farber."

"Of course. That's what you're here for."

"He was telling me tonight about some of the early days. I get the feeling I could listen to him forever."

"I already have," she said, then added quickly, "and enjoyed it."

"And Lord—what a memory!"

"For some things, yes," said Beth. "But he couldn't for the life of him tell you what he had for breakfast this morning."

"Not important, that's why—he remembers what's important."

"Of course."

I turned to Willa and said, "May I ask an indiscreet question?"

"Yes," she said. "If you're prepared for an indiscreet answer."

"He said something before dinner—when we were alone—about Fairbanks and Pickford—about them being here tonight."

"Yes?"

"Well, was that a joke of some kind—or what?"

She looked away for a time, then at me for a longer time. Finally

43

she said, "No, not a joke. A lapse. He has them from time to time. A kind of disorientation from time and place. We were watching an old Hitchcock on TV the other night—*The Thirty-nine Steps*—and all at once Ben said to me: 'Listen, let's go home. I've had enough of London for this trip.' "

"And what did *you* say?" asked Beth.

"I said, 'Fine, Ben. I'll book us on the first sailing.' His doctors tell me it's nothing to be concerned about. They treat him, of course—medication and circulatory stimulation. It may end one day or—" She stopped. "You look concerned."

"I am," I said.

"Why?"

"Well, is it right for me to do business with a man who—?"

"Who *what?*"

"Who isn't altogether—*well.*"

She laughed. "Have no fear. He's well enough for business. His lapses are only personal and social. Just be sure *you're* well enough to handle him."

"No way," I said. (I had *never* used that empty expression. Why did I just now? Of course. Melanie.) "I'm no match for that great man. Actually—and fortunately—I have no authority at all. A messenger boy, as you guessed."

"But I'm so very grateful that Mr. Adani sent such a charming one." She looked at me meaningfully as I tried to decipher her meaning.

"Who is Melanie?" I asked, suddenly.

Willa and Beth both seemed embarrassed by the question. "A friend," Willa said.

"What does she do?"

"Oh—different things," said Beth. "What my mother used to call a 'dabster.' Generally, in that greatest of all American enterprises: public relations."

And some private relations? was the question that formed itself in my mind. Fortunately, I was able to intercept it before it reached my tongue.

"Bedtime," said Willa. "You must be exhausted."

"Not at all. I've had a nap and a swim and a smashing dinner and the most stimulating evening of my life—and you."

She took a beat before she said, "But it's three ten A.M. by your time."

44

"I don't believe any of that," I said. "I believe my watch, which says twelve ten."

"My turn for an indiscreet," said Beth.

"I can hardly wait."

"Do you always carry that case around?"

"Always."

"Why?"

"It makes me look important and mysterious."

"No, it doesn't." She kissed her great-grandmother—could it be?—said, "Good night, love." She gave me her hand, said, "Pleasure," and was gone.

Willa and I got up and started for the foyer. We went up the stairs together. In the upper hall, she asked, "Do you know the way?"

"Yes, I do," I said. "I practiced this afternoon." It was true.

"Good night, then," she said, and offered her hand. I took it.

"Good night," I said. "Thank you so much."

What were her eyes saying? I was in a welter of confusion. Should I kiss her? Gently? Properly? Not at all? Later? Never? I was still considering it when I realized she was gone. I suppose it *was* 3:20 A.M. after all.

I found my way to my suite, went directly to the dressing room, undressed, showered, and got into pajamas. On the way to the bedroom, I stopped in the little office, sat down and wrote up the evening for an hour. I knew that sleep was out of the question anyway and I was trying to digest the remarkable evening.

At about 1:30, I went into the bedroom and found Melanie in my bed.

We clung.

Afterward, she left the bed.

"Where are you going?" I asked.

"Home."

She moved through a panel in the wall and was gone. Now I knew she was part of the game.

Before I could get to sleep—the phone.

"What's about it?" asked Adani.

"I'm on the nine-o'clock flight," I said.

"You stay where you are, you wise-ass!"

"What?"

"You know I was only kiddin'."

45

"The hell I did."

"You *stay*, hear? I'm too tied up here. I've got to go to Washington twice today. You stay. And listen, if he gets too tough you can go up ten percent—twelve."

"I don't think that's going to be the question."

"What you mean?"

"I mean that it's not how much, but *if*."

"Speak English, for Chrissake."

"He hasn't decided—definitely—to sell at all."

"He'll sell. Go up fifteen if you got to."

"I'm seeing him at noon."

"All right. Close it. I'll call you from Washington or someplace." He hung up.

It is possible, I mused, to live too much life in a day. This was one of them. I fell asleep at last.

VII

OTTO DROVE me to the studio. As we approached it, he got on the phone and announced our imminent arrival. We pulled up in front of the administration building, and he said, "Wait here. The old man comes down."

The first things I noticed were the bits and chunks of pieces of gold in the streets. Movie studios the world over are alike, few have any special personality—but Farber Films was certainly different. And so was B.J. Farber.

He appeared and walked toward me, jauntily.

"Sleep O.K.?"

"Perfectly."

"Let's walk."

We started toward the first of the cavernous sound stages.

"Oh," he said, "I wish you could've seen this place in the real days. The action. The work! Now look at it—a sausage machine. But it used to be the best business in the whole world."

"How'd you get into it?" I asked.

He stopped and regarded me. "I told you," he said. "I told you last night. The whole story."

"No, you didn't. I'm sorry."

"You mean you forgot."

"Not a thing. You stopped with your marriage—to Alice—"

"To who?"

"Alice. And the honeymoon to Niagara Falls."

"Alice," he echoed. "Oh, yes. Alice. A sweet girl. She's dead."

We walked again, and he became a tour guide, explaining each department and what it did: props, carpentry, electrical, camera, editing, transportation, casting, art, costumes, on and on. His grasp of the contribution of each was impressive.

After an hour or more, we returned to his office and went directly into his private dining room, where a splendid health food lunch was served to him: broth, steamed vegetables with yogurt, papaya. For me: Mongole soup, hamburger (the best I ever tasted), lyonnaise potatoes, stewed tomatoes, salad, floating island.

Throughout the walk and lunch he interspersed the story he had begun last night. He picked up precisely where he had left off. Talk about continuity of mind! This man was an exemplar of the idea.

VIII

WHEN THEY returned to Dunellen from Niagara Falls, they set to work together to build the business.

For seven months, Alice continued to go to school in Bound Brook. Then she joined him full time. They extended the store hours—first opening an hour earlier, then remaining open an hour later. It cost them no more and improved business slightly. They took separate lunch hours so that the store would always be attended. When Alice became pregnant, hard days began again for Ben.

In the spring of 1908, their first son was born and named Haim, over the objection of the Bohl family.

"What the hell kind of a dumbbell name is *that?*" asked Mr. Bohl. "Nobody'll know how to *say* it!"

"It has to be. It's the tradition."

"But hell, Ben. You don't go for that stuff. You never go to synagogues or any of that."

"It has to be, Tom."

"If you think it's gonna get your old lady back, it ain't."

"It's not that."

(Too bad Tom did not live long enough to see Haim become Higham Farber, which he did the year he entered Harvard in 1926.)

In the year of Haim's birth, the great event took place.

Ben was standing in the doorway of his store early one evening in late spring, deeply depressed. Business was rotten. S.S. Kresge had opened a branch across the street and virtually destroyed the notion part of the Farbers' business. They were now dependent on dry goods alone.

He looked out into the street. The once-a-day street cleaner was late. Probably drunk again. Ben counted the piles of horseballs in the street directly in front of his store. There were four, neatly and symmetrically stacked as though by machine, rather than by nature.

A rueful laugh escaped him.

"Gold in the streets!" he said.

A stranger approached and stopped in front of the store. He looked into the window, then pressed his face close to it and shaded his eyes. He did not seem to be interested in the display, but in the interior.

"Good evening," said Ben.

The stranger nodded and touched the brim of his Panama hat. He was dressed oddly. Not from Dunellen, for sure. A sort of dandy. He walked into the store. Ben could not imagine what he could possibly hope to find there. They did not carry his kind of stuff at *all*. The man walked up and down the length of the store. It was a long store—only twenty feet wide, but sixty feet deep. He went to the end of it and walked back, measuring and counting his steps. What was he? A fire inspector? Insurance man?

"What can I do for you?" asked Ben.

The man smiled, shook his head, and left.

Ben watched him as he crossed the street and began the same routine in Mullen's Hardware Store.

When he came out, he looked into Kresge's window but did not go in. He did spend a long time in Peewee's Diner, and when he emerged, was followed by Peewee himself. They seemed to be arguing about something, negotiating—but in the end, the man walked away. He came across the street and approached Ben.

"Good evening."

"What do you want?" asked Ben.

"Never mind what *I* want. Do *you* want to make three simoleons tonight?"

"What're you talking? I'd like to make three *any* night."

"All right, here's my card."

It read:

**GARDEN STATE
MOVING PICTURE
MACHINE COMPANY**

**22 Broad St.
Elizabeth, N.J.
Main 62**

**Fred Barovick
Exhibition-Sales**

Ben read it, confused.

"What's it got to do with me?"

"Here's the deal," said Barovick. "I show moving pictures. And wherever I go, I need a long store. You got the only one in town, so far as I can see—except for that diner bloke. He's cuckoo—wants a deal I can't give him. So he calls me names. What time you close?"

"Six."

"That's fine. I'll put the signs out. My man comes in about six and sets up. The show'll be seven till nine. We charge a dime, a nickel for kids. Some places—big cities—they charge a nickel, and kids two for a nickel, but a one-horse burg like this, I wouldn't play unless ten and five. So if that's O.K. with you, let's give it a try, and who knows? Maybe if it goes, we can do it regular—once a week, two weeks, we'll see—depends on business. This town looks pretty dead to me, so I don't promise anything. Some towns

49

we do good—others, no. It's hard to say. So what do you say? We on?"

"On. Only one question, please?"

"Yes?"

"What's a moving picture?"

He got his answer that night. He invited all the Bohls—Alice's father and mother, sister and two brothers. He paid for their tickets, Barovick explaining that there could be no free passes.

Signs went up in front of the store:

TONIGHT TONIGHT TONIGHT
MOVING PICTURE SHOW
THOMAS A. EDISON'S
GREATEST INVENTION
THE MOVING PICTURE MACHINE
7:00 P.M. TO 9:00 P.M.
FULL TEN-MINUTE SHOW
ADMISSION: ADULTS 10¢
CHILDREN 5¢
DO NOT MISS THIS ASTOUNDING
20TH CENTURY DISPLAY
YOU WILL NOT BELIEVE YOUR EYES
COME ONE! COME ALL!
—NOT A FAKE—

At six o'clock, Barovick returned with a five-foot-tall grey-haired man. Together, they fastened a white linen screen on the back wall at the far end of the store. At the front end, the little man mounted a projector. It was a large black box, the size of two orange crates, and it made a considerable noise.

All shades were drawn, and a black cloth pinned over the storefront window.

At 6:30, the little man began a trial run. It took ten minutes or more to adjust the focus, as well as the frame, but finally, there were moving pictures. Two prizefighters: the famous "Gentleman Jim" Corbett and Peter Courtney, champion of New Jersey. An Indian war dance. Clips from Buffalo Bill's Wild West Show and Buffalo Bill himself and Annie Oakley.

There were tumblers and tightrope walkers, jugglers, and trained animals. There were even a few shots of the Grand Canyon and Niagara Falls. When the falls came on, Ben and Alice joined hands.

By 6:45, there was a sizable queue out front. Barovick, at the door, sold the tickets. Only thirty people at a time were admitted. Business was brisk and no one was disappointed. There was frequent applause, and the only disturbance was caused by those who came too close to the machine in an effort to fathom its mysteries. Now and then, a shadow blocked on the screen and the projectionist shouted, "One side, please! One side!"

Some watched awhile and left, shaking their heads. Others stayed on and on, watching the show over and over again.

At nine o'clock, it had ended. The Bohls invited the Farbers and the distinguished visitors to their home for coffee and cake.

"Darn good show," said Mr. Bohl. "I've seen 'em before, of course. Moving pictures. Some places don't allow 'em, y'know. Fire hazard."

"My God, is it?" asked Ben. "If it is, we can't do it no more. I'm sure my insurance wouldn't cover a thing like *this!*"

"No danger, no danger," said the projectionist. "I've done over five hundred, and never a mishap."

"Look into it, Ben," said Alice.

"Have another piece, Mr. Barovick—it's Lady Baltimore."

"Thank you, ma'am. Don't mind if I do. I've been to Baltimore. We showed there. Remember, Grover?"

"Sure do. Guy owned the store was a *pill.* And business was bum."

"How did *we* do?" asked Ben.

"Well, I'll show you. No secrets between partners. Here's how we did: one hundred and thirty-four adults, that's thirteen dollars and forty cents. Sixty-six kids—that's three thirty. Total: Sixteen dollars and seventy cents. Not bad. Not great, but for a first time, all right. See, what we're trying is to build up a circuit. If we can get up to three shows a day in seven towns, once a week, that'd be twenty-one shows a week. And if we can average in time, say, twenty-five, thirty dollars a show, that's a gross of six hundred and thirty dollars a week! That's a quite a business, wouldn't you say?"

"Wait a second," said Mr. Bohl. "You said seven."

"That's right."

"You mean Sundays, too?"

"Sure—not everywhere, but somewhere. In New York they do."

"Oh, New *York*," said Mrs. Bohl, with some distaste.

"Nowhere in Jersey, pal," said Mr. Bohl.

"They already did a couple times in Jersey City—not our company, but somebody."

"They'll end up in the clink," said Mr. Bohl.

"Well, even six days," said Barovick. "That would still be—let's see—five hundred and forty dollars."

Another round of coffee and cake. The party was over.

On the sidewalk, Barovick was trying to commit Ben to the following Wednesday.

"I'll let you know," said Ben. "It's the insurance."

"Don't worry about it."

"I'll let you know."

Ben and Alice walked home.

Ben said, "I don't think three dollars is enough if he took in almost seventeen. Well, maybe it is—it's almost twenty percent."

"Maybe we shouldn't do it at all."

"What're you talking? Three dollars every week. That's a hundred and fifty dollars a year—and could be more. Pays the taxes."

Before going to bed, Ben handed her the three dollars and said, "Tomorrow, put this in the savings bank in the name of Haim Farber. It's extra, like found money—so let it be his. For school, maybe college. You can't tell."

Alice laughed, but said, "All right, sure."

Three years later, Haim's savings account totaled some $38,000.

What had happened was unpredictable.

Barovick had returned the following Wednesday evening—but this time, Ben had a week to advertise. A large sign in the show window, as well as posters—made by Alice—tacked up all over town. The gross had been more than doubled, people coming in from the outskirts and the farms. $34.70! Barovick gave Ben $4.00, and they planned to add an hour the following week by beginning at 6:00 P.M.

"Could you get at least a few *different* moving pictures?" he asked Barovick. "There must be a *lot*."

"Sure, but these we *own*. New ones we'd have to *rent*—so down goes the profit."

"But it would be an attraction," said Ben, "if we could say 'with *new* moving pictures,' wouldn't it?"

"Listen, Ben. I know the business. The public's dumb. They'll take what you give 'em. What do *they* know? Wait till they complain, then we'll give 'em something different."

"The public," said Ben, "is not dumb. I'm with the public day in, day out—it's the same public if they buy a yard muslin or a ticket for the show. *Not* dumb."

It was to be a continuing quarrel between them, generally settled by a compromise that satisfied neither party. Still, the business grew. They were selling a novelty, an innovation, to a hungry audience.

The shows became longer—twenty minutes, half an hour. Ben rented, then bought, a supply of folding chairs.

They went to two nights a week, and after eighteen months—to three.

On a buying trip to New York City, Ben saw a nickelodeon on the Bowery, bought a ticket, and went in. Benches. The screen mounted on a platform. It seemed strange without the stock of dry goods all about.

Stranger still was the program itself. Not simply clips and snippets, but three stories, each with a beginning, a middle, and an ending. There was *The Great Train Robbery,* which he had seen on the stage at Jacob's Theatre in Newark years earlier. Also, *Life of an American Fireman,* and *Uncle Tom's Cabin.*

On the trip home, his imagination soared. A moving picture place! Not in Dunellen, of course. Too small. Plainfield? Elizabeth?

From New York to Dunellen was a long journey: trolley car to the 125th Street ferry, ferry to Fort Lee, train to Plainfield, trolley to Dunellen. By the time he reached home, he had made plans. In the course of the next few days, he conveyed them to Alice.

She was not enthusiastic, perhaps because he had wearied her in his overcharged way for hours: between customers at the store, on the walk home, all through supper, washing up afterward, and even now—preparing for bed.

"I don't like it," she said.

"Why not?"

"It's not your business, Ben."

"It's nobody's business yet. It's a new thing. Everybody's learning. That's my best chance—in something new, something beginning. In what's established already, they don't let you in. It's not my business now—but I can *learn,* Allie, and you can help me."

"I don't want to. I'm scared. We're not alone anymore."

"Don't I know it? I want to do it for *him* as much as for us. Don't hold me back, Allie."

"I've *never* held you back!" she said indignantly.

"Who said?"

"Let me sleep, Ben, please. I'm bone tired."

"Sure, sure."

She slept. He tried, but it was no use. He got up, went downstairs, got out a pad and pencil and began figuring.

Alice didn't understand. How could she? A woman. He would talk to Fred Barovick.

After the show on Friday night, he asked Barovick over to the house. They sat out on the back porch, drinking lemonade.

"It won't work, Ben. Hear what I tell you."

"But in New York—"

"New York is New York, Ben."

"People are the same everyplace."

"Yes, but in New York, there's more *of* 'em. And you were right about you have to give 'em different all the time. The novelty's beginning to wear off."

"So you give them different!"

"Where're *you* gonna get different? There ain't that many. Listen, I'll tell you how I know I'm right. About seven, eight years ago, this guy—Alexander Victor—did it."

"Did what?"

"He took a big store in Newark and he put in two hundred chairs and a big screen, and he got from Edison the biggest Kinetoscope and he charged two bits, and in a few months he went broke."

"Koster and Bial didn't go broke. For a long time already they've got a Vitascope there in their Musical Hall on Thirty-fourth Street."

"God damn, you're a stubborn Jew!"

"So are *they,*" said Ben. "Stubborn and *rich!*"

"They don't show *only* Vitascope, you dippy bastard. It's a vaudeville, and the Vitascope is just one of the *acts!*"

"I don't care," said Ben.

He did not discuss the matter again with Alice or Fred—but brooded about it incessantly.

Another sleepless night. He went downstairs, got out his now-bulging file, and began reading through it again. All at once, he stopped. Plans, plans! What good are they? They were like dreams. What was needed was *action*. Such as?

He sat down and began to compose a letter. When he had achieved the sense of it, he enlisted the aid of one of his customers, Sally Herkstroter, a schoolteacher. He paid her a dollar to help him put it into this final form:

March the 12th, 1909

Dr. Thomas Alva Edison
The Edison Studios
144 Elm Street
West Orange, New Jersey

Most esteemed Dr. Edison,
I wish to establish myself in the moving picture business. I am already in the moving picture business part time, but would prefer to be in it full time.
I have many ideas, and I would like to discuss them with you. Is this possible? I am not far and place myself at your disposal for this purpose.
I await your favorable response.

Respectfully yours,
BENJAMIN JOSEPH FARBER

"Very nice," he said. "Thank you."
"There's just one thing," she said.
"What?"
"Are you *sure* he's 'Doctor'?"
"What then? 'Professor'?"
"I don't know."
"A great man like this must be—*or* a doctor, *or* a professor."
"I don't know," she said, worrying.
"So look. So if not Doctor—insulted he wouldn't be."
"You don't think just plain 'Mister'?"
"Edison," he said, "is not a 'Mister.' That I'm sure."
For another fifty cents, Sally had her girl friend, who worked

in the assistant principal's office, typewrite the letter on her typewriting machine.

The day Ben signed it, stamped it, took it to the post office and mailed it seemed to him the single greatest day he had known since arriving in America. He felt himself to be a part of its surging vitality, its audacious invention.

When a week went by with no reply, he reproached himself. What a fool to think he could write letters to Edison! At least, no one knew—no one with the exception of Sally and Mildred, and they were sworn to secrecy.

The lack of response did not, however, dash his hopes. There must be someone else he could find to discuss his plan. The mayor of Plainfield?

Then came the letter. There was no mistaking it. A return address printed in the upper left-hand corner read:

Thomas Alva Edison
Menlo Park, New Jersey

(Not a doctor. Never mind. Read the letter.)

My dear Mr. Farber,
   Mr. Edison has asked me to thank you for your most interesting missive.
[What's *missive*?]
   He is, of course, always solicitous of persons who are interested in the further development of his motion picture machine, since it is very much a part of his continuing work.
   If you will be good enough to present yourself at his laboratory on April 16, 1909, at 4:00 P.M., he will be pleased to listen to your ideas.

Sincerely yours,

WILLIAM EVERETT
Secretary

He read it once, his heart pounding. The second time, he could not keep from laughing. The third time, he burst into tears.

He had not planned to show the letter to Alice, but when she walked in and found him weeping, he had no choice.

"Very courteous," she said. "But nothing will happen."

She handed back the letter, which a few moments earlier had seemed like a U.S. government bond. Now it was no more than a worthless piece of paper.

No more was said on the subject until suppertime. They ate in stony silence for half an hour.

"You're crazy, Ben!" she blurted out suddenly.

"No," he protested.

"Crazy," she insisted, "to think you can sit down with a man like Edison."

"You'll see," he muttered.

"*What* will I see? You wasting your time on scatterbrained schemes. You frighten me, Ben. You really do. I love you, but I'm scared."

He put down his fork and said, "I love you, too. You want I shouldn't go, I wouldn't go."

"*Please* don't!" she said. "People'll hear about it and laugh at you."

"They laugh anyway."

"They'll laugh more."

"All right."

"Thank you, Ben."

But on the morning of April 16, he broke his promise. He could not help it. His mind and his conscience kept ordering him not to, yet he moved relentlessly, recklessly. He dressed carefully in his best clothes, packed his file into a straw suitcase, came down and said to Alice, "I'm going to Edison. Because I have to. I'm sorry. Forgive me."

On the trolley to Plainfield, he realized that he had had no breakfast. Probably just as well, he thought. His stomach was tight. It had loosened somewhat by the time he reached the railroad station in West Orange. He ate a doughnut and drank a cup of coffee, and felt as confident as Columbus.

He walked the two miles to the laboratory and reached it at 3:10. He sat in the shade of a white oak tree and rested.

There it was—the strangely shaped, rather makeshift structure, tacked with black tar paper. The sign over its main door read The Kinetographic Theatre, but in the trade it was already famous as The Black Maria.

57

At five minutes to four, he rose and made his way to the main building.

In view of the momentousness of the occasion, he found himself surprisingly calm.

There were two men at work in the outer office. One of them —in shirtsleeves, stiff collar, and green eyeshade—rose immediately and came to greet him.

"Mr. Farber?"

"The same."

"I'm Bill Everett. Come right in."

Ben went through a small swinging gate and followed Everett to a double door. Everett entered without knocking, Ben stayed close behind him.

"Mr. Farber, sir." He handed Ben's letter to Edison to refresh his memory. Edison read it carefully while Ben studied him and his workroom.

It was a spacious shop, with a small office space at one end of it. Thomas Edison in person seemed to Ben to be the most impressive man he had ever seen. Short, stocky, with a shock of black hair, some of which fell over his forehead. His eyes were an especially arresting feature. Deep-set, dark, and powerful. Doubtless they could see things other eyes could not.

"Come here, young man, come here," he said.

Ben moved to him. Edison held out his hand. Ben took it and shuddered at the touch.

They sat down.

"Thank you for my visit, Mr. Edison. What an honor!"

"Russian?" asked Edison.

"Yes, sir, Mr. Edison."

"Jew?"

"Yes, sir, Mr. Edison."

"Good businessmen, Jews, as a rule. Not much in science. Music, money, yes. Odd."

"I'm a good businessman, Mr. Edison."

"What business are you in?"

"Dry goods. But three nights a week, moving pictures. I have a long store."

"How long?"

"Sixty feet."

"Yes. Long enough. What equipment do you use?"

58

"Edison. Only Edison, Mr. Edison."

"Of course," said Edison, suddenly testy, "but *what* equipment?"

"Vitascope A 101."

"All right. Good machine. We've got a better one now."

"Yes, I heard."

Edison clasped his hands behind his head, leaned back in his chair and said, "Very well. Recite."

Ben did not know the word, but divined its meaning. He outlined his plan to establish a full-time moving picture place in Dunellen, New Jersey. It would operate every night save Sunday, and, like legitimate theatres, might even try Saturday afternoons. His idea was to form a partnership with the Edison Company. He would supply the place and the management, they the equipment and most of the films.

"Who do you see paying the cost of transportation?"

"Me!" said Ben. "I'll pay."

"And what's your idea of the split?"

"Fifty-fifty!" said Ben.

"Terrible idea," said Edison. He rose and walked to the window, looking out. "My Lord," he said, "daffodils already."

Ben thought that he, too, should rise, but found that he could not.

Edison turned back into the room. "Terrible," he repeated. "Ought to be sixty-forty at least."

"Fine," said Ben. "I'll even take thirty."

Edison laughed. "No, no, you greenhorn. Sixty you, forty us. I thought you said you were a good businessman."

"All right," said Ben, dizzy now. "Sixty-forty."

"*If* we decide to do it. God knows we've got the machines and the pictures. It's just that up to now, we've preferred selling to renting. Renting's so damned complicated and who's to do the checking of the receipts?"

"You could trust me."

Edison looked at him carefully. "I daresay I could," he said. "But how many honest men are you likely to find? Look at all the trouble Diogenes had."

"Yes," said Ben, bewildered.

"Long as you're here, let me show you around."

They went first through a great storeroom, where at least one example of every model produced to date was displayed. There was the Zoetrope; the hand-cranked Mutascope, which flipped cards, simulating motion; the Kinetoscopic cylinder; the horizontal projector.

Finally, they stopped in front of a box resembling an ice box. Edison positioned Ben in front of the box, placed a curious headset on his head, with connections to his ears, and had him bend to the viewer. He then released a switch and Ben saw—to his amazement—not only moving pictures, but moving pictures that seemed to *talk!* He was speechless.

Afterward, continuing the tour, he asked, "Why can't that be up on a big screen?"

Edison laughed. "Answer that one, my boy, and you'll be a full partner!"

They went into The Black Maria. It was far more impressive inside than out.

The space had been transformed into a realistic-looking gymnasium, with a basketball court, bunting, and a visitors' gallery. Girls in middies and bloomers were playing basketball.

A tall man stood alone by a camera on a tripod and hand-cranked the camera with great care. The scene ended.

"Very good, young ladies. Sit and rest now. No talking. Reload!"

The cameraman came over.

"Afternoon, Chief."

"Hello, Henry." Edison turned to Ben. "This is Henry Cronjager, who tells me he's the best cameraman in the world."

"I am," said Henry.

"And this is Mr. Benjamin Farber, who is in the moving picture business."

"How do you do, Mr. Farber?"

"How do you do? Say, this is very wonderful. What is it?"

"We don't know yet," said Cronjager. "We've only just begun. We hope it's going to turn out to be a two-reeler. *A Country Girl's Seminary Life and Experiences.*"

"The title's too long," said Edison.

"Has to be, Chief. It's a long picture."

"I like long pictures," said Ben. "I like long pictures better than short pictures."

"Why?" asked Edison.

"Because the people like to get more for their money. Also,

sometimes they come from a long way, so when they get there, it's better if it's not too short, the whole show."

"See that?" asked Cronjager triumphantly. Apparently the matter of length was a subject constantly under discussion. "And didn't George Eastman tell us the other day—?"

"Eastman! To *hell* with Eastman!" shouted Edison.

"Sshh!" said Cronjager. "Young ladies present."

The young ladies giggled.

Edison continued, quietly. "Damned Eastman. Just wants to keep selling us his filmstrips, that's all. He doesn't care what we *do* with them. And anyhow—"

"Ready!"

"Excuse me," said Cronjager, and returned to the camera.

Edison said, "I've got to leave you, Mr. Farber. You're welcome to stay if you like."

"Oh, yes," said Ben. "I'd like."

"You'll hear from us."

"Thank you, Mr. Edison. The greatest honor of my whole life."

They shook hands again, Edison holding on to Ben's longer than common, meanwhile looking him in the eye. Ben was sure Edison was making his decision then and there. What was it? He could gain no hint from that concentrated grim visage or those penetrating steel-grey eyes.

"Thank you for coming," said Edison.

"My pleasure."

Edison was gone. Ben sat to one side and watched, agape, at the making of a movie. Up to now, the process had never occurred to him. He had accepted the finished product as a fact—but of course, it had to be made. Most of the companies were called The So-and-So Film Manufacturing Company. And here they were—manufacturing.

IX

TEN MONTHS later, Farber's Dry, as it had come to be known, became The Happy Hour, playing two shows nightly: 7:00 P.M. and 9:00 P.M. Admission ten cents on weeks nights, five cents for children. Saturday night: fifteen cents for adults, ten cents for children. Saturday matinee: five cents for adults, and children— two for a nickel.

Business built slowly. As the novelty of seeing pictures move on the screen wore off, the patrons of The Happy Hour became more selective. Ben booked carefully, studying the catalogues of the various film companies, looking for films that would attract audiences. He advertised, placed window cards in shops (giving passes for the privilege), and kept the front of the house attractively dressed.

The Redman and the Child (made in Little Falls, New Jersey) proved to be a great hit, and Ben was able to hold it over. Other successes were: *Rescued from the Eagle's Nest,* which an actor named Griffith had made on the cliffs of the Palisades and at the Biograph Studios in New York City; *The Gibson Goddess;* and *The Lonely Villa*—both made in Fort Lee, New Jersey.

Ben thought he could see the future and expanded rapidly— The Happy Hour in Plainfield, another in Bound Brook, still others in Linden and Somerville. He was working around the clock, taking most of his meals while traveling from one theatre to another, and napping instead of sleeping.

Alice continued to operate the little theatre in Dunellen, and although she was delighted by the apparent success of Ben's venture, missed the normal family life she saw all about her.

"When will it stop, Ben?" she asked him one night, after a futile attempt at lovemaking.

"Why should it stop?"

"Our life. We hardly have any life."

He took her into his arms and whispered, "Allie! This is our opportunity. Don't you see it? This is the work time of life—the pleasure time will come later."

"Will it?"

"Sure it will! You'll see—"

"But I'm getting scared, Ben. Nine theatres—but that's all. Everything we have is in the theatres. No reserve. The minute we get a little ahead and something in the bank, you go and set up another one—that's what I mean about when will it stop. Shouldn't we do with what we've got now? . . . Ben? . . . Shouldn't we?"

But her husband was asleep.

A Cowboy Escapade was a success, and Ben began a complex system of renting a film for a two-week period and rotating it through his chain of theatres.

A wild young man who owned a motorbike—Davey Pulaski—was hired to run the prints from house to house.

Business boomed. Ben bought an automobile, a Reo. Alice engaged a maid to look after the house and Haim. Dreams were coming true. Gold in the streets! Then the blow fell.

When a little business becomes a big business, the big businessmen take over. This is the way in which the system operates.

"The Leaping Tintypes," as they were sometimes called, turned the corner and were clearly on their way to becoming a big business indeed.

Competition between the film manufacturers became keen, but Ben remained loyal to the Edison Company.

There were endless patent suits, most of which Edison lost. In time, other companies, mainly American Mutascope and Biograph, were allowed by law to manufacture virtually the same kind of film that Edison had thought exclusive.

As the businesses of manufacture and exhibition grew, the competition became more and more intense, culminating in cutthroat policies that damaged everyone. Eventually, a merger was effected: All the major companies manufacturing film became the Motion Picture Patents Company. Edison was in it, of course, along with his enemies, Mutascope and Biograph. Also, Selig Polyscope, Essanay, and Pathé Frères.

This powerful unit now made the rules: prices and contracts and conditions and licensing fees.

Ben attended a meeting called by a group of exhibitors.

"It's a trust, Goddamn it! It's against the law what they're doing!"

The speaker was Algernon Bragg, the Atlantic City theatre owner. "These bastards are fixing it so we work for *them*. They've got us by the throat. If we don't buy from them on their own terms, we're out of business because we'll have nothing to show!"

"We could buy from Europe," said someone.

"No, no," said Ben. "Some of the things from there are all right, but most, no—not for my people."

"Hell with 'em," said Bragg. "We can join up and manufacture our *own* film."

This idea met with great approval until Ben said, "Sure, but why can't they then open up their own theatres?"

A sober and terrifying pause filled the room. Silence. Then Bragg said, "It's a trust, Goddamn it!"

But he sounded defeated.

Many exhibitors did attempt to make their own films, but failed to produce a product that could compete with the established firms.

Independents attempted to fill the gap. Ben heard of a man named Lasky, who, with his brother-in-law, Sam Goldfish, was making an important film from a Broadway play. It was called *The Squaw Man,* and starred William Farnum, already a movie favorite. It was being directed by Cecil B. De Mille, who was said to be the brother of the famous William De Mille.

Ben went to New York, contacted Lasky and Goldfish, and tried to make a deal.

"Not yet," said Goldfish. "We're not finished."

"When do you think?"

"Who knows? He's in Flagstaff, Arizona. Because that's where they got the real Indians, and he's in California because here these bastards wouldn't give us the cameras. And the film we had to pick up here, there. I don't know what's going to be. This kid, De Mille, he never made a moving picture. I'll have to let you know."

Two months passed. Ben heard from Goldfish by letter. *The Squaw Man* was completed. Would he consider a showing in one of his theatres as a trial run? Of course. They chose the best and the biggest of Ben's theatres—the one in Philadelphia.

When Ben returned home that night, Alice knew at once that something was wrong.

"What happened?"

"Terrible. Something terrible!"

"What?"

"Give me a schnapps and I'll tell you."

Drink in hand, he began: "It started in all right. Then all of a sudden . . . the whole picture . . . it started in to jump on the screen."

"What do you mean 'jump'?"

"I mean all over—up and down and sideways and like a bad dream—and then, all right a minute, and then crazy again, and

64

the people started laughing—then whistling and stamping the feet—so the projectionist stopped it. And we put in another picture . . . but in the booth . . . Lasky was sick and Goldfish was crying like a baby, and the projectionist was explaining—who knows what—something about the sprocket holes was wrong. It was something terrible."

Later it turned out that by using film and cameras from various sources the final print was inconsistent. It took months to repair the damage, but when *The Squaw Man* was finally shown, it was a success.

There were some who believed that the trust had deliberately sabotaged the Lasky-Goldfish effort. In any case, it made others reluctant to attempt production.

Ben tried without success to arrange another appointment with Mr. Edison. Everything had changed.

He played *The Squaw Man,* and as a result, found that he could no longer get films from the trust exchange.

He pleaded with them, he promised to show only their films in the future; they were unrelenting.

He played whatever miscellaneous material he could find, but business fell off badly and one by one, he was forced to close his theatres, then sell them—to the trust, of course—at a loss.

In an effort to save at least *one* theatre, he borrowed carelessly. His credit rating was poor, so he found it necessary to make small loans from several banks in different towns: Rahway, Bound Brook, Paterson. He used the same collateral for each loan, knowing it was wrong, even dangerous—but he was desperate. Six months later, when he was unable to meet his obligations, his notes were called. His only hope was to borrow from his mother. He went to New York but, once there, lost heart and returned to Plainfield. A last-minute loan from the Bohls saved him.

"I can't have my son-in-law in the hoosegow," said Mr. Bohl grimly.

For the next month, sleep eluded Ben. He walked; first around the house, until he found he was disturbing Alice and Haim; then he took to dressing and wandering about the town.

One night, the patrolman found him, at 4:00 A.M., sitting on the curbstone in front of The Happy Hour—now closed and no longer his.

"You all right, Ben?" he asked.

Ben replied in Yiddish, and continued to do so until long after the patrolman brought him home.

The following day he was admitted to the Muhlenberg Hospital, where he remained for five weeks, being treated for what was called a nervous breakdown. Alice and the Bohl family were steadfast.

After his recovery, there was talk of reopening Farber's Dry, but Ben could not bring himself to it.

"I want to stay in the movie business," he insisted.

"*Stay?*" said Alice. "You're not in it *now*."

He stood up, suddenly, from the kitchen table, felt dizzy, pointed at her and said, "I *will* be! I *shall* be! You'll see." He sat down and put his head in his hands.

"You want some more coffee?" asked Alice.

"No. Too much coffee."

"Go lay down."

"Tomorrow," he said, "I'm in New York. Barovick, I'll see."

"Barovick!" she said, scornfully. "That loony. If not for him—"

"Loony he's not. He works for Biograph. No more selling. Now he's mixed up with making."

"Mixed up is right. And that's what *you'll* be, too, if you don't come to your senses."

"*How*, Alice? Tell me how and I'll do it. I swear. I want to make you happy. How?"

"I've told you. Papa's told you. Let's open the store again. And start over."

"Alice, the one thing I know is—to go backwards is no good. Every day in my life I want to go forwards. If not, what's the use?"

"You *went* forwards, so look what happened."

"Too *fast* forwards, maybe," he said. "No more. But the dry goods—no. I couldn't do it. And Alice—between us, between you and me—we have to be honest, no? The business was *not* good."

"We made a living."

"A *little* living."

"So what's wrong with that? What do you want?"

"A *big* living," he said.

66

Later in the day, he phoned Fred Barovick.

"I like to see you, Fred."

"Sure thing. When?"

"Tomorrow?"

"Make it in the afternoon, all right? We're starting a new picture in the morning. Say three o'clock?"

"Yes. Three."

"You know where to come?"

"I'll find it. Don't worry."

"Better I tell you. You'll be coming over on the Hundred and Twenty-fifth Street ferry, right?"

"Right."

"All right. Then walk straight over to Broadway and get on the downtown trolley. You'll have to change at Forty-second, so get a transfer. Then get off at Fourteenth and then it's not far to walk. Number Eleven East Fourteenth Street. Don't go into the studio. Come right up to my office, third floor, I'll be looking for you. Three o'clock."

"I'll be there," said Ben.

The trip from Dunellen to Biograph took over four hours, but Ben felt himself gaining in strength, rather than tiring, as the journey proceeded.

American Biograph, 11 East Fourteenth Street. Ben stood for a time in front of the wide brownstone, looking up at it, his mouth slightly open. For him, it was a shrine. He started up the steps, but stopped suddenly, terrified. His confidence drained out of him. He returned swiftly to the sidewalk and waited uncertainly, trying to rally his strength. He took his watch out of his vest pocket and looked at it. 2:40. Thank God. He walked around the block. On the first corner, a hurdy-gurdy played "Ta-ra-ra Boom-de-ay." He gave the little begging monkey a penny. For luck. On the last corner, a saloon. Did he dare? He went in and stood at the bar.

"Rye," he said. "Beer chaser."

"Yes, sir."

New York, he mused. For fifteen cents, they call you "sir," even, into the bargain.

The sight of the free-lunch counter reminded him that in the excitement of the day he had forgotten to eat lunch. That explained it. That was the cause of the sudden sinking of the heart. Eat something. He piled a plate with pretzels, cheese, ham (an automatic, nervous giggle as he imagined the look on his mother's face could she see him now—or worse, Tante Channah's), pickled tomatoes, salami, and a chicken leg.

Drink first, or food first? Food, or at least some of it. Half. It became an occasion. He ate half the food on his plate, knocked back the rye, exhaled furiously, and took a sip of the beer. He felt better at once. The rest of the food. He ordered another rye. What the hell? In for a dime, in for a dollar. Or at least thirty cents. The rye again, the beer finished. He put half a dollar down on the bar, and wondered, as the bartender took it and rang it up, if he should leave a tip. New York, after all. A dime? A nickel? Then, just in time, the signs over the bar caught his eye:

In God We Trust
All Others Pay Cash.

Work Is the Curse
of The Drinking Man.

"TELL THE TRUTH!"
—Grover Cleveland.

And lettered across an American flag:

TIPPING IS UN-AMERICAN

"Thank you, sir," said the bartender, giving him his change. Two dimes.

"Thank *you*," said Ben. "Delicious."

The bartender seemed surprised. His patrons were rarely polite. He reached down, picked up his own personal reservoir and took a sip.

"You from around here?" he asked.

"No. Dunellen."

"Where?"

"New Jersey. Dunellen, New Jersey."

"Oh, Jersey!" said the bartender forgivingly.

"Yes."

"What brings you to the Big Town?" he asked.

Ben took a deep breath, slipped his foot off the brass rail, stood

68

up straight and said, "Business. I'm in the moving picture business."

This time the brownstone steps of The American Biograph Company presented no threat. Going up them seemed to be the most natural act imaginable. In another sense, it suggested to Ben an ascent to a private heaven.

In a large room on the first floor, a film was being manufactured. He recognized the action, having observed it long ago at The Edison Studio. He watched for a moment, but, remembering Fred's admonition, took care not to cross the threshold.

An excessively tall hawk-nosed man appeared to be in full command. He wore a wide-brimmed hat, which seemed incongruous indoors. He spoke firmly, authoritatively, in a rich, southern accent. Ben's skin tingled as he realized that this was the great D.W. Griffith, many of whose pictures he had played in the days of The Happy Hour.

Another man, also wearing a hat (straw), stood beside him. This man's job seemed to consist of shouting, "Quiet! Quiet, please!" every twenty seconds or so.

I could do that, thought Ben.

"Jesus Christ!" said a hoarse voice behind him.

He whirled about and found himself confronted by his friend Fred Barovick.

"Hello, Fred."

Fred took him by the shoulders, turned him around, and literally pushed him up the stairs.

On the first landing, they stopped and shook hands.

"Jesus!" Fred repeated.

"What'samatter?"

"Didn't I tell you don't go in the studio?"

"I didn't."

"You did. I saw you."

"Not in. *By.*"

"Same thing."

"It is?"

"Me, I don't care. What the hell do I care? But D.W.—Jesus, he's a *hellion.* Every stranger's an enemy. He thinks everybody else in the business is spying on him—you know—stealing his ideas. Of course, sometimes they do. Come on up."

They proceeded to the third floor and into Fred's office. A small room with three cluttered desks. A buxom myopic girl occupied one of them. It was covered with small rolls and strips of film, which she was cutting and assembling.

"Bridget Halloran, Ben Farber," said Fred.

Ben stepped toward her and extended his hand.

Bridget, squinting at a single frame of the strip in her hand, said, "How do?"

"Please to meet you," said Ben, retreating.

"She's Sennett's brain," explained Fred. "She thinks for him."

"Rubbish," said Bridget.

"Who's Sennett?" asked Ben.

"He's the straw hat you saw down there—"

Bridget looked across the room. "You were *down* there?" she asked. "In the *studio?*"

"By," said Ben. "Not in. *By.*"

"Oh."

"He's D.W.'s assistant," said Fred. "Mack Sennett. From Canada someplace. Nice fellow. Jovial."

"Funny how they wear hats inside," said Ben.

"They're Orthodox," said Fred, and howled.

Bridget regarded him pityingly.

"How's Alice?" asked Fred.

"Oh, fine, fine. And the baby, too, thank God. Everybody fine."

"And you?"

"Perfect. Just like before. Just plain perfect."

"I'm glad to hear it," said Fred. "Tell you the truth, I was worried there for a while."

"Me, too. I didn't know *what* happened. Something."

"But you're all right now?"

"Perfect. So, Fred. This is it. I need a job."

"Yes, I know. What kind of a job?"

"Any kind. So long as in the moving picture business."

"The only thing is, Ben—"

"Wait. Hear me out. I can get jobs. I got offered. And Alice, she wants we should open up again the store. But I want the moving picture business—because I want a future. Mr. Bohl, he's against—but what can I do? I told him. I said I would better in the movie business for twenty, twenty-five dollars a week than in the dry goods for forty, fifty. He thinks I'm crazy."

"So do I," said Fred. "The best job is where they pay the most money. That's simple arithmetic."

"Can you help me, Fred?"

"I'll certainly do what—"

Sennett came storming into the tiny space and went to his desk. He stopped and looked around.

"Where the goddam hell's my goddam chair?"

"God forgive you," said Bridget, crossing herself.

Ben sprang up. "Here, sir. Here. I'm sorry."

Sennett took the chair, slammed it down in front of his desk, sat down, and began to sort the papers he had carried in.

Ben stood by Fred, who said, "So like I said, Ben, I'll certainly—"

"If you're gonna *blab*, goddammit," said Sennett, without looking up, "get the hell out in the goddam hall!"

"Sure, Mack. Sure," said Fred.

"God forgive you," mumbled Bridget.

Fred, with his head, beckoned Ben out into the hall. They sat down on the stairs to continue their talk. The door to the office slammed shut loudly.

"Take my advice, Ben. Don't talk about twenty, twenty-five. You'll get no place. You'll cheapen yourself. Forty, fifty, at least."

"I'm willing," said Ben.

"Sennett's the man. He does most of the hiring. We'll tell him —you know, about the theatres—"

"But not about the bankruptcy."

"He wouldn't care about that. Maybe like it. Shows you were in business for yourself."

"Some business. Me, I like the making. Not the showing and the selling."

"Don't I know it? That's why I'm not selling anymore. Also—"

From within the office, Bridget squealed, then giggled.

"Go 'long with you, Mack" she said. "Not now." The sound of a scuffle. "Please. I'm way behind."

"Nothing wrong with *your* behind," he said. "Come here."

"Oh, Mack," she said. "Wicked, wicked."

There were a few more sounds, explicit enough to embarrass the staircase conference into silence.

After a time, Fred smiled weakly and said, "That's how he is."

"So I would have a better chance," said Ben, "if I was a girl, no?"

"Yes. But look here—"

71

Sennett came out of the office and stopped as he saw that he was blocked.

"Got a minute, Mack?"

"For you, Freddie, for you—even two."

"This is my friend, Ben Farber. Mack Sennett."

"Yes, I know," said Ben.

"*Enchanté,*" said Sennett, crushing Ben's hand.

"Ben ran that big chain of theatres in New Jersey."

"I owned them," said Ben.

"Yes," said Sennett. "Until you went on your arse."

"I'm looking for a job," said Ben.

"What can you do?"

"I'm a manager. A good manager. I know money and cost accounting and advertising and inventory and credit and economy and—"

"Hell, that's enough. That's a hell of a lot more than *I* know." He turned to Fred. "You think he could handle a unit manager spot?"

"Yes!" said Ben.

"I asked *him,* not you."

"I'm sorry."

"You don't even know what the hell it is, do you?"

"I could find out."

"Shut up." To Fred: "Could he?"

"I think so."

Sennett examined Ben carefully. Now that he was considering taking him on, he had to get beyond his first impression, which had been unfavorable.

"You're a Yid, aren't you?"

"Yes, sir."

"That's all right. With me, that is. Yids are smart. Business smart. We could maybe use a couple of Yids around here. Trouble is, the old man don't like 'em. But what the hell, he wouldn't have to know. Keep out of his way. If he talks to you, just nod your head, or shake it. Oh—say—how's this? If it comes up, we can say you're Syrian or Algerian or some goddam thing. Who knows how they talk anyway?"

"Thank you," said Ben.

"We'll start you at thirty-five."

Fred gave Ben a hard look.

"No. Fifty, the least."

"Fifty! Go home."

Ben took a breath. "Very well," he said.

"Forty?" asked Sennett.

"I like this company," said Ben. "So I'll come down to forty-five. So long as it's this company. Who else has got D.W. Griffith? And Mack Sennett?"

"All right," said Sennett. "Forty-five. Start tomorrow. Nine o'clock. You'll have to break him in, Fred."

"Gladly."

"Forty-five," said Sennett, shaking his head. "Didn't I tell you these Yids are smart?"

For the first three months, Ben commuted. Dunellen to Manhattan and back each day. He found a route using the New Jersey Central and trollies that kept the trip down to about three hours. He did not mind. The two trips daily gave him time to think and to read. It was his school on wheels. Trade papers: *The Billboard, The Moving Picture World, The New York Dramatic Mirror;* catalogues: Edison Films, Kleine Optical Company (Complete Illustrated Catalog of Moving Picture Machines, Stereopticons, Slides, Films), George Eastman and Company; above all—the newspapers: morning, afternoon, and evening—*The Morning World, The Herald, The Tribune, The Telegraph, The New York Times, The Post, The Brooklyn Eagle, The Evening World.* In time, he was changing from trolley to trolley to train without looking up from the printed page.

Days at the studio were full and exciting. When Ben started at Biograph, the output averaged two films a day. In time, he achieved a system of careful scheduling that raised it to three films a day. He did not in the least resent it when Sennett received and accepted the credit for this development. For one thing, he was still anxious to keep out of Griffith's way. For another, he wanted to make himself valuable to Sennett. What mattered most, however, was the growing self-esteem and confidence he was finding in the recognition of his ability, as well as his ability to learn.

The business mushroomed. Overtime became the order of the day. Ben worked out a system of shooting exterior scenes mornings and afternoons—Grant's Tomb, Union Square, Gramercy Park, Wall Street—and interiors at night, under artificial magnesium light at the Fourteenth Street Studio.

This meant staying overnight in the city more and more.

"The best thing would be, Alice," he said, "moving into New York."

"No," she said flatly.

"Why not?"

"It's dirty," she said. "Where will Haim play? In the streets? In the dirty streets? Four years old—he's going to run around in the streets?"

"No," said Ben. "I see children, nice children. They play in the parks . . . in . . . you know . . . by the schools . . . lots . . . big lots . . . where they play . . . what do you call them? *Please!*"

"Playgrounds," she said, reluctantly.

"Playgrounds!" he repeated. "A fine city. Millions live there."

"That's the trouble," said Alice mournfully, but somehow, in the pause that followed, Ben knew that she would acquiesce.

The flat he found for them was on Twelfth Street, just off Fifth Avenue—an attractive, tree-lined block. Third floor front, with a room for Haim. Alice adapted swiftly, to her own and Ben's surprise.

They went out often, to the theatres on Fourteenth Street and Herald Square. Third floor back, a writer named Porter (who wrote under the name O. Henry) volunteered to look after Haim whenever needed. His only payment: a cigar. They saw Lillian Russell, Joseph Jefferson, Richard Mansfield, Sarah Bernhardt, the Ziegfeld Follies, *The Pink Lady,* the opera at the Metropolitan and Hammerstein's Grand. On Saturday afternoons, a ritual visit to a vaudeville house with Haim, who loved the pace and variety of the programs more than he did straight theatre.

"Too long," he would complain.

Best of all, for Ben, were the constantly available moving picture shows, and in those years in New York, he made it his business to see every single film that was exhibited: *The Life Drama of Napoleon Bonaparte and Empress Josephine of France, The Pullman Bride, The Lonely Villa, A Good Little Devil, A Corner in Wheat, A Tale of Two Cities.*

He had insisted on sitting through *A Tale of Two Cities* twice. Halfway through the second time, Alice fell asleep on his shoulder. He held her close, full of love, yet he could not take his eyes from the screen. He was enthralled.

They walked home. He could talk of nothing but the wonder

74

of what they had just seen. The crowd scenes. How had they been done? The cost? The historical detail!

He was still talking about the film after Alice had turned out the last light in their bedroom and had joined him under the light spring blanket.

The pauses grew longer, but it was clear that they were filled with deep thought.

Ben and Alice were lying on their backs, he with his hands under his head. She moved her hand to his belly, caressed it as she would a fitful infant's in an effort to calm it to sleep, but suddenly desire overcame her. She felt the lubricating moisture being sensuously released between her thighs. She moved her hand downward and gently took hold of his genitals. She waited for them to respond to her signal, far more rare than the times when he touched her.

"And the cutting!" he said. "The best I ever saw. Did you notice like a rhythm? Like a piece of *music!*"

She laughed and withdrew her hand.

"You're laughing?" he said.

"Yes."

"For what?"

"I don't know. Maybe I should be crying."

"Never cry, my dearest. Never."

"I think you love the movies more than you love me," she said.

"Two kinds of love."

"Yes, but which is the stronger?" she asked seriously.

It took him too long to reply, "*You.* You are the stronger."

"You think?"

"I *know.*"

"If you had to give up one—me or the movies—which would you?"

"Crazy question."

"But if? What *if?*" Half a minute passed. "What if?" she repeated.

"I would give up the movies," he said sadly, dutifully. "I swear."

Another silence. His hand went to her nest, fondled it. She turned away from him onto her side.

"No?" he asked.

"Not now. Sleep."

It was good advice. He had an early call. Shooting on Bedloe's Island around the Statue of Liberty. Still, he wondered why she had rejected him after making the initial advance. He thought back, reviewing what had happened (a growing practice in his life), and when he had it before him, he realized that he did not blame her, not at all.

A year and a half after Ben went to work for Biograph, he met D.W. Griffith for the first time. It was inevitable. He was now the chief production supervisor. Mack Sennett, too, had made progress and was directing on his own. The exhibitors constantly called for comedy, a form Griffith considered beneath him. Thus, he turned most of the comedy over to Sennett and to another bright assistant, Frank Powell.

To straighten out a complex scheduling problem, D.W. invited them all to lunch at Lüchow's, down the street. Passing through those doors for the first time, Ben felt that he had entered a Dominion of Success.

The linen, the silver, the service! He ordered exactly what Griffith ordered: oysters (would he be able to down them?), bratwurst and sauerkraut, beer.

"How long have you been with us, Mr. Farber?" asked Griffith.

"Nineteen months," said Ben. "And eleven days."

"Strange we have never met," said Griffith.

"I didn't like to bother you," said Ben.

Griffith finished the last of his oysters. Ben prayed that his would stay down. Griffith sipped his beer out of a large stein and regarded Ben over its rim.

"Where are you from, Farber?"

Ben noted that he had dropped the "Mister."

"From New Jersey," said Ben. "Dunellen, New Jersey. Near Plainfield."

Griffith set down his stein.

"And before that?"

"New York," said Ben. His mouth was dry. He took a sip of beer.

"He's a Syrian," said Sennett. "From Syria."

"He's a Jew," said Griffith.

"Yes," said Ben. "I am."

The waiter, who seemed to be wearing a floor-length tablecloth for an apron, was serving the main course. When he was gone, Griffith said to Sennett, "It would seem that *your* Jew is a *good* Jew."

"Yes, he is," said Sennett.

"I've known a good many Jews," said Griffith, with his mouth full. "Did you know that Haim Solomon—a good Jew—financed the whole damned American Revolution? I don't mean I knew *him,* though."

The three guests laughed a nervous, obligatory laugh.

"My boy," said Ben, "is by the name of Haim. Four years going on five. Very good. My father was Haim also."

"Hold on," said Griffith. "Jews don't name sons for fathers or grandfathers."

"Excuse me, Mr. Griffith. Yes, if dead. Alive, no."

"An odd people," said Griffith.

"Yes," said Ben.

"You've done well by us, Ben," said Griffith. ("Ben"?!) He turned to Sennett. "What's he getting?"

"Sixty-five," said Sennett.

"Give him seventy-five."

"Thank you, Mr. Griffith," said Ben hoarsely.

"Now," said Griffith, "let us consider our plan of battle."

For the next few months, studio matters were superseded by Haim's whooping cough, chicken pox, and scarlet fever. Alice blamed the city of New York and began to talk of moving back to Dunellen.

"Wait," said Ben. "Please wait. Something is in the air. Something splendid, *wunderbar,* wonderful. For all of us."

"What is it?"

"You'll see."

"Tell me."

He took a deep breath and exhaled, "California!"

"Oh, Ben," she said. "Don't be crazy *again!*"

The next day, she took Haim and moved back to Dunellen.

Am I crazy? thought Ben, as he went for his Saturday morning walk to the Fulton Street Fish Market. Sennett had begun to hint at the move more and more. His girl, Mabel Normand, seemed to be urging it. She thought it was time he broke away from Griffith. Mack at first suspected this motive, since it was a known fact that

D.W. and Mabel disliked each other. She was too merry, too frivolous for his taste—and too unmanageable.

Ben adored Mabel. Aside from her beauty and wit and audaciousness, her talent and invention and imagination—she seemed to him to be the most American girl he had ever met.

"Griffith's a peacock," she said to Ben one day. "Strutting around all day, trying to look as though he knows all about it. Hell, nobody knows *anything* much, let alone all. It's a new toy. The way Mack plays with it is more my way."

"Comical, you mean?"

"Sure, let's have some fun, f'Chrissake. What's all this Judith of Bethulia manure?"

"A man of vision," said Ben. "Mack says everything he knows he learned from Griffith."

"Fine. What I say. Time to move on. You can't stay an assistant all your life. You *shouldn't*."

The break came suddenly. Sennett asked Ben to meet him at McGrory's. One ale, one porter.

"I'm going," said Sennett.

"You told him already?"

"Yes. He was fine about it, too. Wished me luck and all. Kessel and Bauman are putting up the simoleons, and may God have mercy on my soul."

"California," said Ben, awed.

"Want to come?" asked Sennett.

"I don't know," said Ben, his hands trembling. "Alice . . ."

Sennett broke into song:

> "When you—
> Wear the Ball and Chain
> Around the ankle—!"

"No, Mack. No. Alice is good. We're together."

"You're henpecked, Ben. And that's a fact. Mabel tries it on me, I kick 'er arse."

"I think *you're* henpecked," said Ben craftily.

Sennett exploded. "Me?!"

"Sure. I notice how you're going. Why? Because *she* wants you to, not because *you* want."

"*I* want, you dumb sheeny! *I* want. That's where it *is*, where it's all going to be. Listen, this is still a secret, so don't throw it around, but the old guy's thinking of a move, too."

"He *is?*" asked Ben.

"The conditions, boy, that's where they got the conditions."

"I'll talk it over," said Ben.

"Get yourself out there and you got a job right off. With me."

"Thank you."

"I'll start you off at seventy-five—like here—first thing you know, you'll be making a hundred."

"From your mouth to God's ear."

"And what's more," said Sennett, enjoying his role of powerful tycoon, "I'll pay half your expenses for the trip."

"Very nice," said Ben.

"One more?" asked Sennett.

"No, no. My head is already spinning with ale."

Sennett raised his glass.

"See you in California," he said.

"What then?" said Ben.

Summer came suddenly. Griffith suspended production for a week and gave the whole company a week off with pay.

Ben and Alice and Haim went to a boardinghouse in Deal, New Jersey, for a week. Sitting there on the porch one evening, studying the sea, Ben said, "That ocean. Same ocean. I came across it, the whole thing, Alice. Now I know what I got to do. I got to go more. That's the story of my people. We got to go . . . wherever we can live . . . whatever we can do. Here is no good for me no more. For us. We got to go."

"Where, Ben?"

"California."

"What?"

"California."

"We can't."

"We're going. The showing moving pictures is nothing. The making, the manufacturing—that's the whole thing, the main thing, and that's where it's going to be. They got there the sun, and all the people who know are going. Will your father lend us? For the trip, only. We'll go in the machine. It will take two, maybe three weeks. But I'll find the way, you'll see."

"I don't know, Ben. I don't know."

"Come with me," he said. They went up to their room and made love for the first time in two months.

In the act, Alice felt his strength and his confidence. She would not stand in his way. They would go.

Two months of preparations. Selling, storing worldly goods. Maps and consultations with the automobile company. Clothing, supplies purchased. Spare tires, tool kits. Food hampers. A small tent to camp out in, if necessary. Also—at Mr. Bohl's insistence —a shotgun and a pistol.

At five o'clock in the morning on May 12, 1912, Ben, Alice, and Haim got into the Reo. The Bohls stood on the sidewalk and in the street. Final goodbyes. Haim began to cry as the motor started. No matter. The car rolled off. Ben, driving, looked resolutely straight ahead. Alice turned and, through tears, saw her family receding. She waved; they all waved back. She turned away, looking with her husband to the road ahead.

The Bohls stood waiting until they could see the car no longer.

Choked, Mr. Bohl said, "I *love* those God damn fools!"

PART II

PIE IN
THE FACE

I

"WHAT A goddam trip!" said B.J. "I still can hardly believe we made it. Three weeks. Some places there was no road from here to the next place, so I had to drive to some other place where there *was* a road to the next place. And the dust! The kid got sick over and over. Who could find gas stations? So we ended up carrying cans in the back and they would leak and stink. I tell you, I look at westerns sometimes—with the covered wagons and so on—and I think to myself: What are *they* suffering? They had it *easy* compared with me!"

We were driving home from the studio. I had spent the early afternoon with four of Farber's controllers, who gave me an inventory that did not remotely match the one I had in my briefcase. I could see there would be massive checking to do before anything could be closed.

Later, I had rejoined B.J., who seemed intent on continuing his story. Was it part of his scheme to build up the value of his holdings by concentrating on its personal, sentimental aspects? Was it simply and plainly a garrulous old man who enjoyed talking, especially about himself? I could not tell.

"We got out here finally—I found us a two-room flat in a little wooden building on Vine Street. I rested for one day and went right away out to see Sennett. He didn't have his big Edendale studio yet with his name a mile high on it. It was still a little lot—like a crazy house. What a world! He had a whole team going all the time—Harold Lloyd, Buster Keaton, Fatty Arbuckle, Mabel Normand—" He stopped, and there was a long pause before he resumed. When he did, he said, "Mabel Normand!" again, and his voice had the sound of an echo.

"Anyhow, we had our meeting. He was glad to see me and said, Oh, boy, how he needed help. All these bastards around him were robbing him blind. So that was going to be me—my job—to watch over everything—everything came in, everything went out. He was a big fellow, Sennett. Sometimes we would hear him singing in his office or in the projection room—if he was waiting for a reel or something. And you know what he would be singing?"

"No idea."

"Opera! He would sing opera all the time. *Aïda, Carmen, Pagliacci.* That's what he always wanted to be—in opera. He was on Broadway, y'know. A singer. He was one of the chorus boys in *Floradora*—a wonderful show. I saw it—I took my mother."

He looked out the window and sang, softly and badly off key:

"Oh, tell me, pretty maidens,
    Are there any more at home like you? . . ."

"But he never made it into the opera. Sennett. He used to tell how he decided he's going to take lessons from the best—a Professor Waldemar in Carnegie Hall. So he went and he sat waiting for his turn, and from the inside, he heard the most beautiful tenor he ever heard. He thought it must be Caruso, the least. So he asked, 'Who is it?' And the secretary told him, 'That is one of the finest artists in the world. He's studied already ten years all over Europe—now he's here.' Mack said, 'In the Met?' 'No, no,' she said, 'not yet. He sings in a beer garden in Yorkville. Imagine it—a great artist like that, and they pay him a dollar and a half a night!' And Mack says he got up and went over to one of those big pier-glass mirrors they used to have and he looked at himself in it and he said, 'Sennett, this is not for you!' And he walked out, and it was the ending of his whole singing career. That's how he got into the movie game—after that. But he used to sing all the time—when he felt good, I mean. Most of the time, he didn't.

"So there I am with him, in his office, and like I said, he's glad to see me and I'm ready to go to work, and he says to me, 'Ben, I'm counting on you, and you do it right, and you got a big future with me.'

" 'Thanks,' I told him.

"Then he says, 'I'm starting you at forty a week. O.K.?'

" 'No,' I said. '*Not* O.K.'

" 'Why not?'

" 'Because in New York, you told me seventy-five. Also you told me you'll pay the half my expenses for the trip—so here's the bill. Half comes out eighty-four dollars.'

" 'Hold on!' he said. 'Hold on! You must've misunderstood me. I said if everything *goes good,* you could *sometime* be making seventy-five—or even more—I never said I could *start* you at seventy-five.'

" 'Yes, you did.'

"He stands up and he walks around and he looks out of his window and he shakes his head and he comes back to me and he says, 'See, Ben, the trouble is your English. You don't speak English too good—or understand it, neither—that's why this misunderstanding. Come to think, I wonder if you can handle this job with your English.'

"I didn't get mad. Who could afford it then? I had in my pocket two dollars and eighty cents, and back in the flat, Alice had our reserves: forty dollars. That's it. That's all. But I said to him, 'Listen, Sennett, English I *don't* talk perfect, but *numbers* I talk as good as *you*—maybe even better.'

" 'Look,' he says, 'let's not fight right in the start. Let's split the difference. I'll go you sixty—believe me, that's big money out here right now.'

"What could I do? I knew sixty was not split the difference. But. 'All right,' I said, 'and what about the eighty-four dollars?'

" 'I never said a damn *thing* about expenses,' he says.

" 'You did,' I says. 'I swear.'

" 'Jesus Christ, I must've been pie-eyed.'

" 'Even so.'

" 'All right, I'll go you fifty, and let's get going.'

"We shook hands, even though I didn't feel like it."

II

"SIXTY DOLLARS!" exclaimed Alice. "You told me—"

"Sixty only to start. It's a good business, you ought to see it."

"See it! I wish I'd never *heard* of it."

"And growing—and pretty soon, it'll be more. And look, we're in California—and the sun. A climate good for the boy and—"

"You shouldn't have tried to climb so high so fast, Ben."

"I know," he said. "I was wrong."

Discussion of this perennial subject was fruitless. Alice held his failure over him like a sentence unserved. He had not yet paid for his crime, but had worked out this method of resignation, admission, confession.

It gave her the upper hand, and she used it.

"I went to the grocery this morning," she said. "The prices! Everything. More than Jersey on every single item."

"We'll make out, darling, you'll see."

"On sixty dollars?"

"I can make extra. There's all kinds work here. You'll see."

There was. He found a night job: ticket taker at the Orpheum on Gower Street. Eight to ten. Two dollars a night. On Saturdays and Sundays, he drove a taxi.

When Sennett heard about the ticket-taker job, he was irritated.

"It don't look good," he said. "My studio manager takin' tickets for Grauman, f'Chrissake!"

"Is that what I *am*, Mack? Your studio manager?"

"No," said Sennett, "you're a ticket taker!"

"I want to learn the whole business. Everything. And around a theayter every night, there's a lot you could find out. The public. I see the public—who they are. What they look like going in— what they look like coming out. It's a lesson every night. The public is smart, Mack. Maybe not always one by one, but together —you should see."

"The public," said Sennett, "is a goddam boob. Give 'em plenty of pratfalls and chases and pie in the face, and they're happy.

Lookit D.W. When he was simple, his pictures raked in the shekels. Now he's gone intellectual and highbrow, he's on his canetta. And another thing—" Ben was sure the subject of his taxi driving was coming up next. He was prepared with an explanation: It was a good way to learn the city. But Sennett said, "—we're using too much film!"

"I know it. I tell them. Keaton specially. He tries every gag six different ways. I told him."

"Leave 'im alone," said Sennett. "*I'll* talk to him."

The Farbers' home life grew increasingly arid. Alice was lonely, had been unable to make new friends. Ben's multiple jobs kept him away far too much. During their time together (6:00 to 7:45, A.M. and after 10:00 P.M. on weekdays; Saturdays and Sundays from 3:30 on. Ben worked from 7:00 to 3:00) they tried to maintain contact, but it was increasingly false. Still, there was no other course that either of them could see. Not for now.

L.A. taxi drivers did not cruise. They waited at a rank for phoned orders.

One of Ben's turns came at 7:15 one Sunday morning. A pickup at an address on Benedict Canyon in the newly developed Beverly Hills area. He found it. A sprawling, impressive Mexican-style house, lush gardens. He rang the bell. A sleepy housemaid responded.

"Be right out," she said.

Ben returned to his taxi and waited.

Twenty minutes later, the door opened. A tall gray-haired man, wearing a red silk robe, embraced and kissed a veiled woman in black. A farewell. It went on for some time. Ben watched and waited.

Finally, the woman was in the cab and gave him the address of her destination: "Fifteen-ten Highland. It's the big apartment house. I'll show you."

"I know it," said Ben.

"Good."

"It's where Mabel Normand lives," he said. "The movie star. You ever hear of her?"

The reply was, "Oh, my God!" And a whoop of familiar laughter.

Ben was so startled that he pulled over to the side of the road and stopped the taxi. He turned to look at his passenger, and of course, there she was—Mabel. She was rolling about in the back seat.

"What's so funny?" asked Ben.

"Life!" she yelled "*Life* is funny. You don't think so?"

"Sometimes."

"Here I am, cheating on the old man for the first time in almost a year, and I take the trouble to make an early getaway at seven in the morning—God, what an hour!—and who should be the taxi driver but his *partner!*"

"I'm not his partner."

"You're not?"

"I work for him. Like you."

"Not like me, dearie, not like me."

Ben turned away, put the taxi in gear, and started off.

"You want the truth, Miss Normand? I'm surprised."

"Come on," she said. "Don't be hard on a girl. I only cheat on him when he's out of town."

"Not nice," said Ben.

"All right," she said. "Pull up to the nearest church—Catholic, please—and I'll knock off a few Hail Marys."

"None of my business," said Ben.

"But I'll bet you turn me in all the same."

"If you knew me, Miss Normand, you wouldn't say a thing like that."

She laughed again. "Under the circumstances," she said, "call me Mabel."

So began their curious friendship, which was to endure until she died, needlessly, on February 23, 1930, at the age of thirty-six.

Mabel Normand had come over to New York from Staten Island, where she was born, to make her way. She was soon a dazzling, popular girl about town. Many considered her to be the most beautiful girl in New York. She became a model for James Montgomery Flagg, Charles Dana Gibson, Penrhyn Stanlaws, and others, and since movies were the new and fashionable thing, she was soon part of them at Biograph in New York; and Mutascope in Fort Lee, New Jersey.

Her wild, hoydenish style—on screen and off—attracted Mack Sennett from the start. His boss, the formidable D.W. Griffith, was less impressed.

He used her in several films, but took a dim view of her future.

"Too inventive," he said to Sennett one day at lunch.

"Comes up with a lotta funny stuff, though."

"I want malleable *clay*," said D.W. "Not Mexican jumping beans."

"She's a beauty," argued Sennett.

"Beauty, my lad, is never in short supply. There has ever been a plethora of beauty. What is rare is *talent*."

"She's *got* talent," said Sennett.

"She's entirely yours, Mack. I surrender my rights."

Who knows what might have happened had the temperamental D.W. taken a different view? Mabel Normand might well have become a true screen star. As it happened, she stuck with Sennett, went to California when he did, and worked with him for seven years exclusively.

She was the one who remembered a comic they had seen at The American Theatre in New York in an act called "A Night in an English Music Hall." At her urging, Sennett brought him out to California. Mabel worked with him in many of his earliest films.

Charles Chaplin was later to say, "I was green and terrified of the camera. She seemed so at ease, and confident. She taught me a great deal. I shall always be indebted to Mabel Normand."

In addition to acting, Mabel wrote and directed. Her creative life was full and fulfilled. The rest of it was less satisfactory.

Her relationship with Mack Sennett was sketchy. He was a complex simpleton, an eccentric. When the money began to roll in, all he could think to do with it was to install an enormous bathtub in a space adjoining his office. Why? Because he liked to take baths —four or five or six a day, often during story conferences or business meetings. His office was in a tower from which he could oversee his domain, in the manner of a perched prison guard.

He and Mabel lived together on and off. The subject of marriage came up from time to time. Marriage was planned, again and again, then abandoned. The truth is that neither of them was keen on the idea.

She would often discuss these and other matters with Ben.

"*You're* married, aren't you?" she once asked him.

"Yes. For five years already."

"So how is it? Give me a hint. Give me a clue."

"Sometimes, yes," said Ben, "sometimes, no. The best thing is my boy. What a boy! Smart?"

"But that ain't marriage," said Mabel.

"What?"

"You're not married to your kid. You're married to your *wife.*"

"Of course."

"So how's that? For her, I mean."

"I do my best," said Ben darkly.

Business got better and better at the Mack Sennett Studios. He dubbed himself "The King of Comedy." The title captured the imagination of the public.

"All you gotta do," he said to Ben, "is sell yourself. Take D.W. What an actor! He's better than a Barrymore! . . . Now listen, I got a problem with this Chaplin geezer—you know, the limey? You gotta help me. Mabel'll raise hell, but the hell with *her.* The thing is—see?—I've given him a couple dozen shots already, and zero. The guy ain't funny. Now *I* know what's funny and what ain't, and he ain't, and that's all there is to it. What's our contract?"

"We've got him for another nine months yet—a hundred and seventy-five a week."

"God *damn,* what a boner! It was Mabel. She kept at me. I wish she'd mind her own damn business. Well, look—talk to the guy and see what you can do. Settle the best you can."

"No, no," said Ben. "I been to *that* fire."

"What fire?"

"You tell me do my best. I do my best—and *you* go crazy."

"Now, lookit—"

"No, no. You tell me what you're willing, and I'll see if I can buy him off."

"Five hundred," said Sennett.

"Five hundred? All right. I'll see."

"What'sa matter?"

"No matter. Nothing."

"You look like you don't think that's good."

"Mack, lemme put it to you like this. We owe him about sixty-three hundred—so we're asking him settle for *five* hundred. Would you, in his place?"

"Why you fatheaded kike—you don't see the difference?"

"No."

"He gets five hundred for *nothing*. For doing *nothing*. For packing his goddam makeup box and getting the hell off the lot. For the six thousand, he'd have to *work*. Every day, if I wanted him to."

"That's just it. He *wants* to."

"But I don't *want* him to want to!"

"I'll see what I can do."

Ben sought out Chaplin and found him in the dressing room he shared with Buster Keaton, Fatty Arbuckle, Hank Mann, and Al Rogers.

"Mr. Sennett wants I should talk to you."

Chaplin smiled wanly. "Yes," he said. "I've rather been expecting a talk." He looked around the room. Only Buster and Roscoe were there, still it was awkward.

"You want us to do a full wings and scram?" asked Arbuckle, a huge, gentle man.

"Not at all," said Chaplin.

Buster looked up from his makeup shelf.

"Tell Sennett," he said, "to go fuck a duck."

"No use," said Arbuckle. "I don't know a duck who'd stand for it."

"And this is a man," said Keaton to Ben, "who knows plenty of *ducks!*"

"Come on," said Ben.

They walked about the lot, in and out of its activity. Seven films were shooting, accentuating for Ben the agony of the job he had been ordered to do. Now and then, as they talked, they would stop in front of a set to watch the action. Chaplin seemed riveted each time.

"Charlie," said Ben, "what do you think?"

"I think I could do it if I got the chance."

"You don't think you got the chance here?"

"No."

"Why not? You've made—what?—fifteen, twenty?"

91

"Thirty-four, ol' cock."

"So why isn't that the chance?"

"Because I've been asked to do as I'm told. Again and again. Keaton does his stuff—jolly fine stuff it is, too. And Ford Sterling."

"Wait a second. Ford Sterling is our biggest star."

"Was he *always?*" asked Chaplin ingenuously.

"No."

"And look at Fatty—he's a personality and he knows it and he knows what to do with it. I'm held back."

"Sennett don't think you're funny."

"I don't think I *have* been very funny—not *here.*" He began to cry, quietly, and continued with difficulty. "But I have been funny elsewhere and I could be again."

It all seemed utterly unreal to Ben—this slight young man of twenty-five, weeping as he talked of being funny. Moreover, directly before him as he spoke, the Keystone Kops were involved in one of their wilder excesses—this time involving pie-throwing against a baseball team, with the baseball team winning every inning.

An idea struck Ben, and he lost no time in voicing it.

"Listen," he said. "Would you like to join the Kops?"

Charlie regarded the scene being shot just as his friend Fatty took a blueberry pie flush in his face.

"No," said Charlie gravely, "I think not." They walked on. "It makes them laugh, all that, but it's not funny."

"What do you mean?"

"It's mechanical. Not human. Other than on the screen, have you ever seen anyone throw a pie or get hit by one?"

"What's that got to do? It's a movie, not life."

"Yes—but somewhere," said Chaplin, "there ought to be a connection. There had better be—if this thing is going to survive."

"Oh, it'll survive all right," said Ben, "only I ain't so sure if *you* will."

"I mean to have a bash at it," said Charlie.

"If you could find an idea for yourself and the Bathing Beauties," said Ben, "maybe you could—"

They stopped to watch Harold Lloyd. He was crawling along on the floor upon which had been constructed the façade of a large building. He simulated effortful climbing and scaling and looking down in terror. Two cameras were photographing the scene. One, from the flies above; another had the cameraman prone, shooting from what would in time appear to be the sidewalk.

Chaplin, drawn to the action, made his way up into the flies and observed the trick shot from that vantage point. He shook his head in wonder and admiration. Now he made his way to the lower camera and stretched out, face down, beside that cameraman. He was again impressed. He got up and rejoined Ben, and they continued their walk.

"No," he said, "I couldn't handle the Bathing Beauties. I'd prefer to work out something with *one* of them."

"Mr. Sennett wants better to settle your contract."

Chaplin stopped. So did Ben.

"You mean I'm sacked?" asked Chaplin.

"What is *that*, 'sacked'?"

"I believe here one says 'fired' or 'discharged' or 'canned,' " he sighed. "It all comes down to the same thing, don't it? Out! Skidoo!"

They walked again.

"You're a young man, Charlie. A lot can happen."

"It already has."

"He wants to be fair."

"Go on."

"Five hundred."

"That's *not* fair."

"You don't think?"

"I can't get back into my act. They've replaced me. No, I've got to work out my contract."

"What if I could get you a thousand?"

"No."

"So what? You expect him to pay you off the whole thing?"

"I don't want the money," said Charlie. "I want the work."

He walked away, leaving Ben with the prospect of reporting failure to The King of Comedy.

Ben found him soaking in a steaming tub, his straw hat on his head, and a cigar in his mouth.

"O.K.?" asked Sennett.

"No, Mack. He don't want to settle."

"Limey sonofabitch! I'll put him in some trick shots that'll break his neck."

"He'll do them gladly. He wants to work."

"All right. Let's work 'im. Let's work his balls off. I want him workin' every day. I want him workin' till he drops—or till he quits!"

The next day Chaplin was told to report to the set of *Tillie's Punctured Romance.* He was told only that he was to play the part of "The City Slicker." He sat in the dressing room, staring at himself in the mirror. "Not funny!" He looked about and saw a pair of Fatty Arbuckle's pants hanging over the back of a chair.

"You going to use those today, Roscoe?"

"No, why?"

"May I?"

"Sure thing."

Chaplin put them on. Keaton laughed. Chaplin next found a discarded frock coat that had been in too many pie-throwing scenes, dry-cleaned, and shrunk. He put it on. Someone's old derby lay on the floor. He picked it up and put it on his head. Shoes. There were a pair of Ford Sterling's on the shelf. Chaplin tried them on. Too big.

"Switch 'em," suggested Keaton.

Chaplin did so, got up, and found it difficult to walk properly. No matter. The walk seemed comical.

His heart was beating faster than usual. His getup felt good, but would Sennett approve? He added a false dress front, collar, and tie. The odd walk suggested a cane. He selected one from a stand containing fifty.

He sat down again and examined his face. "Not funny!" He began to make up. Yellow base, black around the eyes. Ready. He rose, sat down again, and impulsively pasted on a mustache he had seen lying on someone's shelf.

He looked at himself long and hard, then said, "Funny!"

He rose and made his way to the set, practicing his new walk all the way. Everyone he passed laughed.

He went faster and faster. Going around a corner, he found it easier to pivot on one heel.

Onto the set now, continuing his new-found moves. Laughter.

Sennett saw him and laughed, harder than anyone.

"Who's that?" he asked Ben.

"Charlie."

Sennett stopped laughing and said, "Not funny. . . . All right, let's go! Quiet!!"

Sennett was nervous. This was one of his most ambitious projects thus far, a six-reel film starring Marie Dressler, who had just completed a phonomenal five-year run in a play called *Tillie's Nightmare*. Sennett saw no reason not to cash in on this success.

Although Dressler was making her film debut, she was forty-four years old. She towered over Chaplin, who loathed the obviousness of this comic device.

Sennett directed this one himself (with the help of his cameraman, Chuck Hummel), and hectored Chaplin incessantly.

Had it not been for the presence of Mabel Normand in the cast, it is likely that Chaplin would have succumbed and quit. But Mabel was steadfast. Dressler, too, admired Chaplin, although, strangely, he hated her, probably because Sennett made him play passionate love scenes over and over again with this woman, who seemed to him a repulsive gorgon. Also, the fact that Dressler was getting $2,500 a week rankled him.

When they came to shooting a typical Sennett ending—the principals chased by police (his favorite staple) and finally diving off a pier and into the sea—Sennett made Chaplin take his jump some twenty times.

Finally, Mabel said, "Jesus, Mack! Haven't you got it by now? You're wasting film!"

"Film?" said Mack. "Chuck ain't had no film in the camera for the last fifteen takes!" He laughed boomingly.

"You bastard!" Mabel yelled. "You stinkin' rotten bastard!"

Mack made the mistake of striking her. She went off, crying—but returned ten minutes later with a bucket of swill and dumped it all over Sennett from behind. He got up and chased her, but was no match for her agility. She found her way to the prop room and began throwing its contents at him: pots, pans, china, wax fruit, stuffed animals, dummies, a shovel, a hoe, a rake, an accordion. Sennett ordered her to stop. He screamed at his staff and the crew to get her. At this point, the members of the cast came to her aid. The battle that followed outdid the wildest of Sennett's productions. Ben fought on both sides—on Sennett's when Mack was looking, on Mabel's when he was not. Trips, falls, furniture thrown, thrown back, people thrown, mud slung, pile-ups.

All at once, Sennett, looking about him, wild-eyed, realized what was going on and began to shout at Chuck Hummel.

"Roll 'em!" he screamed. "For Christ's sake—roll 'em!"

Chuck tried, but each time, the opposition upended both him and the camera. Ben, pretending to assist Chuck, managed to pull one leg off the tripod. Chuck's attempts to shoot with a two-legged tripod sent Mabel, then Charlie, into paroxysms of laughter.

The battle, which had rivaled Agincourt, ended—but the desperate and hysterical Chuck, fearing for his job, continued his surreal attempts at getting his camera going again.

In the end, the whole assembly stood in a great circle, watching him.

At length, Chuck gave up and stood, panting and dripping.

Sennett approached him. "Did you get it?"

Chuck shook his head.

"None of it?"

Another shake.

"Oh, *shit!*" said Mack Sennett. "You're fired! But not today! Come on, goddamnit, time's a-wastin'. Let's go!"

III

"It was funny," said B.J., "—them two being together as long as they did. Of course, they didn't end up. Maybe they should've, maybe they would've saved one the other. The way it turned out, they both had bad endings. Mack died broke—even though that day, the day she spilled the garbage on him, he was worth maybe six, maybe seven million. And Mabel—also money—but in the end, it didn't help her—she died from too much life. That can happen, y'know. But they were remarkable people all the same —artists. What made it hard to understand them together was— well, like this. They were both common—from nowhere. 'Mutts!' Griffith used to say about them. And Mack liked it like that, he

96

liked being common and vulgar and lowbrow. But she didn't. She used to read everything—classics and Shakespeare and philosophy. The first time I ever heard the name of Freud, it was from Mabel. So that's why I say the two of them—they made such a funny combination. It's a question of character, don't you think so? Like take two fellows used to be around: Sam Goldwyn and Harry Cohn. They both came up from nothing and ended up each one the head of his own company. Goldwyn—a remarkable man. His name was first Goldfish. Then he went into partners with Arch and Edgar Selwyn, from the theatre—high class—and they called their company Goldwyn—later on, Sam liked it, so he took the name for himself. Edgar once told me, 'We *had* to call it Goldwyn because the only other combination would have been to call it Selfish!' . . . What was I saying? Oh, yes. About Sam—what he wanted maybe more than anything was to be a gentleman, and that's what he became. You never *saw* such a gentleman. His clothes were the best. He never carried anything in his pockets— not even money—because it would spoil the fit. And his shoes, and the best of shirts and ties. His office—elegant; and his home and his wife—everything high class. But Cohn—different. If you wanted to insult him, you would call him a gentleman. He *wanted* to be a low-life—he was proud of it—the other thing embarrassed him. So that was Mabel and Mack. They started together in the business, and she was his girl—I think six, seven years. They used to fight something terrible—but then always made up, and he would buy her some jewelry or something. And then, finally, one day, Mack told me they decided at last they were going to get married. I was so surprised, I can't tell you. He told me he asked D.W. to be his best man—but D.W. said he had to be out of town that day. So Mack said he was going to ask one of his brothers, but if *he* couldn't come, he might have to ask *me*. I said fine, it would be an honor, but what about Charlie or Harold or Roscoe? And Mack said no—nobody from the players, because he couldn't play favorites. Then he said, 'And I'm not sure about *you* either, because it's going to be in a church and everything, and I don't know if it's proper to have—you know—one of your kind in a church. I'll have to ask the priest or the minister or whatever the hell he is.' I said to him, 'Listen, you don't sound like *you* belong in a church either—any more than me.'

"The way it turned out, there was nothing to worry, because in

97

the end, it didn't happen. All the plans were made, the date was arranged, and the place, and Mabel bought enough trousseaux for *three* weddings—but then . . ."

IV

"It's a Goddamn good thing Big Nose *did* turn you down," said Mabel. "Because if he'd said yes—you'd've had to find somebody else to be the bride!"

"That wouldn't be hard," said Mack. "There's plenty of 'em after me all the time."

"Quantity," said Mabel, "not quality."

"Anyway, I haven't given up yet, and if I can get D.W., I'm damn well going to."

"Save your breath," said Mabel. "He thinks you're beneath him."

"He's right. I am."

"Well, *I'm* not. I'm as good as he is—*better.*"

They were getting ready for bed. Mabel, at her jam-packed dressing table, was brushing her hair passionately while waiting for the rose water and glycerine to soak into her face. Mack moved in and out of the bathroom during the progressive stages of his seventh bath of the day.

"He's the only man in movies bigger than me," said Mack, carefully blotting his testicles with a large Turkish towel.

"Well, *that's* not so big," said Mabel.

He wadded the wet towel and threw it at her. Fortunately for the evening, he missed her.

"Pick it up," she said.

He was about to tell her to pick it up herself, when he caught a glimpse of her classic bosom. God knows he had seen more than his share of them in the course of his tomcat years, but never one to compare with this one. In his early Broadway days, when he was still a chorus boy, he had contrived, one hot summer's night, armed with binoculars, to peek across an alleyway into Lillian Russell's dressing room in the Weber and Fields Music Hall on

98

Twenty-ninth Street where she was appearing in *Whoop-de-doo*. He saw her as she stood on an ermine bathmat in the full glory of her nakedness, as her maid sponged her down with eau de cologne. Hers was the most celebrated *poitrine* of the century, and his memory carried it indelibly in grateful admiration until the bust of Mabel Normand came into his life. He knew then that he had overestimated Lillian Russell's. It was large, yes. In fact, a bit *too* large and out of proportion. Moreover, the nipples were set in a large dark-brown areola that seemed unartistic. Not so in the case of Mabel's incomparable tits. They protruded in perfect proportion to her head and shoulders, invitingly and maddeningly. They were firm and unusually shaped, jutting symmetrically, triangularly, to a delicious point—and there was no more than the merest rose petal blush surrounding the cherrylike nipples. Beyond all this, Mabel's breasts were alive and responsive and eloquent.

Mack moved slowly across the room and picked up the damp towel. He returned it to the bathroom, came out again, and said, "Sorry, honeybun. . . . Y'know what McCauley told me today? The accountant? He told me I'm worth four an' a half million bucks. Counting everything."

"Throwing things," said Mabel, with dignity, "is infantile."

"*You* do it," he protested.

"Only when I'm infantile," she said.

"Should I put on my nightshirt?" he asked, coyly. "Or are we gonna—you know—*gonna?*"

"I don't know yet," said Mabel. "I'm thinking."

"What about?"

"—wedding."

"It's gonna be grand, don't you worry your little noodle."

"I'm sure of it, but my problem is I'm a kind of ashamed of myself."

"How so?"

"Well, maid of honor. I think of asking Gloria or Edna or one of the Gishes, and then I realize I'm only thinking them because they're stars. By rights, it should be my best friend."

"Marylou?"

"Of course."

"Yeah, well, she sure in hell's no star—and never *will* be. She's a sow."

"She is *not!*" yelled Mabel, and threw her brush at him with great force and perfect aim. As he whirled about to avoid the worst, the silver brush hit him smartly on his left buttock. The brush clattered to the floor. He looked at it.

"Pick it up," he said.

"Pick it up yourself."

He did so, brought it to her dressing table, and put it down.

"She's a sow," he repeated. "And what's more, she's through at the studio at the end of her contract—two more months. God help us."

"Please, Mack," said Mabel. "Don't."

"She's no damn good," he said. "I only put her on because you begged me. You can't run a business on friends and favors. She's just another smick-smack girl, and they're a penny a dozen. Now she's had her chance and she's muffed it, and that's it."

"Mack, please. Don't break her heart."

"She's breakin' *mine. And* my bankroll."

"She'll improve. Harold likes her. Buster, too."

"They like her personally, not professionally."

"Mack?"

"What?"

"*Don't* put on your nightshirt."

The next day, Mack left for San Francisco. He was to be gone two days for meetings with exhibitors.

Mabel went over to Marylou's. They prepared dinner together (chili con carne and beer; lemon meringue pie and coffee) and ate it in the kitchen.

"He's dissatisfied," said Mabel. "If you weren't my best friend, I wouldn't tell you. I couldn't. He says you're too fat—and you *are,* Marylou."

"It's from unhappy. When I'm unhappy, I eat. He gives me rotten parts, the big windbag. Then he blames *me.* That Madeline Hurlock—everybody thinks she's the cat's pajamas. Sure. She gets good parts. Like with Ben Turpin and the lion. If *I* had that part, so I'd be hot stuff, too."

"It isn't that, Marylou. Whatever they give you to do, you've got to hypnotize yourself into thinking it's wonderful. Too much of the time, you look like you *hate* what you're doing."

"I do."

"That's what I *mean*."

They went on talking and searching for the answers and eating, and ended up in tears—both of them.

"And listen," said Mabel, impetuously. "You're going to be my maid of honor!"

"Oh, my God!" said Marylou. "Thank you! Oh—thank you!"

She promised to try harder; Mabel assured her that Mack could be handled.

"Leave him to me," she said.

They embraced tearfully. Mabel drove herself home in the new Stutz Bearcat that Mack had given her, wondering all the way how she was going to go about changing his mind. Stubbornness was one of his most powerful characteristics.

She parked the car in the driveway and made her way to her front door. Only then did she discover that in the emotion and crisis of her parting from Marylou, she had forgotten her handbag.

"Oh, balls!" she said, and trudged back to the car.

It was late now, and traffic was sparse, and she drove much too fast. In front of Marylou's house on Franklin Avenue, she stopped, left the motor running, and approached the front door. She was about to ring the doorbell when she heard the sound of a powerful baritone singing "Toréador, en gardé" from *Carmen*. She froze, listening. A Gramophone? Yes. No. She observed herself as she moved around to the back of the house. Her brain was giving orders which her body refused to heed. Stop! Turn around! Go back! Don't go in! She moved like a sleepwalker to the back of the house, into the kitchen, through the hall, and up the stairs to the rhythm of the continuing song.

In the upper hall, she paused for the merest moment before she opened the door to the bedroom and walked in.

For a full minute, all action was suspended. It seemed to her like one of those freeze-frame shots Buster Keaton had been experimenting with lately.

Marylou, nude, sprawled on the bed, smoking. Mabel noticed a long red scar on her abdomen. Appendix?

At the foot of the bed, Mack—stripped and with drink in hand —could not seem to get his mouth closed. But what held her eyes magnetically was the sight of his erection, which seemed to be pointing at her accusingly.

She watched it with automatic fascination as it melted away into limp detumescence, then she turned away slowly and left. Into the hall, down the stairs, through the kitchen, out—back to the kitchen for her handbag; out again and into the Stutz—motor still running.

She collapsed in tears on the steering wheel and tried several times to put the car in gear and go, but failed.

Mack leaning in.

"Mabel, listen, please—you gotta understand. I told you she was no good—a tramp. She got me drunk. I'm drunk right now —crazy. It'll never happen again—never—on my mother's life. I went crazy—listen, Mabel. We're too important together to each other. And listen, goddamnit! What about you and that fucking William Desmond Taylor skunk? You're no angel, so don't make out like I'm some kind of a— Mabel? Please? Mabel?"

The car took off in a spurt, veering left, and throwing him to the pavement. He yelled at the departing car.

"You bitch! Try to kill me? I'll have you arrested! Come back here! *Mabel!!*"

Marylou watched from the bedroom window as he rose, brushed himself off, and stood uncertainly for a time. Will he come back up? she wondered. Of course. He was wearing only socks, pants, and shirt. He'll *have* to come up for the rest of his clothes—and things. Will he stay? Of course, she told herself, more reason now than ever. Mabel's out. Could I move in? By God, I'm gonna give it a try.

Now she spoke aloud, softly. "Here he comes," she said. Then, louder, "No! Oh, Christ! Where's he goin'?" She yelled after him, *"Where you goin'?"*

He was gone.

V

"You live a long life, like me," said B.J., "—all kinds of things happen to you. Some wonderful, some crazy—but the most un-believable of all was what happened to me one night with Mabel Normand. I told you what a *different* person she was—full of fun

102

and played jokes and tricks on everybody. But then serious, too —and could act and write and direct. The main thing about her, though, was how you never could tell—nobody could—what she was going to do from one minute to the next minute. Even shooting, you would do five takes—she would do it five different ways. Every second, she would invent something new. All right. Imagine this. Put yourself in my place. I'm living in a bungalow near the Edendale Studio. By myself. Alice put it to me—either the movies or her. What could I do? She went back to New Jersey. So I'm living alone in this bungalow. Forty-five dollars a month. And it's late one night and I'm sleeping. Now, I'm what they call a light sleeper—all my life, a light sleeper—and I hear a sound. What kind of a sound? A window is opening. I could hear the sash weights. A burglar? What have I got to burgle? A joke? A mistake? What? I figure out that the best would be for me to make out I'm sleeping and see what or whatever. One eye open, and the next thing, my heart almost stops. Who is standing there right inside of my bedroom? You got it. Mabel Normand. And she says, 'Ben? Ben! Please wake up. I need you.' I sit up, and I say, 'What is it, Mabel? What's going on?' And I start to get out of bed, and she says, 'No, don't move. Stay where you are.' And she goes into the bathroom, and after a while, I hear the shower, and then she comes out wrapped in a towel—carrying her clothes. She hangs up everything—she was always the neatest person you ever saw. And she goes to my chiffonier and she gets out some pajamas— tops only—and she puts them on and comes over and she gets into bed with me and she puts her head on my shoulder and she says, 'Hold me, Ben. Please hold me.' So I do, and then she says, 'Please be my friend. I need a friend.' I said to her, 'Friend? What friend? I love you, Mabel.' And she pulls away and sits up and says, 'No! Don't ever say that! I never want to hear that goddamned word again as long as I live! I *hate* love! It's just another word for lie!' And she comes back and hangs on to me and tells me the whole story of what Mack did to her with Marylou and how it's all over and she never wants anything to do with him and she came to me because she knows he's going to look for her and the one place he won't look is here. Also, she says, 'You attract me as a man. You always have—even in New York. Let's be friends,' she says. 'Real friends.' 'Yes,' I said. So we kissed, and the next thing you know, she was asleep. Not me. She slept maybe two, three hours, and then she woke up and she pulled me over onto her and said, 'Please.' It was like nothing I ever knew about or heard about or read about. It was life. It was what we live for. . . . In the morning, I made breakfast for her—matzo brei; she'd never even heard of it—and we talked. We didn't go to the studio. We talked all day. We decided to leave Sennett and go in business for ourself. She called up Roscoe Arbuckle, and he came over. He'd been having all kinds of trouble with Mack, and so he came in with us, too. We tried for Buster, also—but he said he would never break a contract. What surprised us all was Mack. He said O.K., goodbye and good luck, and I think at the time, he thought he meant it. So that was how it happened. I was in business for myself with two stars—Mabel Normand and Fatty Arbuckle. Mabel got a loan from the Bank of America and we took over a nice little studio in Culver City. We called ourself Fan Films, for Farber, Arbuckle, Normand. And we made a beautyful fan for a —what d'y' call it?—a logo. On the building and stationery and everything. It was like in heaven. My own studio—well, at least, part of it. Something I didn't understand then—I don't understand now—how the better our professional life went—and it went simply great the first year—the worse our personal life. Mabel meant it about she hated love. She wanted excitement and parties and—I'm sorry to say—other men. So it ended for us, and she went to work for Goldwyn and then Mickey Neilan and then to England. A restless girl."

Ben said, "When she came back from London, I tried to get her back into Fan Films, but no use. But Roscoe was still with me, and next to Chaplin, he was the biggest. And Harry Langdon came with us, and—after his accident—Harold Lloyd. He lost three fingers from his right hand doing a trick shot, so Hal Roach fired him. But that Harold! He got a great propertyman to make him like a rubber hand and went on to be one of the biggest. We made about a hundred and twenty pictures a year. Each one cost maybe twenty, twenty-five thousand, and each one took in like a hundred and fifty thousand—so you can see that money was not the problem. I bought a nice house, and my son, Haim, came out and spent two months summer and two months Christmas every year. His mother divorced me and married a paper box manufacturer. Haim didn't like him, but he didn't like me either. A difficult boy —and today, he's a difficult man.

"Then came Pempy."

London. The Savoy Grill. At a corner table Mabel Normand is supping with Mack Sennett.

"And I *thought* about you," he said. "Every single day for the whole two years."

"I don't believe you," said Mabel, chewing.

"Sometimes *twice* a day!" he persisted.

Mabel, eating, said, "That's funny. I haven't thought of *you* at all. Not even twice a day. Not even once."

Mack took a deep breath before speaking, and said, "Mabel— to err is human, to forgive divine."

Mabel laughed so hard that she sputtered.

"Did you just make that up?" she asked.

"You can kid all y' want, Mabel, but you and me, we're *made* for each the other. And you know what I'm worth today? They tell me over *eight million dollars!*"

"That's too expensive for me," said Mabel. "I can't afford you."

"Mabel, listen. Serious. I think we oughta just scrap the whole reel one and start all over. And get married."

"Well," said Mabel, "I think that's a *very* good idea."

"You do?" he said, delighted.

"Yes. There's a fella here in London *I'd* like to marry. Have you got anybody in mind for *yourself?*"

"Honest" said Sennett, "I think you're on purpose tryin' to drive me crazy."

"If I thought I *could*," said Mabel, "I *would*."

"Down deep in your heart," said Sennett, ploughing on, "you know damn well I'm right. You know you love me. And you know I love you. And it's got nothin' to do with business. You're doin' fine. So am I. So from a business point, we don't need each the other, but from a person point, I'm tellin' you we *do*."

Mabel looked up at him and laughed. She laughed and laughed and began to cry.

Sennett hardly knew what to make of this bizarre change of mood until she threw her arms around his neck and through her tears sobbed, "Oh, Mack! Oh, Mack! I've *missed* you *so!*"

A few days later in Mack Sennett's suite, overlooking the Thames, the wedding is about to take place. There are flowers everywhere. Mack is dressed in his best. A British cleric stands by. There are men in uniform, and a number of English film celebrities.

It is half an hour *after* the specified time. The cleric is getting nervous. He has another engagement. Mack finds Pathé Lehrman, one of his assistants.

"Go over to her suite, willya? It's number ten-seventeen. Tell 'er we can't wait much longer. The minister's gotta go. God, that woman probably was late to her own birth!"

"Sure, boss."

Lehrman hustles down the corridor, up two flights of stairs, finds 1017, and is astonished to see the door wide open, and the suite empty. He walks in. He finds a note pasted to the mirror. He takes it down, opens it, and reads:

DEAR MACK: I'VE CHANGED MY MIND AND SO WOULD YOU IF YOU HAD ONE.
GOOD LUCK—TO ME, I MEAN.
TO YOU—THE OTHER KIND.

MABEL

VI

"PEMPY?" ASKED B.J. "What kind of a crazy name is that? Pempy."

"Short for Penelope," she explained.

"Short for Penelope would be Pen," he said.

"Whatever you wish, Mr. Farber."

"Your test," he said. "I like it."

"Did you? Oh! I'm *so* pleased."

He was not telling the truth. He had *not* liked her test, nor had Harry or Roscoe. What he had liked—more than liked—was her. Her cool willowy elegance had bewitched him from their first meeting at a Malibu Beach party given by Thomas Ince to celebrate the completion of his production of *The Wrath of the Gods*. The great J. Stuart Blackton made his customary entrance, this time with a beauty on his arm. Eyebrows bounced when he introduced her as his niece, Pempy Redfern. As it happened, she was.

Ben had brought Mabel, who, in her witchlike way, noticed at once the effect the British beauty had had upon him.

"Let me handle it, will you?" she asked.

106

"Handle what?"

"Our British cousin."

"Stop it, Mabel."

"Stop it, hell. I'm going to *start* it."

Ben watched her as she moved away, and presently was deep in conversation with Miss Redfern. When their attention finally focused on him, he moved away.

Mabel found him. "All right," she said. "Here's your move. Give her a screen test. Sign her. Then bed her and wed her, or wed her and bed her."

Later, when the elaborate picnic lunch was served, he found himself sharing a blanket with Mabel and Jack Pickford and Miss Redfern.

Now he was alone with her.

"Are you an actress?" he asked.

"Heavens, no."

"You should be."

"Why?"

"You're so beautiful."

"Is that all it takes?"

"It doesn't hurt."

"Uncle Stuart says—"

"I don't care what he says. I'd like to test you."

"But I'm leaving for home on Thursday. I have a job, don't you know. I'm a schoolmistress."

"We'll do it tomorrow!"

So it was that less than a week after their first meeting, they found themselves discussing a contract.

"But, of course, I shall have to go home before I can begin."

"Don't go."

"I must."

"I'm afraid you won't come back."

"Of course I will, if I give my word. Besides, this prospect is terribly exciting, really."

"Let me come with you," he said.

She laughed. "How *American* you are!" she said.

They talked their way across the country by train. Six days of exchanging histories, opinions, judgments, and aspirations. The food was surprisingly good, as was the wine. They saw sunsets together and sunrises, held hands, exchanged eyes. They got off the train at every stop, walked, and bought souvenirs. In Chicago, it was necessary to spend the night before taking the special train to New York. They went to the Palmer House. Ben arranged adjoining suites, and it was here, at last, because they both desired it burstingly, that they became lovers, she for the first time.

The train to New York seemed afloat to them.

They went to the Hotel Knickerbocker, where they spent five days and nights before sailing on the *Homeric*.

In New York, they lived a kind of honeymoon—walks and shops and carriage rides; restaurants and theatres and cabarets.

They watched a suffragette parade, went to a thé-dansant at the new Hotel Plaza, and they saw the turkey trot, the bunny hug, and the fox trot performed.

They took in Laurette Taylor in *Peg o' My Heart;* Ethel Barrymore in *Tante;* Caruso at the Metropolitan.

Taken all in all, the days in New York had the feeling of fantasy, and the ocean voyage that followed was similarly unreal. The gentle undulation of life on board the great liner had a hypnotic effect.

Thus, they were even less prepared than others for the shock of finding themselves—quite suddenly, it seemed—in the midst of a country at war. How had it happened? Why? There was hardly time to consider these abstract questions, the awful reality of it all was upon them.

For Penelope, it meant, of course, abandoning any thought of returning to the United States. Her only problem was to decide how and where to serve.

Ben had no choice. All Americans were ordered to leave the United Kingdom at once.

They spent a final wakeful night at Claridge's—comforting and reassuring one another.

"We'll write," she said.

"Of course."

"Constantly."

"I don't think it can be long. It's too crazy. It has to end soon."

"Yes."

"Then I'll come for you."

"Will you?"

"The first possible minute."

"Lovely," she said.

They lay awake in each other's arms until it was time to go, and for the first night in three weeks, they did not make—only felt—love.

He meant everything he said when he said it, but life and circumstances were to intervene.

The voyage home on the overcrowded, understaffed *Mauretania* was a nightmare of anxiety and hysteria. Ben's space was a banquette in the smoking lounge. He stayed in his clothes for six days. Food was minimal—except for the black markets that sprang up, inexplicably, in four staterooms on "A" deck. Rumors abounded: a submarine attack was imminent; there were insufficient lifeboats; the ship was full of spies; the ship had reversed course in the night; there was an influenza epidemic on board. No messages of any kind—incoming or outgoing—were permitted. It was not until the ship docked in New York and Ben went to the Waldorf-Astoria (he could not bear the idea of the Hotel Knickerbocker) and telephoned California that he was apprised of the bad news. Harry Langdon had walked out, the grosses had fallen far short of the expenditures, and the Bank of America was on the verge of foreclosing Fan Films.

Ben made forty telephone calls and managed to buy a little time. He went to New York, where Mabel Normand was on a Red Cross tour.

New York. As part of the Red Cross promotion, a great ball is in progress at the Waldorf. There are booths set up and many of the great film stars of the day are selling kisses.

In a decorative row, each one in her own pretty booth, we see Alla Nazimova, Mae Murray, Lillian Gish, Dorothy Gish, Mary Pickford, Theda Bara, and Mabel Normand.

The way it works is this: You pledge $1,000 to the Red Cross War Relief Fund and you get to kiss the star of your choice. Needless to say, there are dozens of photographers with their flash pans in evidence. There is even a newsreel cameraman at work, and business is brisk. On a balcony, an announcer is relaying to the crowd, through an enormous megaphone, the results of the kiss sale and keeping a sort of score.

Mary Pickford sells five kisses to Alfred Vanderbilt. It is announced with great fanfare.

But a Theda Bara fan, in an effort to outdo America's Sweet-heart, buys *six* kisses.

At Mabel's booth there is a long queue. She performs her duties with dispatch. Next, next, next.

The customer whose turn has arrived asks, "How many do I get for a million bucks?"

Mabel looks up and sees Mack standing there.

"One thousand," she says calmly.

"No rake-off? I oughta get a rake-off for a million bucks."

"This isn't Wanamaker's bargain basement, mister. If you want to buy a thousand, O.K., but give me the money first."

Mack hands her a check for a million dollars and starts kissing her.

The announcer tries to tell the story, but is too befuddled for words.

City Hall. The Mayor of the City of New York, John P. Mitchell, is being photographed in his chambers with Mabel Normand.

In the hallway, a crowd of gawkers. A fat woman approaches one of the policemen on guard and asks, "What's goin' on here anyway? What's all the excitement?"

"It's Mabel Normand," he says. "She's gonna get married to Mack Sennett here any minute."

"Who?" asks the fat woman.

"Mabel Normand, the movie star."

"—never heard of 'er."

"Where do you live, sister? On the moon?"

"And *who's* she gettin' hitched to?"

"Mack Sennett. Mack Sennett. You know, the Keystone Kops, Charlie Chaplin, Fatty Arbuckle."

"I never heard of *any* of 'em," she says, and walks away.

Back in Mayor Mitchell's chambers, he is signing papers while waiting. A few reporters and photographers hover about.

"It must be the heavy traffic," says the mayor.

Mabel replies nervously, "I hope so." The door opens. "Oh!" says Mabel. "Here they are *now*, Mister Mayor."

Henry ("Pathé") Lehrman comes in, walks over to Mabel, hands her a note, and leaves.

Mabel does not open it, but tears it up carefully and drops it into the mayor's wastepaper basket. She goes to the mayor, kisses him, and says, "I'm sorry to have troubled you, Mister Mayor."

The mayor looks up, confused. "Why, what happened?"

Mabel looks at him mournfully and says, "Mack Sennett is dead." She walks out of the room. The reporters run.

On Ben's return to California, he was able to save the studio by selling his house on Alvarado Street, his Malibu property, rights to his existing pictures; taking out a loan on his insurance; and using the money Mabel Normand had advanced him.

He moved into a room at the Hollywood Hotel and began to work sixteen hours a day.

Each day he began by writing to Penelope, but in the first six months of their separation, he heard from her only twice.

The first time, it was a love letter—the only one he had ever received. Then, seven weeks later, an enigmatic cable which read: ALL WELL   STOP   LOVE FROM ME AND GORIOT   PEMPY.

He puzzled over it for days until, in the midst of a sleepless night, it hit him. Goriot. Of course. *Père Goriot* by Balzac. She had urged him to read it as a possible film subject. He had done so, and agreed that it was a superlative story. Her cable meant that she was, or would soon be, in France. He gathered that she had decided on the nursing position after all. He worried.

The invitation to the Seligmans' (black tie!) came as a great surprise. Picture people courted Seligman, and not the other way about. Why would Seligman want *him* to come to dinner?

A.L. Seligman (Ben was to learn later that the initials stood for Abraham Lincoln) was one of the most powerful men in the industry (as it had begun to be known). He occupied a unique position in the community. He did not produce or direct or administer; he owned no theatres or studios; he had no dream of empire. He was, simply and plainly, a financier, a money man. He invested in such projects as he believed would return a profit. There were those who thought him a financial wizard, some even referred to him as a mathematical genius: true, he could add and subtract, multiply and divide, calculate interest and percentages in his head like an adding machine. In fact, Buster Keaton once called him "The Addled Machine." An off-the-mark joke; there was nothing addled about A.L. Seligman. There were many who gave him credit for the swift burgeoning of the moving picture business; William Desmond Taylor once referred to him (possibly because his round florid face was often moist) as "a shiny Shylock." The crack got around and eventually reached A.L.'s ears. He forthwith wrote a formal letter to Taylor, terminating their business relationship, which had been the most successful of all of Seligman's involvements.

Taylor asked to see him. Granted.

"It was a jest, Abe."

"A *libelous* jest."

"Admitted. I regret it. I apologize."

"Thank you. I accept."

"Then we're on again? Let me tell you about the new story I've got for Mary Miles—"

"No," said A.L. "Spare me. We are no longer partners. Go tell your story to Giannini."

"For God's sake, Abe! I've apologized. Abjectly. What more can I do?"

"That's the whole trouble, Bill. There's *nothing* you can do. You are what you are, just as I am what I am."

"You could forgive me, Abe. Couldn't you?"

"Yes, I could forgive, but I couldn't forget. Let's call it quits, Bill. Good luck."

Seligman had been born to wealth. His mother was a Rothschild, his father a respected banker in Hamburg before his emigration.

Seligman's wife, Rhoda, had similarly never known life without affluence. She was a niece of Jacob Leiter, the Chicago merchant and co-founder of the Marshall Field Company.

The Seligmans lived *en prince,* a model for the rest of the community. It was not so much that they had money, it was that they knew how to use it and what to do with it.

Their home, high in the hills, had been designed by the great Louis Sullivan and was perfectly adapted to the atmosphere of Southern California. A low rambling structure set among fruit trees and fountains and gardens, it charmed everyone who was lucky enough to gain entrance.

In a society that numbered a good many nouveaux riches, and its share of upstarts, the Seligmans were the aristocracy.

Why would they invite me? Ben wondered.

112

He was soon to learn.

He sent his tuxedo out to be cleaned and pressed; bought a new dress shirt and wing collar, and dressed fully the night *before* the Seligmans' dinner party by way of rehearsal.

He asked Pathé Lehrman to come over and approve his getup. Lehrman was a Hollywood phony, a European who worked around the Sennett studio. Henry Lehrman, who had been nicknamed Pathé because he had, to get into the business, claimed to be related to the Pathé Frères of Paris.

But phonies, as a rule, know about the social graces, which was why Ben sent for Pathé.

"No good, the studs," said Pathé. "For the Seligmans, should be diamond only."

"Diamond! Where am I going to get diamond?"

"I get them for you," said Pathé. "Not buy, borrow. Also, you got to show more cuff."

"Thank you."

"There will be much wine. Do not drink. Sip. Like a teaspoon at a time. The which fork, knife, spoon is nothing. You watch what the hostess does, or the host, whichever is nearer. How did you get *in?*"

"I don't know."

"Come on," said Pathé. "You can tell me."

"I swear."

"Seligman doesn't ask for nothing. You asked him for backing? Then he wants to look you over."

"No," said Ben. "No backing. I would never go to Seligman, I mean, not yet. He's too big."

"Hey!" said Pathé.

"What?"

"I think I got it."

"Yes?"

"He's got two daughters. One is a beauty, Rachel, looks just like her mother. I hear she's going to hitch with that actor—what's his name?—Barthelmess, Richard Barthelmess. But the other daughter—the younger one—is a pig. Looks like him, like A.L. Sweats. Like him. Her name is Tessa."

"How do you know all this?" asked Ben.

"I keep in touch," replied Pathé. "One of their butlers, they got a dozen, he's a friend of mine. So that's it. That must be it."

"What?"

"He's going to try to fix you up with the pig."

"You're crazy, Pathé."

"You'll see if I am. And say, if you decide you don't want her, see if you can get her for *me*."

Pathé was wrong about Tessa. She was hardly "a pig." True, she did not have the striking, confident beauty of her older sister, but in her own way was attractive and appealing. Her deficiencies were emotional rather than physical. She seemed nervous, apprehensive, frightened of life.

"Now, when you get there," Pathé had advised, "the main thing is nonchalant. Don't show you're impressed by *nothing*. Appreciate? All right. But not impressed. Make out like what you're doing, you do every night. *Nonchalant,* that's your job. And don't forget about the hand kissing."

Ben tried, successfully, he thought, to follow the advice. He did, indeed, bend and kiss Mrs. Seligman's hand when he was introduced to her. Mr. Seligman was cordial and expansive.

Champagne was the only drink served before dinner.

Ben recognized only a few of the guests. He had thought there would be more picture people. These seemed to be politicians, bankers, and judges. From the movie world, only Mary Pickford and her husband, Owen Moore; Maurice Tourneur and Mae Marsh; Wallace Reid and Alma Rubens.

Ben counted. Twenty-two in all.

During dinner, a string trio played Victor Herbert's music exclusively. Ben was seated on Tessa's right. Mae Marsh was on his right. It was hard to do what he knew was the correct thing.

He ate sparingly, sipped the wines, told Tessa the story of his recent voyage from England. She listened, wide-eyed.

"Father!" she said. "Father!"

"Yes, dear?"

"Mr. Farber has just told me something I think would interest all."

"Is that so?"

"Oh, no," Ben said.

"Go on," said Tessa. "Tell it."

Mr. Seligman spoke to the violinist. "Hold it for a few minutes, Josef."

In the terrifying silence that followed, Ben decided to make good.

"I was in England recently," he said, "when I received a call from the American embassy—"

He went on and made good. His recital was the high point of the evening. In the insular movie world, little firsthand news of the conflict in Europe had come through.

The music struck up again. "Babes in Toyland."

Tessa touched his hand. "That was thrilling," she said. "Thank you."

In a large high-ceilinged room, brandy and coffee; then everyone was seated, he still next to Tessa. A pianist (not part of the trio) took his place at the keyboard and provided the score for the showing of *Dante's Inferno,* a five-reel Italian film Seligman had financed.

It was impressive, indeed, Ben thought, but too long. However, it gave him time to consider his situation. He was coming up in the world, no doubt of that. In business, he was in a terrible bind, but it would end. Would it?

Among other things, he noted that the world of the rich was more fragrant than other worlds. Each lady wore her own perfume, and by now—what with the food and wine and excitement —the redolences of the perfumes were blending. One, however, predominated—Tessa's. He sat close to her, their shoulders touching. The scene on the screen was grisly: flames, into which writhing bodies were being consigned. A hurt little cry was emitted by Tessa. She clutched Ben's arm. He took her hand and smoothed it comfortingly. She snatched her hand away, abruptly. Had he blundered? Time passed, Dante's visions continued. Now he felt his hand taken and held firmly. Why? The scenes were now comparatively mild. The music was soft and melodious. He felt his right hand being carried upward, upward, until it was placed upon her ample heaving breast. Both her hands now, pressing his hand to her, closer and closer still.

The film ended. Applause. Comment.

There was dancing then. Not one of Ben's strong points, but he made an effort.

He left with the first of the departees. (Pathé's advice: "Don't hang around till the end; leave early; that means you're serious in work.")

115

He kissed Mrs. Seligman's hand once again. A firm handshake with her husband. He held Tessa's hand as long as he dared, and saw her smile for the first time. The smile revealed another person.

The next day, he sent extravagant flowers and a note to Mrs. Seligman; an old-fashioned bouquet, with no note, to Tessa.

In the course of the two months that followed, Ben was a guest at the Seligmans' on five separate occasions. In addition, he took Tessa out three times. Once to Los Angeles, to *The Red Mill,* once to a piano recital by Paderewski, and once to a ball given by the Motion Picture Directors Association. Each time, he brought her home, came in at her invitation, and kissed her hand when he said good night. No more. His instinct was guiding him unfailingly.

Three months (to the day!) after that first evening, he was asked again.

This time, he was surprised to find that he was the only guest and that A.L. Seligman was entertaining him alone.

Dinner was served, not in the large dining room but in a smaller one, adjoining.

"The girls," explained A.L., "are all in New York, buying clothes. They do that twice a year. In peacetime, of course, in Paris. That's why I have to work as hard as I do."

"I think, Mr. Seligman, that you would work anyway."

"You're right," said A.L. "And by the way, I think it's time you started calling me Abe. After all, we're old friends."

"I'm honored, Abe."

They talked of moving pictures and of the difficulty of achieving accurate accounting from the growing number of exhibitors across the country. Piracy was becoming common practice.

"The trouble is," said Abe, "it would cost more to police the system than you could get back."

"But it's the *principle,*" said Ben. "And the future."

"I don't know," said Abe. "Principle is a funny word—sometimes it can mean stubbornness, sometimes it can mean foolishness. I'm a practical man."

"I have an idea," said Ben. "I would like sometime to tell it to you."

"Why not now?"

During the rest of the dinner, Ben outlined his plan to establish key exchanges that would deal closely with the actual theatres, making spot checks from time to time, and requiring sworn affidavits attesting to the accuracy of the receipts.

Seligman was impressed.

They returned to his study for brandy and coffee.

"You're a bright young man," said Seligman.

"Not so young."

"And I like you."

"Thank you."

"What's more important is that my *daughter* likes you."

The room went round once and stopped. The brandy? Or Pathé's prediction?

"She's a lovely girl," said Ben.

"Where do you come from, Ben?"

"Kovno. In Lithuania."

"Yes, I know."

"So I could never be the president."

"Would you want to be?"

"I would want, Abe, to be the most I can."

"You were married, I understand," said Seligman.

Ben nodded gravely. "Yes, sir."

"What happened?"

"My wife hated the movie business, and I love it."

"More than you loved *her*, I gather."

"She was a fine woman—*is*—but we were a bad match."

"Were you a good husband?"

"I tried to be."

"That's not what I asked," said Abe, harshly.

"Yes," said Ben. "Yes, I *was* a good husband. I provided. Once I had three jobs the same time. And never with other women, no matter what."

"Do you like marriage—that is to say, the idea of marriage?"

"To me, yes. It's important to have a settled life."

"More brandy?"

"No, thank you."

"One sip," Seligman urged.

"Thank you, no."

"Why did you go bankrupt?" asked Seligman.

"I was foolish and went too fast. Like what can happen if you

117

drive an automobile too fast. You have an accident. You go off the road. That's what happened to me. I had an accident."

There was a long silence.

At length, A.L. Seligman spoke.

"I like you, Ben," he said.

The wedding was designed by Joseph Urban, Ziegfeld's art director, who was brought out from New York. Seligman had concluded that there was not yet a Hollywood designer worthy of the assignment.

It was staged by Cecil B. De Mille, the most stylish director of his day, and may have been the first actual wedding to have been completely filmed from beginning to end, edited into a four-reel picture, and distributed to the major participants.

A cable to Pempy's British Medical Corps address:

DEAREST   DISREGARD WHATEVER YOU MAY HEAR OR READ OF ME
UNTIL PERSONAL MEETING WHEN ALL WILL BE
EXPLAINED   STOP   I LOVE YOU   STOP   YOUR BEN

Mack Sennett acted as Ben's best man. During the ceremony, he caught Mabel Normand's eye. She began to cry and continued to do so until the end.

After the reception at the Seligmans', Mack invited Mabel to The Coconut Grove.

They were soon laughing.

"But, Holy Jesus!" he said. "When them papers came out with them headlines about me cooled . . . ! Holy, we *still* ain't got it straight. There's *still* people around look surprised when they see me."

"Oh, sure," said Mabel. "Once something's in the papers, that's it. That makes it so."

"Mabel, you know what I'm worth right now?"

"I can hardly wait to find out. Is it *more* than last time? Or *less?*"

"*Fourteen million simoleons,* Mabel. I'm worth fourteen million simoleons. We can do anything we want. Any pictures, any parts. I'd like to get you off that Mickey Neilan match-up. He's no good for you."

"I'm sorry to tell you this, Mack, but he's a better director than *you* are."

"Who said he ain't? Sure, he's better than me, but he's not better than *you*."

Mabel looked up and smiled.

Mack went on. "Y'know what I'd like to see *you* be doin'? I'd like to see you be makin' all your own stuff, writin' it, and directin' it, and makin' it. Like Chaplin. Look where he's got to. Doin' all his own stuff."

Mabel fixed him with a long look and said, "But he ain't *funny!*"

"Awright, awright," said Mack. "Didn't *you* ever make a mistake?"

"Yes," said Mabel. "In fact, I've made three."

"Mabel, listen, we've *both* made mistakes, plenty of 'em. But let's not make our whole *life* a mistake. Let's, f'Chrissake, do it. Once and for all. Come on. We'll have the biggest, fanciest, jazziest wedding you ever saw."

She looked at him again. "In a church?" she asked.

"Hell, yes! In a *synagogue* if you want it."

"No," said Mabel. "A church'll be all right."

So bemused was Mack that he scarcely realized he had been accepted. All at once, he did.

"Mabel!" he said, as tears came to his eyes.

"Mack?" she said, tentatively.

He grabbed her impulsively and kissed her in the manner of a fade-out kiss.

The church. The wedding. It is every bit as big and glamorous as Mack had promised. All the stars are there. Lillian Gish is the maid of honor. Roscoe Arbuckle is the best man.

There have been countless rehearsals. Parties, really, in preparation for this event. The design, the staging, the costuming, the lighting, are all superlative.

At last, there stands Mack Sennett with Roscoe Arbuckle, his best man, at his side, awaiting the arrival of his bride to the traditional strains of the Mendelssohn "Wedding March." Here she comes, on Buster Keaton's arm. He is to give the bride away. Following, Dorothy Gish and Gloria Swanson and Betty Bronson and Theda Bara and all the others who are acting as bridesmaids.

The ceremony begins. "Dearly Beloved, we are gathered together here in the sight of God and in the face of this company," etc., etc. It drones on, but the guests are interested and somehow carried away by the glamour of it all.

At length, the minister reaches the point where he turns to the groom and says, "Do you, Mack, take Mabel to be your lawful wedded wife? To love and to cherish, in sickness and in health, for richer or poorer, for better or worse, until death do you part?"

Mack takes a deep breath and booms out, "I *do!*" He almost sings it.

The minister then repeats the question. "Do you, Mabel, take Mack [etc., etc., etc.] until death do you part?"

She, too, takes a deep breath and says, "I *do not!*"

Mack fails to register this, as does the minister, who goes on. If ever there was a delayed take, this is it. Five seconds, six, perhaps ten, before Mabel finds it necessary to repeat, "I *certainly do not!*"

She hands her bridal bouquet to the minister, who takes it, flustered. She rips off her wedding veil, plants it on Mack Sennett's head, then flounces up the aisle and out of the church.

Tessa Farber became pregnant as soon as it was physically possible, to Seligman's delight. She was to bear two sons, Abraham L. (named for Seligman) and Gilbert, and in honor of each one, a million dollars was turned over to the Farbers.

Ben often reflected that this was the easiest money he had ever made.

In early 1917, Seligman sent for him.

The usual amenities were omitted. Seligman looked grim.

"My information is," he said, "that we are a matter of weeks, maybe even days, from being involved in this damned war."

Ben was shocked. "I don't understand. Didn't Wilson say—didn't he promise—?"

"Ben!" said Seligman sharply. "You're a bright fellow, but in some things, you're a half-wit! You're not here to give me opinions on world matters, you're here to hear the plan I've arranged for you."

"All right," said Ben.

"There's going to be a Hollywood Victory Committee. Its function will be to place the industry at the disposal of the government. Whatever they want—propaganda movies, stars, selling bonds, morale building, entertainment for the troops. Whatever they want, they'll get."

"Yes?"

"You're going to be the chairman, the coordinator. But it has to be set up before anybody else gets the idea. You're going to be a dollar-a-year man."

"But I don't know if—"

"I've got no time for your 'buts,' Ben. What *do* you want? Be drafted? Be a soldier? Get killed? Get gassed—which is worse than killed? Do what I tell you."

During the war, Ben found it necessary to make a number of trips to New York on HVC business. He generally stayed at the Plaza.

One cold winter's morning while he was having a dreary, unsatisfactory wartime breakfast—no eggs, coffee substitute—the phone rang.

"Yes?" he said crossly. At home, he never had to answer the phone.

"A Mrs. Farber to see you, sir."

"A *who?*"

"One moment . . . your mother," added the receptionist.

Ben sat down, the room spun round.

"Yes!" he shouted. "Yes!"

He had gone cold. This was akin to a visit from the dead. He went out into the hall and waited by the elevator.

In a few minutes, Bessie appeared—a smartly dressed, beautifully coiffed, skillfully made-up New York clubwoman.

A long, wordless embrace. Mingled tears.

In the suite, she took charge and ordered up what she needed to serve a proper breakfast for two.

"I have heard of the difficult situation in these hotels," she explained.

Ben was astonished to hear her virtually accentless English.

She had brought, in a large handbag: smoked salmon, cream cheese, bagels, and a tin of coffee.

Bessie represented a dramatic, astounding transformation. In her Lower East Side years she had become involved with Lillian Wald, then in the process of founding the Henry Street Settlement. She was now Miss Wald's principal associate, in charge of funding and administration.

"Your English, Mama. For God's sake! It's better than mine!"

121

"Did you go to school three years and have private tutors for six?"

"No."

"So?"

"Then you're still—you know—?"

"An allrightnick?" she asked. "Oh, yes! More than before. Mostly real estate—the best investment. You own property, mein gold?"

"Enough."

"Good. In every way, I'm proud of you."

They spent the day together—and were to spend many more, in California and New York and Europe. Bessie became immersed in Farber family affairs and when she died at eighty-nine, in Ben's house, she left her considerable estate equally divided between her grandchildren, great-grandchildren, and great-great-grandchildren—and the Henry Street Settlement.

In the course of the Victory Ball held in the main ballroom of the Commodore Hotel, Mayor Frederick T. Woodman of the city of Los Angeles presented Benjamin J. Farber with a plaque in gratitude for his selfless, tireless wartime service. The governor of the state of California, William D. Stephens, presented him with the state's highest civilian honor, the Citizen's Medal; and the senior U.S. senator, Hiram W. Johnson, delivered a citation to him signed by President Woodrow Wilson.

Ben made a short and modest acceptance speech, after which he introduced his wife, without whom . . .

Seligman watched from a box. He was so engrossed that he had forgotten to light his cigar.

Ben and Tessa now accepted Seligman's gift: a delayed honeymoon trip to Paris, London, Rome, and Madrid. It seemed to Abe to be the only fittingly symbolic one for a union as momentous as this one.

London was the only city that mattered to Ben. It was there that he would meet Pempy in secret.

There had been an exchange of letters. To his dismay, Ben learned that she had never received his cable, thus was in complete ignorance of his new situation. He withheld the news until he saw her personally and convinced her that his marriage was a matter of business. Somehow, he persuaded her not to abandon him—in fact, to join him in California, where everything, he promised, would be worked out satisfactorily. Finally, he insisted, over her violent objections, that she accept a large Bank of America envelope filled with currency.

How to explain her acquiescence to his bizarre scheme? She was in a state of excessive fatigue after four years of involvement in the war; stunned by the news of Ben's marriage; but, above all, in love with him and thus willing to trust him.

Her pride, however, made it impossible for her to accept anything more from him except employment. This he provided during the twelve years she was to remain his mistress. She was, variously, an actress, a coach, a supervisor of the private school for children on the lot, a wardrobe supervisor, and, finally, a story editor. And always believing that her real life with Ben was imminent.

Men of Ben's capacities cannot manage a life with a single partner. At least, that is what he told himself.

We were sitting in his office, having an elaborate tea.

He smiled. "You begin to see now why I didn't want anybody to write about me? I look back on that man did that and I don't like him. Pempy. But she stayed in my life, thank God."

"For how long?" I asked.

He looked vacant and vague, then pressed a button at his side. His secretary, Florence, came in.

"Yes?" she asked.

"Is Mrs. Larner still in her office?"

"I'm not sure, sir."

"If she is, would you ask her to be good enough to step in here for a moment?"

For the next ten minutes, Ben talked, but I could not tell if he was talking to me or to himself. His subject was capital gains taxes as they related to the sale of Farber Films and its many subsidiaries.

The door was opened and a trim, energetic woman who must have been at least eighty came in.

"A high tea!" she exclaimed in a pronounced British accent. "Am I invited?"

123

"Why not?" said Ben. "You're the one started it around here."
She joined us.

"This," said Ben, "is Mrs. Carl Larner, my right lung. I breathe
through her."

"Oh, go along with you!" she said.

We chatted amiably for fifteen minutes. Mrs. Larner was full of
excitement about her forthcoming trip to New York and London
to cover the plays.

I invited her to lunch with me in New York and gave her my
card.

"I might just take you up on that—I just might!" She glanced
at her watch. "I really must be off," she said. "Was there something special, dear?"

"No," said Ben. "I don't think so."

"Good night, then." She kissed his cheek, then to me: "*So* glad
to have met you."

She left. He asked me several questions about Adani—his
origins, his methods, his organization. Suddenly, he changed
focus and asked, "Well, so what did you think of her?"

"Who? The lady who came in to tea?"

"Yes."

"Terribly bright and lively for her age. I always admire that.
Why do you ask?"

"Because. Pempy!"

"What?"

"*She* is *Pempy.*"

I was properly jolted. Their story flashed by me. What life
would she have lived had she not gone to that party in Malibu
with her uncle on that day in 1914?

PART III

"A RECKLESS ROMEO"

I

FOR YEARS Ben had walked the last two miles of the journey home. His driver would drop him at a given point and he would stride along, breathing deeply and thinking.

More recently, at Willa's command, the driver had begun to let him out of the limousine closer and closer to the house. A mile and a half, and a quarter—each day cutting down, until now he was walking no more than a mile or so. At no time did he become aware of the change. As the distance shortened, the breathing became less deep, the thinking more of the past than of the present or the future.

One autumn afternoon, he walked and tried to analyze the reason for the success of *Shampoo*, which he had screened that afternoon. It puzzled him. A dirty picture. Is that what they want? He thought of another daring movie—Garbo in *Camille*. But what a difference! That one had style and subtlety, elegance and taste. This modern approach was too explicit, left little to the imagination. Still, it was a hit. Why? Why? He consoled himself with the argument that there had always been room for all kinds of pictures, always would be. Even now, the great Lubitsch ones would

surely succeed—*Trouble in Paradise, The Merry Widow, Ninotchka.*
He smiled in happy recollection as he recalled the champagne
sparkle of these magical movies made by his great friend and
partner.

As the front gate of his house came into view, he stopped smiling, then stopped walking. He squinted at the sight before him to
make certain that he was seeing what he thought he saw.

A young girl was sitting on the lawn beside the driveway. Blond,
wearing jeans, and leaning on her knapsack, which she had
propped against the stone wall.

In all the years that Ben had owned this house, there had never
been a single trespasser. Should he call the police? The Bel-Air
Patrol?

The girl sprang to her feet as she saw him and raised an arm in
salute.

He approached her slowly, carefully. What was this? What was
going on?

"Hello," she said brightly.

"Good evening."

"Grandpa?"

"What?"

"I'm Beth."

"Who?"

"Beth Farber."

"How is *that?*" he muttered in confusion.

She seemed troubled by her failure to communicate. This was
not the reception she had hoped for.

"I'm Justin's daughter," she said, with a touch of asperity.

"Justin?" asked Ben. "Who's Justin?"

"Are you putting me on, Grandpa, or what?"

"Who's Justin?" he repeated.

"Justin!" she said loudly. "Justin Farber. My father. Higham
Farber's son!"

"You don't have to holler, young lady. They just put new bat-
teries into my hearing aid. It works perfect. From Germany."

She took a step toward him and said softly, "I'm Beth. Higham's
my grandfather. You're my great-grandfather. Hello."

She leaned forward and kissed his cheek. He noted that she
smelled of youth.

"Justin," he said. "Yes. I only saw him once. He was two, maybe
three years old."

128

"He's forty-four now," she said.

"Beth," he said, looking into her eyes. "Beth."

He embraced her. She was astonished by the power in his arms.

"Thank you," she said, and began to cry.

"Don't," he said. "Come in."

The front door swung open as they approached it. Ellen, one of the maids, was unable to conceal her surprise as they entered.

"What's a matter, Ellen?" asked Ben. "You never saw a man with his girlfriend before?"

Ellen blushed and said, "Oh, Mr. Farber!"

"Ask Mrs. Farber if she would be good enough to come down. Tell her I have something to show her."

"Yes, sir," said Ellen.

"Something?" asked Beth, teasing.

"Some*body!*" shouted Ben at Ellen, who was on her way up the stairs.

In the bar, Ben touched a call button and asked, "Would you like a drink?"

"Oh, boy, would I! White wine?"

"Of course. Would you want to wash up?"

"Why? Do I look like I need it?"

"No, no. But sitting in the road like that—"

"Cleanest grass I ever sat on," she said.

"Maybe the ladies' room?"

"Are you trying to get rid of me, Grandpa?"

"Absolutely no."

Chapman came in.

"Good evening, sir," he said. "Ma'am."

"Hi."

"White wine for my granddaughter, please, Chapman."

"Really?"

"Really."

"And a half a scotch for me."

"Very good, sir."

As Chapman prepared the drinks, Ben said, "Sit down, Beth. Sit down. Let me look at you."

She sat into a huge armchair and sank at once into its deep softness.

"Wow!" she said.

Ben sat down opposite her and put on his glasses. He looked at her, blanched, and rose suddenly.

129

"Oh, my God!" he whispered.

Beth got to her feet quickly and moved to him.

"What is it, Grandpa?" she asked.

He tried to speak, failed.

Chapman served the drinks. Ben and Beth touched glasses and drank. Not before he had finished half his drink was he able to speak.

"Alice," he said. "You are Alice."

"I know," she said. "Grandpa always tells me I'm the spitting image of his mother. I don't remember her. I was only three when she died."

"She was beautiful," said Ben. "Inside and out. A good person. The only mistake she ever made—"

Willa's voice: "Hello! Good heavens! What have we here?"

Ben went to her, kissed her and said, "Darling, what do you think? Do you know who this is?"

"Not a clue."

"This is Beth. Beth Farber. Haim's granddaughter."

"And your—*great*-granddaughter."

"Yes," he said. "Right."

Willa went to Beth, put her arms about her, then examined her at arm's length.

"You resemble your great-grandmother," she said. "Alice."

Beth looked at Ben and laughed.

"Yes," she said. "We were just saying."

Chapman served a martini to Willa, who raised her glass and said, "To family reunions. Such joy."

When they were seated, Ben asked Beth, "What are you doing here? Where did you come from?"

"Smith," she said.

"Smith?" asked Ben.

"The college, dear," Willa explained.

"I'm a sophomore. I mean, I *was* a sophomore. No more." She laughed. "Sopho*less*, I guess."

"You left school?" asked Ben.

"Not until it left *me*," she replied.

"What did your parents think?" asked Willa.

"Oh, they don't know. Not yet. I wanted to avoid another screamer, so I thought take off, put some distance between, and then give 'em the ol' fait accompli."

"Oh, dear," said Willa. "I see trouble ahead."

Ben said, "You should've let us know you were coming."

"Yes, but what if you'd said don't?"

"And I think we would have," said Willa.

"How old are you, Beth?" asked Ben.

She laughed and answered, "Eighteen and one day. I waited until my birthday, see?"

Willa and Ben exchanged a look.

"And now what?" asked Ben. "What do you want to do?"

"What *can* you do?" asked Willa. "That's more to the point, isn't it?"

"I'm very bright," said Beth, her face flushed with excitement. "I can type like a mad thing, and I'm a wizard stenographer, and also—"

"Good Lord!" exclaimed Willa. "How on earth did *that* happen?"

Beth smiled. "My father. He insisted that all three of us—my sister, Amy, and my brother, Bruce—that we all learn shorthand and typing. He said it was as important as knowing how to drive a car or brush your teeth right. He said those skills would be an entree to whatever it was we wanted to do. My mother fought him on it, but she lost."

"Are you saying," asked Willa, "that you want a job?"

"Damn right. What the hell do I want with Chaucer? I'd rather hang out with Steven Spielberg or Jane Fonda."

Ben turned to Willa and asked, "What is she saying? Do you know?"

Willa replied, "She sounds to me like a real movie buff."

"You bet," said Beth.

Willa looked at her seriously. "Would you consider going back to school out here? Major in films, perhaps?"

"No, no!" said Beth, firmly, as she stood up. "I've had it with academe. Up to here. I'm hungry for some real world. Starving to death, in fact."

Ben spoke. "We have no openings at the studio at the present time."

"Good!" said Beth. "Because I wouldn't want to work there."

"You wouldn't?" he asked, offended. "Why not?"

"False position," she said. "No. I want a legitimate job, not a sinecure."

"A fancy talker," Ben observed to Willa.

Willa asked, "Would you want to stay here with us until you've settled down?"

"Oh, God, yes! Oh, I thought you'd never ask!"

She went to Willa, dropped to her knees, and embraced her.

"Welcome home," said Willa.

Within a week, Beth found a secretarial job at the William Morris Agency, and after the holidays became an agent trainee. Her apartment on Doheny Drive soon became a headquarters of sorts for an aggressive group of young newcomers and hopefuls.

By spring, she had brought five promising clients into the agency and was rewarded with a promotion to junior agent status. She loved her job and worked long hours.

At the end of summer, she asked for another promotion, but was told to wait. Instead, she applied by letter to seven other agencies. Only two granted her interviews. One of them was Farber-Ross.

Ben's son studied her.

"I don't know," he said. "You may be too pretty for this racket."

"Not at all," said Beth, smiling wickedly. "I use it. You ought to see me."

"How old are you?"

"Old enough," she replied. "I've been trying to figure out what we are to each other. It's tough."

"Well, let's see. I'm your grandfather's half brother. So—well —let's see . . ."

"So that makes us—what?"

"Practically nothing," he said. "I'm your half great-uncle."

"Or my great half uncle. Or how's this: my great uncle once removed?"

"Nice," he said. "That's nice."

"Anyway," she said. "It's remote enough so that neither of us can be accused of nepotism."

"And it also means I can fire you if you don't shape up."

"Correct. And I can quit if *you* don't."

"Hey!" he said. "You're pretty good."

"Not *too* pretty good?" she asked.

They laughed together.

132

Thus began their successful association. Beth soon proved to be remarkably adept at packaging and foresaw the time when she would be offered a partnership. Would she take it? Or would she prefer to go out on her own? On her own sounded better. She felt confident and strong, having made it in a man's world.

II

SATURDAY AFTERNOON. I have taken a place down here at The Beverly Hills Hotel. Bungalow 12. The deal is warming up, and it is essential that I talk to Adani several times a day. I could do it from my comfortable quarters at the Farbers', of course, but I have become increasingly suspicious of that operation. On the surface, they seem respectable, courteous, gracious, and, at times, even faintly naïve. But that reliable minuscule informer who lives inside my head has been whispering warnings. So I drove down here, circuitously, going for what was ostensibly a sightseeing drive, but ended up parking my car on Crescent Drive and meeting my friend, Nick, the assistant manager, at the door of bungalow 12. He has me registered in the name of George Spelvin and understands my need for security.

"Well, for Chrissake, you don' have to live *two* places the same time, do you?" Adani yelled. "What kind a jerk you turnin' out to be?"

"No kind. And listen—if you don't like the way I'm handling this, you can come out and handle it yourself."

"Don't be goddam it tellin' me what to do. What's goin' on?"

"We're talking. We're still talking. That is to say, *he's* talking."

"You make him the offer?"

"Not yet."

"Why the fuck not?"

"I didn't think the moment was propitious."

"The moment was *what?*"

"Propitious."

"What the fuck's that?"

133

"Not the right time. Not the strategic moment. Not yet."

"So why the hell can't you say so?"

"It's moving, Mr. Adani. I think we're going to get it. How close to our way, I can't tell you now, but I've got a strong feeling the key here is *Mrs.* Farber."

"Bullshit."

"I think I'm in a better position to judge than you are."

"Bullshit. I got my informations."

"Some of it's all wrong. And I'll tell you what I'm beginning to think."

"Yeah?"

"I'm beginning to think that your Jack Heller may be playing it both ways."

"I'll have him chopped up!"

"It's a suspicion, not a fact."

"So what makes you suspicion him?"

"I don't know. They seem to know too many of our moves. And listen—for all you know, he's had somebody in *your* files, too."

"Jesus Christ! This is some stinkin' world, you know it?"

"I'm beginning to think so."

"So what's the morning line?" asked Adani.

"Well, he's been telling me his whole story—trying to give me the idea this business means more to him than just money. But that may be a ploy."

"Certainly ploy. These goddam Jews—that's how they do business."

"But, as I say, he's not very tightly wrapped. And his wife knows it. What's more, I think *he* knows it, too. That's why I get the strong feeling that when it comes down to the XYZ, it's going to be her decision. I just know it. He's going to defer to her."

"Then, goddamit, why ain't you workin' on her?"

"Well, goddamit, what the hell do you *think* I'm doing?" Jesus Christ, don't coach me every minute. I'm not a puppet."

"You're not even a puppet, you shithead."

"Listen, Adani, I quit," I said. "I'm checking out and coming home on the Red Eye."

"Don' you *dare!* You stay where you are."

"Don't give me any orders—I just quit."

"You can't quit. You've got a contract."

"Sue me."

"Listen, Guy, come on. You know me. I don' mean nothin'. So whatever I called you, I take it back. I'm sorry, O.K.?"

"O.K."

"When you gonna call me again?"

"When I've got something to tell you, that's when."

I returned to the Farbers' and made a great point of asking everyone within earshot if Mr. Adani had called me.

No.

"Thank you. If he does, I'll be upstairs."

Only the Farbers and Beth and I at dinner tonight. Again, it began with that habitual drink in Ben's study.

"Next week sometime," he said, fixing the drinks, "I want to go through my catalogue with you. Seven hundred and eighty-seven feature pictures."

"Yes."

"But then what I want to see you do is pick out any title you want—anything appeals to you; color, black and white, sound, silent, all talkie, half talkie—anything you want. In fifteen, twenty minutes, I'll have it on the screen for you."

"Interesting, but what's the point?"

"The point? Because that's the merchandise. I want you to see the condition of my product. There's only two people ever been in this business respected the old work—one was Chaplin, the other one is me. It costs a fortune, y'know, to keep these things in shape. The nitrate ones—the old ones—they have to be transferred to the new stock. A fortune. Then, you can't just put them in a can and leave them—it has to be a certain temperature, like wine—and they have to be screened once in a while, so as not to shrink or crack. And they have to be oiled. I go sometimes myself to watch them do it. I love it. And every one of the seven eighty-seven has got a value. What do you think the average value is?"

"I wouldn't have the slightest idea."

He looked at me and his eyes became slits. "If you haven't got the slightest idea," he said, "you shouldn't be here talking to me."

"Sorry. I meant to say I don't have the slightest idea as to what *you* think the value is."

He chuckled. "Very good," he said, "very good. I had some gentlemen come in with computers. They were recommended to

135

me by Max Palevsky—he's an expert. They gave me a projection based on the copyright life—based on the new copyright laws. And I'll tell you the figure they came up with. They came up with seven hundred and sixty thousand a picture. So you can see what those vaults are worth."

"If that figure is correct," I said.

"Well, you're welcome to get your own estimate."

"But, of course, this amount wouldn't be receivable for say thirty—sometimes forty—years, is that right?"

He smiled. "That's right. What's wrong with thirty or forty years?"

"Not a thing."

"So you can see," he said, "that the area Adani's been thinking is way out of line."

I finished my drink in one long, slow draft. Thinking, trying to think, in the glare of those two eyes on me. Levity, I decided. I laughed.

"How do you know what area he's been thinking in?" I asked.

"It's my business to know," he said, "so I know."

"Would you care to set a figure, Mr. Farber, that I could convey to him?"

"No, no. That's not how we're going to do it."

"How are we?"

"You're going to make me an offer. And I'm going to turn it down. Then you're going to make me another offer. And again I'm going to turn it down. Then you're going to keep making the offers and I'm going to keep turning them down until you make the right one, and then I'm going to take it."

"But what if Mr. Adani—?"

The butler appeared. "Dinner is served," he said.

We went in, joined Willa and Beth, and there was no further business talk that evening.

After dinner, we went into the projection room again. Ben seemed impatient to get through coffee and brandy and on with the screening.

"What're we going to see?" I asked.

The Farbers looked at each other and smiled.

"A surprise, rather," said Willa. "A sentimental surprise. Ben and I picked out a few very, very early things. 'Vintage Farber,' you might say. We run them from time to time, but usually by ourselves. They asked for some of them at UCLA a few years ago. Of course, we let them have our best prints, and we went along to see them. An enormous audience, film students, mainly, and they laughed—I mean, they laughed when they weren't meant to laugh. They thought it all ridiculous, quaint."

"Goddam pinheads," said Ben.

"Oh, that's quite strong I think, Ben. But they certainly failed to appreciate the art. And the comedies didn't go well, either. They seemed to bore the audience, and they streamed out."

"That was the last goddam time they ever got any pictures from *me!*" said Ben.

"I won't laugh," I said.

"And I *will* laugh," said Beth.

"You'll laugh, all right," said Willa. "These tonight are all comedies. Buster Keaton, Harry Langdon, Arbuckle, and Harold Lloyd."

As the lights dimmed, I experienced the awful sinking feeling that comes over me when I know I'm in for something boring. How to get through it? How to make time go faster? How to tune out completely? I tried.

It began. The screening lasted for just over an hour, and I am prepared to say here and now that never in life have I spent a more enthralling hour—in or out of bed. How is it that I have come so far in life without knowing the work of these extraordinary, superlative artists? Buster Keaton, who would be called today, I suppose, a deadpan comic, is anything but deadpan. He seems to hold to a single expression, but the point is that the variations are so slight, so subtle, as to rivet one's attention on his eyebrow, or lips, or chin.

Harry Langdon. I had never even *heard* of him. A small man. A baby face. A forlorn countenance. A loser who elicits the last atom of sympathy from the viewer. You feel you want to get up there on the screen and take him in your arms.

Harold Lloyd. All-American. Energetic. But somehow, like the rest of us, getting it wrong almost every time. And unlike the rest of us, getting it right, finally.

Arbuckle, however, was the great surprise. I had vaguely heard of him in connection with some sex scandal, and had relegated him in memory to that long list of physical comedians no longer in vogue. The cross-eyed ones. The stuttering ones. The too-small, too-thin, too-fat—but there was much more than this to Arbuckle. He did not trade on his fatness, but on his grace and agility and sweetness. And in the short I saw, co-starring Mabel Normand, he was as funny and—at the same time—as appealing a figure as I have ever seen on the screen.

The show ended. The lights came on. I heard a strange noise behind me and turned to see Benjamin Farber wiping his eyes, blowing his nose, shaking his head slowly from side to side.

"I can never be grateful enough to you," I said. "What a remarkable experience!"

"Say," said Ben. "We've got more, hundreds more. Haven't we, darling?"

Willa laughed. "Thousands," she said.

"Who's around today can touch those men?" asked Ben. "Nobody. And they did most of the writing, the directing. They were creators. You know what I mean? They created."

"Yes," I said.

Willa said good night and went up to bed. Shortly afterward, Beth kissed Ben and said, "I'm seeing you tomorrow about the Warren Beatty thing—so get out the boxing gloves!"

Ben seemed overstimulated by the evening's entertainment, and asked for a glass of warm milk.

"And you better a drink," he said.

"By all means."

We moved out to a small adjoining terrace. There was a bright moon, and no artificial light was required.

And so we sat, I with drink in hand, he sipping his warm milk in silence.

Finally, he spoke. "That Roscoe," he said. "He was my partner, y'know. But what's more important, he was my friend. And a terrible thing happened to him. Even now, it's almost sixty years ago, I still can't understand what or why. We all stood around, sat around, and watched our friend being crucified, and there was nothing we could do. Some tried but it was no use.

"I remember it all started like a party, like a little vacation. It was Labor Day, the Labor Day weekend, nineteen twenty-one, and everybody was going someplace. Some to Yosemite. Some to the desert. Some up to Big Bear. A lot of them, the ones with boats, they used to go to Catalina. We had a lot of invitations, Tessa and me. The one thing she loved was boats, sailing. Me, I

138

always got sick right away. So we made up that weekend *she* was going to go with the Barrymores on his boat, and I was going to go up to San Francisco with Roscoe and a wonderful actor by the name of Lowell Sherman—he was a director, too, very fine—and two or three other fellows. Everybody loved San Francisco. There was a lot to do there, and Roscoe, he was crazy about cars. He owned maybe six, seven, and he'd just bought this new one, a Pierce-Arrow. So we drove up. Some drive! They didn't have the big concrete highways, like now, or the freeways. Still and all, it was a nice trip, right next to the ocean all the way. And we stopped and had a picnic and stopped and took a swim, and finally towards the evening, we got to San Francisco. We went right to the St. Francis Hotel, there, on Union Square. And Roscoe, he knew how to do these things, he had arranged a whole part of the twelfth floor for all of us. And we all went down and had a fine Chinese dinner in Chinatown, and then we came back and went into Roscoe's suite and we had a few drinks. Now, of course, you remember it was still Prohibition, so it wasn't so easy to get. But that Roscoe, leave it to him. And by now, everybody was pretty tired, so we all went to bed. And the next morning, we slept late, it must have been eleven, eleven thirty, my phone rang, and it was Roscoe, and he said, 'Where the hell are you, Farber? Your ham and eggs are getting cold.' That was a big joke with him, because he claimed I still hadn't eaten my first piece of ham yet. But I put on a robe and slippers, and went on over. And there was Roscoe and Lowell and Al and Chuck Hummel and two fellows from San Francisco—one was an agent, one was an exhibitor—and here was this big buffet of all kinds of food and champagne. And everybody was drinking champagne mixed with orange juice. So I did too. And there was a lot of eating and drinking, maybe a little too much for so early in the morning, but anyhow, it got to a point where Roscoe—he was still wearing his pajamas, too, and a big robe—he started in telling stories about how he started in the show business, in vaudeville, and what he was, you know, was a singer. That's right. He was a beautiful singer. In fact, Caruso once heard him sing, and he said that if Arbuckle wanted to, he could train and go into the opera. That was always funny to me, how a man who was such a fine singer made a success where nobody could hear his voice. Maybe that was the reason whenever there was a little party like this, or a gathering, he always used to like to get up and sing. And this particular afternoon he said he was going to do his whole act for us that he used to do in the vaudeville. And Lowell said, 'Get the hook.' And we all said, 'No, no. No vaudeville.' But Roscoe, he just lined up all the chairs like seats in the theatre, and by God, he did his whole act for us—singing and dancing. You wouldn't believe how delicate a big man like that moved when he danced. And then he did his jokes, very bad, and he sang 'After the Ball,' and he finished with a big dance."

III

ROSCOE DANCED off, nimbly, into room 1220. Applause. He returned at once, taking his bows, then went through the elaborate old routine of a vaudevillian milking one bow after another: keeping his hand on the proscenium, seeming to be ready to do an encore, going off and returning with a ukulele, and so on.

Despite the reluctant audience, the act had gone wonderfully well. It called for another drink. While this was being consumed, the phone rang. Roscoe answered it.

"Alcatraz!" he said. "Hey, ol' pal! What say? How are you? . . . You are? . . . Sounds hotsy-totsy. Wait a second." He put his hand over the mouthpiece and turned to the others in the room. "Girlies. Anybody interested in girlies?"

The men responded with whistles, applause and stamping of feet.

Al Semnacher returned to his table in the dining room of the Palace Hotel beaming. He sat and rejoined his two companions.

"We're all set," he said. "He's having a little party and he wants us all to come on up."

"Who else is there?" asked Maude.

"What the hell do *you* care who else is there?"

Maude Delmont was the older of the two women. She was dressed flamboyantly and was made up so heavily that she succeeded in adding at least ten years to her actual age.

140

"I'd like to know," she said. "I gotta right to know."

"You gotta right to *nothin'*," said Al. "Who the hell you think you are, for Christ's sake—Mrs. Leland Stanford?"

"I just asked who else is gonna be there," she said, beginning to choke up. "What's wrong with that?" She was crying.

"What's wrong is, I'm doing the best I can for you and you're being a pest, and don't give me all that eye-pissing either, I'm sick of it!"

"Leave 'er alone," said the other girl. She was Virginia Rappe, somewhat younger than Maude, but in her getup and makeup, achieving the same age. It had taken her over an hour this morning to get herself looking what she considered "presentable," because she was ill. Her complexion was sallow, the shades under her eyes deep and purple, and there was a profusion of skin blemishes which she had skillfully camouflaged.

"I'll leave the *two* of you alone in one goddam minute," said Al. "What the hell *is* all this?"

Both women were by way of being Al's clients, although the commissions he had received from them in the past two years would scarcely have paid for the breakfast.

Maude had apparently seen her best days as a small-part player in shorts and serials. She now worked only intermittently a few days at a time whenever a friend with sufficient power was able to provide the work.

Virginia had had more of a career, based on the fact that she had become involved with Pathé Lehrman and had lived with him on and off for several years.

Unfortunately, he had promised far more than he had been able to deliver, and on the way had introduced her to dope and booze and dissipation. His amorality proved to be contagious. Even in the days when they were sharing an apartment, he would frequently bring other women home to spend the night. This led her, too, into strange paths of behavior and her reputation was soon that of a "pushover," in the language of the day.

"I think he said Lowell Sherman was there," said Al.

Maude stopped crying and brightened. "Lowell Sherman?" she repeated, awed.

"Yeah, that's right. Lowell Sherman. So what're you getting your drawers all damp for?"

"Lowell Sherman," said Maude, "is class. *You* wouldn't know

141

about that. He's a great actor. He's from the legit. And a director, too. But listen, if it's Lowell Sherman, I have to change my clothes and everything."

"Why?" asked Al. "Why bother? You want the truth? You look as good now as you're *ever* gonna look."

Maude ignored him and said, "I think my navy blue. Don't you, Ginny?"

"Sure, that would be great," answered Virginia absently.

"How the hell long is this gonna take?" asked Al. "We haven't got all day."

"Five minutes."

"Banana oil! You know what I learned in life? There's no such thing as five minutes. Somebody says to you they'll be over in five minutes, it's usually half an hour. Somebody says they have to see y' for five minutes, it's at least twenty."

"So come up with me," said Maude, "and time me."

"Don't think I won't." He snapped his fingers in the air. "Check, please!"

Upstairs in Maude's room, she moved in and out of the bathroom, in various stages of dress and undress, in and out of her closet. She changed her hairdo and her makeup and managed a surprising effect of respectability. So absorbed was she in making this transformation, that she appeared to be oblivious to what was happening on her large bed: Al and Virginia lying there, fully clothed, but with enough undone to share what Al called a quickie.

In suite 1219–1221 at the St. Francis, the party was winding down. Most of the food had been removed. Roscoe, Lowell, Chuck, and Ben were getting sleepy, although it was not yet one o'clock.

Roscoe began to sing: " 'Three o'Clock in the Morning!' "

" 'Three o'Clock in the Morning,' " said Lowell. "Most appropriate."

"To me," said Ben, "it feels more like five."

Roscoe began the song again: " '*Five* o'clock in the morning, we've danced the whole night through!' " He looked at his three friends, variously sprawled in different parts of the room, all still in pajamas and dressing gowns.

"Which one of you clodhoppers can waltz?" asked Roscoe.

"Not me," said Ben.

"I gave it up for Lent one year," said Lowell, "and never took it up again. The tango, yes. The waltz, no."

"Me?" said Chuck. "I don't believe in dancing, it's only a substitute for the real thing, so why not the real thing?"

Roscoe approached Ben. "Come on, Ben. On your feet."

"I wouldn't dream of it."

"Come on." He grasped both Ben's wrists and pulled him to his feet.

"Cut it out, Roscoe," said Ben. "No fair."

"He's right," said Lowell. "Why don't you pick on somebody your own size?"

Roscoe put on one of his famous plaintive expressions, and said, "Because I can't *find* anybody my own size!"

In the general laughter that followed, he and Ben began waltzing about the room with surprising grace and agility. Roscoe provided the music. There was a sharp knock at the door.

"Let 'em in," said Roscoe, "I'm busy."

He continued to dance as Lowell went to the door.

Two beautiful young showgirls, Alice Blake and Zey Prevon, entered, accompanied by a dress salesman named Ira Fortlouis.

The greetings were loud and raucous. Fortlouis was carrying a bottle of gin, which he began to open at once, and before long, Alice was waltzing with Roscoe, Zey with Ben.

Twenty minutes later, another knock. Another party arrived. This one was composed of Al Semnacher, Maude Delmont and Virginia Rappe. Maude and Virginia regarded Zey and Alice and bristled. Zey and Alice went into a corner and whispered, then giggled.

Roscoe was on the telephone, ordering masses of food from room service. Virginia joined him as he hung up and asked, "How about a little music? Haven't you got a piano or a Gramophone or anything?"

"Leave it to me," he said, and picked up the phone again.

Another arrival. This time it was a local bootlegger named Jack Lawrence with two helpers. They brought a case of scotch, a case of gin, and a case of bourbon. Roscoe insisted that they stay and have a drink.

"A charming conceit," said Lowell. "It reminds me, rather, of the days when emperors had official tasters who would partake first of food and drink and, of course, if they expired on the spot, the emperor would send the stuff back. Drink up, gentlemen, drink up."

Before leaving, Jack Lawrence made a date with Virginia Rappe, to take her out to a Chinese restaurant across the bridge. She asked if she could bring her friend Maude. Why not?

"I'll see if I can get someone for her," said Jack.

Lowell need not have been suspicious. The booze was splendid. Maude was so impressed by the quality of the scotch that she had ten in the course of two hours by Ben's count. He was amazed at her capacity.

Virginia drank Orange Blossoms: gin and orange juice. Roscoe saw to it that the orange juice was freshly squeezed before each drink.

By four o'clock in the afternoon, Zey and Alice were asleep on two sofas. Maude was wearing a pair of Lowell Sherman's silk monogramed pajamas.

"More comfortable," she said.

The Gramophone was playing "I'm Just Wild About Harry."

A few minutes later, Virginia garnered the biggest laugh by far of the laugh-filled afternoon, by coming in to 1220 from 1219 wearing a pair of Roscoe's pajamas.

"Take those off!" shouted Roscoe. "Take those off at once, they're not insured."

Playing Pola Negri, in a manner that demonstrated her deficiencies as an actress, Virginia unbuttoned the pajama jacket and tossed it to Roscoe. As she revealed that she was circumspectly underdressed, the laughter increased and turned to applause. Now the pajama pants came off, but instead of tossing them to Roscoe, she threw them out of the window.

Ben got on the phone and asked the bell captain if he could possibly retrieve something that had fallen to the sidewalk.

"What is it?" asked the bell captain.

"A tent," said Ben. "A Barnum and Bailey circus tent."

Lowell and Maude retired quietly to room 1221.

The music was now "A Pretty Girl Is Like a Melody." Roscoe and Virginia were dancing gaily and especially well.

A bellhop came in carrying the lost pajama bottom. Roscoe tipped him five dollars, took the garment, and magically trans-

144

formed it into a kind of sheik's kúfiẏah. The seat over his head, one of the legs swung around his neck, the other down his back. Now, with a comic flourish, he swept Virginia off her feet and into his arms in the manner of Rudolph Valentino's handling of Agnes Ayres.

He sang out the publicity slogan that had been used for the film: "Shriek—For the Sheik Will Seek You, Too!"

In a falsetto voice, Roscoe then spoke the catch phrase that had gained such wide currency: " 'I am not afraid with your arms around me, Ahmed, my desert love, my sheik.' "

The act was going well. Even Zey and Alice awoke to appreciate it.

Roscoe began to sing the celebrated song inspired by the picture: "The Sheik of Araby." Ben provided the comic obbligato that tough kids were singing in the streets: " 'Wit' no pants on.' "

Roscoe: " 'I'm the Sheik of Araby!' "

Ben led the rest of the room in the obbligato: " 'Wit' no pants on!' "

Roscoe: " 'Your love belongs to me!' "

The group: " 'Wit' no pants on!' "

Roscoe: " 'At night when you're asleep—' "

The group: " 'Wit' no pants on!' "

Roscoe: " 'Into your tent I'll creep.' "

The group: " 'Wit' no pants on!' "

Roscoe: " 'The stars that shine above—' "

The group: " 'Wit' no pants on!' "

Roscoe: " 'Will light our way to love!' "

The group: " 'Wit' no pants on!' "

Roscoe: " 'You'll rule this land with me—' "

The group: " 'Wit' no pants on!' "

Roscoe: " 'The Sheik of Araby!' "

The group: " 'Wit' no pants on!' "

As the number ended, Roscoe made an exit, missing the door by two or three feet and crashing, with his arms full of Virginia, into the wall. He caromed off, bounced against a piece of furniture, into another wall, back to the door, missing it again. Virginia began to scream. He swung about, stumbled into 1219, and slammed the door.

From inside the room, Virginia could be heard yelling, "Put me down! Put me down, you fat slob!"

145

Roscoe's voice: "Now, now, take it easy."

Virginia's voice: "I'm sick! You've got me sick. Where's the god-dam toilet?"

IV

"SOME TIME went by," said B.J. "I don't know how long. I have to tell you the truth. We were all drunk. Even me—and I've never been a drinking man. I would drink sometime but never drunk. This time was one of the few times it was different. Anyway, Roscoe came out and he said to us, 'Where's Maude? Or somebody. I think Virginia needs some help. She's sick.' So Zey and Alice went in. I, too. The girls went into the bathroom, to Virginia. We waited around. After a while, they brought her out. There was no question, she was in bad pain and she started in ripping her clothes off. And there was a lot of screaming and hollering and Roscoe told them to shut up or he'd throw them out of the window. He was drunk, mind you, and annoyed, but she kept on screaming. Pretty soon Maude came in and Lowell also, and it was decided that the best would be to send for a doctor. So they did. But in the meantime, Roscoe said to me, 'Let's get her out of here!' So I called up the manager and asked him if he had another suite someplace because one of the guests was sick. Pretty soon the doctor came. Then *another* doctor. The whole excitement pretty much sobered everybody up by now and we went for coffee. One of the doctors got me and Roscoe to one side and said, 'This woman's pregnant. Did you know that?' Well, we just looked at each other and if that wasn't a big enough shock, he said, 'And she seems to be sporting quite a case of gonorrhea.' And Roscoe started to laugh. Now, I'm not defending the bad taste—somebody laughing at somebody's sickness—but the way he laughed, I knew what he was laughing. He was laughing that he hadn't had anything to do with her in that way, if you know what I mean. Maybe he thought of it. Maybe it was on his mind. But the first place, I think he was too drunk to function. And the second place, he was laughing that if he *had* managed it, what

146

might have happened to him, what he might of wound up with. So that's why he was laughing. And it was that that convinced me then, and I'm still convinced, that the worst thing Roscoe did that day was get drunk."

"But the girl died," I said. "Didn't she?"

"Yes, but not for several days after that. We were all back already in Hollywood, and she was in the hospital. And there were all kinds of arguments what should be done, arguments among the different doctors, that is. And they gave her several treatments, and then they operated. And several days later, yes, she passed away from some kind of kidney failure. A sick girl, who probably shouldn't have had one drink even, let alone six or seven. And all the dancing and excitement. But this woman, this Maude Delmont, had it in for Roscoe and she made up all kinds of stories and then she got that son-of-a-bitch Pathé Lehrman all excited, too. He wasn't even there; he was in New York. But it was that Maude, she was the one who went ahead and she swore out the complaint against Roscoe Arbuckle.

"And they came down and they arrested him. He called me up right away. He couldn't believe it. I couldn't believe it either. But the next thing you know, we were all embroiled up there in San Francisco with the lawyers and depositions and the newspapers and the photographers.

"There were plenty of pressure groups in those days, just like now, and Hollywood had a bad name. We were all supposed to be immoral and having a bad influence on young people. And Roscoe became a scapegoat, that's all. The papers were terrible, unbelievable. The way they played it up, the way they made it seem. Goddamnit, I was *there,* I saw what happened. It was just a wild party, that's all. And like a lot of wild parties, it had a bad ending. But to put it all on him, to blame it all on him?

"Anybody could have looked back on his record for all the years he'd been around and nobody could find anything against him, no matter how they tried. The prosecution sent people all over the country to try and dig up bad stuff on him, and they found just nothing. But here's maybe the most important point of the whole story—you know, by the way, he went through three different trials. The first one it was something awful, with the publicity and the demonstrations. One time when he came into the court, there was a whole bunch of women there, maybe a

147

hundred, from the Women's League for Decency, and the minute they saw him they all started in to applaud, automatically, to applaud, till one of them—a leader—screamed out, 'Women of America, do your duty!' And they all begin to spit, and they spit all over Roscoe. The look on his face, those eyes, it was something I can never forget.

"We tried to get Earl Rogers to be his lawyer. He was the most famous criminal lawyer there at the time. His daughter, Adela Rogers St. John—a very good writer—she worked for me, but Rogers right at that time was sick with a heart condition, and he couldn't handle it. But he gave a lot of good advice. One piece of advice was, he said, 'Get ahold of Frank Dominquez. Let him do most of the courtroom appearances.' And when we asked him why, he said, 'Because he's a big fat guy, like Roscoe, so Roscoe won't stand out so much, so he won't be so conspicuous.' Well, we did that, we got Frank. He was a fine lawyer from a well-known family, California family, and he did most of the courtroom work. But of course, there were five, six other lawyers also. To me, it was like life or death. If Arbuckle went down, it was me with him. He was by then Fan Films only asset. And what was I saying before, about the most important point of the case? Oh, yes, now I remember. This goddam bitch, this Maude Delmont, she was the one swore out the complaint, and right through the seven months it took for the three trials, that was the last was ever heard of her. She never testified in court, she was never there. There was a hung jury the first time, and a hung jury the second time. And in the meantime, Roscoe couldn't work, he used up all his money, Joe Schenck loaned him some. All his friends stood by him, stuck with him. Buster Keaton, Harold Lloyd, Chaplin, Mary Pickford, Joe Schenck.

"But then, on the other hand, there were some who were against him. They were worried this whole case was going to give Hollywood a worse name than it had already, and that it would hurt business. The business part, naturally, worried them more than the name part.

"Roscoe had been separated from his wife, Minta, but when the trouble hit, she came back and stood by him right through the whole time.

"The bigger the case got, the more headlines, the more sensationalism, the more everybody wanted to get into the act. There were prosecutors, and they had political ambition, so they didn't stop at anything. They bought witnesses, they had spies, they used pressure. And Roscoe simply had his spirit broken.

"By the third trial, by the time the third trial got under way, he was like a zombie. He didn't eat, hardly; he couldn't listen; he found it hard to talk. He was just the pawn of the whole thing.

"Finally, there we were back in San Francisco, and we went back to the St. Francis Hotel. You can imagine how painful that was, but the lawyers said that strategically and psychologically it had to be. If we went to some other hotel, it might be like some kind of admission. And poor Lowell Sherman, what happened to him. Just because he'd *been* there, he was suddenly, all of a sudden, blacklisted, too, and couldn't get work, not as an actor, not as a director, nothing, and he went broke.

"The third trial, to tell you the truth, after sitting through the first two, I didn't have too much confidence. But the lawyers did. They had found out so many things about the prosecution's witnesses, about the people who had been swearing to this and that.

"Like, for instance, there was one guy they had as a witness, and he swore that a couple of years before, Roscoe had tried to bribe him. That was while he was working as a watchman around the studio—that Roscoe had tried to bribe him with ten dollars or twenty dollars to give him the key to Virginia's dressing room, because he said Roscoe told him he wanted to play a little joke. But what it said to the jury was that Roscoe was hot for this girl. Think how stupid all this was. Here he was, one of the most successful comedians in the world, and she's nothing, a bit player. So even if he *had* wanted her, if he *had* been interested in her, he wouldn't have had to bribe a watchman for the key to her dressing room. That wouldn't have been the way to go about it, anyway. But they believed this bastard, and it was just another thing that weighed against Roscoe.

"But by the time the third trial came around, Roscoe's lawyers had found out that this watchman was a crook, an ex-convict, he'd been involved in all kinds of crime, and spent some time in psychiatric institutions, and was a completely unworthy and untrustworthy human being. So his testimony was worth nothing.

"And *still* they didn't call that goddam Maude. And the trial went on.

"Mabel Normand, of course, was wonderful. She used to call

149

Roscoe on the phone practically every day. And I think the reason she didn't believe a word of any of this stuff was because she knew him, you see. That's what's so interesting. All of us, the ones who knew the man, knew that he *couldn't* have done all the crazy things they were suggesting, and all of the innuendo and the double meanings in the newspapers. The real man and the one they invented in the papers and in the gossip were like two different people. That's what they mean, I suppose, when they talk about image. That's why my publicity men are always so careful how they present somebody, what kind of pictures they send out, what kind of stories. Because, see, the public doesn't know these people. The public is not acquainted personally with Marlon Brando or with, say, even John Travolta, or with Robert Redford. So what do they know? They only know what they're told in the papers or on the radio or on the television. And they make up their minds. So what you had here was some kind of phony picture being built up, and, naturally, it affected almost everybody.

"We made a terrible mistake on the first trial. The lawyers weren't as careful as they should have been when they were putting together the jury, and they let one woman get on. I'll never forget her name—it was Hubbard. Hubbard. I can't remember her first name. Mrs. Hubbard. If not for her, Roscoe would have been acquitted. It was only later, we found out that her mother-in-law was one of the Daughters of the American Revolution, and that her husband was a lawyer, and a friend of the D.A. And her mind was made up even before the first witness was called, and it was this one woman that meant there had to be a second trial.

"And, of course, by the time the second trial came up, it was hard to get a jury who didn't have an opinion one way or the other. And by the time of the third trial, my God, it was even worse. And you could just see this man and his spirit being eaten away, day after day, by the injustice and by the humiliation and the aggravation. There were so many times when we would sit and talk, and I could tell from the look on his face that he wasn't listening to anything I was saying. He was a beaten man.

"But there was no way of stopping things now that they had gone this far, and so it went on and on."

V

ALL THREE trials of *The People of the State of California* vs. *Roscoe C. Arbuckle* were conducted in four separate and distinct places: in the San Francisco courtroom; in the press from coast to coast; in the minds of the public; and in the power structure of the motion picture industry.

Adolph Zukor, the head of Paramount Pictures, was by way of being the self-appointed head of this establishment. It was he who called the conference and the meetings.

"Gentlemen," said Adolph Zukor, "I hope it is not necessary for me to remind you all that this is a confidential session, that nothing said here or done here or discussed is to be mentioned to anyone on the outside. I do not refer to the press only, but even to your other business associates, and if I may say so, I do not think it should be discussed with your wives—or even with your mistresses."

There was a sprinkling of laughter around the huge shiny table, which mirrored the heads of the eighteen most important men in the motion picture business.

Zukor went on. "We are faced today with a situation so serious that I can see it developing to a point where a substantial part of our business will be closed down. I assure you this is not an exaggeration. Also, if something is not done, and done very fast, I can see our entire business, as it now stands, being wiped out."

"Now wait a minute, Adolph," said Joseph Schenck. "Speaking for all my partners at United Artists, we think it's a good idea to face the facts, but there's no reason to panic."

"I'm sorry I have to disagree with you, Joe, but I think there *is* a reason to panic."

"Go ahead," said Schenck, "let's hear the rest of it."

"The rest of it is," said Zukor, "that up there in San Francisco, it's not only that son-of-a-bitch Arbuckle who's—"

"Mr. Zukor," said Ben, rising from his chair, "I have to object, and object very strongly—"

151

"Sit down, Ben," said Zukor. "This ain't a court of law and you ain't a lawyer."

"Let me finish," said Ben. "I object, I object very strongly, with all my heart, the way you just referred to Roscoe Arbuckle. You called him a very bad name. I'm not the most educated man in the world, but I know that in this country and under the system of law in this country, a man is innocent until he is proven guilty —*proven!* So far, there's a trial still going on, and nothing has been proven yet."

He sat down, trembling, reached out, poured a glass of ice water with some difficulty, and drank it.

"What's been proven," said Jesse Lasky, Zukor's partner, "is that our grosses are off anywhere from twenty-eight to thirty-three percent."

"Well, is that Arbuckle's fault?" asked Sam Goldwyn.

"You're goddamn right it is," said Lasky. "Who's else? He's got the whole country against the movies—the churches, the women's clubs, the newspapers—and I say—"

"Just a moment, gentlemen," said Zukor. "Let's have some order here. You'll all get a chance to speak and to give your opinions. I don't want this to be a disorganized argument. I am looking here for an orderly discussion. . . . Now, where was I? . . . I was trying to point out to all of you that what is on trial up there in San Francisco is not just Arbuckle, not just a man, but this whole entire business that we love and that's been so good to us. So all right, like Ben says, 'innocent till proven guilty.' But suppose it turns out guilty? *Then* what are we going to do? And shouldn't we prepare for it now? The worst thing of all is that the way it's gone up to now, even if it should be possible that it would come out up there *not* guilty, our troubles are the same, maybe even worse. Maybe the press and a lot of people would say, Sure, those movie bastards can get away with anything because they're rich and because they're powerful, and I have to say this gentlemen—you'll forgive me—and because they're Jews."

"I'm no Jew!" said Winfield Sheehan, the florid head of Fox Films.

Light laughter again.

"I know that, Winnie. I know that. And by the way, you're not missing a thing. . . . I'm not talking about what's real, only about what people *think*. Now, what can we do? I have several ideas, and one I would like to propose definitely. Do you realize that this year alone, there have been over one hundred censorship laws introduced into the legislatures of thirty-seven states? Do you realize that the state of New York has already set up a system to license movies?"

"For God's *sake,* Mr. Zukor!" said Ben. "I can't let you tell it in such a way. That New York State thing happened last *August,* way before anything happened in San Francisco with Roscoe."

"You don't seem to understand," said Zukor. "I'm not talking about Arbuckle only. I'm talking about ourselves. Sure, even before Arbuckle, we were in some kind of trouble, but he sure in hell brought it to a head. Maybe we could have bumbled along somehow and quieted them down, but now, on account of him, they're all screaming for blood. *Our* blood. Listen, the last time I was in Washington and I sat down with President Harding, he told me himself how worried he was about the movies. He said we've got to stop making dirty movies."

"What we should have done, years ago," said Sheehan, "is set up our own control system. And see, if *we'd* had that, maybe you wouldn't have those hundred goddam laws after us."

"That's what I'm coming to," said Zukor. "Exactly, Winnie. That's just what I'm coming to. We have got to form our own organization and we have got to censor our own pictures ourselves. I talked the whole thing over with President Harding, and he thinks it's a good idea. He said the best would be if it didn't look like it was us doing it ourselves, that it ought to be like an organization that saw to it that nothing bad was ever in movies. It ought to be, or ought to look like, it was independent. Of course, *we'd* have to set it up and finance it, but that shouldn't be hard. And then, like if this organization gave the O.K. to a picture, then it meant that it was O.K. And nobody would dare to question it. It's like we all make a contract, an agreement, that certain things are not going to be in pictures."

"Like what things?" asked Goldwyn.

"I don't know yet. That would have to be decided by the person in charge."

Louis B. Mayer of Metro-Goldwyn-Mayer spoke.

"What kind of person?" he asked. "Who?"

"I don't know yet," said Zukor. "But the President suggested somebody."

"Who?" asked Mayer.

"Well, he recommended Will Hays."

"Who?" asked Schenck.

"Will Hays," said Winnie. "He's the Postmaster General of the United States, for Chrissake! Don't you even know who the Postmaster of the United States is?"

"No, I don't," said Schenck. "I don't know and I don't *give* a good goddam."

"Well, he certainly sounds perfect to run the movie business," said Lasky. "A Postmaster General. Jesus!"

"Wait a second," said Zukor. "He wasn't always a Postmaster. He was the chairman of the Republican National Committee. He's the one who got Harding elected."

Lewis J. Selznick now spoke for the first time. "How old is he? This Hays?"

"I don't know. About forty or so," said Zukor.

"I hope he's a Catholic," said Sheehan, "because that's the bunch raising the most sand."

"No, he's not," said Zukor. "He's some kind of a Presbyterian, I think. Mind you, he's only a candidate. We can discuss a lot of others."

"There's something in this, Adolph," said Selznick. "It's like what the baseball guys did last year. When they had that crooked World Series, they were in trouble. The public lost confidence and the whole baseball business could have been wiped out, but they set up an association and they got that Judge Landis to run it and now everybody thinks they're pure."

"I still think a Catholic would be better," said Sheehan.

"Kenesaw Mountain Landis," said Goldwyn. "Some name!"

"Mind you, he's only going to be one guy, whoever he is. The head," said Zukor.

"And it should be a whole board, like a board of directors, don't you think so?" asked Mayer. "I mean, it should have on it everything, Jews and Catholics and Mormons even. We've got to cover everybody. Maybe a couple of priests and ministers and rabbis."

"And lawyers," said Selznick. "You've got to have some lawyers to make sure it's going to stick."

"The idea is," said Zukor, "that we set up like a constitution, like a set of rules and regulations."

"It's not a bad idea," said Lasky. "Not bad at all."

154

"And like I said," said Zukor, "this is something we should do no matter *how* it comes out up there in San Francisco."

Up there in San Francisco, matters were going well for Roscoe Arbuckle. His team of lawyers had prepared their case thoroughly and brilliantly.

The prosecution, conversely, was clearly depending upon the sensationalism involved. They were shakily organized. Worried that their principal witness, Maude Delmont, was untrustworthy, they decided not to call her.

Moreover, the district attorney, Matthew Brady, obviously a man with political aspirations, saw in this trial of the century an opportunity to make a name for himself and to present to a wide public a figure of law and order and decency. His zealousness in this direction became easily apparent day after day and influenced the jury against him.

In Matthew Brady's office an important conference was in progress. Brady had called in his assistants, Isadore Golden and Milton U'Ren.

"Have you talked to those two tramps today?" asked Brady.

"I talk to them every day," said U'Ren.

"What I want to know is—which one of them do you think we ought to put on? That Alice Blake? Or the other one? What's her name?"

"Zey Prevon," said Golden, "also known as Sadie Reiss. Also known as Zey Prevost."

"Holy Jesus," said Brady. "I think we better go with the other one."

"No, wait a minute, boss. I don't think so. Blake is a real high-class girl. Her folks've got money. She's been to college. The other one, Prevon, is just a little pisspot. And she's gonna be a hell of a lot easier to break down."

"All right," said Brady. "Whatever you say. And you're sure nobody's been able to get to them?"

"I'd stake my balls," said Golden. "We've had them under lock and key this whole time."

"All right, then. Let's go with Prevon."

The questioning continued before the coroner's jury.

"U'Ren: "What was her condition? What was she doing?"

155

Prevon: "She was laying on the bed and she started in to moan. Hair all down. I said, 'What's a matter with you?' She says, 'Oh, I'm dying. I got pains. I know I am dying.' I said, 'You're not gonna die.' So then Alice comes running in."

U'Ren: "What did she do then?"

Prevon: "Virginia? She didn't say anything more. She just kept on moaning, moaning. She got up in bed then and started to tear her clothes off of her. Like crazy. She pulled her waist nearly all off of her. And stockings and garters. And she says, 'I got a pain.' "

U'Ren: "What part of her body was it she referred to?"

Zey Prevon put her hand on her left breast. "Right here. She says, 'I got a pain around my heart.' So Alice says, 'I think she's got gas pains.' So Mrs. Delmont went to put her dress on in the other room and I got some carbonate of soda. No. We got Virginia all undressed first and the bed was all wet, so we took her from one bed to another bed. Then we tried to put the carbonate of soda down her, but she threw it all up."

U'Ren: "Were these the words she said? I'm reading from a statement you gave to Mr. Vernon, the official notary public stenographer: 'Oh, I am dying. I am dying. He has killed me.' "

Prevon: "No! She did *not* say, 'He has killed me.' "

U'Ren took a deep breath, stepped away and glanced over at Matthew Brady, who made a fist of his right hand and pantomimed a series of short punches. U'Ren returned to his witness.

U'Ren: "You realize that you are under oath?"

Prevon: "Yes, sir."

Sitting on a bench directly behind the defense counsel's table, Minta reached over and took Roscoe's hand. He turned to her and made every attempt to smile, but only one side of his mouth made a faint movement upward.

U'Ren: "Didn't you, upstairs, less than half an hour ago, state that she said, 'He has killed me'?"

Prevon: "No, somebody must've wrote that in."

Brady flushed, coughed, pretended to make a few important notes, then glanced up at the presiding judge. His worst fears were realized. The judge was looking straight at him.

U'Ren again looked over toward Brady, who beckoned to him. He walked to the prosecutor's table and leaned over. He and Brady and Golden had a swift whispered conference.

U'Ren returned to his witness and hammered away with persistence and power along these lines. He had been taught that if a

156

question is repeated again and again it becomes subliminally an answer in the collective mind of the jury.

At last he could see that Zey Prevon was beginning to get confused. He reminded the members of the jury that under the rules of evidence, *they* were permitted to ask questions.

U'Ren: "Did you not state that in Mr. Arbuckle's presence in room twelve nineteen Miss Rappe was yelling, 'I'm dying, I am dying. You killed me!' "

Roscoe sat looking up at the witness, aghast. Could she? Would she be forced by this battering to swear to a lie? Also, he thought, why are they asking only her? The room had been crowded. Ben had been there, and Lowell and Chuck. Along with Alice and Maude. Why was it all hanging on what Zey would say?

Prevon: "No, she did *not* say, 'You killed me.' She only said— 'I'm dying, I'm dying, I know I'm dying. I'm going to die.' "

She tried to continue but could not. She collapsed in a flood of tears and sat weeping hysterically. When she recovered sufficiently, she said, "I don't remember."

Matthew Brady beamed. At last, she was beginning to crack. A juror spoke.

The juror: "Did you notice any marks on her neck?"

Prevon: "No, sir, I did not."

Another juror: "Are you in the movie business?"

Prevon: "I used to be. Not now."

Another juror: "What clothes were on Miss Rappe when you went into the room?"

Prevon: "She had all her clothes on."

Juror: "A skirt?"

Prevon: "A skirt and a little green blouse and a little white blouse underneath it."

U'Ren held up a palm, signaling to the jury that he wished them to hold further questioning for a time.

Now Isadore Golden rose from his chair at the prosecutor's table and moved toward the witness. They were using the well-known San Francisco detectives' method of questioning suspects, spelling one another so that the questioner was always fresh while the suspect became more and more fatigued.

Golden: "Did Miss Rappe ever say, 'You killed me'?"

Prevon: "Not that I remember, no. 'I'm dying. I'm dying.' That's what she yelled."

Golden: "Did Miss Rappe ever use the words: '*He* killed me'?"

157

Prevon: "No."

Golden: "Did you ever tell anybody that Miss Rappe said, 'You killed me'? Yes or no, please."

Prevon: "I don't know."

Golden: "If you did, have you forgotten?"

Prevon: "I must've forgotten."

She burst into tears again. But the questioning continued relentlessly. Finally, she was exhausted, disoriented, and hysterical. Brady threatened her with prison for perjury, but she stood firm.

The next day, she was back on the stand. It took two more days and finally the prosecution had to settle for a compromise. For the words 'He killed me' Brady somehow forced her into saying that she had heard Virginia say, 'I'm dying. I'm dying. He hurt me.'

On the basis of this flimsy and forced evidence, the coroner's jury indicted Arbuckle not for murder but for manslaughter.

When the verdict was read, Arbuckle looked over at Ben, who sat impassively, although tears were streaming from his eyes. He could not believe what he had just heard.

Manslaughter!

VI

"WE COULDN'T believe it," said B.J. "Any of us. We went there to a room near his cell. His brother, Arthur, and his sister, Nora, and Minta and me, and they let us visit for a few minutes before locking him up. And all of a sudden, his sister went up to him and put her hands on his shoulder and looked at him and asked him, 'Did you do it, Roscoe?' and he looked back at her and he said, 'No, Nora, I didn't. I didn't touch the girl.'

"The next morning, Zukor and the whole bunch insisted that I should take him off salary and the reason, officially, legally, I should give was that Roscoe was in breach of contract because he didn't show up for the first day of shooting of a picture by the name of *The Melancholy Spirit*. I said, 'Listen, Mr. Zukor, and listen, Jesse, how can I *do* such a thing? How could the man show

158

up for work when he was locked up in jail?' They just looked at each other and then at me, and then they told me that I should fire his lawyer, Frank Dominquez. 'Why?' I asked them. 'He's a great lawyer. We couldn't get Clarence Darrow because he couldn't get into California without getting arrested himself, and we couldn't get Earl Rogers because he had a heart condition.' And they said, 'Never mind.' They thought Dominquez should have gotten him an acquittal, and so long as he didn't, he was out. And if not they were going to walk out on me altogether. So I changed lawyers, but I didn't take Roscoe off salary. I told them I did but I didn't.

"I want to tell you another thing, an interesting thing, but crazy. For years and years, the story was—everybody knew it, every college kid repeated it, every taxi driver, everybody knew that what happened was that Roscoe took a Coca-Cola bottle and shoved it up into this girl, and that's what killed her. Now as I say, it's a story that—like everybody *knew*. So here's what's interesting. There were three trials over a time that lasted more than seven months. And dozens and dozens of witnesses were called and testified. And somewhere in the files, I've got all the transcripts. I've got every word that was said by everybody and anybody on that case. It's more than nine thousand pages long—could use some cutting by the way—and in the whole nine thousand pages, there is *not even one mention by anybody at any time of any Coca-Cola bottle at all!* How can you explain a thing like that? Later on, you began to hear it was a *champagne* bottle! I suppose that must have been for the class trade. A champagne bottle, not a Coca-Cola bottle. Well, there wasn't any goddam champagne bottle mentioned in the nine thousand pages either. It comes down to a story of what happens when you begin to get a mob spirit working. One thing leads to another.

"In the middle of everything, that bitch, Maude Delmont, she wound up in jail herself. She was locked up for bigamy, and the prosecution never mentioned her name again, even though you have to remember, she was the one who signed and filed the original complaint. When she got out of jail, she went into vaudeville. She was one of those sensational acts they used to book: The Woman in the Arbuckle Case. They must have paid her thousands of dollars a week. And she would go on and just talk or be questioned by somebody. She was some number, that one.

159

If not for her, there wouldn't have been any case at all, ever. But anyway, the second trial went on, and this time we all know it would be all right.

"The second trial lasted almost four weeks, and it was practically a remake of the first trial. And the worst thing was that between the second trial and the third trial, the terrible William Desmond Taylor murder happened. This great English director was shot to death in his own home, and there was all kind of suspicion. Did one of his girls do it? Like Mary Miles Minter. Or maybe even Mabel Normand? She was the last one who saw him alive. But many people thought it was the mother of Mary Miles Minter, because she didn't like what Taylor was doing to her daughter. And there were all kinds of theories, but to this day, it hasn't been solved. But why it was bad for Roscoe was that it was again one of those things that was giving the whole movie business a bad name. We were all dope fiends and drunkards and murderers and rapers and God knows what else. So the whole atmosphere was bad. And this time, I wasn't so confident as I was the other times, even though this time—the third time—we finally got a really great lawyer. His name was Gavin McNab. He was brilliant, and you could see that even the judge, Judge Louderback, who was still the judge, the same as he had been the other two times, was impressed by him.

"He brought out, with plenty of truth, the kind of person Virginia Rappe was, and the kind Roscoe was. Did I tell you that the prosecution had over a hundred people all over the country, going around, looking for evidence about Roscoe's life in the past? They went to New York and Chicago and every place where he had ever been or where he had ever played, all the people he had worked for, or worked with. And they couldn't find one damn thing. Say, maybe this will be interesting to you. You remember that writer, that fine writer, Dashiell Hammett? He wrote *The Thin Man* and a lot of things like that that made big hits. Well, at that time, he was working for the Pinkertons in San Francisco, and they put him on the case to find out if he could find out anything bad about Roscoe. So he went all over and he couldn't find anything, but he got interested in the case, just the same. And he told everybody that he was absolutely convinced that Roscoe was innocent.

"Anyway, McNab did a splendid job and gave a whole different

160

color to the case. He put Roscoe on the stand and Roscoe was great.

"There was something so sad right in the middle of the third trial—Roscoe had a birthday. It was his thirty-fifth birthday. Just imagine it. Such a talent. Only thirty-five years old, and a career practically ruined. But we all believed, all his friends, that if only he could be acquitted the way he was supposed to be, maybe it would die down, and he would go back to work again.

"Well, anyway, it wasn't till April that the trial was over, and I remember it was late one afternoon . . ."

VII

JUDGE LOUDERBACK finished his charge to the jury.

Ben looked up at the courtroom clock and saw that it was ten minutes after five. He would go back to the hotel, he thought, perhaps have a drink and dinner with the Arbuckles and Buster and Buster's wife. Would there be time for a nap before dinner?

He looked across the room at Roscoe, who stood talking to McNab, and wondered if McNab would like to come to dinner? How would they know when they had a verdict? Of course, it might not be until tomorrow.

Ben was tying his shoelace, which had come loose, when he became aware of a stir in the courtroom. He looked up, along with everyone else, and saw that the jury was coming back into the room. Was this a good sign or a bad one? He could not tell. Everyone sat. Judge Louderback, hastily summoned, returned to the bench, buttoning his judicial robe. Everyone rose again, sat again, Apparently, the jury was going to ask for clarification on certain points, but so soon? The question or questions they asked might provide a clue.

Judge Louderback spoke. "Ladies and gentlemen of the jury, do you require further information or instruction?"

"No, sir," said the foreman, Edward Brown. "No, Your Honor. We have reached a verdict."

161

The judge seemed stunned, as did the courtroom. The clerk of the court went at once to the jury box. Brown handed him a piece of paper. The clerk of the court carried it to the judge, who adjusted his glasses and read: "We the jury find Roscoe Arbuckle not guilty of manslaughter."

On the word "not," the courtroom exploded. There was cheering, applauding, and whistling. The clerk called for order. Brown asked the judge if he could read a statement that the jury had signed unanimously. He explained that they had taken an immediate standing vote upon entering the jury room, and that the five minutes had been spent in writing out the statement.

"You may proceed," said the judge.

Brown read quietly, but firmly, to a hushed courtroom: "Acquittal is not enough for Roscoe Arbuckle. We feel that a great injustice has been done him. We feel also that it was only our plain duty to give him this exoneration, under the evidence, for there was not the slightest proof adduced to connect him in any way with the commission of a crime.

"He was manly throughout the case, and told a straightforward story on the witness stand, which we all believed.

"The happening at the hotel was an unfortunate affair for which Arbuckle, so the evidence shows, was in no way responsible.

"We wish him success, and hope that the American people will take the judgment of fourteen men and women who have sat listening for thirty-one days to the evidence, that Roscoe Arbuckle is entirely innocent and free from all blame."

Brown looked up and added, "This statement has been signed by every member of our jury and also by our two alternates."

Again the spectators cheered and yelled, but this time, there was no way of getting them to subside.

The seven-month nightmare was over.

Ben and Minta and Buster and Buster's wife rushed over to Roscoe, who seemed dazed and unbelieving.

Despite the release from strain and the deep feeling involved, there were no tears, there was only laughter.

Gavin McNab came to dinner after all. In the circumstances it was decided to take a private dining room at the St. Francis.

There were toasts and speeches. Dinner took three hours. Afterward, when the party broke up and everyone had gone home or up to bed, Ben and Minta and Roscoe sat up all night, discussing the realities.

The phone kept ringing.

They heard that Joseph Schenck had released a statement saying, "I hope Arbuckle will return to the screen at once, and I think the public will welcome him."

Jesse Lasky's release was more restrained. He wrote: "The manner in which the public receives his next picture will determine whether Arbuckle is offered another contract."

Adela Rogers St. John phoned and read Matthew Brady's statement: "I am an American citizen and I take off my hat to the verdict of an American jury."

What meant far more to Roscoe were the calls that came in throughout the night from Charlie Chaplin and Douglas Fairbanks, Mary Pickford and Mabel Normand.

The following day, theatres throughout the country showed Arbuckle movies to packed houses.

When the scandal had first broken, Sid Grauman's Chinese was playing *Gasoline Gus*. He had taken it off immediately. Now he put it on again.

As dawn was breaking over the city, Minta kissed Ben, shook hands with Roscoe, and went to bed.

Roscoe went to the window and looked out over Union Square.

"I'm broke, Ben," he said.

"Maybe money broke, yes, but that's not what matters. You've still got your talent. We'll make money again."

"Will we?"

"Certainly. Maybe more than before."

"I sure in hell am going to need it."

"Yes, that's true."

Roscoe turned back into the room and asked, "How do I stand, Ben? Give me the bad news."

"Why don't you wait till tomorrow? We'll sit down in the office and we'll go over everything."

"Where do I stand, Ben?"

"You really want to know?"

"Yes."

"Right now?"

"Yes, please."

Ben took some folded papers out of his breast pocket, looked

163

at them carefully, then said, "Right now, you owe about seven hundred and twenty thousand dollars."

Roscoe gave his head a violent shake in the manner of a prize-fighter who has just received a solid blow to the head.

"Wow," he said. "Will they wait? Will any of them wait?"

"What else can they do, Roscoe?"

"You're right, even if they cut me up and sold pieces, they couldn't get *that* much back."

Ben got up. "Get some sleep, Roscoe. So will I. It's going to be a hard day today, so let's start it as late as possible."

"All right."

They shook hands, then embraced.

Ben said, "Don't worry, everything's going to be all right."

On Thursday, April 13th, Ben stayed all day in San Francisco with Roscoe who was writing out statements, giving interviews, holding a press conference and answering the telephone. There were dozens of offers, but Roscoe and Ben had decided to wait a few days before making definite plans.

At 11:00 P.M., Minta and Roscoe and Ben left San Francisco and drove through the night to Los Angeles.

On Friday, the 14th, they repeated the San Francisco experience: interviews, press conferences, statements, receiving callers.

On Saturday, they went out to Malibu and spent the day with the Fairbankses.

Sunday, April the 16th, was Easter Sunday. Roscoe, with Minta, and with his brother Arthur, and sister Nora, went to church in the morning, then spent a quiet day at home.

On Monday, he met with Ben early in the morning at the studio. They began to formulate plans and a schedule for the year to come.

On Tuesday, April 18th, Will H. Hays issued an order barring Roscoe Arbuckle from the screen.

Representing the newly formed MPPDA—Motion Picture Producers and Distributors of America—he ruled that Arbuckle could not be employed in the industry in any way. He could not act or write or direct. Moreover, none of his pictures could be shown anywhere.

A heated meeting was held at Charlie Chaplin's home. It was attended by many of Arbuckle's friends and supporters. There

164

were some who thought that Hays's action was illegal and unen-
forceable. Indeed, the view was expressed that the MPPDA itself,
by setting itself up as a pre-censoring instrument, existed in violation of the Constitution of the United States. Even so, there
seemed to be little enthusiasm for litigation.

Buster Keaton said, "I don't see the point of setting up a war
between us and them. We've all got to live together if we're going
to work together, and what the hell, there are always rules of the
game. All I think is they ought to let Roscoe go back to work. Now
how can we get them to do that?"

It was not to be, not for some time. What was at stake was
business. Public opinion had been manipulated to the extent that
it had affected the box office. Few people in Hollywood believed
that Arbuckle was guilty, yet so much smoke had been generated
that a clear view of the truth was obscured.

In later years, Will Hays claimed that the ban was not his idea,
but Zukor's. Zukor told him that regardless of the verdict in San
Francisco, the industry had to bend over backwards now to show
good faith, and banning Arbuckle—in spite of the verdict—
would do precisely that. Hays related that he thought it would be
better if Zukor made the announcement, but Zukor insisted that
it should come not from him personally but from the whole association.

"Well, I guess I'll be going," said Minta. "Maybe tomorrow."
"Where to?" asked Roscoe.
"Oh, back to Martha's Vineyard, I suppose."
"You won't stay? Maybe for a few more weeks?"
"No, dear. There's nothing more I can do for you here. It's just
you against life now. I hope you come out all right."
"That was real fine, what you did, Minta, coming back, sticking
with me."
"I like you, Roscoe, and I'm sorry for you. You got a bad shake.
But for us, for you and me, it's all over, and we both know it."
"I'd try again, if you would."
"No, Roscoe, I'm too tired. I wish you could let me have a few
thousand, though. I know you're in bad shape. You don't have to
tell me."
"Oh, hell, Minta, you don't have to go on about it. I understand.
And sure, I'll get it for you. I'll get you more. I'll borrow it from
Ben or Mack. I can't ask Joe Schenck anymore. I'm into him for

I don't know how many hundred thousand, but I'll get it. And believe me, you've more than earned it, Minta."

"Yes, I have," she said.

VIII

"NOTHING GOOD happened for him anymore," said B.J., "from then until he had the good sense to die eleven years later. In the meantime he traveled around. He went to China, Japan. But wherever he went the scandal followed him. And then around Christmas time Hays made *another* announcement. The ban had been lifted.

"But you know, some of those bloodthirsty reformers and vigilantes wouldn't give up. They kept raising hell and it wasn't any one group, it was all kinds. It was priests and some rabbis and the WCTU and up in Sing Sing, the warden said ban or no ban he wouldn't allow any Arbuckle pictures in the prison because they might be a bad influence. Papers over the country, even *The New York Times,* were absolutely vicious. And now that he was *allowed* to work, he wasn't going to be able to *get* work. One minute it looked yes, the next minute no."

IX

BUSTER KEATON picked up Roscoe and drove him over to Ben's office. They walked around the lot for a while, stopping in on various sets to see what was doing. A great deal was doing. Production was proceeding in high.

Roscoe became increasingly gloomy. Finally, they wandered over to Ben's office where the three friends sat drinking coffee and discussing the difficult situation.

"How would it be," said Buster brightly, "if you just changed your name? My first idea was that you should take off about

166

two hundred pounds and bill yourself as *Skinny* Arbuckle. Why wouldn't that be good?"

"This guy's a comedian," said Roscoe.

"Oh, is he?" said Ben. "I'm glad you told me. I wouldn't know it from his jokes."

"No, that idea's no good," said Buster. "But a name change is. And I've got the name you should go by."

"Go ahead," said Roscoe with a sigh.

"Will B. Good," said Buster.

Roscoe and Ben laughed. Suddenly Roscoe said, "Can I borrow your secretary, Ben?"

"Of course, what for?"

"For immoral purposes," said Buster. "He wants to take her up to San Francisco for the weekend."

"Button your lip, Buster," said Roscoe. And to Ben: "Could I?"

"Of course."

"I want to dictate something."

Ben buzzed for his secretary, who opened the door.

"Would you come in, please, Miss Peterson, and bring your book?"

"Yes, sir."

A few minutes later, Roscoe was pacing about the room slowly, dictating: "To the editor *colon* I am not only wholly innocent *comma* but more than that *period* There is a higher law which deals with the spiritual side of mankind *comma* and surely this Christmas time should not be the season when the voice of the Pharisee—"

"Would you spell that please?" asked Miss Peterson.

"Pharisee," said Roscoe. "P-h-a-r-i-s-e-e-."

"Thank you."

"—when the voice of the Pharisee is heard in the land *period*."

"What the hell's a Pharisee?" asked Buster. "Some special kind of a homosexual?"

"Shut up, Buster," said Ben.

Roscoe, concentrated and intent, heard nothing. "*Paragraph*," he said. "It is not difficult to visualize at this time of the year *comma* which commemorates the birth of Christ—"

"Would you spell that please?" asked Buster.

"*Comma* what might have happened if some of those now who heartlessly denounce me had been present when the Savior *capi-*

167

talize forgave the penitent sinner on the cross *comma* in words that have more influenced the human race than any other words ever uttered *period* Would not some of these persons have denounced Christ and stoned him for what he said *question mark paragraph* No one ever saw a picture of mine that was not clean *period* No one ever saw a picture of mine that was not wholesome *period* No one will ever see such a picture of mine *period* I claim the right to work and service *period paragraph* The sentiment of every church on Christmas day will be *quote* Peace on earth and goodwill to all mankind *period unquote* What will be the attitude the day after Christmas to me *question mark.*"

At the breakfast table, Tessa was reading from *The New York Times* to a disconsolate Ben. "And then it goes on," she said. " 'Among the differences which separate members of the human race is that between those who get away with it and those who get caught'—and so on and so on and so on. Now listen to this: 'An odor clings to him and it will cling no matter how he sprays himself with Biblical analogies.' "

In Will Hays's office he lay stretched out on a sofa, resting, while his secretary read his mail to him.

"And this is from the General Federation of Women's Clubs," she said.

"How many members have *they* got?" asked Hays.

"Oh, about three million or so."

"And what do *they* say?"

She read from the postal telegraph form. " 'This organization stands ready to help any individual to rehabilitate himself, but not at the expense of the ideals of the nation. The youth of our country must be protected from a revival of interest in the degrading details of his trial and from continued discussion of immoral living associated therewith.' "

From his pulpit in the Calvary Baptist Church in New York, the Reverend John Roach Straton proclaimed, "You cannot purify a polecat! You cannot denature a smallpox epidemic! You cannot reform a rattlesnake! You cannot cure the organic disease of film corruption with soothing syrup!"

In San Francisco at a meeting of the Vigilantes, Mrs. W.B. Hamilton was on the platform.

"Where is your forgiveness?" she cried.

And from the unruly audience came cries of, "Get off!" "Sob stuff!" "Sit down!"

Mrs. Hamilton, a distinguished and well-known matron, waited patiently for quiet, then went on. "I do not believe in taking the whole pound of flesh out of Arbuckle," she said.

From the audience: "He's got plenty! He can *spare* a pound."

Prolonged laughter. Mrs. Hamilton continued with some difficulty since booing, hissing, and whistling had begun.

"Why should he be made to pay for the sins of the whole moving picture industry? As your representative, I attended the Arbuckle trials, and I know that he could not have been convicted of manslaughter on the evidence presented. As long as he has been reinstated, what can be done about it? And why not give him his chance to make good as a man anyway?"

Dr. Mariana Bertola, a firebrand, leaped to the platform, pushed Mrs. Hamilton aside and shouted hysterically, "Arbuckle can prove himself a man in some other way. We have no objection to his running a teahouse in Japan or anywhere else. What we do object to is having him paraded before little boys and little girls to be idolized and emulated. I believe this move on the part of Will Hays is just a feeler to test women's sentiment and believe that it would be fatal to the cause of decency to weaken in our demands for the punishment of these lurid offenders now!"

She had struck home. The audience cheered her. Mrs. Hamilton left quietly.

Directly after Christmas, Roscoe started shooting a two-reeler called *Handy Andy.* Astonishingly, the year away from the cameras and the emotional upheavals he had endured did not in the least dull his inventiveness. In fact, he seemed more inspired than ever before. The day he finished the picture, the customary wrap party was in progress. Roscoe and Ben stood around drinking and joking with the crew.

A uniformed chauffeur approached them and handed Arbuckle a folded note. Roscoe and Ben read it. Roscoe nodded to the chauffeur, and said, "Excuse me," to his friends. He and Ben walked off the set and onto the driveway. There on a back seat of

169

an enormous Packard limousine sat the tiny but formidable Adolph Zukor.

"I appreciate it if you fellows could come with me for half an hour or so. It looks like we got a crisis."

"Shouldn't I *change* first?" said Roscoe, indicating his comic getup. He was wearing a red-checked shirt and too-tight overalls; a green bow tie the size of a watermelon and big white shoes.

Zukor took his watch out of his vest pocket and looked at it. "He'll bring you back here to change later," he said pointing to the chauffeur. "I think it would be better if we could go now, he's waiting for us."

"Who?" asked Ben.

"Will," said Zukor. "Will Hays."

In Hays's office, the members of the strangely assorted group sat regarding one another. Here was Zukor, the Hungarian immigrant, the former fur salesman, now a powerful and determined motion picture executive. And there was Will H. Hays, the product of successful American conservatism who had never dreamed of earning $150,000 a year. And Ben, who had made it from Kovno via Ellis Island. And finally, the fat, young comedian from Smith Center, Kansas, the heartland of America, who had waddled his way into show business and movies and success and fame and fortune.

"Tell him, Will," said Zukor.

Hays looked as if he were about to throw up. He took a deep breath, tried a smile, and said, "You know I like you, Roscoe."

"Thank you."

"What's more, my children like you. And my grandchildren, too. We all like you."

"Thank everybody," said Roscoe.

"What Will is trying to say," said Zukor, with no little impatience, "is that none of this is personal. It's got nothing to do with you personally. It's come down to being a question of the whole industry."

"Yes," said Hays, "the whole industry."

"Sweet Jesus!" said Roscoe. "Don't tell me you're going to ban me again. Please, please don't tell me that."

"No, no," said Hays reassuringly. "Of course not."

"Who said ban?" asked Zukor.

"Because I don't think he could stand it," said Ben. "Not again. I don't know how he got through it the first time, if he did."

Roscoe was sweating now, profusely. "I think I'd rather die than go through that again," he said.

"No, no," said Hays.

"It's getting to me, this on again off again gone again Finnegan. I mean in or out permanently, but not in and out, in and out, in and out."

"Calm down, Roscoe," said Ben. "We're all friends here."

"Well, some of us are, I guess."

"Would you like some water?" asked Hays.

"No, I would just like to know what I'm doing here."

"Well," said Hays, "you're probably aware of the storm that's been raised by your reinstatement."

"Yes, I am," said Roscoe.

"It wouldn't have happened if he hadn't been banned in the first place," said Ben.

"Well, that's neither here nor there," said Zukor.

"Neither here nor there," said Hays. "Now, as I said, there is no intention, no question of a ban again. But for the good of the business and your fellow players and artists and for all the rest of us, we feel, all of us, that since the whole situation is most harmful and if it goes on, it's going to ruin the business and for all I know ruin a lot of your friends—"

"What we would recommend to you," said Zukor, "is that you stay in the business, but as a director or a writer. Anything. Just so long as you are not on the screen. For the time being, anyway."

"D.W. Arbuckle," said Roscoe grimly.

"As a matter of fact," said Zukor, "we also think that maybe you shouldn't use your own name. For the time being, anyway."

"That's all right with me," said Roscoe, "I *hate* my name." He got up, looked at Zukor, and said, "Did you say he'd take us back? Your driver?"

"Yes, of course," said Zukor. "Then would you send him back here for me?"

Ben got to his feet with some difficulty. He felt poisoned. He started out. Roscoe followed him.

"Yes," said Roscoe, "I'll be glad to do that . . . send him back. Good-bye, Mr. Hays. . . . Good-bye, Mr. Zukor." And as he walked out, slowly, he added, "Good-bye, Mr. Arbuckle."

X

"HE DIRECTED several small movies," said B.J., "but he used his father's name—William Goodrich. He was good, he always had been. He went out to play in theatres and nightclubs. He needed the money. He owed. He owed Mabel and Joe Schenck and Buster. He still had to pay Minta. He paid her regularly, as long as he lived. He got married again, several times, I believe, and he worked around, odd jobs here and there—helping Buster with a picture, going to New York and trying a play. He did whatever he could, but he was never Fatty Arbuckle again."

"That's an awful story," I said. "One of the worst I've ever heard."

"Oh, but that kind of thing happened over and over again. We've always had scandals, we always will. It happened again in different ways with Wallace Reid and Clara Bow. It happened with the Hollywood Ten and then later with that wonderful little Marilyn Monroe. And I used to think in the days when there was such a furor about that lovely Ingrid Bergman and the women's clubs again and the banning of the pictures, I used to think— why, it's Fatty Arbuckle all over again. But I suppose if you live a public life, you have to put up with things like that. It's still a great business, the best. Let me ask you a question."

"By all means."

"Why do you think he wants my company? Your boss. Mr. Adani?"

"Because it's a great business, the best."

"I think I heard that someplace," said Ben, "from a very wise man."

"Yes."

"But tell me, seriously, if you know. Does he like movies? Is he interested in movies?"

"Oh, I think so."

"But why? I know he owns manufacturing companies and coffee plantations and tobacco fields. I know he owns shopping centers and an airline and ships. What does he want with a movie company? What is he going to do with it?"

"Why, he's going to run it, I suppose."

"*He's* going to?" asked Ben, astonished.

"Not directly, no. In fact, he'd be more than pleased to have you continue in any supervisory capacity you choose."

"I choose nothing. I choose to get out, if I get out, if I sell. See, it would be different if my sons had turned out different. But my oldest son, Haim, he never was interested. With him the only thing he liked was luxury and society. So you get what you want in life. He married a high-class society girl with plenty of money and social standing and I want to tell you how high class she is. She is so high class that I've only met her twice in my life. Once at the wedding and once since then and that's all. And the other boys? Well, Ernst is a fine man but I never could get him interested in this business either. He got interested in these pictures that you see hanging around the house, and he studied them over and over, and he became one of the best in his field, an art historian. And his brother Gilbert was with me in the business a long time, but he's like me. He can't be a partner and can't be an assistant, so it didn't take too long. He went out on his own and he did not bad. And now, God should only forgive him, he's in the television business. Very big in the TV. . . . And my other one —Abe? Well him let's not talk about."

"The grandchildren?" I asked.

"Grandchildren, of course, not only grandchildren, but I have three *great*-grandchildren. Beth and two others. And I'll tell you a secret if you promise you won't tell anybody. I even have a great-great-grandchild."

"Is that so?"

"You know what that means? You've got any conception?"

"I think so."

"I bet you haven't. It means that my grandson has a grandson. Are you married?"

"No, sir."

"Have you ever been?"

"Yes, sir."

"Well, then you *can* imagine. Suppose you have a grandchild and now that *grandchild* has a grandchild—and you're still around!" He smiled. "That's me!"

173

PART IV

THE SILENT LOVERS

B.J. FARBER and Guy Barrere did not meet for the next two days because Ben was involved in committee work as well as the annual meeting of the Motion Picture Relief Fund, of which he had long been chairman.

Guy continued to meet with other studio officials and had three valuable middle-of-the-night sessions with Jack Heller.

On both evenings of Ben's absence, Guy had dinner with Willa and Beth. Afterward, the ritual movie. During the first screening, he found himself holding Beth's hand. During the second, it was Willa's. Both were enjoyable. Beth seemed to him a rare girl: vibrant, humorous, intelligent. It was clear, however, that she had no interest whatever in him. He wondered why. Suspicious? Probably.

The second film was a raunchy Clint Eastwood number. When it ended, Beth giggled as she said, "Am I glad Grandpa wasn't here for *that!*"

"PG," said Guy. "That's not so bad, is it? Parental Guidance."

"Don't mention it," said Willa. "If there's one thing he objects to more than what he calls 'dirty' pictures, it's the rating system.

He says it makes no sense because all parents aren't the same, nor all children."

"And he's just damn right," said Beth.

They were still discussing the rating system when Ben returned at 11:00.

"There's a lovely chicken sandwich in your study, dear, if you want it," said Willa.

"I do," said Ben. "Troubles always make me hungry, especially *other* people's troubles. Come in with me, Guy. I'll give you half."

"Lord, no!" said Guy. "I had a dinner here that ought to last me until Christmas, at the very least."

"Well, come anyway," said Ben, "and watch me eat. It's quite a sight."

"Go ahead," said Willa. "Beth and I have some important women-only matters to discuss, anyway."

"Two suffragettes!" said Ben.

In his study, Ben found a supper tray. He began to eat at once.

With his mouth full, he said, "What's this Willa tells me, for God's sake? You're leaving us?"

"Yes," said Guy.

"Why?"

"Well, I can assure you it isn't the food—or the service."

"Or the price," added Ben.

Guy laughed. "No, no, it's just that my boss wants me to. And he's the boss."

"What's he afraid of?" asked Ben craftily.

"Nothing."

"My opinion," said Ben, "we're making progress. With me, you know by now, after the whole week we've been negotiating—talking. With me it's not so much how much, but *should* I."

"I believe you."

"I'm ninety-*two*, for God's sake! What do I want with money? What I want more is everything should be neat, with no loose endings."

Guy spoke slowly and carefully. "But by the same token, Mr. Farber, what do you want with a studio?"

Ben chewed his food reflectively. He swallowed and said, "I don't know. I wish I knew. I don't. Something inside. I can't let go."

"Would you like me to ask Mr. Adani to come on out? It's no trouble. He owns his own jet."

Ben thought for a moment and said, "In-ter-est-ing. I never met in my whole life one person owned their own jet that I liked."

"Oh, you'll like Mr. Adani."

"I don't think so."

"Why not?"

"Because he wants to buy me."

"No. Just your studio."

"But *that's* me!" cried Ben. "That's all I *am!*"

Guy took Ben's eyes and began to press skillfully as he lied. "You could go on running it as long as you like."

"For him?" asked Ben.

"Well—" Guy began.

"No, if I decide to sell—if I sell—then it's lock, stock, barrel, and good-bye."

He began to weep, softly at first, then convulsively.

Guy watched him helplessly, trying to think of something to do, to say.

Ben recovered, wiped his eyes, blew his nose, and continued. "Oh, yes, I'll unload, I suppose. I mean sell." All at once, he was weeping again.

Guy became tense with strain.

"Can I do anything?" he asked.

"I don't think so. You see, my trouble is—I don't want to *die!*"

"Of course not."

"Maybe greedy. I've had a good life . . . a long one—some think *too* long."

"No."

"Yes," Ben insisted. "Even some of my children think too long. Maybe they're right—maybe people *shouldn't* live so long as I have. But what can I tell you? I don't want to die. Not yet."

"You're not going to."

"Get yourself another drink," said Ben.

Guy rose to do so.

"And me, too," said Ben.

Guy turned and regarded him questioningly.

"Go ahead," said Ben. "Do what I tell you. It's *my* booze, ain't it?"

As Guy prepared the drinks, Ben added, "Some writer I once

179

had said a good one: 'Moderation in everything—including moderation.' "

Guy laughed and said, "I'll remember that."

He served the drinks. They drank.

Ben looked at his guest carefully. "Listen," he said, "honestly, what's the sense you moving out? We *like* you, the both of us. It's like it was before the children all got out. Poor Willa. She's heard all my stories a hundred times."

"I'm glad I haven't," said Guy. "It's been—well—a sort of education."

"For me, too, you know it? Remembering so much. The more I tell it, the more I understand it."

"What *I* still don't understand," said Guy, frowning, "is how Farber Films got to be in the first place."

Ben frowned, trying to remember.

"Well, after the Arbuckle trouble, you see, I was in bad shape. Fan Films was down. But we'd made a lot of good product, and I still owned a lot of great material we hadn't made yet. Also, by now I had a reputation. So when L. B. Mayer called me up personally and said M-G-M would like to maybe buy me out, I thought it was my lucky day.

"I said, 'Are you talking merger, L.B.?'

"He hollers—he was a hollerer—he hollers, '*Merger?* M-G-M and you and your little two-holer? It's like that horse-and-rabbit stew. They make it with one horse and one rabbit!'

"I said to him, 'But how do you know it ain't the rabbit that gives it the flavor?'

"But he didn't get it. What he did get was Fan Films, and me. They gave me a little money and some stock and a lousy contract and a fine title: executive producer. What did I care? I was still in the movie business—it was my *life!*"

Guy asked, "And why did you *leave* M-G-M?"

Ben sighed and said, "It's a long story." He laughed. "And every time I tell it, it gets longer."

"Please?" Guy urged.

There was a pause as Ben thought it over. "Garbo," he said.

"What?" asked Guy, failing to make the connection.

"Greta Garbo," said Ben. "Of all the greats, she was the greatest."

"Do you really think so?" asked Guy, wondering if Farber was off the track again.

"I *know* so," said Ben. "I'm not talking her beauty only. That *everybody* knows. But talent. And courage. And work. Character. A great woman. A great career. And they finished her when she was thirty-six years of age."

"How?"

Ben thought before going on. "One of the main things I learned through the years was—I wish I'd learned it sooner—was that the main trouble with the movie business is that it's too much an art. And the main trouble with the movie art is that it's too much a business. . . . Garbo. Greta Garbo. There's a perfect case. God Almighty, I remember the day she arrived in Hollywood. How could I forget it? I was there. Nineteen twenty-five, that's— what? My God!—fifty-five years ago. I don't believe it. It's true, but I don't believe it. . . ."

II

AN AFTERNOON in September 1925. The Pasadena Railroad Station. It is what Californians call "a typical California day." Strong, relentless sun, deep blue skies with clouds designed by D.W. Griffith, Billy Bitzer, and Worth of Paris; a languorous breeze that never exceeds the speed limit; and a fragrance in the surrounding air in which the pungency of orange blossoms predominates.

On the platform, Ben Farber, thirty-seven, stands talking to a group of M-G-M press agents. Reporters and photographers are milling about. A Brown Derby catering truck stands by. Three waiters are dispensing food and drink, with astonishing expertise.

Ben leaves the press agents to join Ruth Waterbury of *Photoplay* magazine, and Adela Rogers St. John of Hearst International. They have been looking through the promotional material recently furnished them by the M-G-M publicity department.

"Is this right, Ben," asks Adela, "or a typo?"

"What right?"

"His first name."

"Mauritz. M-a-u-r-i-t-z," says Ben. "Mauritz Stiller."

"With a t-z?"

"Correct," says Ben.

"How come?" asks Ruth. "Is that the Swedish spelling, or what?"

"No, no. Stiller's not Swedish. He's they say the greatest Swedish director, but he's not Swedish."

"What is he, then?"

"Russian."

"Jewish?"

"I don't know," says Ben. "Maybe. Ask him."

One of the photographers approaches and says, "Hello, Ruth. Can I get a shot of you with Mr. Farber?"

"Sure," she replies, "but fast, huh?"

She moves to stand close to Ben, who straightens his tie, flattens his hair, and asks, "What's this *for?*"

"*Photoplay,*" says the photographer. "Every month we run little shots of Miss Waterbury with bigshots."

He sets off his flash powder and takes a picture.

"Say!" says Ben. "You should be writing titles. Comedy titles."

"The photographer grins and asks, "Is that an offer, Mr. Farber?"

"No," said Ben. "Just a rotten idea."

The photographer takes another picture and says, "Thanks." He gets out his notebook and, pencil poised, asks, "Do you like Benjamin J. or just B.J.?"

"Why not D.W.?" asks Ben.

The photographer emits a dutiful laugh.

"No," B.J. says. "Use whatever you want."

The photographer, writing, says, "B.J. And could I have your exact title?"

"Certainly. Executive Vice-President in Charge of Worldwide Promotion, Exploitation and Sales."

"Long title," says Adela.

"It's a long job. Twelve, fourteen hours a day, every day."

"Thanks," says the photographer, leaving.

A waiter approaches, serves Ruth, Adela, and Ben.

"See," says Ben, "what happened was I merged my company with Goldwyn and Mayer."

"But I understand Sam Goldwyn isn't *with* the company," says Adela. "Is he?"

"No," Ben answers, "only his name. He's an independent guy and he wanted to be independent. Lots of fights. At the end of one of them, Sam said, 'You wait and see. Some one of these days, I'll buy you bastards out—and then you know what I'm going to call the new company? I'm going to call it Metro-Goldwyn-Mayer and *Goldwyn!*' It was funny how the split happened. What happened was—"

"Ben!" calls a brassy voice. Ben looks off. "Come here!" the voice orders.

"Excuse me," says Ben. "I'll tell you later."

"Of course," says Adela.

Ben walks away swiftly, almost running. Adela and Ruth exchange a knowing smile.

"When the great Louella calls there's no 'Wait a minute,' is there?" says Adela.

Ben approaches Louella Parsons, the doyenne of the Hollywood press corps. She is sitting on the back seat of a top-down Pierce-Arrow touring car. She, too, has the publicity material.

"Hello, Louella," says Ben. "I want to personally thank you for coming. I'll tell L.B. you were here. Personally."

"Do that," she says firmly. "And there's something *you* can tell *me.*"

"Anything."

Louella beckons him closer. He moves in. She looks about, leans toward him, drops her voice, and says, "You know me, Benny, I need inside stuff—not this puff everybody else gets."

She tosses the publicity kit at him, a little harder than necessary.

"Anything I can do, Louella, you know that. I'll do."

"All right then," she says. "This female he's got in tow, what's her name again?"

"Garbo. Greta Garbo."

"That her real name?"

"So far I know, yes."

"And what is she? His girl friend?"

"That I *don't* know," Ben replies.

"Come on, Ben," says Louella testily. "Don't give me that applesauce."

"I swear," says Ben desperately. "I swear on my mother's life!"

"Swear on L.B.'s, then maybe I'll believe you."

"I'll see if I can find out for you, Louella. O.K.?"

"When?" she replies and sulks.

"As soon as I see L.B."

"Can't you call him up? I've got a deadline!"

Ben glances at his watch. "Please," he begs. "The train. It'll be here any minute!"

In a drawing room of the Sante Fe Chief, Mauritz Stiller and Greta Garbo sat opposite one another. Between them a table was laden with books and pads and objects. An English lesson was in progress.

Stiller was a tall, black-mustached, broodingly handsome man of about forty-two. He thought of himself as important and gifted, which indeed he was.

Garbo was nineteen and had not yet become the most beautiful woman of the century. She was plump, awkward, and plainly terrified. She held up an orange, showed it to Stiller.

"Ah-*rintch*," he said confidently.

"Yes," said Garbo. She pointed out the window and asked, "What—is—there?"

Stiller looked out, thought hard. Suddenly, happily, he cried, "Ah-*rintch!*"

"No," said Garbo.

"No?" he echoed, bewildered.

"No." She pantomimed profusion remarkably. Stiller understood.

"Ah," he said, "*much* ah-*rintch!*"

"No," said Garbo patiently. "Many orange-*es.*"

Stiller, perspiring, repeated, "Many ah-*rintch!*"

"Ez!" she added.

"Ez!" he said.

"Many orange-es," she said again.

Stiller sighed wearily, and said, "Many ah-*rintch*. Ez!"

"Yes," said Garbo, and patted his hand. He leaned across the table and kissed her. She picked up some cutlery and held up a spoon.

"Spoon," said Stiller. She nodded and held up a knife.

"Night!" he said brightly.

She shook her head and said, "Kni*fe*."

"Yes," said Stiller, "kni*fe*."

"Night," she said, "is—" She conveyed the idea of night. He nodded, understanding. She held up a fork. "And this?" she asked.

184

"Fok?" he asked.

"Fawk."

"Fook?" he asked.

"Fork," she said.

"Fark," he tried.

Carefully, she enunciated, "Fork."

"Fuck!" he cried triumphantly.

The Santa Fe Chief approaches the Pasadena Station. The press agents, old hands at the game, have determined a precise point of detraining for the distinguished visitor, since lighting equipment and platforms have had to be arranged for the newsreel cameraman. The welcoming party moves to that point and assembles itself in a semicircle. The train pulls in and comes to a noisy, puffing stop as if fatigued from its long journey. Porters alight, baggage is thrown, a few mortals get off, confounded and stunned by the unexpected hoopla.

Flashlight guns explode, the newsreel camera begins to grind. There is a smattering of applause from the welcomers, led by the well-rehearsed M-G-M claque.

Mauritz Stiller comes down the train steps and raises his hand in a salute he has borrowed from King Gustav of Sweden. He stands for a moment, aware of the cameras and their angles.

He is disappointed, having expected a larger crowd. Moreover, there is no music!

Behind him, in the shadow, stands Greta Garbo, frightened into immobility. She is wishing that the train would turn around and go back at once.

Stiller moves to the crowd. Garbo follows hesitantly.

(If only she could have known, at that moment, as she moved into the bright sunlight that she was entering one of the most memorable and distinguished and unforgettable film careers of all time.)

The crowd surrounds Stiller, who is shaking hands with Ben.

Ben steps up onto a small platform and reads from a prepared statement. "Mr. Mauritz Stiller, on behalf of Metro-Goldwyn-Mayer and indeed, the entire American motion picture industry, it is my honor and pleasure to welcome you to the United States. We know that your genius will enhance our screen and that you will make lasting contributions to the art of the film.

And now, the ladies and gentlemen of the press have a few questions."

Stiller, panicked by his inability to understand calls out, "Var är Greta?" Louder, "Greta!?" Louder still, "GRETA!?"

Garbo is standing outside the circle and would remain there, but for the hypnotic and commanding sound of Stiller's voice. He has trained her over the years to respond automatically to his direction, in the way a private soldier obeys his captain. She moves through the crowd quickly and forcefully, joins Stiller.

He introduces her to Ben with signs and mumbles.

"I'm so glad to meet you, Miss Garbo. Mr. Mayer ran your picture at his home the other night—that one—what's the name?" Rolf, the studio interpreter, moves in and says to Stiller, "Han vill veta namnet pa din film."

Stiller to Ben. *"Gösta Berling's Saga."* Rolf translates, *"Gösta Berling's Saga."*

"That's *it,*" says Ben. "Yes. Very strong. And you photograph not bad."

He claps his hands to get the attention of the crowd. "Ladies and gentlemen," he says, "this is Miss Greta Garbo—the great Swedish star of *"Gösta Berling's Saga*—" Stiller claps him on the back and points to himself. Ben goes on: "—which was directed —I should say, *brilliantly* directed—by Mr. Mauritz Stiller."

"Can we see it?" asks Ruth.

"Yes, when?" from Adela.

"Absolutely," says Ben. "I'll arrange a screening."

An elderly reporter asks, "What's your first picture going to be, Mr. Stiller?"

Rolf and Stiller have a brief whispered conference.

Rolf says, "I have several projects—all great—which I shall submit to the M-G-M studio. Each one has a principal role for my protégée, Miss Greta Garbo."

"When are you two gonna get married?" asks Louella in her loud and brassy voice.

Garbo is painfully embarrassed. Rolf, mortified, conveys the question to Stiller, who, in a burst of temper, insults Louella in Swedish.

Louella laughs. There are further questions and many more photographs taken until Ben mounts one of the platforms and says, "Thank you, ladies and gentlemen. M-G-M appreciates your fine courtesy and cooperation. Please send tear sheets direct to the studio."

The crowd disperses as the photographers make a few final shots.

Later that evening, Garbo would write home:

> Dearest Nisse: We are here at last and the only question is, which of us is the more unhappy. At the railroad station there was a stupid welcome organized by the studio. A pleasant, likable man named Farber was the representative, but even *he* could not control the jackals of the press.
>
> One rude fat woman—she is said to be powerful—actually asked Moje when he and I were to be *married!* The implication was clear. We were illicit and such things are not countenanced in this purer land.
>
> Moje insulted her violently—fortunately in Swedish—else we would probably be on our way home by now. Secretly, I wish we were.

The studio welcome is over. The party moves to the parking lot beside the Pasadena Railroad Station.

A small number of cars are parked; Packards, Paiges, Model T's, a Cadillac roadster and one Rolls-Royce.

In the midst of all, an incongruous van. Standing in the rear of it, an even more incongruous man. He is dressed in native Swedish costume: short yellow knee pants, black wool jacket, gaily caparisoned hat. He is Victor Seastrom, the celebrated Swedish film director, recently arrived in the States. He peers off, jumps into the van. As he disappears, he shouts, "Gor er fardiga! Dom kommer!"

Stiller, Garbo, Rolf, and Ben trudge into the parking lot followed by two porters pushing a cartful of luggage. The Rolls-Royce belongs to Ben, and the studio has provided a small truck for the baggage. Stiller and Garbo are clearly depressed. But as they approach the lot, twenty-three members of the Hollywood Swedish colony come pouring out of the van. They are *all* dressed in native costume. The musicians they have brought swing into the Swedish National Anthem, "Du Gamla, Du Fria" ("Thou Old, Thou Free"). Stiller and Garbo find themselves suddenly surrounded. Hugs and kisses. Tears and laughter. Garbo smiles for the first time. Among the friends are Lars and Karin Hanson;

187

Edythe Seastrom; Guje and Kaje (the Seastrom children); Einar Hanson; Jean Hersholt; Nils Asther; Anna Q. Nilsson; and Svend Gade.

A folk dance begins in the Pasadena parking lot. The song is the traditional folk tune "Raven Raskar Over Isen" ("The Fox Runs over the Ice"). Singing breaks out. The dance is a circular chase pattern. Garbo merrily kicks off her shoes and joins the dance, as does Stiller. The singing and the dancing and the laughter become inreasingly boisterous.

Ben is enjoying the event, which seems to be taking place in a foreign country. He looks up, startled, as a loud siren is heard approaching. A police car comes tearing in. The singing and dancing grind to an awkward halt as two police officers get out of their car and advance toward the party.

"What's goin' on here?" asks the sergeant.

"Sir?" asks Seastrom.

The patrolman speaks. "You in charge?"

"I organized, yes," replies Seastrom. "A welcome for these new friends here. They come to America."

"You got a license?" asks the sergeant.

"Pardon?"

The patrolman becomes officious. "You can't have no demonstration without a license. Don't you know that? Where d'you think y'are? Back in *Russia?*"

The sergeant is already writing out a citation. Ben steps in.

"Just a moment, officer," he says. "This is not a demonstration, only a celebration."

"Who you?" asks the patrolman.

"I'm Benjamin J. Farber—"

"Beat it!"

"—vice-president of M-G-M," Ben adds.

The policemen freeze. "How do you do, Mr. Farber?" says the sergeant.

"Pleased to meet you," says the other patrolman.

The sergeant takes off his hat, the patrolman follows suit. They shake hands with Seastrom. The sergeant tears up the citation.

The patrolman speaks to Seastrom. "Go ahead, folks, do your demonstration."

"*Celebration,* you pinhead," says the sergeant.

They move off to their car.

188

"That's what I said," says the patrolman.

"You did not."

"Did."

"Did not."

They get into their car, throw a salute to Ben, and drive off.

Ben touches Seastrom's shoulder and says, "Go ahead."

"You think?"

"Do what you were doing. It was nice."

"Thank you." He turns and calls out to the group. "Allt gick bra, vi borjar om igen!"

The singing and dancing begin again, tentatively—and before long, Pasadena becomes Malmö once again.

In Ben's Rolls-Royce, he sits between Garbo and Stiller. Rolf is on the front seat beside Ben's chauffeur, Archie, an enormous, handsome Negro.

Garbo and Stiller are looking out at the scenery with interest. It is a topography new to them.

"Forty, forty-five minutes, that's all," says Ben, "and we're there."

Stiller nods as Ben continues. "See all the palm trees?"

"Titta pa alla palmerna?" Rolf translates to Stiller.

"Ja," says Stiller.

"Yes," says Garbo.

"Yes," says Rolf.

Ben is becoming irritated by this mindless routine.

"Listen," he says to Rolf, "tell them English. The main thing is they got to learn English. Otherwise, how can they work? They got to read scripts, don't they? And stories? And on the set, directions. If everybody has to go, for Chrissake, from English to Swedish and Swedish to English, everything is going to take double the time. *English!* It's not impossible. It's not even hard. I didn't know English neither when I came here to America—but I learned it—*everybody* learns it. You know how? By *studying* it, that's how. They're going to have coaches. A man for her, a lady for him. Thalberg likes it better that way, so they don't get to imitate too much. The studio will pay, but *they* got to work—eight hours a day, the least. Four with the teacher and four hours alone. What's the best, I found out, is to read the papers out loud every day, the whole paper, and the trade magazines because that's interesting. Also, with each other, they should make a rule—only English, even in *bed! English!*"

Rolf is shocked—but Ben is unaware of it and goes on.

"They got to learn English—to speak and read and write and understand, understand?"

"Yes, Mr. Farber."

"So tell them."

Rolf begins to tell them, in Swedish. As he does so, Garbo nods, seriously. She knows that Ben's idea is unassailable. Stiller, on the other hand, becomes increasingly angry.

All at once, he leans forward and shouts at Rolf—something in Swedish.

Rolf, startled, shouts the translation at Ben: "I am a director, sir!"

More from Stiller, louder.

Rolf to Ben, louder: "An *important* director!"

Stiller yells, out of control and shaking his fist at Rolf.

Rolf apes him: "I come here to *give* directions, not *take* directions!"

So it goes. Stiller to Rolf to Ben, who is given no chance to reply.

Garbo follows the scene, her head swiveling. Suddenly, she bursts into uncontrollable laughter. It ends the bizarre encounter.

The three men look at her. She laughs.

It will be some time before she laughs again.

III

BEN FARBER was never happier than when conducting a studio tour. He felt a personal affection for every sound stage, for every piece of equipment, for all the players and technicians, for every acre of the vast backlot. Even the studio's inanimate objects had life to him.

He had become expert at showing visitors about: financiers, exhibitors and distributors, theatre owners, dignitaries from abroad. He had polished his spiel so that it was succinct, witty, enthusiastic, and to the point. It always went well.

Today was an exception. The visitors were Mauritz Stiller and Greta Garbo and Rolf. They moved about the lot, Ben talking animatedly, Rolf interpreting and unconsciously mimicking Ben's excitement. Stiller and Garbo grew increasingly glum.

In a sense, the tour was a cruelty. They had made the long and arduous journey, not to *see* this magnificent toy but to play with it. What did it matter how efficient and up-to-date and superior the machinery, if they were not allowed access to it?

Stiller spoke to Rolf, who conveyed his expression to Ben.

"Patience," said Ben. "You got to have patience more." Rolf translated simultaneously. "My God, it's only a week you're here and already—"

Stiller whispered to Rolf, who said to Ben, "He says eleven days. Not a week, eleven days."

"All right," said Ben, "so eleven days. He's got time, tell him."

Rolf told him.

"He's only forty-three years old."

Rolf told him. Stiller spoke.

"He says forty-*two*," said Rolf.

"I apologize," said Ben.

Stiller, every inch a gentleman, bowed forgivingly.

"Here we are," said Ben. They stopped at the entrance to Stage 4. A red light was blinking over the entry and a forbidding sign read:

CLOSED SET
NO VISITORS

Ben opened the door. Garbo went in, then Stiller, then Ben, then Rolf.

Stage 4 seemed to be two areas. The first, a brightly lighted set; the second, the dim work space surrounding it. An assistant director spotted Ben and his party and rushed at once to provide chairs for them. They sat and watched. Garbo, in wonder; Stiller with disdain.

On the set, King Vidor was directing Lillian Gish, M-G-M's newly acquired star, and John Gilbert in *La Bohème*. The set represented Rodolphe's grand apartment.

Rolf found it difficult to explain the action, since this M-G-M version had made some changes from the original, with which

Mauritz Stiller was intimately familiar, having made a version of his own some nine years earlier. The grand apartment was explained by the fact that in M-G-M's version, Rodolphe was a great success at the end of the story, rather than a great failure, as in the original.

The action being photographed from several angles was Mimi's death scene. Vidor had been shooting it for three and a half days and was now concentrating on Miss Gish's close-ups. She was in costume. John Gilbert incongruously wore tennis clothes, since in this angle he was off camera. The customary set noises floated about. The crew was an exceptionally noisy one.

Rolf explained the action and identified the people: Vidor, Gilbert, Gish, and William Daniels, the cameraman.

Garbo found herself staring at John Gilbert, undoubtedly the most attractive man in Hollywood. He was smoking and smiling.

"Hurry up and die will you, Lilly? I'm starving."

"Why don't you eat your mustache?" suggested Lillian.

"Good Lord," said Vidor, "it's like working with Weber and Fields." He turned his attention to the makeup man, "She ready?"

"Ready," said the makeup man.

"That's a marvelous effect, Lil—those parched lips."

"I should hope so," she said. "I haven't allowed a single drop of liquid of any kind to touch them for three weeks."

"Not even a liquid kiss?" asked Gilbert, with an irresistible show-business leer.

Rolf translated this exchange with a swift whisper to Stiller and Garbo. Stiller stared straight ahead, stonily. Garbo found it impossible to suppress a radiant, wicked smile.

"Honestly, Jack," said Lillian, "you *can* be revolting."

"*Can* be? I *am!*" asserted Gilbert.

The makeup man regarded Lillian's lips glumly and said, "I coulda done it just as good with *makeup*."

Vidor turned to his assistant and said tensely, "All right now, let's make it."

"Quiet, please!" the assistant called out. "*Quiet!*"

The noise on the set subsided a bit. "Listen, you monkeys," he shouted, "when I say 'Quiet,' I don't mean just a little less noise —I mean *QUIET!!*"

The set fell silent.

"Music, please," said Vidor, in a whisper.

A superlative string trio set up a few feet from the camera began to provide the mood music. Appropriately enough, they used part of the Puccini score for *La Bohème*. They had been doing so all through the filming. Now for the death scene they played Mimi's touching aria—"Addio, senza rancor" ("Farewell, I Wish You Well").

A nod from Vidor. The assistant said, "Camera!"

The camera rolled noisily. The musicians instinctively provided a crescendo.

"Speed!" from the camera operator.

The slate man held his slate in front of the camera, took it away. "Action," said Vidor.

Ben and his guests watched the filming with interest. Even Stiller seemed impressed.

Vidor knelt near Lillian Gish and spoke softly: "That's lovely, Lillian, lovely. Just perfect . . . take your time." He pointed to Gilbert, "Go, Jack."

Gilbert, playing beautifully, indeed as if the camera were focused on him, spoke his lines, " 'My love, my love, do not leave me—we have known *that* agony—' "

Vidor. "A little to the left, Lil. Left." Lillian turned her head left, toward camera. "No, no," said Vidor, "go back." Lillian responded. "Again. Much slower. Much." Lillian took direction admirably. Vidor pointed at Gilbert, who went on with his lines.

" 'There is no life for me without you,' " he said.

Vidor. "Open your eyes, Lil. Open. See if you can catch the key light." He pointed to it. Lillian caught it precisely. "Good," said Vidor, "great. All right, now—*die!* Take your time and die. They're watching, all those millions, they're watching you die. Talk, Jack, say something, anything. She's dying."

"I love you," said Gilbert. "My Mimi, I love you. Don't die."

"Die!" said Vidor.

"I love you. I love you," said Gilbert.

The crew held still. Vidor checked the camera operator, who was watching through the finder. He nodded reassuringly to Vidor, who returned his attention to the scene just as Mimi died.

"Cut!" shouted Vidor. The noise on the set resumed automatically. Vidor moved at once to Lillian and took her hand. "Wonderful, Lil," he said. "Wonderful."

"Beautiful, Lilly," said Gilbert, meaning it.

Lillian Gish could only whisper, "Thank you."

"Perfect," said Vidor. "Couldn't be better! . . . Let's do one more."

"One more," shouted the assistant.

The slate man, weary, erased the number 18 after the word "Take" on his slate and chalked 19. The makeup man moved back in, the cameraman adjusted a few lights. Ben and his group rose and started out. Garbo could not keep from throwing a sad and envious look back at the set.

On Stage 9, *Go West* was shooting. A film written, directed, produced by, and starring another of M-G-M's stars, Buster Keaton. Ben and his party came on to the set to watch.

They saw Buster performing a scene with Brown Eyes, a beautiful brown and white cow, the co-star of this great-to-be film.

He was rehearsing the famous milking scene. Buster, a city slicker, was dressed in ill-becoming cowboy garb. He had been told to milk Brown Eyes. A born and bred city boy, he believed that the phrase "the cow gives milk" was literal, thus he was having some difficulty.

Buster Keaton was remarkably inventive and graceful and elegant. All those things a great comedian must be.

Ben's party watched with amusement, and even Stiller smiled.

As Buster reached the climax of the scene, Ben and his group burst into laughter.

Buster Keaton stopped the rehearsal and looked over at them, annoyed. He signaled *Out!* with his head. Ben hurriedly gathered his party and left.

Stage 2. Ben and his party were paying another visit to another set. On this one, Constance Bennett, Sally O'Neil, and Joan Crawford were making *Sally, Irene, and Mary,* directed by the powerful and eccentric Edmund Goulding.

Again, chairs were swiftly provided for the important visitors, and the scene was shot.

It took place in a chorus dressing room. Constance, Sally, and Joan played Broadway chorus girls of the picture's title. The whole chorus rushed in to make a quick change. Goulding had skillfully turned it into an erotic picnic.

As Garbo watched, she could not help but wonder if she was going to be asked to do this sort of scene.

IV

BEN CONTINUED in memory. His face was suffused with intimations of the past. Guy was riveted. As it happened, Greta Garbo was one of the few figures in Ben's long recital of whom he had heard; indeed, had seen, both on the large screen and on late-night TV.

"At first," said Ben, "they lived over there in that Commodore Hotel, but they didn't like it. So I found them a place in Santa Monica at the Miramar. It's still there, I think."

"But what about work?" asked Guy. "I mean for either one of them."

"What could we do? We had nothing ready. We were looking; the whole studio, the whole story department. But naturally, she was not so easy to cast. You couldn't put her in just any old thing. And with him, it was still a language problem. So all the time I kept telling them, both of them, learn English, talk English, study English."

V

THE MALIBU colony in 1926 was not yet overpopulated, overbuilt.

On the patio, in front of a modest, charming cottage, Mauritz Stiller and Greta Garbo, its tenants, sat. Stiller, a dandy, wore formal city dress. Garbo was in a flowing frock. They sat in the shade under a large beach umbrella, each holding an identical copy of *The Los Angeles Times*.

Garbo read aloud, slowly but accurately, in a pronounced Swedish accent, with many mispronunciations, but with instinctive feeling. As she read, Stiller attempted to follow the text with his finger on *his* copy, now and then mouthing the words along with her.

Garbo read: "Al*thow* the war sens are . . . nature-ally pre-dome-in-ant in *The Big Parahde* . . . the picture *its*elf is . . . essence-ally a luff story . . . and a supremely stirring one at that. Reneé Adorée—who *app*ears for a very short time . . . in the eerly part of the story . . . and again at the finish—manages to impress herself so *vit*-ally on the audience . . . that her presence . . . in the dim back*ground* . . . is never for an in-stant forgotten. Both she and Joan Jilbert are brilliantly . . . effective." She heaved an exhausted sigh and fell back into her deck chair.

Stiller read. "Bahth she and Jean Jil*bert* [the French pronunciation] are brill-iant-ly e-fec-tive." He smiled, delighted with himself and his progress.

In the M-G-M makeup department, the makeup man, his assistant, the hairdresser, and her assistant, were applying finishing touches to the subject in the makeup chair. One by one they stepped back to admire their handiwork. As they did so, the young woman in the chair was revealed. Who was she? Ben Farber wondered as he came into the room. It took him ten seconds to realize that it was Greta Garbo. She had been transformed into the then current M-G-M image—a cross between Joan Crawford and Norma Shearer, two of the studio's most successful stars. The cosmeticians exchanged congratulatory and self-congratulatory looks, and all of them put their attention on Ben. He was puzzled, but then thought, *What do* I *know?* He nodded approvingly. They were all astonished when Greta Garbo, examining herself in the mirror, burst into tears. She felt, with reason, that she had been turned into someone else, someone she did not recognize. She was in misery, physically uncomfortable in her skin.

A few days later, in the M-G-M executive projection room, Farber sat with Irving Thalberg and Louis B. Mayer. They had finished watching the day's rushes and were now looking at the screen tests.

Irving Thalberg was twenty-six, and the wonder of the motion picture business. He had begun some ten years earlier as an office boy in the New York City headquarters of Universal pictures. Attending night school, he had acquired shorthand and typing, and had maneuvered himself into the position of acting as Carl Laemmle's secretary whenever that head of the studio came to

New York. Before long, Laemmle was so impressed with his young secretary's taste and judgment and imagination that he invited him to come and work in California. Thalberg was soon one of Laemmle's most valued assistants and, to the astonishment of the industry, was made studio manager at the age of twenty-one, and head of production a year and a half later.

It was said by the backbiters that Laemmle promoted Thalberg in this fashion mainly to torture his own young son, Carl Laemmle, Jr., who had rather disappointed him by not being able to take over the reins of the studio at the age of eighteen.

There were Laemmle/Laemmle, Jr., jokes by the score, most of them apocryphal. A favorite had to do with a cable Laemmle, Jr., had purportedly sent from Paris reading: "DEAR PA PLEASE CABLE $5,000 GEORGE V AT ONCE. ENTERTAINING IMPORTANT FRENCH MOTION PICTURE COUNT THIS WEEKEND. LOVE, JR." To which, it was said, his father replied: "NOT ONE CENT UNTIL YOU LEARN TO SPELL. POP."

Thalberg's success in running Universal was spectacular, and what was even more important to the powers—profitable. Thus, a few years later, he was offered the job of running Metro-Goldwyn-Mayer; a proposal he found alluring. It would give him, he realized, an opportunity to produce what he had labeled "prestige pictures," movies made not for profit but for an uplift in standards. In this way, Thalberg reasoned, the base of the motion picture audience could be widened. In the twenties, kids went to the movies, usually on Saturday afternoon; ate popcorn, hissed the villains, whistled, stamped their approval at the arrival of the cavalry, hung in suspense as desperately as Pearl White hung from the cliff at the end of Episode 11, and made loud kissing sounds when the action on the screen provided the opportunity. Maids and their boyfriends; nursemaids and policemen; the flood of immigrants who, yet unable to understand English, were able to follow the stories on the silent screen perfectly. The upper middle classes and the snobbish upper classes, the intellectuals, the academic community shunned the movies as something beneath them. Thalberg saw no reason why the motion picture, as a literary form, could not take its place beside all the others. For this reason, he championed prestige pictures.

Louis B. Mayer, his partner/colleague/adversary, was something else again. A self-made tycoon from Brookline, Massachusetts, he had risen in the new industry swiftly by means of auda-ciousness, persistence, hard work, and ruthlessness. He had little understanding of, or feeling for, art in any form. The movie business was, above all, a business, and a good one. The talent involved was simply a necessary evil. The brilliant men and women who wrote and produced and directed and acted and photographed and designed and composed the product were no more, in Mayer's eyes, than the bricks and mortar that went into the building of a structure. But his business acumen and daring were among M-G-M's most valuable assets. He was older than Thalberg by seventeen years. An overweight, steely, tough, mean, humorless man.

They sat on opposite sides of Ben Farber. They never liked to sit next to each other.

Garbo's test came on the screen.

"Who's this?" asked Thalberg.

"You know who," answered Mayer. "That girl. Stiller's girl."

Ben spoke. "She's got a name, L.B. Greta Garbo."

They returned their attention to the screen to watch Greta Garbo's first test. She moved about awkwardly, wearing an un-suitable dress, and was obviously responding to someone's off-screen direction. She showed or tried to show, anger, jealousy, happiness, sadness in too swift succession. All at once, she cried. Not realistically, but theatrically. The lighting in the test was in-different, the camera work sloppy.

"Good God!" said Thalberg.

"You don't like her?" said Mayer.

Thalberg turned to Mayer and said, "I don't *know* her, L.B. It's not a question of liking *her,* it's the creature we're projecting onto the screen."

"My opinion, Irving," said Ben, "she's got possibilities. Real possibilities."

"We can't sell possibilities," said Mayer.

Thalberg pressed a buzzer. The test disappeared from the screen. The lights came on in the room. Thalberg paced about, thinking. The pause was long and awkward.

"She's got a nice ass," said Mayer. Thalberg looked at him sharply. "For a Norwegian, I mean."

"She's Swedish," mumbled Ben. "I think she's got possibilities. *Real* possibilities."

198

Thalberg stopped in front of him and said, "That may be, Ben, this business of ours is full of imponderables. But if we're talking about now, about today, I'll give it to you in one word. She's *unusable.*"

"Maybe you should run *Gösta Berling*," Ben suggested. "That's a picture, this is just a test. Not even *much* of a test. By the way, I think we ought to look into our test department. Their work gets worse and worse. How can anybody tell *anything*? This thing we just looked at, I couldn't even tell if it was the same actress I saw in *Gösta Berling*, and, by the way, that was a hit. A big European hit. Look it up."

"No, no," said Thalberg, who moved away impatiently. "She's not what I'm looking for, not right now. I need a girl for *The Torrent* opposite Ricardo Cortez—and you know how difficult he can be."

Mayer lumbered to his feet and said, "What the fuck's *he* got to be difficult about? The son-of-a-bitch named himself after a *cigar*, f'Chrissake."

"He did?" asked Ben.

"A cigar!" Mayer repeated. "You didn't know that?"

Thalberg returned to Farber and asked, "What are we paying this woman?"

"Woman!" Ben laughed. "She's twenty years old."

Mayer threw him a withering look.

"What are we paying this girl?" asked Thalberg patiently.

"Nothing," said Ben. "Three hundred and fifty."

"For how long?"

"One year, with options."

"Options," said Thalberg. He turned to Mayer. "Did you negotiate it?"

"Listen, Irving," said Mayer shaking his stubby forefinger, "don't hector me! I *had* to take her to get Stiller. He wouldn't come otherwise."

"Oh, don't be silly," said Thalberg.

Mayer, a habitual overreactor, screamed, "Don't you call me silly, you little tin Jesus, you!"

"I didn't say you were silly, Louis,"

"Yes, you *did!*" He turned to Ben. "Didn't he say I was silly? You're a witness."

"No," said Thalberg. "I said what you *said* was silly."

"Oh," said Mayer, accepting what he deemed an apology.

"Of course, he'd have come without her," said Thalberg. "There's not a team that ever was that couldn't be melted by pouring a little hot currency over it."

"What's the use fighting, boys?" asked Ben. "We've got her—so we'll do something with her."

"Something?" asked Thalberg. "What?"

He stormed out of the room. Mayer turned to Ben and said, "All right, see if you can settle with her."

Ben smiled and mused, "Chaplin."

"What?" asked Mayer.

"Just like Chaplin."

"Who?"

"Garbo," said Ben absently.

"You crazy, Ben?"

"A little. In this crazy business, aren't we all?"

Mayer stormed out of the projection room in a poor imitation of Thalberg.

Ben sat and buzzed the projectionist.

"Yes, sir?" came the projectionist's voice over the intercom.

"Run that test again, will you, please, Chuck?"

"You bet."

The lights in the room dimmed, the whirr of the projector was heard, Ben settled back to watch. The test came on again. It seemed even worse than before.

In Malibu, Stiller and Garbo were still working over what to them had become the most important document of all, *The Los Angeles Times*.

Stiller read aloud with firm and confident fluency:

" 'But at his news . . . conference today . . . President Coolidge declared that the . . . busyness of America is busyness. Indeed . . . busyness has become a national obsession.' " He threw the paper aside in a burst of frustrated fatigue.

Garbo began to read from a copy of *Photoplay*.

" '. . . and to have "It," the for-tun-ate posses-sor must have that strange mag-net-ism which attracts *both* sexes.' "

She raised her eyebrows before continuing.

" 'There must be physical attrac-tion, but beauty is unneces-sary.' "

After an exhausted sigh, she and Stiller looked at each other and tried hard to exchange a smile.

The next day, they were sent for. It appeared to be a matter of importance, since Ben Farber sent a car and driver to bring them to the studio.

Stiller, his usually faultless instinct conveying to him that the great moment had come at last, got himself up in special style. He wore his best Gelot derby, a boutonniere, and selected his finest walking stick. Upon arrival, he strode confidently toward the main entrance. A step or two behind him, Garbo, in a lovely summer frock, followed.

They entered the building, and soon were sitting in Ben Farber's office.

It was a beautifully appointed room, as befitted a top executive, but had been carefully arranged so as not to challenge the grandeur of L.B. Mayer's headquarters.

Ben sat behind his desk; Stiller and Garbo in large comfortable visitors' chairs across from him.

"Yes," said Ben, nervously, "Malibu is *very* nice. The ocean. And so forth."

He rose suddenly, walked to the window, and looked out for a time. Then he said softly, "I'll come to the point."

"If you please, sir," said Stiller.

"Say, that's good!" said Ben, turning. "Your English is *good!*"

"My English," said Stiller haughtily, "is *not* good. My English it is *excellent!* As well as so is Miss Greta Garbo's English is."

"All right," said Ben. "Here it is. The test is *no good.*"

There was a pause, filled with incomprehension, mystery, and irritation.

At length, Stiller spoke. "Test?" he asked. "Which of test?"

"Mr. Thalberg hated it," said Ben.

Stiller looked at Garbo, agape. He got up, took a step toward her, and asked, "*Test?*"

Garbo was trembling. She wet her lips and said, so quietly that he could barely hear her, "They said me a surprise, Moje. For you."

Stiller, pale, took a deep breath and said, "Good. I am a surprise."

He was having difficulty staying in control.

Ben spoke. "So what he wants—Mr. Thalberg—is that he wants to settle her contract. Miss Garbo's. Not yours, Mr. Stiller. Only hers."

Garbo sat quietly, passively. She had expected this, knew that the test had been a failure. But Stiller was on the verge of an outburst.

He spoke evenly. "I shall not angry. To make one test without me—it was bad—it was . . ." He turned to Garbo and said, "—*misstag!*"

Automatically, she corrected him. "Mistake."

"It was mistakes," he said. "Now *I* will make."

"No," said Ben, "I don't think so."

"Why no?" asked Stiller.

"No more test," said Garbo.

"He won't O.K. it," said Ben. "Mayer. It costs too much money."

Stiller moved to Ben and said, "*Me!* I pay the too much money. I pay. I talk Mayer. I talk *all.*"

VI

"AND I'LL be goddamned if he didn't," said Ben. "He paid the bill for the whole thing. And mind you, he didn't have all that. Probably had to borrow."

"And what happened?" asked Guy.

Ben laughed. "Well, it took him three days, I remember. He worked like a crazy man. It was the most expensive test I think maybe ever made. . . . He wasn't easy to get along with, this Stiller. These days, they call it 'difficult.' But you know what I found out in seventy years in the movie business?"

"What?" asked Guy. "I'm interested."

"I found out that everybody who's good is also difficult. Those klutzes who just do what you tell them, they're always second rate."

Guy laughed. "Well, I'll try to be a little more difficult from now on."

"Yes," said Ben, "you do that. . . . Of course, remember this:

202

It's possible you can be *too* difficult. And that's what it turned out in the end Mr. Mauritz Stiller was."

Guy leaned forward. "But about Garbo. After his test—the one *he* made—*then* did you all realize what you had?"

"You want the truth?"

"Of course."

"No. Nobody thought, not even her. Nobody imagined she would become the biggest international star in the whole world."

VII

IN THE makeup department, Stiller supervised a careful, discreet hairdress and an extremely subtle makeup. He had long since learned that Garbo's talent extended to her skin, and that the less interference, the better.

In the costume department, he had overseen the creation of a flowing frock that moved beautifully. Stiller spent hours having Garbo move, turn swiftly, sit, stand, dance, lie on a sofa, on a chaise longue, on a bed, and each time ordering careful adjustments from the fitters.

At last they were on the set. Stiller took charge of the lighting. He used no stand-in, but insisted that Garbo remain in position for the hours of lighting from every angle. He ordered the set cleared of pictures and flowers and props, which he considered distracting.

A tall bit player named Gary Cooper had been recruited to play opposite her.

He rehearsed them until they were exhausted.

At length, the scene was ready to shoot.

Garbo and Cooper played a skillful, graceful scene of seduction, perhaps a bit more daring than would have been permitted on the 1926 theatre screen.

Then came two weeks of cutting and of Stiller working over the prints in the laboratory, of carefully choosing takes, of substituting others. He worked through the night—several times.

They waited. Mayer yawned sleepily and put his head back on his seat, resting his eyes. Thalberg read a script.

Stiller, who had been in the projection room checking the equipment and the projector, now came into the room and said, "We are ready, gentlemen." He exuded unshakable confidence.

The test began. Mayer fell asleep. Ben was thrilled. Thalberg, who had come as a matter of courtesy, was forcibly struck by the very first shot, an astonishing, living, breathing close-up of one of the world's most incandescent faces.

In the next shot, as she whirled about the room, with Cooper in clumsy pursuit, she appeared to rival the great Pavlova. And as she conveyed the sense of a woman being pursued with the intention of being caught, and was, and was embraced, then returned the embrace, Thalberg heard himself say, "Remarkable!"

Mayer awoke.

"She's *extraordinary!*" said Thalberg.

"See that?" said Mayer. "What did I tell you?"

"What you told me was that you had to sign her to get Mr. Stiller. Was that true, by the way, Mr. Stiller?"

Mayer rose indignantly. "You should have more respect," he said. "I'm older than you." He started out of the room and added, "You'll be sorry someday, Irving." He was gone.

"I'm sorry right now," muttered Thalberg and returned his attention to the screen. The test ended on a typical Stiller embrace. A close-up kiss and the camera moving up up and away until finally the viewer was convinced that he saw more than he was actually seeing. Fade-out.

Lights came on. Thalberg rose at once, went to Stiller and offered his hand. Stiller got up, took it, and bowed formally.

"Congratulations, Mauritz. We all have a great deal to learn from you."

"Thank you," said Stiller calmly.

"You'll hear from me," said Thalberg, "soon."

They left. Farber and Stiller shook hands, delightedly. Stiller sank into a chair, put his head in his hands and sobbed.

"And listen, Mauritz," said Farber. "Another thing. You're not paying for that test. I don't care how much it cost. I'm going to see to it. You're not paying, not a penny. I'll pay. M-G-M will pay. That is some goddamn test!"

A week went by without communication. Stiller remembered distinctly that Thalberg had used the word "soon." But what did "soon" mean? He was not certain. He looked it up in his dictionaries, and was even less certain.

After lunch one day, they continued their daily reading. They had abandoned *The Los Angeles Times* and were now following the various trade papers. Garbo read: " 'Lawrence Weingarten announced today, on behalf of M-G-M, that Ricardo Cortez will play the coveted role of Rafael Brull in Irving Thalberg's production of *The Torrent*. Greta Garbo will make her American film debut under—' " Stunned, she looked up at Stiller. "Greta Garbo," she said. "In the paper! Here. In *The Moving Picture News*. Here. It says: 'Greta Garbo.' "
"Wonderful," said Stiller, "wonderful."
Garbo went on. " 'Greta Garbo will make her American film debut in the part of Leonora, under the direction of—' " She stopped and could not go on.
"Yes?" asked Stiller, pale.
" '—under the direction of Monta Bell,' " she said.
In all his years, Stiller had not been dealt such a blow. He sat for a time uncomprehending, bitterly disappointed, but not defeated. Garbo looked at him and felt his pain. Tears welled up in her eyes.
They said nothing more for an hour.

The next morning, she found him walking along the beach. She joined him, held his arm tightly, and said, "Idioter! Dom vill visa att dom har makten, det är allt!"
"Please, Greta. In English. Yes. Even in a hell time such like this."
"The story," said Garbo. "I have just read it. Stupid. The part, foolish. I will say no. I would worry on it even if *you* were going to direct, Moje."
"I am not," he said. "But you must."
"No."

"It is not the end of all," he said. "Be good. Thalberg finds me something. I will be good. Too. Then we shall—together."

On the screen of Grauman's Chinese, the premiere of *The Torrent* was coming to an end. The lovers parted, forever. The end title scrawled on. The audience applauded politely, and a number of voices could be heard shouting, "Garbo! Garbo!"

VIII

"IT WAS a nothing," said Ben. "A schnitzel. But she got them right away. I've seen it happen dozens of times. Right away. Marilyn Monroe, John Garfield, Hepburn, Humphrey Bogart. It only takes a half a minute, and the audience recognizes a star just as if they would be an old friend.

"So we put her right away into another one. This time with Stiller. But trouble. He hated the leading man, Antonio Moreno. And Moreno hated him, so it was just one fight after the other fight. What could we do? In the middle of the whole everything, we had to get rid of him—Stiller—and put on Fred Niblo. Fast, experienced with American crews, which Stiller was not. A good cast. Lionel Barrymore, even.

"And Garbo? She hated the picture, and Moreno and everybody, especially after Stiller left. But the way she worked, you couldn't tell. What a professional! Till the end, a great professional."

IX

ON THE set of *The Temptress*, a fierce blowup was in progress. Stiller and his leading man, Antonio Moreno, were in the midst of a violent quarrel. Garbo stood between them, trying to make peace. The men were on the verge of coming to blows. Moreno, about to land the first punch, was deterred by members of the crew. Stiller ordered Moreno off the set. Moreno left. Stiller sank into his chair, his hand on his chest. Garbo gave him a glass of water. They exchanged a look. He nodded. She reached into her pocket and from a small silver pillbox extracted a Digitalis capsule. He took it.

X

A few days later, everything was proceeding as before on Stage 9, *The Temptress* set, but in the director's chair, which was clearly labeled "Mauritz Stiller," sat Fred Niblo.

Garbo, Moreno, and Barrymore were playing a scene of bitter recrimination.

"Cut!" called Niblo. The adversaries suddenly stopped acting. The crew stepped in to adjust makeup, props, and lights. Fred Niblo, a gentle hypnotist, put his arm across Garbo's shoulder, and spoke softly to her and to Moreno.

"Mean it," he said to Moreno. "Mean what you say when you say it. Talk to her, not to Garbo, talk to her."

Antonio Moreno had not the slightest idea what Niblo was talking about, but he nodded automatically.

To Garbo, Niblo said, "Whatever you do, Greta, don't cry. Let us know that you *want* to cry, that you *feel* like crying, that you're fighting with everything you've got to hold back the tears, but don't let me see one, not a drop, not a glitter. Do it all in your head. I want the exterior absolutely calm and unruffled, but we've got to know. We've got to know that if you let go, you'd burst into floods of tears. I wouldn't ask everyone to do that. I know how hard it is, but *you* can do it. You're the best there is. At least, I think you're *going* to be."

Garbo turned away, embarrassed. Lionel Barrymore reached out and touched her cheek.

"She's a Barrymore, you know, Fred."

"What?"

207

"Of course. She's one of the *Swedish* Barrymores. Greta Barrymore. Why she changed her name, I'll never know."

"All right, let's make it!" said Niblo and returned to his chair. The Klieg lights burned on. The crew made ready for still another take.

Seven months later, *The Temptress* opened at the Capitol Theatre in New York, the great new M-G-M flagship.

For the first time, the name Greta Garbo appeared above the title along with Antonio Moreno and Lionel Barrymore. She had begun to develop a following in New York, and several of the more important New York film critics, among them Robert E. Sherwood and Gilbert Seldes, had singled her out for praise.

The Temptress seemed more distinguished than it actually was, due mainly to Garbo's presence.

It built to its melodramatic climax, and then began its descent into the slow, sad ending: Elene (Garbo), defeated by life and by love, was seen in a Paris dive, overpainted, her beauty gone; drinking and carousing with a coterie of apache men and demireps. Although she is debauched and degraded, her beauty, or the memory of it, somehow shines through. Fade-out. The End.

The handkerchiefs were out, the reaction enthusiastic. At the back of the theatre, manager J.B. Glendon was dictating a memo to the home office. *"The Temptress,"* he said. "No walkouts. Garbo steals it. (Don't tell Moreno.) Opened soft, but personally have faith will build, mainly due to G.G. What's next? See if you can find her a manly man to play opposite her. She is one powerful Katinka. Regards, Glendon."

In John Gilbert's portable set dressing room, he sat being made up, and chatting with his friend Lionel Barrymore. He was stripped to the waist, displaying a powerful physique. He was the handsomest, most dashing actor in the business.

"Do you realize, Lionel," he said, "that this bozo here actually gets paid for gilding the lily?"

"Some lily," says the makeup man. "New wrinkles to worry about every day."

Gilbert sends an elbow into the makeup man's stomach, playfully but powerfully.

Barrymore is having a drink. "And let me tell you, Jack," he says, "this girl can act. Nobody around this loony bin knows more about acting than I do, so keep it in mind. You can get a lot from her. More than you've been getting from those floozies they've been saddling you with."

"I'm damn glad to hear it. I love acting, but with actors and actresses, not with store-window dummies. I know a lot about store-window dummies, I used to be one myself." He laughed. "Pour me a shot, will you, Lionel? Just a wee one. A little whistle-wetter."

"Certainly not," said Barrymore. "You want to ruin your voice for the day?"

Gilbert's voice was indeed one of his great charms. It was light and low; manly and attractive. Moreover, he articulated beautifully. His mother and father had owned and operated a successful stock company in Salt Lake City, and he went on the stage at the age of four. While still in his teens, he broke away and came west, where he worked in every area of the budding film business; as a stagehand, electrician, cameraman, assistant director. What interested him most, however, was writing. In fact he had contributed a number of creditable scenarios. However, his astonishing good looks and unique personality trapped him, finally, into acting. Without any particular effort, he found himself one of the three most important stars in Hollywood.

He reached for Barrymore's drink and said, "Come on, ol' boy, be a sport."

Barrymore snatched the glass away and held it out of reach. "Nothing doing," he said.

"Please," said Gilbert. "I'm as nervous as a cat—as a nervous cat."

"Yes, well, there are better ways of calming down than sloshing this bootleg rotgut."

"I know there's a better way," said Gilbert, "but I don't have time for it just now."

He flashed his celebrated smile.

"You're choosing one hell of a way to start a new picture, my boy," said Barrymore.

"A nip?"

"A nothing," said Barrymore. "You're going to get Clarence sore as a boil. There's a straitlaced man if I ever saw one. God, he reminds me of my aunt, Mrs. Drew."

"Clarence drinks," said Jack. "I've seen him. I drink *with* him."

"Not on the set."

"I'm not on the set, you dippy bastard, I'm in my dressing room."

"Well, then, *dress!*"

Gilbert laughed, rose and began to dress. "Eddie!" he called. "Ready."

The makeup man left, as Eddie, Gilbert's dresser, came in and began to assist him. Eddie was a shriveled little old man, but as active as a flea.

"I've been watching that Miss Garbo," he said. "She's *beautyful!*"

"Oh, do you think so?" asked Gilbert.

"I really do," said Eddie sincerely.

Gilbert turned to him pugnaciously. "Well, lay off, Eddie. I'm warning you, or you're going to have trouble with me. Maybe even a duel, like the one I fight in this picture; which, by the way, I win."

"Good," said Eddie.

Barrymore said, "It's a fine story, Jack. You'll have a rouser."

"What's the title mean, Mister G?" asked Eddie.

"*Flesh and the Devil*. Well, see, she plays *Flesh* and I play the *Devil*. Or, maybe I'm *Flesh* and she's *the Devil*. They haven't told me yet."

"You've met her, haven't you?" asked Barrymore.

"Yesterday. I've seen her around, of course, but it wasn't until yesterday that we were introduced. Formally. She held out that lovely hand and I swear, I was afraid to touch it; I thought it might break. The truth is, Lionel, I think I'm gone on the girl. I mean, I hardly know her, that's true, but I've seen every inch of film she's ever shot in every language; and I can see that it's possible—to fall in love with a shadow. Jesus, they tell me a lot of them fall in love with mine!"

Barrymore laughed and said, "You're just like my brother Jack. . . . Say, *here's* a thought. Maybe all you Jacks are alike. He was being interviewed the other day—"

"Interviewed, ugh!"

"—by some hoity-toity theatre arts type, and she asked him, 'In your opinion, Mr. Barrymore, does Hamlet actually have sexual intercourse with Ophelia?' And Jack said, 'In my company, always!' "

They shared a show-business laugh in which Eddie joined.

Stage 9. *Flesh and the Devil.* The working set was a nineteenth-century boudoir, brilliantly designed by Cedric Gibbons and Frederick Hope. The set dressers were supplying the finishing touches.

Garbo, beautifully gowned and coiffed and made up, was reclining on a slant board, designed to keep the wrinkles out of her costume.

Clarence Brown, the director, stood chatting with her.

"I hope, Miss Garbo, that you don't mind starting with the boudoir scene."

"As you wish, Mr. Brown. I know my whole part, of course."

"That's most commendable. Thank you."

"Not at all."

"You see, it's been my experience that if you can kick off with a major scene—it breaks the ice, don't you know."

Garbo, confused at these idioms, said, "Yes."

"Anyhow, thanks. We'll have a shot at it."

Gilbert walked in, in full military regalia. He was resplendent.

"Good morning, Mr. Gilbert."

Brown examined him from tip to toe and said, "Well, I must say—*you* look pretty ravishing!"

"*Must* you?" asked Gilbert.

Brown laughed and Garbo wondered why.

"Rehearsal, please!" called Brown.

"Quiet for rehearsal, please!" yelled the assistant director. "Quiet!"

Brown, Garbo, and Gilbert walked onto the set. Brown explained the required action, as the cameraman, William Daniels, watched through his camera finder.

Brown spoke to his players quietly and confidentially. Even his script girl was able to catch only a word, now and again, or a phrase. "On the floor . . . free . . . your purest instincts . . . unconventional . . . and completely free . . . completely . . . learned long since that the best direction is the *least* direction . . . All right, then, whenever you're ready."

Brown left the scene as Gilbert assisted Garbo. She sank to the pillowed floor and lay back. Gilbert knelt beside her. Brown took his place in his chair beside the camera and signaled his assistant.

"All right," the assistant called out. "Settle down for rehearsal."

There was instant quiet. Brown was one of the most respected

211

directors on the lot, and his crew knew that he brooked no non-sense. Further, he was one of the few who insisted upon actual dialogue being spoken, even though the film was silent. Many directors permitted the players to ad lib and improvise. Not Brown. It had been observed that a man saying, "Mary," produced an attractive expression. Similarly, a girl saying "John," made a pretty face. So, as a general rule, all leading men were addressed as "John," and all leading ladies as "Mary."

Brown would have none of this. Garbo in *Flesh and the Devil* was Leonora and Gilbert was Leo.

Brown could not help but observe, as Garbo and Gilbert rehearsed, that the crew, including the propmen and the flymen, were especially attentive and interested. He smiled to himself. One of the difficulties of working in films was the absence of an audience. Thus, one had to make do with the crew or casual onlookers. As they rehearsed, Brown experienced that rare shock of recognition, experienced when an important team is born.

" 'Come! Come and be close to me,' " said Leonora/Garbo.

Leo/Gilbert, rather awkwardly, lay down beside her. She took his head in her hands and pulled it to hers. She faked a succession of simulated rehearsal kisses, kissing his face again and again. Then, he simulated kissing her on the lips.

He spoke mechanically and tentatively, in the manner of a player who is not sure of his lines. " 'How I have longed for'—the —the something of—of something—oh, shit!" He looked up at the script girl and asked, "What is it, Adele?"

" 'Food,' " said Adele. " 'Love'—'the food of love.' "

" 'Food,' " cried Gilbert. " 'Love'—God damn it—I *knew* it this morning. Food, food, food. Love, love, love. 'The food of love.' Sorry, Clarence. Nerves, I expect." He spoke to Garbo. "You mind if I go back, Miss Garbo?"

"Go back," she said quietly.

He began again, a trifle more confident this time. " 'How I have longed for that. The—*food!* of love. How I have hungered.' "

" 'No longer, my love.' " Garbo acted full out, as was her way. " 'We are together—as surely God and nature intended—' " Gilbert provided another screen kiss and looked up.

"Hey, Clarence," he said, "do you want to check Miss Garbo's lip makeup?"

"Makeup!" cried Brown.

"The thing of it is," explained Gilbert, "I don't want to smear it."

"No," said Garbo, "and I don't want you to."

"Thank you."

Ernie, the makeup man, stepped in, kneeled down and examined Garbo's lips.

"What do you think, Ernie?" asked Brown.

"Might be all right. If they're careful."

Gilbert's famous temper flared. "Careful? What the hell do you —how can we be—? Oh, for Christ's sweet sake! Excuse me, Miss Garbo, but—"

"Easy, Jack, *easy*," said Brown. "Let *me* run it." He stepped into the shot and knelt beside them. "What we'll do is this," he said. "We'll do the two shot right through the kiss, then Jack's close-up, and if the two shot's smeared him, we can clean him up just ahead of it, and the same, of course, for Miss Garbo."

"Should I powder her down anyway?" asked Ernie.

"Do you mind?" Brown asked Garbo.

"I prefer no, especial for the close-up, but I promise—I never smear."

"That may be," said Brown, "but you've never been kissed by John Gilbert."

There was a mild company laugh. Ernie powdered Garbo's lips. As soon as he turned his back, she licked the powder off.

Gilbert spoke. "Let's shoot it, Clarence, could we?" he asked. "All this horsing around is giving me the screaming meemies. *Jesus!* Excuse me," he said to Garbo. "Talk, talk. Arrangements, arrangements. Let's *do* it, for God's sake."

"As you wish," said Brown, as great a diplomat as he was a director. "All right with you, Miss Garbo?"

"Surely, yes."

"Right," said Brown, and to his assistant: "Take."

"Hold it down for a take!" shouted the assistant. "This is a *take*, everybody. A *take*."

The crew sprang into action. Every department did its sudden stuff. Makeup, wardrobe, props, set.

"Clear, please!" yelled the assistant. "Clear it!"

The crew cleared at once.

Surprisingly, no one left the camera position. The crew formed a large semicircle around it.

Brown spoke to the players. "Remember now, we open on a wide two and ride in slow on the big kiss to a double close-up."

"I understand," said Garbo.

Gilbert smiled saucily and said, "I think I can handle that, all right."

Brown turned to his assistant and said, "Now."

"Let's have a bell!" yelled the assistant.

A loud bell clanged and kept clanging until absolute quiet was achieved.

"Ready?" asked Brown. The assistant nodded.

"Go."

"Roll 'em!" cried the assistant. The camera whirred.

The slate man knelt in front of Garbo and Gilbert. His slate read:

> **DIR: BROWN   CAM: DANIELS**
> **"FLESH AND THE DEVIL"**
> **SCENE: 82   TAKE 1**
> **29 Oct 26**
> **EASTMAN 87B STOCK**
> **MGM**

"Speed!" called the camera operator. The slate man stepped out.

"Music," said Brown quietly.

Near the set, but screened off, a string quartet made up of members of the Los Angeles Symphony Orchestra began to play "The Girl with the Flaxen Hair" by Debussy.

"Action," said Brown.

There was a pause, too long to suit Brown, until he realized that Garbo was gaining concentration, collecting her thoughts, preparing. At length, she took a deep breath and closed her eyes. When she opened them, the transformation was complete. She had, indeed, become someone else—Leonora.

She spoke. " 'Come! Come and be close to me—' "

Leo/Gilbert lay down beside her. Something about her playing, the way in which her eyes took possession of his—something about the hypnotic, magnetic quality of her movement mesmerized him, and he moved to her gracefully, sensually, as if in a dream. She took his head into her hands tenderly, and began to kiss his face—but not at all as she had done in rehearsal.

Now she was bestowing tantalizing gifts of love and desire and invitation. The fleeting angel kisses were far more eloquent than words ever could be. All at once, not as rehearsed, he took charge, embraced her powerfully, rolled her over and kissed her truly. She responded. The camera moved toward them slowly.

Brown was as astonished as he was delighted. For once he did not resent the fact that his careful direction had been ignored.

In the scene, the kiss ended. Reluctantly, hesitantly, unwillingly.

Leo/Gilbert continued with the text, but in a new voice, and with stunning reality. " 'How I have longed for that—the—' " He kissed her again, although it was not in the script. Finally, came away, as though in slow motion—" 'the food of love.' " Another series of abandoned kisses followed. He kissed her eyes, her ears, her neck, and her throat, then her lips, one at a time. She responded, becoming a part of him.

Their positions reversed. She kissed him. He held her head in his powerful hands and said, " 'God Almighty! How I have hungered.' "

He kissed her now for fair. She went limp in his arms. Her hands moved upward, floating at first in supplication; and finally, in surrender. She held his head and they conjoined.

Clarence Brown and his crew became statues as they watched. They had never before seen anything like this, not on a movie set.

Brown turned to his assistant, who was kneeling beside him, and said, "I'm not directing this damn thing. *God* is."

In the scene, the kiss ended and she spoke. Her voice sending shivers down most of the spines of those watching. " 'No longer, my love, we are together. As surely God and nature intended.' "

An inspired exchange of kisses followed. A back and forth, a give and take. A perfect sexual exchange. It ended in a climactic, orgasmic, earth-shattering kiss.

(This was the very scene the M-G-M flacks were later to exploit as: 89 KISSES IN A SINGLE SCENE!)

The camera reached the planned double close-up position. The operator looked at Daniels, Daniels looked at Brown, who signaled, No, not yet.

The kiss in double close-up continued to breathe, to live.

Brown waited it out. Finally, he said, "Beautiful. Cut."

The kiss continued.

"Cut!" said Brown, somewhat louder.

The kiss continued.

Brown stood up and shouted, "Cut!!"

But Leonora and Leo or Garbo and Gilbert were still deep in their kiss. The lights on the set began to go out one by one. The crew started to move about. The bell clanged. The music stopped. The customary set noise returned.

The kiss did not end.

Later that afternoon, at Tillie and Mac's, across the street from the studio, the lunch-hour crowd had assembled. This was the diner across the street, frequented mainly by stagehands, bit players, and extras. The food was basically Tex-Mex.

In one of the booths, the slate man, Brownie, and Adele, the script girl, were having lunch with two extras from the set of *Beverly of Graustark,* a handsome girl, and a pretty boy wearing flamboyant Graustarkian costumes. Her hair was encased in protective cheesecloth. His collar was stuffed with pieces of toilet paper to guard it against the makeup. All four were eating large bowls of chili.

"So finally," said Brownie, "he hollered 'Cut!' I mean real *loud* —and still nothing."

"Listen," said the Graustark girl, "don't tell *me* about that Gilbert. He was *born* horny. He'd hump a snake if he could hold on to its ears."

"And he's hollering," said Brownie with his mouth full, " 'Cut! Cut!' Boy, it was *funny.*"

"I thought it was beautiful," said Adele softly.

"They done the close-ups yet?" asked the Graustark boy. "I'm gonna sneak a peek."

"Finished," said Adele. "With Miss Garbo, there's hardly ever more than one or two takes."

"Sounds to me," said the girl, "like you couldn't do more than two of those. Not in one morning."

"Speak for yourself, toots," said the boy. They all laughed and Brownie said, "It's like the one about the man-wife vaudeville act. They say to the booking agent, 'We got a great act. We come out and do it right on the stage.' And the agent says, 'Great! But then what do you do for an encore?' "

216

The boy and girl howled at the joke they have heard many times before. Brownie laughed, too.

Adele did not laugh. She was looking off in a reverie, beginning to remember, forever, the remarkable sight she had seen that morning.

On the M-G-M lot, one of the most impressive structures was the large, sprawling building known as The Marion Davies Bungalow. It had been built on the lot by William Randolph Hearst for his mistress, at a 1924 cost of $420,000. A large sign over the entry identified it:

MISS MARION DAVIES
Cosmopolitan Pictures

In its dining room, Miss Davies, dressed in the glittering costume she wore in *The Red Mill*, was lunching with her director, Roscoe Arbuckle. A maid and a butler attended them. The servants were removing the soup course, vichyssoise, and serving an elaborate seafood salad.

Close to the table, on an elaborate console, the Atwater Kent radio, with its conical parchment speaker, was receiving a broadcast from the Los Angeles Biltmore. A small jazz combination was playing "Baby Face."

Marion spoke with her entrancing stutter, about which she had no self-consciousness whatever. "And even though they all n-n-know about Jack and what a t-t-tomcat he is—they were surprised, b-b-because it usually t-t-takes him a few d-d-days."

"Jack's all right," said Roscoe.

"Will you have coffee, Mr. Arbuckle?" asked the butler.

"Goodrich," said Roscoe.

"Beg pardon?"

"My name is William Goodrich."

"It *is?*" asked the butler, confused.

He had long been a Fatty Arbuckle fan.

"Yes, Adams," said Marion. "Mr. G-G-Goodrich is my new director."

"Yes, ma'am," said Adams as he left, frowning in confusion.

"I'm with *you*, Roscoe," said Marion. "I'm all for J-J-Jack; it's that big Swede gives me a p-p-pain. All that hiding away, behaving

217

like a k-k-queen. Hell, she's just like the r-r-rest of us. But guess who thinks she's the c-c-cat's p-p-pajamas?"

Roscoe, preoccupied and distant, finally looked at her and asked, "Who?"

"Mr. Hearst," she replied. "Isn't he one un-p-p-predictable b-b-bastard?"

"I should say so," said Roscoe. "When I was in my trouble . . . he and all his papers . . . why, they were the *worst*. They were all bad—but, he was the worst. His papers I mean, but he must have been behind it. And here he hires me to be your director in *The Red Mill*."

"*I* hired you, Roscoe," she said.

"Yes, I know, of course. Thank you. But *he* had to approve."

"He d-d-does what I want," said Marion forcefully. "If not—" She stopped.

"Yes," said Roscoe, understanding.

He returned to his plate and began to eat ravenously.

"On the other hand," said Marion, "this Garbo-Gilbert thing c-c-could be one of Strickland's hot ideas—you know—b-b-build up some off-screen screwing, and those d-d-dummies out there think they're seeing it on the screen."

The music on the radio switched to "The Sheik of Araby." A tenor's voice came on singing the chorus. The voice: "I'm The Sheik of Araby."

Roscoe sang automatically, "Wit' no pants on!"

"What?" asked Marion.

He failed to hear the question, and went on eating.

On a grassy knoll near the exterior set for *The Scarlet Letter,* on the backlot of the M-G-M studios, Greta Garbo and John Gilbert were having an elaborate picnic lunch. Gilbert owned a superb piece of equipment for outings such as this: a picnic basket from Abercrombie and Fitch in New York, which had cost him just over $1,000.

On a spread blanket, there were sandwiches, hard-boiled eggs, caviar, a little basket of crudités: celery, cherry tomatoes, raw cauliflower, carrots, and radishes. An overflowing basket of fruit. A bottle of champagne. Cake and cookies. And one large platter of Swedish delicacies: gravlax, Jansson Frestelse, pytt i tanna, and stettekaka.

John Gilbert had long known that the proper ammunition was required for a successful hunt.

He had also brought along a portable phonograph and it played Ruth Etting's recording of "Shakin' the Blues Away," by Irving Berlin, from The Ziegfeld Follies of 1926.

They ate in silence, studying each other, enjoying their food, comfortable in one another's company.

Garbo nibbled on a hot dog, the first she had ever had. Gilbert watched for her reaction. He was chewing on the pytt i tanna, loathing it and pretending to love it.

All at once, she looked away swiftly. He continued to stare at her, and in a few moments her eyes returned to his. A smile was exchanged.

Now his eyes asked, and hers responded.

The music ended. Gilbert removed the needle, turned over the record, wound up the machine with its crank, and replaced the needle. In a moment, Al Jolson's voice was heard singing, "Five Foot Two, Eyes of Blue." Garbo and Gilbert continued to eat and to look at one another. There seemed to be no need for words.

A Hollywood night at Grauman's Chinese. The premiere of *Flesh and the Devil*. Searchlights, limousines, radio announcers, photographers, bleachers for the fans, and fans for the bleachers.

A studio limousine drove up. Ben Farber appeared. John Gilbert stepped out, beautifully attired in white tie and tails. He put his hand into the limousine and brought forth Greta Garbo. A vision.

The crowd cheered, whistled, and stamped its feet until Taki Galanos, whose firm had erected the bleachers, began to worry that they might collapse.

Garbo and Gilbert stood posing for the photographers and waving to the crowd. She smiled her most radiant smile. Gilbert leaned over and whispered into her ear. She laughed. The crowd cheered even more wildly. They had scarcely ever seen her laugh. Clearly, Greta Garbo was happy. Happier than she had ever been.

Now Mauritz Stiller stepped out of the limousine. He looked ill and fatigued, but was playing the good sport. The oddly assorted trio moved across the red carpet, arm in arm, into the theatre— and triumph.

Ben followed, confidently.

XI

BEN SAID, "That was the biggest picture—*Flesh and the Devil*—that we ever had up to that time. You see, no matter what they want to tell you, you listen to me. Who makes a hit is not the producers, or the actors, or the directors. Who makes a hit is the public, and the public, well, they simply went wild for them—for Greta Garbo and John Gilbert. Not only for them, but for the picture, too."

"And what happened to Stiller?" asked Guy.

"Well, that, I'm almost ashamed to tell you. We lost him. What happened was he went over to Paramount and he made them a terrific smash hit—but not with her, not with Garbo. In fact, Irving Thalberg admitted later that he'd made a mistake. And believe me, he didn't admit that often.

"So what was decided, it was decided to put them right away, the same year, into another picture—the exhibitors were hollering for it. So Irving, after a lot of conferences, he picked out to do *Anna Karenina*. Only it was decided to call it *Love*."

Guy smiled and said, "Good title."

"Well, to tell you the truth," said Ben, "I like better *Anna Karenina*. But they all said, who can say it? So—*Love,* that *everybody* can say. But before we could get started—trouble."

XII

TROUBLE, INDEED. It was taking place in L.B. Mayer's office, where eventually all the important trouble was dealt with. Present were Mayer, Garbo, Ben, Rolf, and Harry Edington.

Edington was a small, dark, wiry man who had recently become Garbo's agent, at the suggestion of John Gilbert. He had cleverly agreed to represent Garbo, for no commission whatever, believing that the prestige of an association with her would be commission enough. She, a shrewd businesswoman, recognized that this arrangement added 10 percent to her income.

Mayer and Edington had been sparring for half an hour. Rolf sat beside Garbo and interpreted. Her English was excellent by now, but in matters of business she preferred to be absolutely certain sure.

"A classic," said Edington, "that's all, a classic. An all-time, goddamn classic."

"Classics!" said Mayer dourly. "They can sometimes lose a bundle."

"Not this one, L.B., and you *know* it!"

"We'll see, we'll see," said Mayer impatiently. "It's early yet, first run. How will it go in Paducah, in Dayton, Ohio, in Brookline, Mass., my hometown. And who knows foreign yet?"

"*I* know," said Edington. "A smash. She's a bigger star there than here, isn't she?"

Mayer, who knew that Greta Garbo was the greatest international star of the day, ignored the question, but said, grudgingly, "It's a good picture. Who said not? Should do well. Why not?"

"After all," said Ben, "it also had John Gilbert. And he's our biggest. And what about Mr. Clarence Brown? You can't do better than that, than him. And we had on it some of our finest writers who—"

"Oh, sure," said Edington, "but the little girl here helped. Wouldn't you say?"

Mayer smiled for the first time in an hour and said, "Little?"

Rolf quickly translated the nuance of Mayer's remark. Garbo was understandably miffed.

Edington asked, "So what do you say, L.B.? Let's negotiate."

"Negotiate? I have a contract with this woman—with this ungrateful woman. Tell her when she can talk English, I'll consider a raise."

At this, Garbo stood up and moved resolutely to L.B.'s desk.

"I can speak English excellently, Mr. Mayer," she said. "So how much?"

Ben laughed. Mayer turned on him. "You think that's funny?" he asked.

"Sure," said Ben. "Just like when Laurel and Hardy fall in a hole."

"Do me a favor," said Mayer, "go back in your own office."

"Not on your life," said Ben. "I want to see how this thing comes out."

Mayer was thrown and showed it. He touched the five tips of the fingers of his left hand to the tips of the five fingers of his right. He bounced them off each other for a time, then asked Edington, "What's she getting now? See? I don't even *know*."

"Six hundred," said Edington.

"No," said Garbo in a voice louder than any of them had ever heard from her.

Edington turned to her and asked, "No?"

Garbo said, "A *lousy* six hundred!"

"Where does she pick up language like that?" asked Mayer.

"From Jack, probably," suggested Ben.

"What's the difference?" asked Garbo.

Mayer held on to his head. "Six hundred!" he exclaimed.

"Sure," said Ben, "don't you remember? We raised her from three fifty after *The Temptress*."

Mayer rose. "My God, we've doubled your salary, and you're still kicking?"

"No," said Garbo. "Doubled would be seven hundred."

In a sudden reverse, Mayer decided to attempt charm. "All right," he smiled, "you want seven hundred, you *got* seven hundred."

Garbo turned away in disgust.

"Come on, L.B.," said Edington.

Mayer came out from behind his desk. This was meant to signal courage and fearlessness. "I've got a contract!" he shouted. "I don't have to give her *anything*."

"And she doesn't have to show up!" yelled Edington, topping him.

Mayer dropped his voice to a near whisper, and said, "Is she threatening me?"

"No," said Edington, "*I* am. You've got to be fair—"

"*Fair!*" Mayer said, as if Edington had uttered a dirty word. "Fa-*ir!* I've *gambled* on this woman. I risked. I discovered her. If not for me—where would she be?"

"I don't know," said Edington, "maybe Paramount?"

Ben moved closer to the fray and said, "All right, Harry, what's *your* idea of fair? What do you want?"

"Me?" said Edington. "I want nothing. I think you gentlemen should know I represent Miss Garbo for gratis. I receive no commission of any kind. This is entirely a favor to Jack."

"Thanks," said Mayer bitterly. "Thanks very much."

Ben asked, "So what does *she* want?"

Before Edington could reply, Garbo, standing near the door, turned into the room and said, "I want five thousand dollars a week."

There was a silence that signaled the end of the world. Ben whistled softly. Garbo stood her ground defiantly. Edington was confused; Mayer, on the verge of apoplexy. Instead a burst of laughter escaped him. He laughed and laughed, returned to the great chair behind his desk. He laughed and laughed some more. He wiped his eyes.

Edington spoke to Garbo. "Wait a second, Greta. I thought we said *four* thousand."

"Yes," said Garbo, "but the insults I have here today—it is changed. *Five!* And if he does not stop to laugh at me—this buffoon—it will be *six!*"

Mayer stopped laughing at once. He clicked an intercom.

Thalberg's voice came on. "Yes, L.B.?"

"I got here in my office Garbo," said Mayer. "Also her big new agent, Edington, that Gilbert put on her. I want to ask you a little question, Irving. What do you think they just now asked for? In money."

"Ten thousand a week?" guessed Thalberg.

Mayer yelled, "What're you, Irving, *crazy?*"

Thalberg's voice. "I can't continue this, L.B., you just broke my machine." A clicking sound. Mayer stood up and said, "Very well. In the circumstances, I will recommend to the Board of Directors an adjustment to two thousand a week."

"Don't bother," said Edington.

"Would you consider three?" asked Ben.

"No," said Garbo. "Five."

Ben turned to Edington. "You said negotiate, Harry. So come on, bend."

"I surrender," said Edington. "This girl needs an agent like she needs more sex appeal."

Mayer came out from behind his desk again, a changed personality, and approached Garbo. "My dear girl," he said, "you must be reasonable. We are building a career for you. We are putting the resources of this entire great studio behind you. We want to pay you, of course. We all get paid. Even me. But, for God's sake, five thousand dollars; it's out of the question. The Board of Directors would laugh at me."

"You pay John Gilbert ten thousand a week," said Garbo.

"But he's a great star already."

"I know," said Garbo, "and my role in *Karenina* is the same big as his—bigger. And *he* thinks I am worth five thousand. Ask him."

"Ask him?" shouted Mayer. "I'll kill him!"

"Please do not," said Garbo. She started out, Rolf following.

Ben turned to Edington and pointed to Rolf. "What does she need *him* for?" he asked.

"Wait!" shouted Mayer.

Garbo kept moving as she said, "When you call me, I am ready to start. You have my number, Hollywood six-oh-six-one."

She was gone. There followed an oppressive silence. After a time, Edington said, "Well . . ." waited half a minute, and left.

Ben and Mayer sat quietly, unable to look at each other. Ben got up abruptly and padded out of the room. Mayer sat alone, and precipitously burst into tears.

The marquee of the Capitol Theatre in New York read:

TOGETHER AGAIN
JOHN GILBERT
and
GRETA GARBO
in
"LOVE"

"Steamier than FLESH AND THE DEVIL*"*
N.Y. Times

At the Fifty-ninth Street entrance of the Hotel Plaza in New York, Garbo came out surrounded by five M-G-M public relations men. Several reporters descended upon her. The PR men were no match for them. She was trapped.

"How long will be you be in New York, Miss Garbo?" asked a reporter.

"Two more days," said a PR man.

"What's your next movie?" asked another reporter.

"It hasn't been decided," said a second PR man.

A third reporter said, "Hey, come on! Can't *she* talk?"

A third PR man said, "Yes."

The fourth reporter asked, "What is she? Deef and dumb?"

The reporters were milling about, blocking her way, but the PR men managed to get her across the sidewalk and close to the waiting limousine.

Another reporter, one of the most aggressive, put his body between Garbo and the entrance to the limousine as he asked, "When are you going to marry John Gilbert?"

There was a silence, as all the reporters waited for her reply.

Garbo said calmly, "Listen to me. Mr. Gilbert is a fine actor and a splendid man. We are friends. We are partners. We are fellow artists. I am not going to marry Mr. Gilbert. I am not going to marry anyone. Never."

A reporter leaned in and asked, "When you say partners, just what does that mean, exactly?"

Garbo lost her temper. "Oh, go away," she shouted. "Leave me *alone!*" She got into the limousine. The PR men joined her. The car drove off.

"What'd she say, Artie?" asked one of the reporters.

"She said"—Artie attempted an imitation of Garbo, as he continued—"I vant to be a-*lone.*"

The reporters all jotted it down.

XIII

"WELL, BY NOW," said Ben, "you can imagine, we had something fantastic going. We put them together again into *The Green Hat*, a big Broadway hit. Only we called it *A Woman of Affairs*. My *God*, what a success we had! The business was unbelievable all over the country. Of all our assets, and we had plenty, that team was the biggest."

XIV

AT THE bar of The Coconut Grove, which served only Moxie, Coca-Cola, Canada Dry ginger ale, and lemonade, John Gilbert sat with Lionel Barrymore. In the background, Paul Whiteman and his orchestra were playing Irving Berlin's "Blue Skies." Gilbert took a silver pocket flask from his hip pocket, poured some of the scotch it contained into his glass of ginger ale and into Lionel's.

He said, "You don't understand, Lionel. Maybe *I* don't understand—but this time it's different."

"You've said that before, my boy."

"I know I have, but this time I *know*. I care more about *her* than I do about myself!"

"Say, that *does* sound serious, Jack. What are you taking for it?"

"It's no joke to me. Sure, I've been married—three times, three mistakes. I've knocked around, what else is there to do? But this time I can see a whole life, a life I want. A family. And work. Lionel, she's the most glorious, the most satisfying, and most forever girl I've ever known."

The normally cynical Barrymore was touched.

"Can I tell you a secret?" asked Gilbert.

"No."

"Three weeks from next Sunday, September eighth, King Vidor and Eleanor are getting married."

"So I hear."

"At Marion's house in Beverly Hills."

"And may God have mercy on their souls," intoned Barrymore.

"All right now, here's the secret—" He looked about to make certain there were no eavesdroppers, leaned forward and added, "I've asked Greta to make it a double wedding—and she said she'd think about it. And, Lionel, the way she said it, the way she said she'd think about it, I *know* she's going to *do* it!"

"Just *how* did she say it?" asked Lionel.

"Christ, you're about as funny as Boris Karloff."

"What makes you think—?"

Louella Parsons and her husband came by. Both were pleasantly plastered.

"Jack," cried Louella. They kissed. "I've heard a rumor—"

"Rumor, tumor," said Dr. Martin.

"Be quiet, Harry."

"Is that so?" asked Gilbert.

"I heard a rumor that you and Garbo are secretly hitched."

"I know, I started it," said Jack.

"Well, *are* you?" persisted Louella.

"Come on now, do I *look* married?"

"Married, harried," said Dr. Martin.

"If you let anybody scoop me, Jack, you'll regret it."

"Louella, Greta and I are not getting married. I swear it on my mother's life."

"Life, wife," said Dr. Martin.

"Well," said Louella, "that's good enough for me. I'm going to bash some of those sources of mine with a baseball bat. See you later." She and Gilbert kissed again, after which she said, "Hello, Lionel."

Lionel said, "*I am* marrying Garbo. There's a scoop for you."

"Scoop, poop," said Dr. Martin.

"Oh, be still," said Louella.

"I'm hungry," said Dr. Martin. They moved on.

Lionel looked hard at Gilbert and said, "You astonish me."

"How so?"

"How can you swear on your mother's life?"

"Because my mother's dead, you dumbbell."

"Touché!" shouted Lionel, and began to laugh so hard that he had trouble keeping his drink from spilling.

In the spacious gardens of Marion Davies's house in Beverly Hills, preparations for the double wedding were complete. Even the weather had cooperated. It was a cool, bright, sunny summer's day. There were glittering wedding decorations, cages upon cages of lovebirds and doves, bowers of flowers, and eighty carefully selected guests. Among them: Norma Shearer and Irving Thalberg, Mr. and Mrs. L.B. Mayer, Joan Crawford, Mr. and Mrs. Benjamin Farber, Douglas Fairbanks and Mary Pickford, Mr. and Mrs. A.L. Seligman, the Gish sisters, Buster Keaton and Charles Chaplin.

In a corner of the garden, Ben stood chatting with Buster Keaton and the Seligmans.

"Well, they seem to have the perfect day for it," said Seligman.

"If it wasn't for the wedding," said Buster, "it would be a *perfectly* perfect day."

Ben looked about and said, "My God, *everybody's* here."

Keaton said, in all seriousness, "You know why? It's because King isn't only a fine director but a fine man. Everybody in this town loves him. Him and me. We're the only two."

Across the garden, Vidor was standing with Gilbert, who looked at his watch every ten seconds.

He realized that the assemblage was becoming noticeably restless. He saw people asking questions and getting shrugs instead of answers.

He strolled away quickly, and a few minutes later King Vidor saw him from afar on the telephone, shouting angrily. King was about to join him when the minister caught his attention and indicated his watch. Vidor nodded, and went off to find Gilbert in the library, flushed and furious.

"Jack—" said Vidor.

"Leave me alone. Get out of here."

"But listen, Jack—"

"Will you get the hell away from me, or do I have to *belt* you?"

Vidor left the library.

Within ten minutes, Gilbert was in the bar, pouring.

L.B. Mayer came in with Eddie Mannix and Ben. "Come on, Jack," said Mayer, "they're starting."

"Out!" said Jack.

Mannix, an experienced and accomplished fixer, moved to Gilbert and said, "Come on, Jack, be a sport."

"No," said Gilbert.

Mayer tried. "Marion says—and don't forget you're a guest in her house—" Jack knocked back a drink and poured another. He laughed.

"That's a hot one," he said. "A tramp sends a bum to teach me manners."

"Don't talk like that, Jack," said Ben. "It's not nice."

"I forgive him," said Mayer, all dignity, "because he's drunk."

Gilbert bowed and said, "I accept your apology."

"What are you building the whole thing into a whole Dreyfus case, for God's sake?" Mayer bellowed. "She's only another piece. So just because you're laying her, doesn't mean you have to marry her, does it?"

Gilbert, incensed, went berserk and leapt across the bar. Mayer ran off, yelling. "Crazy! The man's crazy. Get him away from me!" He stumbled into the bathroom and slammed the door, but before he could lock it, Gilbert threw all his weight against it. The door flew open. Ben and Mannix tried to hold him back, but failed.

In the bathroom, Mayer was cowering in a corner. Gilbert locked the door, grabbed him, and began banging his head against the tiled wall. Mayer's glasses flew from his head and shattered in the basin. He was screaming. The door was finally forced by Ben and Mannix. There was blood. Whose? Ben and Mannix managed to pull Gilbert off and away. Mayer sank to the toilet seat, shaking. Gilbert was still trying to get at him, held back by Ben and Mannix.

"You bastard!" he screamed. "You son-of-a-bitch bastard!"

Mayer got up with some difficulty, regained his breath, and said, "Gilbert—you are *finished!* Finished for good. I'm going to ruin you if it costs me a million dollars."

"So what?" said Gilbert. "You'll no doubt charge it to the company, you cheap crook."

He left, spent. Mayer indicated to Ben to follow him.

XV

"I stuck with him," said Ben, "for the longest time. After all, a man in that condition, he might do anything. Also, remember no matter what L.B. said or what he threatened, John Gilbert was still one of our biggest stars. So we got into his car. My God, I must have been taking my life into my hands. He drove around. And this was funny—not recklessly, but very, very carefully. And finally, we drove right up to *her* house, to Garbo's house. We drove in and we stopped. We got out, we went to the front door,

229

rang the bell, and the maid opened the door. We talked to her for a minute, and then we went inside. He just went right upstairs and walked all over. I don't know what he expected to find or to do. He wasn't being sensible, but while he was prowling around, the maid told me everything. She told me that Garbo was getting ready to go to the wedding, but then at the last minute she lost her nerve and she ran away someplace. I begged her to tell me where, I offered her money, but she honestly didn't know.

"So then when Jack came down, I tried to explain to him, but he wouldn't listen. He kissed the maid and hugged her and we went off. Where we went, you wouldn't believe. We went from one speakeasy to another. There was one by the name of Joey's and one was The Wonder Bar, another one Ruby's and The Tent and The Hole and, of course, Jack got drunker and drunker. He was starting to stagger, even. I swear to God, I didn't know there were that many speakeasies in Hollywood, but he knew them all. One after another. I could have stopped him, I suppose, but why should I? The man was in pain. He was in agony. He saw his whole life collapsing. I honestly thought that if he was left alone, he might kill himself. So, this way, just getting drunk, was better. But finally, I put my foot down and I said to him, 'This is it. No more driving with you if you drive. You want to kill yourself, kill yourself, but not me.' So he let me drive, and would you believe where he insisted to go?"

"Where?" asked Guy.

"To Marie's Place."

"What was that?"

"You never heard of Marie's Place?" asked Ben, surprised.

"No, never."

"My God, I thought everybody had heard by now of Marie's Place. It was a famous whorehouse, with a great angle. Every one of the girls there was got up to look like one of the great movie stars of the day, and—"

"I don't get it," said Guy.

"Well, let me try to explain you. To begin with, you see, the girl had to have *some* kind of resemblance. And then Marie, I don't know who she was, or what her name was, but she was known as 'Marie Dressler.' She was the madam, and she had there a 'Joan Crawford,' and a 'Theda Bara'—'the Gish sisters'—a 'Mary Pickford'—and, of course, a 'Greta Garbo.'"

Guy laughed.

"Oh, it was funny all right," said Ben.

"You mean to say it really worked?" asked Guy.

"Well, you got to remember," said Ben, "they kept their lights there pretty dark—and everybody was always drinking—so it wasn't too hard to imagine whatever you wanted to imagine. If you wanted to."

XVI

MARIE'S PLACE. Ben and Jack sat at the best table in the house. Jack looked about the room. Each one of the "stars" was trying to make good with him, to catch his eye, to be chosen. He looked at "Crawford" and flirted outrageously; at "Clara Bow," then looked at "Garbo." She smiled at him, winked, beckoned him with her head and indicated the stairs. His eyes were glassy. He took his attention from her and put it on "Theda Bara." "The Gish sisters." He was drawn back to "Garbo." She was mouthing enticing endearments.

Gilbert looked fuzzily from one to the other. The dim lights did indeed buttress the illusion. Moreover, the drinks served at Marie's were strong, and a man's willingness to fantasize in sexual matters became even stronger.

Jack stared at "Garbo," who was becoming more real to him by the minute. All at once, he turned and crooked a finger at "Joan Crawford." She rose and joined him. Ben and Jack got to their feet as "Joan" came up. She kissed Gilbert briefly and shook hands with Ben.

"Where've you been, Jack?" she asked. "I've missed you. We've *all* missed you."

"Sit down, 'Joan,' " said Jack. They all sat. A drink was served. "I've been busy being jilted, stood up."

"Joan" laughed. "Well, *that* doesn't take long," she said.

"You'd be surprised," said Jack sagely.

"Joan" looked from him to Ben. "What's this going to be—a threesome?"

231

"No, no," said Jack. He looked off and saw "Mary Pickford."
"Garbo." "Mary" again. Back to "Garbo." Gilbert beckoned to
"Mary," who jumped up eagerly and joined his party.

"How are you, Mary?" asked Ben.

"Oh, working hard, as usual. Selling."

"Doug O.K.?" asked Ben.

"He's in New York." She turned to Jack.

"What's new at *your* sweatshop, Jack?"

"Oh, you know," said Jack, "like everywhere else these days,
worrying about the talkies. Not me. What have *I* got to worry
about? I'm a *stage* actor, after all."

"I hate those damned talkies," said "Mary."

"Joan" looked at Gilbert and said, "I loved you in *Woman of
Affairs*, even though you had to wrestle the big Swede." She
looked across the room at "Garbo," who was blazing with jealousy.

"Mary" said, "They should've called it *A Man of Affairs*."

"I asked them to," said Jack, "but I'm in purdah since my trouble with L.B."

"*Now* what trouble?" asked "Joan."

"You haven't heard? He asked me to marry him and I turned
him down."

"Why, for heaven's sake!" said "Mary." "You'd have made a
lovely couple."

"Half a lovely couple," said "Joan."

"No—I couldn't—" He looked across the room and flashed his
dazzling smile at "Garbo." She looked back at him long and hard,
finally relented and smiled. His eyes proposed to her. Her eyes
considered it.

While this silent flirtation continued, Ben said, "The Warners
are in the talkies because it's their only chance to stay in business."

"I'm not worried," said "Mary." "Don't forget, *I* was a Belasco
actress."

"You were?" asked "Joan."

"Damn right," said "Mary," "before I ever came out here."

By now, Gilbert's campaign was apparently successful. "Garbo"
nodded, almost imperceptibly.

Gilbert returned his attention to his table and said, "I *couldn't*
marry L.B., because I'm going to marry G.G."

"When?" asked "Joan."

Gilbert stood up unsteadily, raised his glass and shouted with gleeful madness, "Tonight! Right here!" He walked over to "Garbo," knelt before her, took her hand, and kissed it.

In the parlor of the whorehouse, the mock wedding was in progress. Ben, holding the Los Angeles telephone directory, was acting as the minister. Gilbert had gotten him up for the part by turning his collar around. Marie had provided a coat that looked enough like a cassock.

All the girls and a few stray patrons were present and had arranged themselves in the manner of a wedding party.

Enoch, the Negro pianist, was providing appropriate music.

John Gilbert stood in the groom's position with the uniformed doorman, who was acting as best man.

Enoch struck up "Here Comes the Bride." "Garbo" and the bartender, who had been pressed into service to give the bride away, came down the aisle. She was in an improvised wedding gown made from one of "Mary's" nightgowns, and a veil made of cheesecloth hastily borrowed from the kitchen. She carried a bouquet of flowers gathered from the front yard.

Despite the nonsense and the mockery, the scene was attractive, affecting. "All brides are beautiful."

The bride reached the groom. They regarded one another solemnly. They knelt on the pillows before the minister. Enoch segued from "Here Comes the Bride" to Irving Berlin and played "Always."

Ben spoke under his breath to Gilbert. "Now what?"

Gilbert prompted softly, "Dearly beloved—"

"Dearly beloved—" Ben repeated.

"We are gathered together in the sight of God and in the face of this company."

Ben plowed on gamely. "We are gathered together in the sight of God and in the face of this company."

The spectators were rapt. They were beginning to be caught up in the illusion.

Gilbert rattled on. "To join together in holy matrimony this man and this woman."

Ben rattled, too, in imitation. "To join together in holy matrimony this man and this woman."

By now "the Gish sisters" were hanging on to each other and crying official wedding tears.

233

Gilbert, still prompting, said, "And so forth, and so forth, I don't know, something, and so forth. Rise, please."

Ben repeated. "And so forth, and so forth, I don't know, something, and so forth. Rise, please."

The bride and groom rose. Jack and Ben continued their echoed exchange. Jack said, "With this ring I thee wed and with all my worldly goods I thee endow."

"With this ring I thee wed and with all my worldly goods I thee endow."

"In sickness and in health, for richer, for poorer, forsaking all others until death do us part."

"In sickness and in health, for richer, for poorer, forsaking all others until death do us part."

"I now pronounce you—Garbo and Gilbert."

"I now pronounce you—Garbo and Gilbert."

"Make that Gilbert and Garbo," said Jack.

Ben obliged. "I now pronounce you Gilbert and Garbo."

Jack kissed his bride, exquisitely. All kissed the bride. Applause. Music. Gilbert and "Garbo" rushed up the aisle. The wedding party followed.

In the lower hall, at the foot of the staircase, Gilbert swept "Garbo" off her feet and started up. Halfway up, he stopped; she flung her bouquet. It was caught in tandem by "the Gish sisters." The bride and groom disappeared.

Ben watched the farce with mixed emotions. He knew that he had seen the beginning of the end of the great John Gilbert.

XVII

BACK IN Ben's study, remembering has restored a youthful glow to his countenance.

"It was like a crazy dream. The whole thing."

"Amazing," said Guy.

"And then, the next thing you know—there was no more discussion yes or no—the talkies were here. No more arguments about novelties or gimmicks or the economics. The pictures'd started talking and like a baby, who learns to talk, is not going to shut up. Of course, some of the actors and actresses, they just quit. They said the hell with it, and they quit. Chaplin said he didn't care what anybody else did, he was going to go on making silents. And he did—for years and years—but he was, after all, *Chaplin*. One night he came over and told me a whole story, a whole wonderful story about where he was going to play a deaf and dumb clown in a circus. Naturally, in love with a bareback rider or something. And the way he was going to arrange it was that everybody else in the picture talked, except, of course, him. He was very excited about this idea. In fact, he said maybe he would develop it into his new character, and make a whole bunch of pictures like that. I thought it had possibilities, but, I don't know, he never did it. Come to think of it, all of us don't make more pictures than we *do* make. A lot of other people thought Chaplin's idea was crazy. But look how they handled it with Harpo, with the Marx Brothers. Nobody ever heard the sound of his voice on the screen, and he was certainly one of the greats. Well, what can I tell you? They were crazy days. Hardly anybody was sure exactly what to do. With Gilbert, we put him into a picture called *His Glorious Night*. It was a very fine Molnar story. And we gave him Lionel Barrymore to direct. It looked like it was going to be fine, but something happened. I don't know what, for sure, but something. As the years've gone by, God *Almighty*, the stories we've heard! The mystery. The double-crosses. What L.B. did. What Lionel did. God only knows. The truth is that nobody knows the truth, but they all know what happened. And what happened was something terrible.

XVIII

ON STAGE 9, Lionel Barrymore was arranging the setup with the cameraman, Percy Hilburn. The stand-ins were in place being lighted.

In Gilbert's portable dressing room, he was having a row with Howard Strickling, M-G-M's chief publicist.

"The hell I did," said Gilbert.

"Would I lie to you, Jack?"

"Why not? You lie to everyone else."

Strickling controlled his temper. Controlling his temper was part of his daily job. He took a deep breath and said coolly, "It was at Pickfair—don't you remember? And I asked you as a personal favor to do just one interview—*one*—"

"When you get Garbo to do one, just *one*; I'll do one, just *one*."

"And you said yes," said Strickling.

"Christ, I must have been plastered."

"You may have been at that."

"And you want to hold me to a drunken promise, you louse?" asked Gilbert.

"Jack—help me, will you? I've got a job to do." They looked at one another. Strickling had apparently struck a nerve.

Gilbert sighed and said, "All right—where is the silly bitch?"

"She's *not* a silly bitch," said Strickling. "She's Ruth Waterbury, editor-in-chief of *Photoplay* magazine."

"Two cheers," said Gilbert.

"You want her in here?"

"I don't want her at all. But, no—not in here, for God's sake."

He rose, put on a silk Japanese kimono, glanced at himself in his makeup mirror, made a few vital adjustments, and moved out of the dressing room, followed by Strickling.

Strickling led him to a quiet part of the set, away from the camera position. A trim and proper young lady stood there, waiting.

Strickling made the formal introduction. "Miss Ruth Waterbury, Mr. John Gilbert."

"How do you do?" said Miss Waterbury.

" 'Miss'?" asked Gilbert. "Did I hear him say 'Miss'?"

"Yes."

"Well, how on earth has a dish like you eluded holy matrimony?"

"Oh, really!" said Miss Waterbury, flushing.

Gilbert turned to Strickling and whispered loudly, "Is that buttering her up enough?"

Strickling produced a mirthless laugh and moved away. Miss Waterbury and Gilbert sat on camp chairs. She got out her notebook.

All professionalism and efficiency, she began. "Now, this is your first talkie, I believe."

"Yes, and that's what *I* believe, too."

Strickling, watching from a distance, was aware of Gilbert's discomfiture. Miss Waterbury was not.

"Are you worried?" she asked.

"Hell, no!" said Gilbert. His expletive shocked her. He noted it and smiled wickedly as he continued. "Why should I be, for Christ's sake?" She was shocked again and showed it. "I'm a stage actor, I'm no movie dummy. I'm from the legitimate theatre."

"You are?"

"Of course. I was on the stage when I was *four*."

Miss Waterbury was writing furiously. "Really. Four? How was that?"

"Well, my mother and father, don't you see, were both on the stage. The Pringles. The finest third-rate stock players in the country."

Miss Waterbury glanced up at him from her notes, wondering if he was pulling her leg, or if she should show her disapproval. He went on.

"Yes. They ran this stock company in Salt Lake City, and I went on whenever they needed a child for the play."

"How fascinating," she said.

"Yes, isn't it? . . . I recall once taking a curtain call with my parents after the first act of the play—we took calls after each act in those days. My mother was wearing a long dress with a bustle and a train. The play was *The Fatal Wedding*."

Miss Waterbury was writing as swiftly as she could. "*The Fatal Wedding*, yes?"

"Well," said Gilbert, "she stepped forward to take her solo call. We had one of those roll-up curtains—it rolled up and down like a window shade—and somehow, I don't know how, the train of my mother's gown got caught in that roll curtain." Miss Waterbury continued to write and to listen, apprehensively. Whatever could be coming next? she wondered. Beads of nervous perspiration formed on her brow, as Gilbert continued. "So up up up it went, and do you know—?" He stopped and looked off, his eyes misty with memory. Miss Waterbury stared at him, pencil poised. "And do you know," said Gilbert, "that was the last time I ever saw my mother's ass!" He continued to stare off into the distance, remembering the scene in Salt Lake City, long ago. He looked back at Miss Waterbury, but she had fled. Gilbert leaned over and spoke to her empty chair. "And do you know?" he said, "that was the last time I ever saw an interviewer's pad."

The assistant director approached and said, "Ready, Mr. Gilbert."

"One moment, please," he said. "I'm just finishing." He made contact with the chair again. The assistant director waited calmly, nothing surprised him. He had been at Metro for years. Gilbert continued speaking to the chair. "It's been so nice getting rid of you, Miss Waterbury," he said. "We must do it again sometime." He rose and walked away with the assistant director.

On the set, Lionel Barrymore was talking to the leading lady, Catherine Dale Owen. She was an excessively beautiful blond actress, but rather wooden. She played Princess Orsolini, opposite Gilbert's Captain Kovacs.

"Want to run the words, Jack?" Barrymore asked.

"Not unless you do."

"You, Cath?" asked Barrymore.

"I'd rather do it."

"With anyone special?" asked Gilbert.

Miss Owen tapped him with her fan.

"Take," said Barrymore to his assistant.

Again the familiar shout from the assistant, "Quiet! This is a take." A loud bell sounded. The crew made ready, and when all the details, necessary and unnecessary, had been attended to, he called, "Roll 'em!"

The camera was a new sort. A monstrous machine enclosed in a presumably soundproof booth. The operator and the focus man wore bathing suits inside the booth, where the heat was oppressive.

On the set, the slate man now had the additional job of providing a noise to assist in the later synchronization. The slate read:

DIR: L. BARRYMORE		**CAM: HILBURN**
	HIS GLORIOUS NIGHT	
SCENE 93		**TAKE 3**
EASTMAN SOUND		**X-177**
6 JULY 1929		**MGM**

The players in position, the camera rolling, the slate man called out, loud and clear, "*Glorious Night,* scene ninety-three, take three." He then banged the striped clackers together and retreated. The players made ready. Miss Owen ran her tongue over her lips swiftly to moisten them. Gilbert cleared his throat noisily.

Barrymore said, "All right now, from 'You said you wanted to speak to me.' Now. Action!"

Owen/Orsolini: "You said you wanted to speak to me. What about?"

Gilbert/Kovacs: "You're going away tomorrow."

Owen/Orsolini: "Yes."

Gilbert/Kovacs moved closer to her as the behemoth camera booth was propelled forward by a crew of eight.

Gilbert/Kovacs: "Would you mind very much if I were to come with you?"

The players were standing now in a tight two-shot, the camera close to them.

Owen/Orsolini: "Have you bought your ticket already?"

Gilbert/Kovacs: "Yes."

As the scene continued, one began to spot microphones hidden in every possible place on the set. In a vase of flowers. In a row of books. Behind a photograph. From time to time, when the camera operator would signal that he could see one of the microphones, a property man crawled on his hands and knees, or slid on the floor on his belly and moved the microphone into another position. The overhead microphone boom was yet to be invented. The scene continued.

Owen/Orsolini: "Where did you buy it?"

Gilbert/Kovacs: "Why the porter bought it for me."

Owen/Orsolini: "I see. . . . You mustn't come to Venice."

Gilbert/Kovacs: "I only thought . . . as an escort."

The crew watched with interest and admiration. They were seeing a new John Gilbert, less a cutup, more an actor; less a playboy, more a professional. Lionel Barrymore followed the scene, playing both parts. He mouthed the lines, created the expressions, and seemed in turn to become both the Princess and the Captain.

Owen/Orsolini: "We're traveling with my father."

Gilbert/Kovacs: "I have the honor of knowing His Highness, your father; we've often walked together in Karlsbad last summer."

Owen/Orsolini: "You will not walk together in Venice. You will even avoid Italy for the present."

Gilbert/Kovacs: "I love you! *Desperately!*"

On the set, the scene had played smoothly, colorfully, in a highly sophisticated style. When Gilbert had spoken the climactic line, the effect was dramatic and startling.

In the theatre, the effect was something else again, something terrifying. Unnerving. And, as it was to turn out, killing.

As the line was spoken, there came the shattering sound—the worst imaginable to actors and actresses, directors and authors— the sound of an audience laughing in the wrong place. The reason was eminently clear. Gilbert's voice, which had sounded perfectly acceptable on the set, was, as recorded and projected, thin, high, almost effeminate, completely out of character with the image of the great lover on the screen.

In Loew's Hollywood, the preview audience had been suppressing giggles for half an hour. Now a few of the more rowdy invitees, particularly those from other studios, and perhaps a few plants, began to laugh in earnest. There seemed to be a fierce, sadistic pleasure being taken in seeing a screen idol emasculated in public.

On the screen, Owen/Orsolini was saying: "That, my boy, is precisely why I . . ."

Gilbert/Kovacs: "I am *not* a boy!"

The line came out of the speakers as a high-pitched petulant whine. The audience howled.

John Gilbert sat in the audience beside Greta Garbo. All about them, the laughers were having a whale of a time. Garbo sat horrified. Gilbert was slack-jawed and numb. He wanted to run out of the theatre, but was, for the moment, immobile.

From the screen, his voice: "My hair will be turning grey presently." For some reason, this got the biggest laugh.

In another part of the theatre sat the executives. Thalberg with Norma Shearer. Thalberg was utterly confounded. Directly behind him, flanked by Mannix and Ben, Mayer was smiling broadly. He poked Mannix with his elbow. Mannix turned to look at him. Mayer winked. Ben saw the exchange. From the screen, Gilbert's voice: "This is my last chance to tell you about it."

The prophetic words caused the wicked rowdies to let go with all they had.

Gilbert could take no more of the torture, left his seat, and stumbled up the aisle, followed by Garbo. The executives watched him leaving. Mayer was still grinning. Gilbert and Garbo were gone.

In the executive section, Mayer turned to Ben and said, "Well, this was not *his* glorious night."

"He was right, Louie," said Ben, "you *are* a son-of-a-bitch!"

"You watch out," said Mayer in an angry whisper. "You'll be the next."

"A son-of-a-bitch bastard," said Ben. "Just like he said." He got up and left.

Mayer continued to look at the screen. His smile was apparently frozen on his face, but now strangely dampened by rolling perspiration. No matter, he felt bathed in triumph.

XIX

GUY WAS shocked by the account.

Remembering it in such vivid detail had agitated Ben, and he now strode about the room. From time to time, picking up an object and slamming it down.

"We couldn't find him for two and a half weeks after that," he said. "And when we did, we had to put him into St. John's Hospital to dry him out. Some said the whole thing was a mistake in the sound department, and some said no, that's how he records. He's got some kind of trick voice. Then, of course, there was some said it was L.B. himself fixed it. It was interesting. Irving—Thalberg, I mean—he stuck right by Gilbert; he did his best. But the crazy thing was that even when his voice was fine in the next picture, the audience still laughed. At what? It was only that they believed all the stories they'd heard about that first picture. Even if they'd seen it, or even if not."

"Jesus," said Guy shaking his head.

"So, finally, of course, L.B. had his way. The way he used to have in most things, and Gilbert was out. He made a few more pictures here and there—not for us—and pretty soon it was over. Drinking. *That* didn't help either. Years later, *many* years later, Garbo insisted to hire him for a part with her in *Queen Christina* —imagine it, she made them fire Laurence Olivier to put in Gilbert. But it didn't work out. The audiences didn't care anymore. The critics, they were pretty harsh. Even *he* admitted to me one day that he was just about shot. It was so crazy, I can't even believe it myself. It was a lunch, we had lunch together at The Brown Derby, and he ordered a lot of things, and so did I, and neither one of us ate *anything*. And I remember the last thing he said. He said, 'Isn't it great? Isn't it wonderful, what's happened for Greta? Some people have success and don't really deserve it, but there's one who really does. She's the greatest. Wouldn't you say so, Ben? Simply the greatest. And now she'll go on and on.'

"Well, there was a lot of us believed it. Still and all, we didn't know how the talkies were going to work for her, and that Irving —boy, did he make a project out of it! He considered maybe twenty, thirty different combinations, different stories, different ideas, concepts, and finally he decided *Anna Christie*. He didn't want to take any chances, he wanted like one of those tailor-made parts, so he decided *Anna Christie*."

XX

In Irving Thalberg's office, a tense meeting was in progress. It involved only two people: Irving Thalberg, who sat relaxed behind his desk, and Garbo, who stood before him.

"Please sit down, Greta."

"I can't."

"Why not?"

"I'm too upset."

She walked away from the desk.

"Come on, now," said Thalberg. "Sit down and we'll talk it out. Reasonably, intelligently. Why not?"

Hesitantly, reluctantly, she came to his desk and sat.

"But one thing clear," she said, "we are *not* going to talk about that terrible *Anna Christie!*"

Thalberg smiled a gentle smile and said, "You *are* being unreasonable, you know. It's the greatest play by our greatest playwright. He's our Ibsen. The finest actresses in America have played that part, and have scored in it. Lynn Fontanne, Pauline Lord, Laurette Taylor. And the silent, a few years ago, Blanche Sweet. It never fails. I want something surefire for your first talking picture."

"Those great actresses, yes, but they were not Swedish."

"What's the difference?" asked Thalberg. "Anna Christie is."

"If I would do it, I could never go home again—never!"

"What are you talking about? Why not?"

"Because the whole thing, it shows Swedish people to be low-lifes—drunkards, whores, degenerates."

"Now really, Greta, I'm surprised at you. Who put this nonsense into your head? Stiller?"

Garbo was on her feet at once. "Stop it! Don't speak of him. My Stiller. My poor Stiller is *sick*. Perhaps very sick. I don't talk to him of trouble, not now. And you may not know it, Mr. Thalberg, but I have my own mind."

Thalberg stood up and asked, "Do you admit it's a great part?"

"A great *wrong* part. I don't play that whore no matter *what* you say."

She turned and started out of the room with long determined strides. As she reached the door, Thalberg called out sharply, "Miss *Garbo!*"

She stopped and turned.

Thalberg moved toward her with resolution. A soft, gentle, diffident man had metamorphosed into a determined, powerful boss. "Look here, Greta, I try *never* to use suspension as a weapon." She was, all at once, worried. "We are, after all, on the same side."

"Yes."

"I honestly believe that I'm a better judge of what's good for your career than *you* are." She began to reply, he silenced her with a look. "Your reaction to this fine material," he said, "is emotional, personal, and absolutely wrong-headed. Will you please come back and discuss it sensibly?"

"No," she said. "You will talk me into."

She turned to the door again and was about to open it when his powerful voice stopped her.

"Garbo!" he said firmly. She turned, startled at this uncommon form of address.

Thalberg said, "I was hit hard financially by the failure of the Bank of America last week." Garbo looked surprised. "And so were you, Greta."

She stiffened and in an attempt to brazen it out said, "How do you know that?"

"It's my business to know such things." He moved closer to her and put his hand on her shoulder in an avuncular way. "I intend to get out of the hole by doing my job. What do *you* intend to do?"

"I don't know," said Garbo, visibly frightened.

Thalberg took both her hands in both of his and said, "Greta, you're my greatest. You're an artist. I kiss the feet of talent. For God's sake, don't make me punish you. It's not my way, not my style. But if I'm forced to do it, I will. What do you say?"

On the screen at the Capitol Theatre in New York: the bar scene, directly preceding Garbo's now-classic entrance. The door opens and through the swinging doors she appears, carrying that straw suitcase. Applause, during which she moves across to a table in the foreground and sits. Johnny, the proprietor, approaches her.

Anna/Garbo: "Give me a visky—ginger ale on the side—and don't be stinchy, baby!"

Another spontaneous burst of applause from the amazed and delighted audience.

XXI

BEN WAS recreating the historic moment for Guy.

"One line," he said excitedly. "Think of it, that's all it took. One line—" He attempted an imitation of Garbo. " 'Give me a visky—ginger ale on the side—and don't be stinchy, baby.' And that was it, that did it. Home free. In! Still the biggest star in the business."

The telling had exhausted him and he sat breathing hard.

"But no such luck for Gilbert?" asked Guy.

Ben shook his head sadly. "No, not at all. It was soon after, he died. Imagine it. Thirty-seven years of age."

"What did he die of?" asked Guy.

"Of Hollywood," Ben replied. "He died of Hollywood. How can a man go from being the biggest to being nothing—and in the same place—with everybody looking at him? And you want to hear something crazy? The day after he died, houses all over the country played any of his pictures they could get ahold of."

It was no exaggeration. In New York, at the Rivoli, the enormous electric sign and the marquee proclaimed: JOHN GILBERT IN "THE BIG PARADE."

In Chicago, at the Oriental, the front of the house was plastered with posters from *The Merry Widow,* starring Mae Murray and John Gilbert.

In Plainfield, New Jersey, the audience applauded as the main title: JOHN GILBERT AS "CAMEO KIRBY" came on.

In a theatre in Paris, *A Woman of Affairs* was being shown with French subtitles.

The front of the largest movie palace in Tokyo, on the Ginza, displayed four twenty-four sheets of "LOVE," WITH GRETA GARBO AND JOHN GILBERT.

Back in Ben's study he handed Guy an 11 x 14 still framed in gold. "Here it is," he said. "That famous shot."

Guy examined it carefully. It was the still from *Flesh and the Devil.* That famous first kiss in which they created, for a time, a world of their own. The kiss that would not, could not, be interrupted. Guy handed back the still. Ben replaced it and said, "A tough business, tough. Maybe I've had the best of it." He paused in reverie and remembrance and regret. "Maybe I *will* sell."

Guy bounded from his seat and said, "That's *great,* Ben. Because I talked to Adani this afternoon and he's authorized me to offer—this will surprise you, I promise you—he's authorized me to offer—"

There was a discreet knock at the door.

"Yes," said Ben.

Chapman came in and said, "Dinner, sir."

Guy laughed ruefully and said, "Right on cue!"

"Good," said Ben. "I'm starving." He started out, Guy following.

245

In the sumptuous hall, they started for the dining room. Ben took Guy's arm and said, "All this remembering, it makes me hungry. You don't find it the same? Probably not—after all, a young man like you, you haven't got as much to remember. Well, you will—if you're lucky, like me—you will."

They disappeared into the dining room. The doors closed.

XXII

THE FARBER boys—Abe, eleven, and Gilbert, eight—returned from Jackie Coogan's birthday party exhausted.

Half an hour later, Abe threw up and made Gilbert laugh. Within twenty minutes, it was Abe's turn to laugh and Gilbert's to throw up.

When they had calmed down, Tessa asked them about the party.

"Fine," said Abe.

"He's got a boat," said Gilbert.

"What do you mean, a boat?"

"A boat in the pool, and you can get in it and row it around and everything."

"How come *we* haven't got a boat in *our* pool?" asked Abe.

"I don't know," Tessa replied. "Ask your father."

"Not I," said Gilbert.

"Why not?" his mother asked.

"Because what's the use? *He* never listens."

Abe giggled. "Tell 'er the joke you did on him," he urged. "Tell 'er!"

"No."

"Go ahead."

"What joke?" asked Tessa.

Gilbert blushed and shook his fist at his brother and said, "I'll get even with you, don't you worry!"

"What joke?" Tessa persisted.

"It was nothing. It was last Friday when he came home. So he came in our room and we were doing homework, and he said,

246

'How are you, boys?' And I said, 'The doctor says I've got scarlet fever.' And *he* said, 'Fine. That's fine.' And skidooed."

"That was the joke," said Abe.

"That was *no* joke," said Tessa. "You ought to be ashamed of yourselves, both of you."

"Not me!" cried Abe. "I didn't do it. *Nothing.*"

"*Any*thing," said Tessa.

"*Any*thing," he repeated.

"So what about the boat?" asked Gilbert craftily. "Do we get it or not?"

Tessa regarded her sons worriedly. "You know your trouble, you two?" she asked. "You're *spoiled.*"

Abe took a step toward her and yelled, "I am *not* spoiled!"

Gilbert held his ground and said, "I *like* to be spoiled."

"Me too!" chirped Abe, and when his mother looked at him with reproach, amended, "*I* too!"

Tessa broached the subject of the boat that evening during dinner, having learned that her sons were tenacious types and that she would have no peace until they had achieved their desire.

"Jackie Coogan has a boat in his pool," she said.

"You don't say," said Ben. He took a sip of his wine and went on. "It looks like *The Battle of Verdun* is going to make it after all. Irving scrapped the whole last half of the whole picture practically, but Vidor's new stuff is beautiful, and the preview looks like it was the sensation of the year."

"So can I get them a boat?" asked Tessa. "The same as Jackie's?"

"Sure, sure. This ham is excellent, dear. From Virginia?"

"How should I know?"

"You want to go to New York for the opening?"

"What opening?"

"*The Battle of Verdun* I've been telling you. They're going to have an orchestra in back of the screen and a special score to fit the picture—like maybe by Herbert Stothart—and they're even talking about what they call 'sound effects.'"

"What's that?"

"You know, guns and cannons and so forth. Airplane noises."

"What a mistake," said Tessa. "People go to the movies for peace and quiet."

Ben took another sip of his wine and asked, "What do they need a boat for?"

The boys enjoyed the boat daily for over a week. It was bigger than Jackie Coogan's, and they called him up to tell him so. He came over to see for himself.

They rowed about, all three.

"Yours could only take *two*," Gilbert taunted. "Three would *sink* it!"

"*Sink* it!" yelled Abe.

Jackie looked from one of his companions to the other, seriously, before asking, "You fellas ever played Shipwreck?"

"Shipwreck? What's that?" asked Gilbert.

"Oh, it's a swellelegant game."

"How do you play it?" asked Abe.

"Well," said Jackie slowly, "you smash up the boat and then you cling to the debris."

"All right," said Gilbert, "let's go over to *your* house and play it."

Jackie shook his head sadly. "No use," he said. "We played it at my house yesterday, so no boat."

He lied well. He was, after all, an actor.

Within minutes, the destruction of the boat had begun, and soon the pool was littered with debris. Clinging to it, however, proved to be dull sport, and the boys gave it up in favor of making competitive ice cream sodas and sundaes at the soda fountain in the pool house.

Later, the pool man reported the event to Tessa.

She sent for her sons.

"Jackie did it," said Gilbert.

"All by himself," Abe confirmed.

Tessa spoke sternly. "You're not to have him here ever again."

"No!" said Gilbert. "Because then we can't go *there*."

"To Jackie Coogan's," said Abe tragically.

"Oh," said Tessa, reflecting. "That's *right*. Well, let me talk to your father."

"You know what those sons of yours did today?" Tessa asked Ben as they prepared for bed that night.

"When you tell me so then I'll know."

"Guess."

"F'Chrissake, Tessa, I'm tired out. I'm half asleep, and you want me to play guessing games with you."

"*Half* asleep? You're *all* asleep. You're always all asleep!" she exploded.

Ben buttoned his pajama top slowly and said, "So how come I'm running a whole studio if I'm all asleep?"

"Around here, I mean!" she shouted. "Around here asleep. You're like some kind of a ghost—that's right, a *ghost!*—at least to me. You could be dead, even—for all the good I get out of you." She stalked out to her dressing room and returned a minute later. "All right, I'll tell you. You know that boat you bought them? Well, today they had over Jackie Coogan, and he smashed it to pieces. That's what they say. If you ask me, they helped him. They're such goddam liars, those little scamps."

"Ghost!" said Ben absently.

"What?"

"You said 'ghost' just now. My God, that's a *wonderful* idea! I remember it. Somebody made it. I can't remember who. *The Legend of Sleepy Hollow.* But maybe two, three reels only. It should be a full length. By Washington Irving, that's who."

"He made it?"

"No, no. He's already long dead. Somebody. What an idea for a remake! Thanks, Tessa. I'll tell everybody it's *your* idea."

"I've got other ideas too," she said. "Better. Only *you* don't seem to be interested."

"Tell me."

She looked at him, conveying hungry frustration.

"Oh," he said, understanding. "Listen, let's go someplace for the weekend. Santa Barbara. Someplace. Would you like that?"

She nodded, unable to speak.

A few minutes later, she asked, "What about the boat?"

"What boat?"

"The boys' boat, for the pool."

"I *bought* them a boat," said Ben. "Didn't I? What do you *want* from me? What do *they*?"

"They broke it, I told you. They smashed it."

"Yes," he said, "I heard about that. You told me."

"So?"

"So buy them *another* boat."

249

In bed, in the darkness, all was still for a time until Ben laughed.

"What?" asked Tessa.

He moved closer to her and embraced her.

"Ben," she said.

"And it's in the public *domain* yet," said Ben as he rolled over to go to sleep.

PART V

THE SCARLETT
O'HARA WAR

I

Guy had been talking to B.J. for half an hour, brilliantly, seductively. His subject, tax avoidance by means of stock transfer, was one on which he was as knowledgeable as anyone in America.

B.J. listened, apparently enthralled. When Guy sensed that he had made his point, he stopped. He had learned long ago the perils of overselling.

"I don't know," said Ben. "Things like that—they always look better on the paper than how they come out for real."

"How do you mean?"

"Like the time—after Buster left me and I went on alone with Farber Films. And doing fine. Wonderful days. One day, I get a call from L.B. Mayer himself. Imagine it. We hadn't spoke in I don't know how many years. He tells me let bygones be bygones and he's got a proposition. He comes over—that was already a sign—him to me not me to him. And he and Eddie Mannix and two big M-G-M lawyers, they sell me the idea they should take me over—Farber Films over. How the capital gains is in my favor and so on and so on. Something else. It was some kind of satisfaction, them taking me back in after throwing me out. Who knows? What can I tell you? I made a mistake. A greedy mistake. The money, yes—I got it. But it wasn't worth what it cost me. To lose my own independence. A mistake. Three years I suffered, but finally, in the end, thank God, I bought back my name. They kept a lot of the assets—properties and so on. But that day I went on my own again, I tell you that was the happiest day of my whole entire life. And that was the day I made up my mind—never again. Never partners, never mergers, never nothing. On my own. Independent. That's my favorite word that I know. So you see what Farber Films has gone through all these years. Up and down. In and out. Sickness and health and so forth. That's why it's like a child to me. One of my children. My favorite, is a fact."

"I appreciate all that, Ben. But this isn't capital gains I'm talking about. This is a stock transfer."

" 'The Last of the Mohicans,' " said B.J.

The non sequitur startled Guy.

"What?" he asked.

"Me," said B.J. "That's me. The Last of the Mohicans. They're all gone—all the rest of them."

He began to count, pinching a fingertip for each name. "Adolph Zukor, tiny but tough; Sam Goldwyn, he once called me up to tell me he wasn't speaking to me! B.P. Schulberg, Carl Laemmle, L.B. Mayer, Jack Warner, Harry Cohn, David O. Selznick. Selznick, now *there* was a *giant!* Well, they were *all* giants. Some of them little giants, some of them big giants. Selznick, he was younger than the rest of us. It was his father, Lewis J., was in our bunch. He went broke and died from it. But David took his father's place real good—and sometimes real bad. Still and all, listen, the way he handled that *Gone With the Wind?* If he never did one other thing, that would give him a place in the history. . . . One day, I remember, he invited me to have lunch with him, so I knew it was something big. He wouldn't come to my place. He didn't have the nerve to ask me to come to his, so it was settled to go to The Vendome on Sunset, very big in those days, very high class. And even though I knew there was going to be some problem, some difficulty, I looked forward, because David—he was never boring. Listen, none of those fellows were, the ones I just told you, at least not to each other. You know why? Because we all had this one big thing in common. We all loved the movies and *making* movies. That was our life, and we loved our life. . . . Well, I got there first, right on time. In fact, five minutes early.

I've got plenty of faults, but in my whole life I've never been late. Not for an appointment or a train or a plane or a theatre. Ten minutes late, he comes in. David. While we're shaking hands, he looks around the room and says, 'Sit here, Ben. Do you mind? I'll sit there. Maybe he won't see me.'

" 'Who?'

" 'Myron.'

" 'Your brother?'

" 'Yes.'

"Now why a man wouldn't want to see his own brother, don't ask me. But he didn't. His brother, Myron, was at that time the biggest agent in the whole business. So he orders a drink, David, a double scotch. I was having a ginger ale, a single. Drinking in the middle of the day, I never could do it. So David asks me about Willa and the boys, and Willa's sister, Oriana. You see, there was a time there he used to go out with Oriana, and we thought it might develop serious. But something happened. I don't know what, and a little later he married Mayer's daughter, Irene. . . . Anyhow, he finishes his drink and we order, and he asks for the wine list, and he picks out something expensive, and finally he looks at me like he is in some kind of a pain, and he says, 'Ben, we're in terrible trouble.'

" '*We* are?' I ask him.

" 'Yes.'

" 'What is it?'

"And he looks at me very stern, and he says, 'You've got an actor, and I want him.'

"I laughed."

II

B.J. LAUGHED The sheer audacity of the approach delighted him. "I love it how you use words, David."

"That's my business—words."

"You're a smarter talker even than your father, and believe me, he was some talker."

"He was more than a talker, ol' boy. He was the most creative producer this business has ever seen. He failed because he had a soft heart, and when the bastards found it out, they all ate him alive. Not you, Ben. I don't mean you."

"Thank you. I know what you mean, though. But Lewis J. Selznick would've said, '*You've* got an actor, and *I* need him.' You said *want* him. What a difference!"

"What about it, B.J.? Are you going to make it hard for me? How hard?"

"Are we talking about Gable?"

"We are."

"For Rhett Butler in *Gone With the Wind?*"

"Exactly."

"It's a fine role, David, almost surefire, but there are problems."

"Many?"

"Well, let's see. One, we never—never in the history of the company have we loaned out Gable. He's our biggest. They don't call him 'The King' for nothing. It's not that he's The King around the studio. He's The King around the box office."

"I don't need him for box office," said Selznick. "My *property* is all the box office *I* need. I need him for his talent and personality and presence."

"It would be a perfect piece of casting, David. I can see that."

They ate in silence for a time, relishing their food.

"There's one thing I like about you, David. You're a knife and fork man, like me."

"When it's good," said Selznick. "Like here."

"Yes."

"So that's the first problem, that you've never loaned him out before? That's not a problem. People who're afraid of doing anything for the first time are doomed."

B.J. thought for a moment and said, "You're perfectly right. The next problem is a little more serious. Something for nothing."

"Quid pro quo?"

"If you want to say it fancy—like a lawyer—*yes.*"

"What if I gave you the distribution?"

"You would?" asked B.J.

"I said *what if?*"

"Interesting," said B.J. "Interesting."

Selznick laughed.

"What?" asked B.J.

"I can just hear your brain clicking away. You're figuring,

'Gable's worth three, four hundred thousand a picture, and what's the distribution worth?' "

"Exactly," said B.J. "You don't think that's a legitimate calculation?"

"I do. Of course, I do. And you'll be way ahead—*way* ahead."

"If you *really* thought that, David, you wouldn't be offering it."

"I do, Ben. This is going to be the greatest motion picture of all time."

"You say that every time . . . and so do we all."

"This time I mean it. I feel it in my bones."

"There's another question, though."

"Go ahead."

"Your subject matter, David. It worries me because—"

"Don't you think I ?"

"Wait a second!" said B.J. sharply. "I haven't finished."

"Sorry."

"I was saying it worries me, because the Civil War is tough to sell. Since *Birth of a Nation* every single try has failed. And I doubt you could put *that* one over today. In its own time it had other things going for it. The first real long picture, and spectacle, and so on."

"I know all that," said David impatiently. "When you deal with a classic, it's all the rules out the window. And this is the greatest American novel of all time."

"But the point of view, David. Who are you for? Which side?"

"I'm on the *story's* side."

"That's just stalling, David. We've got a divided country, still. You know that. So if it's pro-North, you'll get killed in the South, and the other way around."

"Leave it to me," said Selznick.

"And what about the girl? What's her name—?"

"Come on, Ben. Don't play games. You know her name perfectly well."

"I did, but I forgot."

"Think."

"Yes. Something like Scarface."

"That's right," said Selznick. "Scarface O'Hara!" He slapped the table and howled. "That's worthy of Goldwyn."

"You want an advice?" said B.J. "Go around and say Sam said it, and it'll be all over the country in a week. Good publicity."

"No, no," said Selznick. "I couldn't do that to Sam. I *like* Sam."

257

(Later that day, David Selznick told his staff that Sam Goldwyn had phoned and asked, "Who've you got for Scarface O'Hara?" The line was, indeed, repeated throughout the country.)

"So, who are you thinking?" asked B.J.

"I'm thinking of everyone and anyone, and so are they. My phone never stops. They call me themselves, some of them, or their agents, or husbands, or beaux, or girl friends, or mothers, or fathers. They've all checked in, one way or another. Bette Davis, Hepburn, Jean Arthur, Lana Turner, Shearer, Maggie Sullavan, Lombard. Charlie's on me about Paulette Goddard. Tallulah phones every hour on the hour."

"Joan Crawford?" B.J. suggested.

"Not yet, but she will."

"She would be fine. Maybe the best. Also, if you took her, it might be easier for me to deliver Gable."

There was a pause.

B.J. laughed. "Now I hear yours clicking," he said.

"I can't give Gable casting approval in writing," said David, "but *you* know and *I* know that he's got to have it to make the combination work."

"Careful. You give him the say, and he'll turn down everybody but Lombard. I understand that's very serious."

"Oh, I doubt it," said David. "She's too ballsy for him."

"Just the same."

"Anyway, before I make *that* decision, I've got a scheme. I'm going to launch the greatest talent search in the history of show business. We're going to scour this country from border to border and coast to coast. We're going to look in every bush and behind every tree and under every rock. We're going to cover schools and stores, factories and farms, we're going to find Scarlett O'Hara. We know she's out there somewhere."

"You don't really *mean* that, David, do you?"

Another sip, a wink. "Of course not, but isn't it *sensational?*"

B.J. shook his head in admiration. "You're some showman, kid. If he was alive, your father would be proud of you."

"He *is*, Ben! He *is*," said a new, gruff voice.

Ben shuddered. All at once he was aware of a large florid man leaning over the table and laughing. It took him a moment to recognize Myron Selznick, who said, "Hey, chaps, want to hear a great joke I just made?"

258

"No," said David. "This is business, Myron."

"It got a hell of a laugh at my table. Didn't you hear it?"

"No," said B.J.

"Well, I'm lunching with Walter Wanger and Scott Fitzgerald and Sheila and Merle and Ronnie Colman. How's that for a bugger's muddle? Anyway, Walter looked over here at you two and he said, 'I'll bet nothing good comes of *that* meeting.' And I said, 'No, but I'll bet it'll make a pisspot full of money!' "

He doubled up with raucous, inebriated laughter, upsetting David's wineglass.

"Jesus, Myron," he said. "Will you calm down?"

"Oh, did you say sit down? Sure, but I've only got a minute."

He took a chair from an adjoining table and sat down. The waiter came over.

"Courvoisier and soda," said Myron.

"Yes, sir."

"So what do you say, Ben?" asked Myron. "You going to give him Gable? What's *he* going to give *you?*"

"I know what I'm going to give *you,* you pain in the ass," said David to his brother. "A bust in the mouth."

B.J. spoke quickly. "This is one case, Myron, where I really think you should mind your own business. We're in the midst of a very serious negotiation here."

"What you pirates seem to forget," said Myron, "sitting here trying to figure out ways to screw each other, is that I *represent* Mr. Clark Gable and he doesn't make a move without me."

"Go 'way, Myron," said David.

Myron addressed himself to B.J. "My brother's problem is that Scarletts he's got coming out of his ears. Scarletts are a dime a dozen. I've got four clients—*four*—who can handle it to perfection, but there's only one Red Butler, and his name is Clark Gable."

Selznick laughed. "No, his name is *Rhett* Butler."

"What?"

"Rhett, not Red, you ignoramus."

"Well, I never read the goddam book. I mean I never *rhett* the goddam—" He was in hysterics again.

Selznick said, "Ben, how do we get rid of this pest? Any ideas?"

"Sign Gable and Lombard and I'll go," said Myron.

"There are many actors who could handle it," said Selznick.

"Who?" asked Myron challengingly.

"Bill Powell made a brilliant test."

"Oh? So what are you sitting here kiss-assing Farber for?"

"Errol Flynn would be brilliant."

"Sure, with a fifteen-year-old Scarlett."

"Freddie March."

"How about Freddie Bartholomew?"

The waiter brought the brandy and soda.

"Mr. Selznick will have that at his own table," said David.

Myron rose, unsteadily. "Goddam right he will," he said. "It's a damned sight jollier than *this* table." He took a step and stumbled. The waiter steadied him.

"Thanks," he said. "Remind me to remember you in my will. Codicil." He turned to his brother. "I'm in no condition today, David, but remind me to kick the shit out of you tomorrow."

He was gone.

"I'm sorry, Ben. I apologize."

"What's it got to do with you?"

Selznick ordered a Napoleon and coffee.

"Just coffee for me," said B.J.

"When can I know, Ben?"

"Give me time. So many details. Terms, dates, extensions. Let me talk to the boys. Also, I got to feel out Clark. Who knows? Actors are funny. What if he says no?"

"If he says no, I don't want him," said Selznick.

On the following Sunday, Myron Selznick and Clark Gable went duck hunting on the outskirts of Gable's ranch in the Encino Valley. They sat in a blind, drinking beer. The world seemed far, far away.

"I haven't finished it yet," said Gable. "It's a *hell* of a long book!"

"That's just the point. If he's only going to do some of it, *which* some of it? If I know David—and I do—he'll lean on the romance, on the sex stuff."

They each took a shot and missed.

"Trouble is," said Gable, "with Cukor directing, it's bound to turn out a woman's picture."

"Not with *you* in it, Bozo."

"And by the way, who *is* the woman?"

"Nobody yet."

"I'd like to know."

"All in good time. If this thing hots up, I'll get you approvals. I'll get you any damned thing you want. I'll get you a night with Irene. This guy's desperate."

"What about Carole?"

"I can fix that, too, but give me a break, will you? One thing at a time?"

Another pair of shots. Nothing.

"She'll be sensational," said Gable. "She's got it all. The looks, the craftiness, the sex, the wickedness, and the youth. That's one of the main things. The youth. Jesus, some of the ones I've heard mentioned—Shearer, Bankhead, Hepburn. They're too old! They're in their *thirties*."

"Goddam, Clark. You really are a lummox. Do you know how lucky you are to have me to do your thinking for you? Where do you get all that hot information?"

"In the papers," said Gable doggedly. "I read papers."

"What the hell do the papers know out here? They know what we tell them, that's all. Don't you see what that glandular brother of mine is doing? He's building the bloody thing into a *cause*. He's getting everybody involved emotionally. He's turning it into a goddam horse race. Now stop bellyaching, and let me go in there and make the deal of a lifetime for you. We've got them by the balls. So don't let go."

"Well—" said Gable, frowning.

"Here's the strategy. You tell B.J. you don't want to play the part."

"I don't?"

"No, not yet."

"I don't get it."

"You don't have to. *I* get it."

Gable, irritated, took two more shots. A dead duck fluttered to the ground. He grinned happily and said, "Hey, see that?"

Myron took another shot, and missed.

At David's home, out by the pool, the make-or-break meeting was under way. Myron, carefully sober, and B.J., tense, were listening to David. "And the day I start giving approvals, any kinds of approvals, to anyone—actors, directors, Schencks, anyone—that's the day I leave this business and go to Ischia or Majorca and write great novels, which is what I ought to be doing anyway."

"Where's Ischia?" asked B.J. absently.

"Don't get hot about nothing, David. The guy wants to know who his leading lady is."

David was on his feet. "When the fucking time comes," he shouted, "I'll *tell* him! I promise you, and I promise him, I won't keep it a secret until the picture's finished. I'll tell him. Right now, it's nobody's business but my own. Cukor doesn't know. Jesus, *Irene* doesn't know."

B.J. caught the implications in the outburst. "But you *do* know, David?"

Instead of replying, David dove into the pool, swam its length furiously, and returned. He leaped out and stood, dripping and triumphant. "Of course I know. What do you take me for?"

"Would you tell us—in confidence?" asked Ben.

"No."

"Would you tell *me?*" asked Myron. "In private?"

"*Especially* not you," said David. "I'd sooner tell that gardener."

"But what's the point of all this mystery, Dave?"

"The point is, my dear man, that I'm in charge and no one else. And I'm going to run this show my own way. So here it is. As to the part of Scarlett O'Hara in the David O. Selznick production of *Gone With the Wind,* the chosen actress will be announced at the appropriate time and not before. As to the role of Rhett Butler, it has been offered to Clark Gable. If he accepts, the film will be released by the company to which he is presently under contract. I thank you."

"Let me ask you, David," said B.J. "Whoever she is, does *she* know?"

"She does *not* know. No."

"One more question."

"Yes?"

"A big star? Will there be billing problems?"

"There will be no billing problems."

"But, David, if you've made up your mind, why are you making ten, twelve tests a day, every day?"

"Because I want to."

Myron rose. "There's only one man in the world knows you, David. Really knows you, and that's me. You remember the apartment on Eighty-sixth Street in New York? We slept in the same bed for four years. I know you, David. The good and the bad. I know about your education and what you're good at. I've been through all your love affairs and helped you with your troubles."

262

"Come on, come on," said David. "What's the point?"

"The point is, my beloved brother, that you're as full of shit as a Christmas turkey."

It would be told otherwise when it was told, but the fact is that David swung first. Myron must have been right about knowing him, since he easily anticipated the pass and sidestepped it neatly. The force of David's swing turned him around completely. Myron stepped in and with both strong palms on David's back, shoved him forcefully in the direction of the pool. Off balance, David felt himself going in. On the way, he grasped at Myron's knees, caught them, and dragged Myron, fully clothed, in with him. They sank, wrestling, then surfaced, laughing so hard that it took them five minutes to get out of the pool.

When, after several more minutes, they had calmed down and David had retrieved Myron's eyeglasses for him, and the brothers had caught their breath, B.J. got up, looked at them, and said, "So what do you say, gentlemen? Have we got a deal?"

This set them off again, and B.J. left without getting an answer to his question.

III

EARLY IN life, Lewis J. Selznick had begun to inculcate his sons with certain basic rules for living. "Read!" was one of his first orders. To that end, he brought books home daily—singly and in sets. Soon there was a library. David read *David Copperfield, Huckleberry Finn, Little Women, A Tale of Two Cities, Anna Karenina, The Adventures of Tom Sawyer, Little Lord Fauntleroy, The Prisoner of Zenda.* In years to come he would make movies of them all.

Once Lewis J. Selznick had said to his sons, "And whatever else you do or don't do, boys, you see to it that you find one hour in every day for *thinking*. It may be hard sometimes, but do it. Morning or afternoon or evening. No compromise. Don't think you can do it out walking or later on, when you drive—you can't. Or with music playing. Find a spot, close the doors, sit down in a chair or on the floor, and *think*. Think about what you're doing and about what you *should* be doing. Think audaciously. Plan. Make an inventory of your friends and of your enemies. See if you can find a way to turn your enemies into friends. Consider your options and your choices. Are you doing what you want to do or what *others* want you to do? Are you doing it to impress or to express? Think! Your opinions. Are they your own based on your own knowledge and experience and instincts or are they secondhand? Something you heard somewhere? Read somewhere? Do you believe what you believe, or what you *think* you should believe? I want you to develop into original thinkers. That could mean that sometimes you won't agree. That's fine. Maybe you'll even fight, you two. That's fine, too, so long as it's about something important. But the main thing is not to deviate from the plan. The main thing is to make it a habit. When you're a little older, I want you to make friends with William James on the subject. He teaches that in the making or breaking of a habit the thing to beware of is the *single exception*. After a while, you can maybe learn to think outdoors or in some special private place. That may change. But what must *not* change is that hour. Not forty-five minutes and not two hours, but an hour. You understand?"

"Yes, Pa," replied Myron, aged thirteen.

"Sure, Pa," said the eleven-year-old David.

They shook hands solemnly all around.

David put in his first hour of thinking on the very same day, sitting up, fully clothed, in the bathtub of the bathroom of the seldom used guest room, and he had done his hour almost without exception through the years.

Myron, conversely, thought it nonsense from the start (as he did most of his father's ideas) and hectored David about it, without cease.

"Try it," said David. "Why don't you try it before dismissing it?"

"I do my thinking while I'm screwing," said Myron. "That comes to about an hour a day. Don't bother me, will you?"

David became attached to the ritual in a quasi-religious way, and, in fact, passed it on to his own sons when the time came.

In the past year he had discovered, quite by accident, an ideal thinking place. It was not more than a ten-minute drive from his home on Summit Drive, but it might have been deep in the wilds of New Hampshire.

High above Beverly Hills there is a reservoir, surrounded by woods and glades. Looking for a lost dog one Sunday morning,

David had come upon this area. He never did find the dog, but he did find this singular retreat, and returned to it often. It took some exploration to find a place within the place: a small dry cave overlooking the calm water. David had appropriated the spot as his own, feeling what Peary or Ponce de Leon might have felt at the moment of discovery. It was here that he came to think, sometimes stopping on his way to the studio, other times on his way home. In times of crisis, he would often leave his office and make his way to the cave. It was here that many of his ambitious projects were conceived, some of his momentous decisions reached, a few of his grandiose plans abandoned.

Today he sat in the cave, thinking hard on the subject of his most recent meeting with Ben Farber. He would get Gable, felt confident on *this* score. Farber was no fool. The fact that he had not turned down the idea out of hand was a good sign. "Talk to the boys," was no more than a euphemistic stall for time. The boys would do as Farber recommended. Now then, with Gable, who? Chemistry! Chemistry—that ineffable, indefinable combination of qualities that made one pair electrifying and another not. Should he run every Gable picture and see with whom it worked and with whom not? No. This time out, he wanted a fresh brand-new team, one that had never been seen together. That ruled out Lombard. Who else? Shearer. They had made *A Free Soul* together and most successfully. Jean Harlow? Out. Not right, anyway. Good, but common. Scarlett has to have class. Otherwise the key seduction scene loses power. Kate? Yes, definitely. Sullavan? Maybe. Bette? Not bad. Goddard? Possible. Jean Arthur? Cute, not beautiful; petulant, not passionate. He closed his eyes and pictured each one of them with Clark Gable, embracing, kissing, making love. Ben Hecht had once said, "Chemistry—there's only one way to test it. Would you like to see them actually doing it or not? I mean *really* doing it? That's how you can tell. The only way."

David closed his eyes and gave it this test until it began to unnerve him. He opened his eyes and saw Joan Crawford standing there before him. Her hair was braided and ribboned in the Southern manner. She wore a long white cotton dress buttoned down the front and in her right hand carried a champagne bucket filled with ice and cradling a bottle of champagne; in her other hand, two champagne glasses. David was visibly irritated.

265

"What the hell're you doing around—?"

"Don't be mad, David. Relax. Look, can you open this? It's one thing I've never learned to do."

She fell to her knees, charmingly, and pushed the bucket toward him. Resigned to the moment, he began to prepare the bottle for uncorking.

"What the hell am I doing here?" she said. "Is that what you asked? I want five minutes with you. Without agents or—"

He popped the cork into the air. She held out the glasses. He poured. They sipped.

Thirty-five minutes later, she was saying, "And besides which, for God's sake, they've *seen* Davis in that part when she did *Jezebel*. So what's she going to do that's new? She would be the *worst* idea."

"So far they're *all* the worst idea, according to you," said David, smiling. "Now tell me the *best* idea."

"I think," said Joan Crawford, "that it comes down to three. Paulette Goddard, Tallulah Bankhead, or Joan Crawford."

"In that order?" asked David, wryly.

"Not necessarily," said Joan. "Goddard's got the fire and the youth and the looks. The acting's *her* weak spot. Sure, George could help her, but enough? I don't know . . . Tallulah's good. Her big thing, of course, is the Southern. I mean, after all, she *is* Southern. You can't take that away from her."

"No, you can't," said David, grinning.

"But she's a *stage* actress. She's never made it on the screen, and who knows if she ever will?"

"So that leaves who?"

"The one it was written for. Me."

"It was?"

"I mean, she didn't know she was writing it for me, but she was."

"I see."

"That's what I was born for, to play Scarlett O'Hara."

"Is that why they named you Lucille Le Sueur?"

She poured the last of the wine and they finished it slowly. David studied the remarkable, classically photogenic face before him. Those eyes. The most sensual mouth ever seen on the screen.

"What're you thinking?" she asked.

"I'm thinking," David replied, "would I like to see you and Clark Gable in action. In the hay."

"Well," she said, "I know *I* would."

They laughed together. And as they did, they knew what the next hour would bring.

"There's only one worry," said David.

"What's that, darling?"

"The Southern. I think the public is going to demand an authentic Southerner."

Joan Crawford became another girl as she softened and said, in a mellifluously accurate, upper-class Georgia accent, "Why, don' y'all trouble yo little haid 'bout that, Mister Man. Ah was born 'n' raised right here on Peachtree Street."

David looked at her, astonished. He had done a thorough, scholarly job of research on Southern accents and could by this time distinguish not only the real from the phony but Tennessee from Georgia from Alabama.

"Jesus Christ, Joan," he said. "That is *great!*"

"Sho 'nuf, honey," she said. "This is Geohgia y'all hearin'. That Bankhead pussun, why, she's Alabama—where the white trash come from."

"How'd you *get* that?" asked David, genuinely interested.

Joan became Joan again. Tough, pragmatic.

"How the hell do you think, you jerk? By working on it. By sweat, and blood, by going to Atlanta, Georgia, and working ten hours a day for two weeks with three coaches, that's how!"

"Well, I'll be a son-of-a-bitch," said David. "I wouldn't have thought it possible. I've always thought Shaw was full of banana oil with that *Pygmalion.* I mean, the guy picks up a Cockney girl and turns her into somebody who passes for a blueblood. Christ, talk about suspension of disbelief! Even when I've seen it well done, I thought it was a mindless little fairy tale. But *you've done* it!"

"*Now* what? Gable. Will *he* say yes?"

"He's got nothing to say."

"But you want to keep him happy, don't you?"

"Of course."

"All right, leave him to me."

"Watch your step, Joanie. That Lombard is tough."

"Carole? I love her. I adore her. She's the greatest. Do you know what she said to me? She said she wouldn't play it if it was offered to her."

"She did?"

"In front of Clark she said it."

"But why not?"

IV

"BECAUSE I don't want the fucking responsibility," said Carole.

"*Every* part's a responsibility these days, Carole," said Ben Farber. "With the way costs are mounting up."

They were playing croquet; she and Clark Gable, Gilbert Farber and his bubbly wife, Agnes; Charlie Chaplin and Paulette Goddard, Abraham Farber and Lana Turner, David O. Selznick and Joan Crawford, Ben Farber and Tallulah Bankhead, recently arrived in Beverly Hills and staying with the Farbers.

Croquet at the Farbers' was a Sunday tradition in Beverly Hills circa 1938. Food and drink were served all day long and matches were played on three separate lawns.

As this match proceeded, various combinations of players found themselves in conversational proximity; playing or coaching, or watching and waiting.

Carole continued. "Not like this one, sweetie," she said. "It's gotten all out of hand, too big. Those little shoes are impossible to fill. I've got a hunch the first Scarlett isn't going to be the last. Go ahead, shoot."

Ben's attention returned to the game. He did not participate in many sports, but croquet was a passion, and across the years, with the help of lessons, he had become an adept.

Gable, Bankhead, Lombard. Tallulah was on her fifth mint julep. "Goddamn, they get worse, these bloody juleps."

"Why don't you switch to Bloody Marys?" suggested Carole.

The joke cracked Tallulah up, and she laughed raucously. "Jesus, I may have to. Who've they got mixing these things out there—a rabbi?"

Selznick and Crawford. "Did you hear that?" she asked.

"Hear what?"

"That crack. That anti-Semitic crack?"

"That's not anti-Semitic," said David. "They *have* got a rabbi doing the mint juleps."

Joan hit him with her mallet and they laughed.

Goddard and Chaplin. "And what did *he* say?" she asked.

"Well, you know David. Cagey, crafty, noncommittal, devious."

"God, he sounds just like *you.*"

"Right now," said Charlie, "I think our only trouble is that Bankhead woman."

"No, no. She's too old."

"That's what *you* think. What matters is what *he* thinks."

"He'll think what somebody smart tells him to think. He's got no mind of his own. He knows you're smarter than he is and richer and more powerful. Work on him."

"I am, dear. I am."

"*I* don't see it. All I see is *you* working on *me.*"

Charlie hit his ball with such force that it went right off the lawn. He went after it, fuming.

Farber and Crawford. "But is it definite? Gable?"

"Why don't you ask *him,* Joan?"

"What makes you think he'd tell me?"

"What makes you think *I* will?"

"Because you love me."

"I do?"

"Of course, didn't you know?"

"Why, no. I thought I loved my wife."

"Don't tell me you're one of those *little* men. Big men can handle two at a time, or three, or four."

"My goodness, and you know some like that?"

She looked around. "There are three right on this lawn," she said.

Ben scanned the area. "Yes," he said, "I see them."

"So how about it, Ben? Tell me. The truth. Have I got a chance?"

"You've *all* got a chance until he makes up his mind definite."

"Who's all, Ben? Who's in the running? You can tell me *that,* can't you?"

"For that, you have to get right inside of his head."

"All right, I will."

Tallulah Bankhead and Paulette Goddard. "He's begging Charlie for me, but you know Charlie."

"No, I don't, but I'd like to. Is he any good?"

"Ask Mildred Harris."

"So old Chinchilla Head wants *you*, does he?"

"But Charlie's got other plans for me. They say it looks like Crawford."

Tallulah emitted her celebrated baritone guffaw. "Scarlett O'Hara, the well-known Charleston dancer."

Paulette joined her in hilarity. "That's rich, Tallu, that's really rich."

Tallulah grabbed Paulette's upper arm and drew her close. "So he wants you."

"Yes," said Paulette defiantly.

"But Crawford's got it."

"So they say."

"Well, then, you silly little tit bouncer, tell me something."

"What?"

"Why the God damn hell did he send for *me?*"

"He did?"

"And all expenses for me and my maid and the car, and a chauffeur, and a personal wardrobe being made, and my own makeup man from New York, and all the time I want, and Gable's going to test with me. Have you got the question?"

"Yes," said Paulette, pale.

"And what's the answer, you pot?"

"Leave me alone," said Paulette, pulling away.

Farber and Selznick. "I don't know, Ben. Charlie's offered me a stupendous United Artists release and personal cooperation and a piece of his new picture."

"But Paulette Goddard," said Ben.

"Yes, and no Gable. I'm thinking of Bogart. Bogart and Goddard. I like the chemistry."

"You're not thinking of Bogart and Goddard."

"I'm not?"

"No," said Ben. "You're thinking of Gable and how to screw Ben Farber."

V

THE STUDIOS at station KNX. Jimmy Fidler, the popular Hollywood columnist, is on the air, spouting breathlessly.

"And from where *I* sit, it looks like the great search for Scarlett is over before it begins. I have it on the highest, confidential authority, and I am sworn to secrecy as to the source and so my lips are sealed, but here it is, ladies and gentlemen. And *don't* forget where you heard it first. Scarlett O'Hara, the most coveted role in the history of the movies, will be played by none other than the lovely—*Miss Joan Crawford.* The deal has been set, signed, sealed, and delivered. And—"

Paulette Goddard, her nightclothes flying behind her, rushed through the upper hall of the Chaplin house, down the stairs, through the sitting room, into the garden, past the pool and tennis court to Charlie's cottage. As Paulette approached the cottage, Charlie could be seen acting a part. He was in there with an assistant, Robert Florey, and a secretary. Paulette burst in and screamed, "Crawford! It's Crawford! Signed, sealed, and everything!"

Charlie, caught in mid-gesture, held his pose and asked, "Who says so?"

Paulette collapsed in tears onto a sofa as she cried, "Fidler! Jimmy Fidler! On the radio. He said it on the highest authority."

Charlie, still in his pose, said, "Jimmy Fidler is a horsecock. Now get the hell out of here. I'm working."

"But he said—"

"I'm *WORKING!*"

One would not have thought it possible for a man as small as Chaplin to produce, unamplified, the volume of the explosion that filled the room, startling the secretary, causing Florey to drop his glass, and driving Paulette from the premises as though wafted out on the shattering sound waves. Charlie picked up the

271

scene precisely from where he had left off. It was the ballet-with-the-globe number from *The Great Dictator*.

The studios at radio station KLAC Los Angeles. The moon-faced bulk whose head is stuffed with nothing but gossip, innuendo, rumor, and handout is on the air. She is reading from 4 x 6 cards with large print. "This is Louella Parsons, and here is my first exclusive. Never mind what you have heard, are hearing, and may be hearing in the next few days, weeks, or months. David Oliver Selznick, *your secret is out!* A darling little birdie has told me all, and I must say, David, I *congratulate* you."

She drops the top card to the floor, and continues from the text. "After a full week of the most comprehensive screen-testing in the history of our town, David and his entire staff have agreed that Scarlett is going to be brought to life by the Scarlett of her own time, a true daughter of the solid South."

She drops the card and goes on to the next. "Yes, you have guessed it. None other than the lovely *Miss Tallulah Bankhead!* You can read all the details of this great exclusive tomorrow morning in my column in all editions of *The Los*—" She drops the card before continuing. "—*Angeles Examiner.* . . . My next exclusive—"

The next morning, David routinely phoned Joan.

"Hello, sweet," he said.

"You son-of-a-bitch! You fat, four-eyed, no good, lying, filthy prick!"

David laughed and asked, "What *is* all this?"

"*Bankhead*, you bastard. That lard-assed piece of cornpone. Her over me? *ME!!*"

"Who says?" asked David.

"You didn't hear Parsons tonight? Is *that* what you're pretending?"

"Parsons? Now, really, Joan. Do I look to you like a man who has time to listen to all that ladled crap? What'd she say?"

"You can read it in her column tomorrow morning."

"Why should I? I'm only interested in what she writes about me or my studio, and she never writes anything we don't give her. Come on, Joan, you've been around. You know the game."

"She got it from *somebody* at your place."

"Of course, you half-wit, she got it from *me*."

Joan was stunned, but suspicious. "It isn't true?"

"Of course not."

She softened, turning back into Miss Jekyll from Miss Hyde. "But how do you dare? I mean, what happens when she finds out?"

"Oh, I changed my mind. Circumstances beyond my control. Artistic differences. And in the end, who cares? There's nothing as old as yesterday's newspaperwoman."

"Tell me the truth," she said.

"You *know* the truth."

"Me? Is it me?"

Time stood still. "Say it," she said, in a choked voice. "Let me hear you *say* it."

"It's you," he said.

She began to weep tears of relief, but through them, managed to say, "But, Jesus, if you'd lie to Louella Parsons, why wouldn't you lie to me? Changed your mind. Circumstances beyond. All that. How do I know?"

"How do you know I may not die in the next ten minutes?"

"Don't," she said, and stopped crying.

Hedda Hopper on the air. "Tallulah," she said, "you can go home now. I hear you have a lovely apartment in New York and a house in the country, and they're going to get a lot of use soon. Oh, yes, Joan. David meant well, but in the end he couldn't resist the blandishments of the greatest blandisher of them all—Mr. Charlie Chaplin himself. So, it's you, Paulette, as if you didn't know. And dear listeners, don't be surprised if the next announcement isn't Charlie, oh—excuse me—isn't *Charles* Chaplin as Rhett Butler!"

Early the next morning, Tallulah, still in evening clothes, stormed into Hedda Hopper's office, smashed a chair, threw everything off the top of the desk, got out a siphon of soda and symbolically pissed all over the place and everyone in it. The police were called, but when they arrived, she had another siphon ready for *them*.

Half an hour later, Hedda, her staff, one of the policemen, and Tallulah were sitting around having coffee and Danish, telling stories of similar escapades in the past.

After due consideration and a talk between Hedda and her

lawyer, Jerry Geisler, it was decided to hush up the whole affair. What the hell. Fun's fun.

VI

It had taken Russell Birdwell, David Selznick's masterful press agent, three weeks to set up this press conference. It was held on Stage 5 of The Selznick International Studios. A massive buffet lunch was served, the menu firmly Southern: gumbo soup, fried chicken, reed birds, sugar-cured ham, yams, collard greens, prawns, sugar cane, pecan pie, watermelon. A bar serving only bourbon in all forms, mint juleps, Southern Comfort, and corn likker. The stage had been decorated under the supervision of William Cameron Menzies to resemble a large and lovely Georgia garden, honeysuckle bushes and roses, wisteria trees, porches, columns—a notable success.

Abraham Farber hovered about, presumably because he was Menzies's agent; actually because he made it his business never to miss a Hollywood party of any kind.

Birdwell had imported the caterers, the maître d', the bartenders, and the complete serving personnel from Atlanta. Predominantly black, they wore the traditional white linen jackets and white gloves, and waited on the guests with a deference known only to the hospitable South.

Every invited guest was presented with a copy of *Gone With the Wind* personally inscribed by Margaret Mitchell. A blowup of the book jacket, twenty-four-sheet size, hung behind the platform from which the announcements were to be made. Russell Birdwell moved about inside the mass of trade-paper representatives, newspaper and magazine writers, radio people, and the motley horde known vaguely, but importantly, as the Hollywood foreign press corps.

He made careful note of all who had not received a copy of the book and promised that it would be forthcoming soon. It was.

No one managed these affairs better than Birdwell. He observed the action of the crowd, and when he decided that the appropriate temperature had been reached, he sought out David.

"Let's go," he said.

Selznick glanced at his wristwatch. "You think? How about waiting a—?"

"Right now," said Birdwell. "Don't coach me."

He rounded up Ben Farber, Cukor, Menzies, Sidney Howard, who was writing the screenplay, Kay Brown, the story editor, and Jock Whitney, the money. He whispered a few secret instructions to his assistants and sent them scurrying.

The assembled group, led by Birdwell, mounted the platform and took preassigned seats. There were three chairs significantly vacant. Scattered, tentative applause, and the hum of discreet murmuring as the guests helped each other in identifying the people seated on the platform. Birdwell went at once to the microphone, praying that it would work. Amplification was new, and he had never before used it in these circumstances. He waited for silence, complete silence, then said, "Ladies and gentlemen, your host—Mr. David O. Selznick."

Selznick lumbered to the platform, slowly and humbly, as Birdwell had directed him: "Give the applause a chance to mount." It did, and reached a deafening crescendo as David took his place before the microphone. This was the signal for the sixteen people, strategically spotted, to rise. In twenty seconds, the whole audience was on its feet. David stood quietly, nodding.

Ben leaned over to Jock Whitney and said, "Isn't this great? And he hasn't *done* it yet. This is just for telling them he's *gonna* do it."

"Birdwell," said Whitney.

Silence.

Selznick began. "My friends!" Why not? If it was good enough for Roosevelt, it was good enough for him. "An ancient sage once observed that in a journey of a thousand miles, what matters most is the first step. My vast and loyal army of coworkers are about to embark with me on the single most important work of our individual and collective lives. We have set ourselves a mutually agreed upon goal which is simply this: to create the greatest motion picture of all time. [*Applause*] A man's reach should exceed his grasp," he intoned, "or what's a heaven for?" He hoped, secretly, that some would credit him with the creation of this quotation. Many did. "Joining me on this platform this afternoon are just a few of the key people who have a part in this historic adventure." He introduced each of them with lengthy, fulsome remarks. This, too, had been part of Birdwell's plan. "Keep the early part so dull that the later part'll seem exciting by comparison."

The last one to be introduced was Ben, who came forward and joined Selznick at the microphone. "Ladies and gentlemen," he said, "it is most generous of my friend and colleague, David O. Selznick, to let me have the honor of making one of the important announcements today. Many people have the impression that we movie people are fierce competitors. The only thing wrong with Sam Goldwyn's remark, 'In this business it's dog eat dog, and nobody's going to eat me!' is that Sam never said it. Some smart aleck said it and pinned it on Sam. I, myself, have been in this wonderful business for more than thirty years, and I can tell you that I have known every kind of kindness and cooperation. People, many people, have helped me, and I am glad to say that I have sometimes been in a position to help others. We are announcing today—my company and Selznick International—a remarkable, unprecedented arrangement in connection with *Gone With the Wind* which we, too, believe will be the greatest picture of all time. [*Applause*] Our company is proud to announce that we will be the releasing and distributing organization for David O. Selznick's epic production, *Gone With the Wind*. [*Applause*] We are also proud and happy to announce that for the part of Rhett Butler, David O. Selznick has chosen our great star, *Mr. Clark Gable!*" [*Prolonged applause*]

Now, down the center aisle, came one of Birdwell's planned, electrifying moments—The King himself, striding down toward the platform, flashing his famous smile, waving his most generous greeting, twinkling his dimples.

An ovation.

Meanwhile, set decorators and propmen swiftly constructed a small but luxurious office on the platform—a massive desk, three chairs, the walls papered with book jackets of *Gone With the Wind.*

Clark Gable mounted the platform, shook hands with Ben and with David. The set-type lighting flooded on. The motion picture cameras started grinding, the still photographers crowded in and began popping flashbulbs. The platform party circled the desk in the White House–inspired manner; Gable in the center chair with Ben on his left and David on his right. Birdwell directed the

276

action from the floor. Documents (prop) were produced and the signing ceremony went on with all the emotion and sense of earthshaking import as an international tripartite treaty.

Birdwell hustled it along, anxious to keep the momentum going. He snapped his fingers at the wings. The set disappeared, the party took its seats again, leaving Gable at the microphone. Birdwell handed him a note. Gable read it and nodded. The lights returned to normal except for a flattering pink spotlight on the star. He held up his palm. Instantaneous silence. He took a long, dramatic pause, then said, "All *I* want to know is, who's gonna be my Scarlett?" He winked and produced a few volts of the sexual electricity that had brought him fame and fortune. As Clark Gable left, retracing his steps, there was wild applause, cheers, and from the audience shouted suggestions. Many of them were indistinguishable, but one could hear, "Hepburn! Hepburn!" From another part of the room, "Davis, Bette Davis!" And an organized chorus began to chant, "We want Crawford! We want Crawford! We want Crawford!"

Selznick looked over at Ben suspiciously. Ben shrugged, but convinced no one, not even himself. A new voice. "Maggie Sullavan!" Another "Minnie Mouse!" "What's the matter with Bankhead? *She's all right!*" "Marie Dressler!" screamed a drunken voice. Its owner was quickly located and hustled out with the wiseguy who had yelled "Minnie Mouse."

Selznick took the microphone again. He held up a palm as Gable had done, but *his* palm lacked the magic. The crowd became unruly. Two fistfights broke out on the floor. Birdwell was troubled. He signaled a security officer who pressed a button that set off a series of wildly clanging bells, but the ideas from the floor continued.

In time, order of a kind was restored. "Exactly," shouted David. "We *all* see her! We *all* care! And so today, I make this pledge to the American people. No effort and no expense will be spared in order that we may achieve the perfect result. The *real* Scarlett O'Hara!"

Names screamed and yelled from the floor again. "Yes!" shouted David, pointing in the direction of each suggestion. "Yes! Yes! They're all under consideration, *each* and *every one*. And now I beg you to be quiet and listen to the most important announcement of the day."

His words had little or no effect. The rowdy crowd had begun to revel in its rowdiness. Birdwell jumped up onto the platform. Two cameramen, with hand-held Eyemos, joined him on the platform, one at either side. They were photographing the audience, panning slowly around the room. Russell shouted, "Now listen, you people!"

The combination of the sound of his voice and the choleric look on his normally placid face was enough to achieve a modicum of quiet. He continued, "You will note, I trust, that I did not refer to you as ladies and gentlemen. . . . This is a professional occasion, and you were invited here because you claim to be professionals. Now I expect you to behave accordingly. The hoodlums among you are being recorded, and those of you who do not, or will not, cooperate will be barred from this lot henceforth. Is that clear?"

The scene resembled a high school auditorium with a stern and strict principal chastising an unruly student body. There was a burst of solid, legitimate applause from the majority of the crowd, who had begun to fear the consequences of the riotous acts. A few people left, some of them shielding their faces.

Selznick again. "Thank you, Russell." To the crowd: "I, personally, am thrilled by the passion and emotion generated by the question, but for God's sake and mine, let's keep it in control; let's keep it civilized. Now. I want to announce on behalf of Selznick International that we are about to launch the greatest talent search since the motion picture industry began. I direct your attention to the screen on your right."

The lights were dimmed, and a huge map of the United States was projected. David went on, "We propose to divide our great country into four sections: Northeast!" On the screen the Northeast corner turned yellow. "Southeast!" Blue. "Northwest!" Pink. "Southwest!" Green. "We are sending an experienced talent-scouting team into each of these sectors. They will interview and make preliminary tests of all qualified candidates. Now listen to this. The door is open to any American girl who thinks she can play Scarlett O'Hara. No one will be turned away, because we firmly believe—"

A strong Southern-accented voice rang out, "Now how 'bout y'all stop this shit, Yankee boy?" Its owner leaped to a chair and went on, "How 'bout you just stay right there in the blue part, in the *real* South!" Six security officers converged on the speaker, who calmly drew a pistol and brandished it expertly. Screams preceded the crush away from this apparent madman. Abraham Farber leaped up onto the platform, took his father's arm, firmly, and led him as far away from the action as possible. "He's a nut," said Abraham. "Never monkey with a lunatic. Anything can happen."

"Thanks, Abe. This was very nice of you."

The nut was given a wide berth, and in a flash was flanked on the adjoining chairs by two companions, also armed. All three donned Confederate army field caps and held up Confederate flags. Someone laughed. The speaker fired a shot into the air. There was no further laughter. He went on, directing his address to the platform. "If you think you're fixin' to insult the glorious South, Jewboy, you got yourself another think comin'. You keep them goddamn coonhounds out of that yellow part and red part and green part. They ain't gonna find no Scarletts up in there. Don't y'all know that, Yankee boy? You try to pass off anybody but a Southern belle and we'll keep your God damn movie out of the South and blow it off every screen wherever. This has just been Warnin' Number One. There'll be more."

The three intruders jumped to the floor, emitting, as they did so, the blood-curdling Rebel yell. They began to back off. "The South shall rise again!" shouted the leader as he and his accomplices backed into the sudden arms of twenty members of The Los Angeles Police Department. The three were quickly disarmed and handcuffed. As they were led away, they burst into song, performing a spirited rendition of "Dixie." It trailed off:

> "In Dixieland I'll take my stand
> And live and die in Dixie.
> Away, away, away down South in Dixie.
> Away, away, away down South in Dixie!"

All of Selznick's considerable charm, coupled with Birdwell's extraordinary skills, was not enough to reconstruct the meeting.

At length Birdwell took the microphone and said, "Well, folks, I guess you got enough copy for one day. Unfortunately, it's the wrong copy for us. However, even Babe Ruth struck out once in a while. Please don't leave without a complete kit and please ask

279

for any help we can give you with hometown papers and special regional campaigns. Also, there will be—"

He realized that he had lost them, and trailed off. He switched off the microphone and said, "Oh, fuck it!" The words boomed all over the sound stage. He had switched the mike to High Amp instead of Off.

"Well, anyhow," he said later to David, "it got the biggest laugh of the day."

"What should we do about those three maniacs?" asked David. "Something? Nothing?"

"Don't bother me with stuff like that now, Yankee boy. I've got a record-breaking migraine coming on."

In David's beautiful office, which bespoke taste and class of the highest order, he and Ben were having a postmortem. David was having a drink, Ben a glass of what he still referred to as seltzer water.

"I thought," said David, "that Gable's reception was fantastic, didn't you? I mean genuine, heartfelt. They were voicing their approval in a real, not phony, way. Didn't you think so? Weren't you pleased?"

"I thought it was very nice," said Ben. "Also, I thought what he said and the way he said it was fine."

"Oh, sure," said David. "That was Birdwell."

"It was?"

"Sure. Birdwell told him what to say."

"Oh?"

"Birdwell's a guy doesn't believe in leaving anything to chance."

Ben rose. "David, between us, now that we seem to be partners in a way—"

"In a way?" David laughed.

"I believe that to be frank and open and aboveboard is very important."

"No argument there."

"There should be—between us at least—complete, what's the word—complete—Willa says it all the time—"

"Candor?"

"Candor! That's it. There should be, between us at least, complete candor."

"Of course."

"About today, David. It was a tremendous event. I can't tell you how impressed I was. The whole organization of it. Not only the conception, but the execution—brilliant."

"Thank you. It was mostly Russell Birdwell, a genius in his field," said David.

"How a man thinks all that up. It's beyond me."

"What the hell, Ben, that's his business."

"Yes."

"So what's all this about candor?"

"I'm coming to that. Good as it was, David, I think this time you went too far."

"How do you mean?"

"Those three bums at the end. That you *didn't* need."

The remark brought David to his feet.

"Do you think—?" he began. His voice went up two tones. "You mean to tell me you—?"

"Yes," said Ben, doggedly. "I do."

David turned away. "I'm insulted, Ben. I'm really insulted. That was absolutely on the level. Do you think I'd allow gunplay? That I'd invite people in, then terrorize them?"

"Maybe not you—maybe Birdwell."

"No, no. He clears everything with me—everything."

"Sure. Tomorrow it'll be in all the papers. Maybe out here and in *The New York News* and *Mirror* on the front page—and radios, magazines, and so forth. Great publicity. But do you think, David, the right kind? You don't think it could maybe begin to stir up troubles?"

"God damn right, I do. It was a disaster for me—a disgrace.

Ben studied him. "I still think you did it, David. I'm sorry. But all right, if you regret it, so let's forget it."

"Ben, I swear to you. I had absolutely nothing to do with that ruckus."

"I'll tell you what I'm going to do, David. I'm going to try to believe you."

"Thank you."

"Let's change the subject. My son Gilbert was over for dinner last night. He says he can't see anybody but Kate Hepburn in it. What *about* her? She and Gable—my God! I mean in case you decide not to go with Joan."

"Kate," said David, "is a strong candidate. But what would the Southerners say? She's a celebrated Connecticut Yankee."

"You see," said Ben, "your head is poisoned already. Well, good night."

"Good night, Ben."

At the studio a test was made of a young Warner Brothers contract actress named Lana Turner, who, with the considerable assistance of a sweater, had made a success in *They Won't Forget*. Her agent, Abraham Farber, insisted that Selznick test her, and for politic reasons, Selznick agreed. The test was farcical, like so many of the others.

In Boston, over six hundred young women stormed the Statler Hotel ballroom. The efficient team of talent scouts weeded them out and made miniature personality tests of five of them.

One, a striking Wellesley girl from Savannah, was sent to Culver City to be seen by David O. Selznick personally. The team moved on to New York, then to Chicago.

In Atlanta, another team spent three weeks and saw over two thousand girls who responded to the newspaper ads and the radio announcements, before going down to Florida. Of the Atlanta group, thirty minitests were made and six girls were sent to California. One of these was a peach named Margaret Tallichet, who did not get the part but who stayed on in California, met and married William Wyler, and lived happily ever after.

In Seattle, the pickings were slim. A widely read columnist named Dick Moran denounced the search for Scarlett as a tacky publicity stunt and stated that he had it from an impeccable source that Katharine Hepburn had been signed for the part. Pressed for proof by his editor, he revealed that his sister-in-law worked at Western Costume in Los Angeles and had told him that a complete Scarlett O'Hara wardrobe was in the works there for Katharine Hepburn.

As it happened, this much was true. David had ordered the wardrobe, using her forms there, in a desperate attempt to lure Hepburn into testing, which she had up to now categorically refused to do.

So Seattle was mild; about a hundred and fifty interviews, six little tests. No one sent down. On to Portland.

In Dallas, a beautiful girl had herself delivered to the scouts in a huge box made in the form of an outsized copy of *Gone With the Wind*. She popped out, dressed as Scarlett, and recited a page and a half of the text of the book before she could be contained.

Houston was worse. Bribes were offered and a few accepted. David found out and rushed to Austin where fists flew. A new team continued on to Fort Worth. Eight would-be Scarletts left for California.

Other players were beginning to be signed. Leslie Howard, Olivia de Havilland, Thomas Mitchell. GWTW became a trademark as swiftly identifiable as Coca-Cola or Rolls-Royce. Not a day passed without news or rumors or denials or reports or statistics on the subject of GWTW. Birdwell lost thirteen pounds in three months. Sets had been designed and were being built. That important penultimate scene, the burning of Atlanta, was in the hands of the special effects department, the stuntmen, William Cameron Menzies, and The Culver City Fire Department.

Three weeks after the team left Reno, Nevada, a small display ad appeared in the Reno *Courier*.

SCARLETT O'HARA
Second Audition!

Only those candidates not previously interviewed may apply. Call 499-6161 for appointment.

8 x 10 glossy and resume required.

The response was solid if not overwhelming. Was The Search beginning to pall?

This new team was composed of two men, Harold Fuller and Stewart Page, and one woman, Louann Hutchins. The men were in their forties, both of them fleshy and outgoing, well and conservatively dressed in a style foreign to Reno. Miss Hutchins appeared to be their efficient executive secretary.

"Only about eighteen today," she said. "How do you want to work it? The call-backs tonight or tomorrow?"

"Let's see what we get first," said Fuller. "Let's see how many live ones come to the—"

"If any," said Miss Hutchins.

They had taken five rooms at The Silver Dollar Motel, including one large meeting room which they had converted into a small motion picture studio, complete with camera and lights.

The interviews proceeded swiftly. Of the eighteen, only four were worth call-backs. They were scheduled for the same evening at 7:00, 8:00, 9:00, and 10:00 o'clock.

"Is that your real name?" asked Page. "Laurie Lee?"

He was interviewing her alone in the improvised dressing room made of a bedroom adjoining the studio. She was a small dark stunner with a spectacular bosom.

"Half of it is," she said.

"Which half?"

"Laurie. The Lee is really Levi."

"I see. And is it true that you're a direct descendant of General Robert *E.* Levi?"

"Absolutely," she said.

"Well, that puts you ahead. *Way* ahead."

"Thank you."

"Have you read our book, Miss Lee?"

"Oh, yes. Five times."

"And you see yourself as Scarlett?"

"All I want is a chance," she said, with a dry tongue.

"Well, that's all you're going to get," he said.

"Thank you."

"Now, I take it you're familiar with the corset-lacing scene?"

"Oh, yes. I love it."

"Uh-huh. Well, maybe we'll have a shot at *that*. What I want you to do is just look over the scene in the book, but when we make the test, use your own words and, of course, sound as Southern as you can."

"Oh, Ah can do thayat," she said.

"All right, then, do it—but don't *over*do it."

"Ah won't."

"Miss Hutchins will help you with your costume."

"Now?" asked Laurie, suddenly terrified.

"Why not?"

Louann came in. Page withdrew.

"All right," said Louann. "Get out of your clothes. Shoes and stockings, O.K."

After a moment's hesitation, Laurie began to undress slowly, nervously. She had not expected it all to happen so swiftly, so abruptly.

"Hurry up," said Louann, holding up a period corset.

In another dressing room–bedroom, Harold Fuller was studying an excessively pretty winsome blonde who knew exactly what to do with her wide violet eyes. She was doing it.

"The basic trouble," he said, "as I see it, is your youth. How old are you?"

"I'm twenty-two," she said. "And Scarlett goes from sixteen to twenty-two."

"You're not twenty-two."

"Twenty-one," she said.

He stared at her. "But damn it all, you're so *right*. I'm going to take a chance. Who knows? Later, maybe, if we get up there, the makeup men can do something. They're terrific, you know."

"Yes, I know," she whispered. If only she could keep from fainting!

"Now. Are you familiar with the corset-lacing scene?"

In the studio, Page was completing his test of Laurie. Miss Hutchins was standing in for the part of Mammy. Laurie, to Page's astonishment, had turned out to be a resourceful actress. She attacked the improvisation with the innocence of the amateur and made a considerable impression.

"Cut!" he called out.

"Very good," said Miss Hutchins.

Laurie burst into tears. Page approached her and put his arm across her shoulders.

"Excellent," he said. "Really excellent."

"So *nervous!*" she said, still weeping.

"All right, Miss Hutchins. Get her dressed. I believe Mr. Fuller needs the corset." He laughed. "Wouldn't you think that a company as big as ours could afford *two* corsets?"

"Would you mind, Mr. Page?" asked Louann. "I have to go help Mr. Fuller."

"Oh, sure," he said easily. "I'll handle it. Go ahead."

He led Laurie, still in tears, into the dressing room. He closed and quietly locked the door. He began to unlace the corset.

Laurie stopped crying, collected herself, and said, "I can do it. Really. I'll be fine."

"No, no," he said. "This is complicated. I do it all the time. I've gotten to be quite an expert. There."

The corset off, he put it aside and began to rub her sides. "Too tight," he said. "She had it on too tight."

"Yes, I think so."

Laurie stood now in her loose camisole. Page put his arms about her, comfortingly. "You really all right now?"

"Oh, yes."

He took her face in his hands and said, "You surprised me, you know it?"

"I surprised myself," she said softly.

"Listen," he said comfortingly. He sat down on the edge of the bed and drew her down beside him. He held her hand and continued. "I'm going to be absolutely honest with you. Based on what you did here tonight, if it was up to me—I'd make a full-scale test of you in Hollywood."

"Hollywood," she breathed.

"But I'm not all that important, unfortunately." He handed her his card. It read:

SELZNICK INTERNATIONAL
4000 Pico Blvd.
Culver City, California
3664/5/6/7/8/9

Stewart Page
Talent Coordinator

She looked at it and blinked. Was this the glass slipper?

"Thank you," she said.

"Would you *like* to come to Hollywood?"

"This says Culver City," she said.

"Well, you know—it's all Hollywood."

"Yes," she said. "I would. Very much."

He put his arm around her again. "I'd look after you down there. By the way, do your folks approve?"

"Well, it's just my mother, and she's in Denver. I'm just here working."

"What do you do?"

"I'm a manicurist. At the Reno Ritz."

"Think of that. Boyfriends?"

"Well, *you* know—"

"Free-lancing. Is that it?"

"Yuh. I guess you could call it that."

"I'll tell you the truth, Laurie. I've seen hundreds of girls and made dozens of tests, and you're the best—the best by far. I'm very, very proud of you."

"Thank you."

He smiled. "Would you let me kiss you? Just for luck?"

"If you want to," she whispered.

"No, it's no good unless we both want to."

There was a pause filled with whirling thoughts and colliding feelings. Finally Laurie said quietly, "Yes."

He kissed her with expertise she had not yet encountered. It was all too exciting. Did he really like her, this great man from Culver City—or Hollywood? She found his touch unexpectedly tender. She was accustomed to coarser, less practiced approaches. She found herself lying down. What was happening? The lights were out. Her camisole was being removed, gently, firmly.

"Wait!" she cried.

"Please," he said.

She began to weep softly.

"No, Laurie. Don't, Laurie. I'm going to make you happy."

His head seemed to be floating about and above her body, stopping from time to time here and there and here to bestow a kiss of greeting.

Laurie stopped crying.

In the other dressing room, Fuller was unlacing the corset from the pink blonde's body. She was reading his card.

METRO-GOLDWYN-MAYER
10202 West Washington Boulevard
Culver City, California
Tel. 2244

Harold Fuller
Casting Director

"You were sensational!" he said. "The best yet. I think you just might have a shot at this thing."

She looked at him carefully. "You wouldn't shit me, buster, would you?"

"I would if I could, baby. I would if I could!"

"You a New Yorker?"

"Why do you ask?"

"You got that New Yorky line," she said.

"No, I'm from Hollywood."

"Originally?"

"Originally Chicago."

"Well, Chicago lines ain't bad either."

He tossed the corset aside and asked, "Did she have it on too tight? She usually does." He came to her and touched her sides. "Any welts?"

"See for yourself."

She reached down and brought her slip up over her head, revealing a body that outdid her erotic head. Fuller, goggle-eyed, attempted to gulp away his shock. He could not take his eyes from her unsettling nakedness.

"God damn!" he said, "and I'd have sworn you were a *real* blonde."

"Never mind. Just so long as you're a real casting director."

"Why? You doubt it?"

"Not at all. What I want to know is what's the score? Do I get to go on up there?"

"There's a good chance."

"What does it depend on?" she asked.

"A number of things."

"Oh." She was disappointed.

288

"What's the matter?"

"I was hoping it was just one thing."

"You're some number," he said, shaking his head.

"Listen, fella," she said, "I'm no dumb blonde. As you can see for yourself, I'm not even a *blonde*. You don't think *I* think anybody's going to give me the part of Scarlett O'Hara, for Christ's sake, do you? If I thought that, I ought to be put away someplace. No, what I'd like to get out of all this is a trip up there and a try—for something. For anything. Maybe a bit, even an extra."

"Well, hell, honey—that's no problem. A bit? I can get you all the bits you want."

"Well, then," she said, "what're we waitin' for?"

She sat down on the edge of the bed and began to remove the last remaining articles of clothing she had on—her garter belt and her stockings.

Twelve days later, two FBI agents appeared at the M-G-M front gate. They looked as though they had been drawn by James Montgomery Flagg for an Arrow Collar ad. After properly identifying themselves, they were escorted to Ben Farber's office. There they produced a warrant for his arrest on two charges of violation of the Mann Act.

Ben laughed and said, "Why, this is without a doubt the absolutely craziest thing I ever heard of. All right, leave it and I'll take it up with the legal department."

The agents exchanged embarrassed looks, then the taller of the two said, "I'm sorry, Mr. Farber, we're under orders to take you in."

"What *is* this?" he asked. "Some joke? Some kind of one of those Hecht and MacArthur jokes? If it is, I swear—"

He buzzed Henry, his secretary, and said, "Get some lawyers up here—whoever's free."

"Yes, sir."

Ben turned to the FBI men. "Sit down, gentlemen, sit down." They did so. "Coffee?"

The three lawyers, after examining the warrant and discussing the matter with the agents, agreed that there was, for the moment, no course other than to comply. The senior lawyer, William Jesperson, said, "Would you excuse us for a few minutes, please?"

The other lawyers and the agents left the room. Jesperson turned to Ben. "Of *course,* this is ridiculous, Mr. Farber, but if you want the truth, most legal procedures are."

"I don't want to hear your theories," said Ben impatiently. "What the hell's gonna happen now, right now, this minute? I'm going to be locked up in a jail or what?"

"Oh, no. Good heavens, nothing like that. But we do have to enter a formal reply. The FBI is involved, you see, because the Mann Act is a federal statute."

"You mind telling me what is the Mann Act?"

Jesperson blushed. "Why—uh—it's a law that makes it a federal offense to take women across state lines for immoral purposes." Ben thought hard. He walked to the window and looked out.

"Well, for Chrissake!" he said. "I haven't done *that.*"

"Of course not."

After a moment, Ben added, "Not *lately.*"

When Ben, along with Jesperson; an associate, Mrs. Angevin; a bondsman; and the agents arrived at the office of the clerk of the federal court in Los Angeles, they found David Selznick and a similar group already there. They also saw two extremely attractive young girls; one small and dark, the other pink and blond.

Ben went to David at once. "David," he said, his forefinger almost touching David's face, "if this turns out to be another of your goddam stunts—or Birdwell—I swear to God I'm going to call off the whole goddam deal!"

"Are you *mad?*" asked David, with an English accent.

"Mad? I'm goddam *furious!* In my whole life I was never arrested, and I'm fifty goddam years old."

"What about *me?*" said David. "You think *I* get arrested every day?"

"You *ought* to be!"

"Calm down, Ben."

"No! And I *still* think you hired that Goddamn Confederate army that day!"

The legal technicalities were handled with dispatch. The parties involved then went into a conference room for a discussion of the realities.

The girls were accompanied by an intense young myopic attor-

290

ney from the Legal Aid Society named Jaime Rodriguez. "Go ahead," he said to Sally. "Keep going. Tell it all, the whole truth."

"Well, see," said Sally. "We didn't mind puttin' out for those boys. At least, *I* didn't. I thought they were on the level. They sure did it all great, I must say. Didn't they, Laurie?"

"Perfectly."

"Anyway, I always heard that kind of stuff was par for the course in the movies."

"What nonsense!" said Ben. "People will believe anything."

"So when they got us up *here*," Laurie explained, "and we were all together in this nice house in Pasadena, and they said everything was going fine at the studio, but it was going to take a while to get all the arrangements arranged and in the meantime, wouldn't we like to make some money? Some real good money. And—"

She began to cry. Sally picked up.

"It turned out this Hutchins woman, or whatever the hell her name was or is, was nothing but a plain, common, ordinary madam. And those two guys? They worked for her. Pimps."

"I'm afraid," said Jesperson, "they're more than that. Worse."

"We tried a raid on the Pasadena place," said Rodriguez, "after the girls got out, but we were too late. So the only way we could involve the authorities was to charge the companies of origin, you see."

"You got some nerve, young man," said Ben.

Jesperson glowered at the young lawyer. "You may be flirting with a false arrest matter here."

"No, sir," said Rodriguez. "I think not. All you have to prove is that these perpetrators were not in your employ, and I'm sure you can do that."

David said, "I'll see those bastards are tracked down if it costs me a hundred grand!"

Ben looked at him. "On that one, David, we're *not* partners."

"You young ladies," said David, "have certainly been victimized, no doubt about that, and I'm going to do whatever I can to make some kind of restitution." He looked at both of them carefully. "Come and see me tomorrow."

Sally turned to Ben and said, "Is this guy really David O. Selznick?"

"I think so," said Ben, if there *is* a David O. Selznick."

Both girls were, indeed, eventually bit players in *Gone With the Wind.* Laurie stayed on afterward and pursued a quiet, respectable, if unspectacular, career, married a great cameraman, and had five children, one of whom became a big star.

Sally returned to Reno, acquired financing, and opened a small but exclusive whorehouse which she and her third husband still operate, now legally.

VII

THE GREAT party was Myron's idea. But David and Ben gave it as co-hosts. Cocktails and first courses at the Selznicks'; dessert and entertainment at the Farbers'. The theme was as far away from *Gone With the Wind* as possible. A New England shore dinner: clam chowder, baby lobsters, corn on the cob, sliced tomatoes and cucumbers, a selection of pies—lemon meringue, apple, and blueberry—white wines, red wines, champagne. Lobster bibs, dress informal, a down-home country band flown in and square dancing planned. Clearly, the party had nothing to do with *Gone With the Wind,* even though it was being given jointly by the Selznicks and the Farbers. David and Ben worked on the guest list with the greatest care. It was made up entirely of those actresses who were being considered for the part of Scarlett. Each one was expected to turn up with her husband or lover or beau.

"Did we leave anyone out?" asked Ben.

"God, I hope not. Let's check it."

David began to read: "Paulette Goddard, Bette Davis, Miriam Hopkins, Tallulah Bankhead—"

"I hope she doesn't get plastered," said Ben.

"I hope *I* don't," said David. "—Joan Crawford, Jean Arthur, Carole Lombard, Katharine Hepburn."

"*She* won't come."

"Why not?"

"She's too smart."

"She'll come," said David confidently.

"What did we decide about Ann Sheridan, finally?"

"No."

He crossed her off the list and went on. "Margaret Sullavan, Barbara Stanwyck . . . Lana Turner?"

"Oh, no."

"No it is. Evelyn Keyes?"

"Not if you've already decided on her for the sister."

"I have."

"Then no."

"Norma Shearer, Irene Dunne, Jean Harlow."

"She's out, too, isn't she?"

"Well, yes," said David. "But let's have her. It's always a better party with Harlow. She's a bombshell."

"No objection."

"God, I'm beginning to see it," said David. "Fabulous."

"I can hardly wait," said Ben, laughing.

When Willa Farber saw the list, she looked grim, and said to her husband, "Has it ever occurred to you, Ben, or to the Boy Wonder, that this thing may backfire?"

"Why would it? It's all in the spirit of fun," he said.

"Yes, well, *his* idea of fun may not be someone else's."

"Oh, don't make so much of it, Willa. It's a party, that's all."

"It may turn out to be more than that. Or less."

Irene Mayer Selznick studied the list, pale. "You've had some harebrained ideas in your time, David, but this *may* be—no, this *is* the worst."

"Don't worry about it."

"I think you should."

"I know what I'm doing."

"And I know what *I'm* doing. I'm going to Palm Springs."

Paulette Goddard and Charlie Chaplin were the first to arrive. They lived right across the street.

"Clam chowder!" Charlie shouted. "I could smell it all the time I was dressing. I *love* it!"

"Everything flown in from Maine," said David.

"What's it in celebration of, anyway?" asked Paulette, carefully. "Anything?"

Before David could reply, Clark Gable appeared with Carole Lombard. "Clark!" Paulette screamed. She ran to him, embraced

293

him, making sure that David saw them together, then hugged Carole. "Oh, congratulations," she said. "Wait until you see what Charlie and I are giving you for a wedding present."

"We could use one," said Carole.

Charlie and Clark were shaking hands grimly. Charlie suddenly became an English music hall comic and in fruity Cockney said, "You know what a bachelor is, mate? Ask me what a bachelor is, mate."

Clark, laughing, said, "All right. What's a bachelor, mate?"

Charlie: "A bachelor, mate, is a man who never makes the same mistake *once!*"

To punctuate the joke he performed one of his celebrated spins and falls.

Carole looked off as Tallulah, escorted by a handsome young Negro, came in, followed by Jean Arthur and her husband, and Miriam Hopkins with Russell Birdwell.

Carole took Clark aside. "Do you get it? Couldn't you *die?*"

"Get what?" asked Clark.

"Oh, my God, you're dumb. Is it too soon to get a divorce?"

"Get *what?*"

"All the Scarletts. They're all *Scarletts.*"

"Come on, honey," said Clark. "You can't call Jean Harlow and Norma Shearer starlets."

"Holy shit! Not only dumb but deaf, too." She leaned to his ear and said, "*Scarletts*—not starlets. *Scarletts!*"

Clark looked and saw them all. By now they were all there, all except Hepburn.

David wondered. Had Ben been right, or had he tipped off Kate, a special pal?

Birdwell was saying to Tallulah, "And there they were, the *six* of them, waving pistols and Confederate flags. Did you hear about it?"

"*Hear* about it? I *sent* them, you jackass. They're all my *cousins.*" Her wild laugh rang through the room.

The first course was served on the loggia at a long wooden country table covered with a red-checkered tablecloth. The chowder was so delicious that it became the topic of conversation. Only Jean Arthur failed to taste it. She sat not far from David, who noticed it.

"What's the matter, Jean?" he asked. "Don't you like clam chowder?"

"I like clam chowder," she said in the husky voice that was her trademark. "But I don't like *you.*" She stood up and glared at him. David continued to have his chowder, calmly. Jean went on: "Is this your clumsy, stupid idea of a prank of some kind?"

"O.K., Jean," said her husband, "take it easy." He attempted to get her back in her chair. She slapped him. He got up and left. She started after him but returned at once, picked up her large bowl of chowder and, before anyone realized what was happening, moved over and dumped the contents over David's head. As exit business, she smashed the empty bowl on the tiled surface of the loggia, and ran off. David followed her, caught her, grabbed her. Her husband appeared and pulled her away. David swung at him and missed. Her husband landed a glancing blow that did little damage but did knock off David's glasses. Ben and others came between them. Jean and her husband left. David went up to change.

Later, the lobsters were served in the dining room, country style, all the food on the table and passed around.

"She was right," said Margaret Sullavan, sitting beside Ben.

"This is a stinking idea," said Bette Davis. "We're all embarrassed. I may throw up."

"People are losing their sense of humor," said Ben. "We just thought so much talk, too much, on the subject and with so much excitement, we thought it would be friendly and professional to all get together."

"All the losers, you mean," said Barbara Stanwyck.

"No, no, not at all."

The table was suddenly quiet.

"I notice," she said, "that Miss Hepburn isn't here, and the word is she's got it."

The room became a still picture. David rose, a lobster claw in his hand, and began an oration.

"Friends, Romans, and countrymen, lend me your ears. Miss Stanwyck is wrong. One hundred and one percent wrong. I have declined to discuss this matter for sound professional reasons, but the situation this evening compels me to break my silence. Miss Katharine Hepburn will definitely, positively, irrevocably, certainly, absolutely, indubitably *not*—I repeat *not*—n-o-t—play the part of Scarlett O'Hara in David O. Selznick's magnificent production of *Gone With the Wind.* And I think I can also say, without fear of contraception—" He paused for the laugh that did not come. He plunged on, "that another absotively, posilutely no, as of this evening, is Miss Jean Arthur. Which means that no decision has yet been made and, at the risk of sounding like Agatha Christie, I can say I would like to say that Scarlett O'Hara is right in this room."

In the long pause that followed, looks and smiles and winks and glances and stares of every description were exchanged.

Dinner continued. As it was ending, Myron staggered into the room, pulled a chair over to the table and squeezed in. The food had been removed.

"Hey!" he said to one of the butlers. "Bring me some dinner!"

"Scram, Myron," said David.

"How *dare* you!" said Myron, attempting to rise.

Carole leaned over and said, "Listen, Myron, were you *invited* to this party?"

Myron rose and with outraged dignity said, "Not only was I *invited* to this party—but I *declined* the invitation!"

Before the guests moved to the Farbers', Miriam Hopkins and Tallulah Bankhead had an unfortunate run-in. They were aware, as was everyone else, that they were the only two contenders who were authentically Southern. They flaunted their accents all evening in an attempt to outdo one another. Miriam said something.

"What did you say, sugar?" asked Tallulah.

Miriam repeated it.

"I declare, sugar," said Tallulah, "I can't understand a word you're sayin'."

"Well, I find you a bit of a mushmouth myself."

"Mushmouth, mushmouth. Is that a white-trash word?"

"Yeah. And can I ask you something?"

"Why, you can ask me any ol' thing. How else you gonna learn?"

Miriam asked, "Have you *always* been a baritone?"

"Why, no, bless your little heart, only since the day I got the shock. When I found out I've got a touch of the tarbrush."

"Oh," said Miriam, "everybody's always known that." She looked at Tallulah's black companion and said, "But I must say your little brother's just as cute as paint."

The bitchy colloquy got the expected responses, and, in fact, the participants appeared to be enjoying it. Thus it came as a shattering surprise, as the party prepared to move on to the Far-bers', that Miriam and Tallulah out on the front lawn began swinging at each other. Finally, Tallulah got a firm grip on Mir-iam's hair with both hands. Miriam returned the compliment. The efforts of Birdwell and Tallulah's partner were of no avail. When Birdwell got the impression that the young man was being too rough on Miriam, he spun him around and punched him in the chest. The young man went into an automatic prizefighter stance and knocked Birdwell cold with a single right hook.

The women stopped their hair-pulling. "Oh, shoot!" said Tal-lulah. "This is terrible. I should have told you all that Bobo is the lightweight champion of *Texas!*"

The evening progressed with growing tension at the Farbers'. Charlie got Farber into his study.

"If that's true, Ben, what that big blowhard says, then I tell you there's no contest. I know this business as well as anyone, and I tell you Paulette's the one. Did you see her in *Modern Times?*"

"Of course, Charlie, of course."

"And she's going to play the lead in every picture I do from now on."

"That's fine."

"So what do you say?"

"Charlie. If it was up to me, we'd have a deal right now."

"Is that a fact?"

"Yes, but the creative side—that's him. You know that."

"Well, will you work on him?"

"Yes, of course. Everybody's working on him."

A pause.

"Where was Irene tonight?"

"I don't know, Charlie. I honestly don't know."

"If you put *me* in the part, David," said Jean Harlow, "you're a horse's ass."

"I know more about it than you do."

"You don't know more about *me*, though. I could never do that stuff. That scene, the morning-after scene, when she's had her first good bang?"

"What about it?"

"Well, Jesus, man, can you picture *me* being so surprised and delighted and happy and all? In the morning?"

"Yes, the way we'll do it—"

"David, listen. If you give me the part I'll take it, but, oh, *boy,* will I stink!"

Another part of the forest—the garden, actually. Joan Crawford and Clark Gable are walking, slowly.

"But we're old hands at this game, Clark. We know what's what. This is all a lot of whistlin' Dixie, a lot of jerkin' off."

"Hey!" Clark was shocked.

"It is. You know and I know that when the chips are down, *you're* the one that's going to decide."

"Me?"

"Damn right."

"Hell, if it was me, I'd want Carole."

"Sure, but she told me she doesn't want it, and I believe her. Neither does Norma. This fathead, he's so drunk with power, he thinks everybody is willing to lay down and die for it. But he's wrong. I guess that little Jean Arthur showed him tonight."

"Listen," said Clark, "he's so goofy he might just give it to her *because* of that."

"No, there's more to it than that. That's an old romance."

"It is?"

"Was. Old, old. And she figures she ought to get it without competing."

"Oh."

They stopped walking. "Take *me,* Clark," said Joan. "You'll never regret it. Take me. Come on. We'll have a whale of a time. Weren't we great together in *Dance, Fool, Dance?*"

"We sure were."

"And what about *Laughing Sinners* and *Possessed* and *Dancing Lady* and *Chained* and *Love on the Run* and *Forsaking All Others?* Jesus, we're practically a *team,* Clark!"

"Yeah. We were good, all right."

"We were *great.* On *and* off, weren't we?"

"Sure were," he said, blushing.

She reached up, grasped his head, pulled it down, and gave him a reminder. As it proceeded, a wicker chair came flying in and hit them. Clark and Joan went down. The words which followed, wrapped in screams, were indistinguishable. The party rushed out to find Joan, hurt. Clark and Carole were at the peak of a furious row. As Joan came to, she began to scream, "Police! I want the police!" She rushed at Carole, who belted her. Ben got into it somehow, then David, but not Birdwell. He had had enough for one mad night.

The others, believing that the police *might* be coming, began to leave. Those who remained took sides. There was a good deal of pushing and shoving. More furniture was thrown. Running away from it all, Clark Gable went right through the plate-glass picture window that separated the loggia from the sitting room. Blood. Too much blood. Carole rushed to his aid, looked at him, emitted one final scream and fainted.

Tallulah took charge marvelously, applying tourniquets with skill and efficiency.

The ambulance and the police arrived simultaneously.

Two A.M. Willa had gone to bed. Selznick was on the phone. Ben sat drinking a glass of milk.

Selznick said, "Thank you, doctor, thank you." He came to Ben, picked up his drink and said, "Nothing serious. Three or four stitches in his lower right arm. Face is O.K."

"But I guess," said Ben, "we better forget about Crawford, right?"

"Yeah, I'm afraid so."

"And Shearer? She *really* said no?"

"And meant it."

"I heard what Jean Harlow said to you."

"Yeah. She's right."

"So where are we, David? Where are we?"

"I wish I knew, Ben. God *damn*, how I wish I knew!"

Ben brightened. "Say, David, listen. I got a *great idea!*"

"What?"

"Let's you and me give a party."

"What?"

"Yes. Let's you and me give a big party and invite each one of the contenders."

David was laughing.

"Nothing Southern, you understand, so we don't give it away. Maybe a New England party."

"Cut it out," said David, in hysterics. "Please."

Ben went on. "Clam chowder and lobsters and—"

David ran from the room. His voice was heard from the hall. "God *damn* it, Ben!"

"What?"

"I've pissed myself."

It was Ben's turn to laugh.

VIII

IN HISTORY, the burning of Atlanta took five days and nights. In *Gone With the Wind,* the preparation and execution of the burning took a total of fifteen days and eleven nights spread over a period of six weeks. Multiple cameras were used for each section of the great conflagration. Every safety precaution was taken. Some cameramen wore asbestos suits. Injuries and accidents were numerous, and the first-aid station was busy at all times.

Overseeing the whole operation was David O. Selznick himself. Dressed in boots, rain gear, and a red fire chief's hat, he seemed to be everywhere at once. Every leftover set from every old David O. Selznick production had been taken out of the scene dock and consigned to the flames. He and his chief assistant, Danny O'Shea, were now negotiating for other studios' old sets.

Night after night on the back lot of the Selznick Studios in Culver City, Atlanta burned. Doubles for Clark Gable and the yet uncast Scarlett escaped the burning city again and again.

It all added up to one of the most spectacular sequences in Hollywood's history, and soon became a social occasion in a community suffering a paucity of evening action. "One thing about Hollywood," Oscar Levant had observed, "no matter how hot it gets in the daytime, there's nothing to do at night."

But while Atlanta was burning at Selznick's, there *was* something to do; that was, if one could wangle an invitation. Friends, families of crew members, agents, journalists, all vied for admittance to the spectacle. The observing crowd grew larger every night.

"If the picture does as well as the fire," said Danny O'Shea to Gilbert Farber, "we'll have a smash."

On the third evening, the most immense shots of all were being made.

David, in his fire chief's hat, his face sweating and streaked with soot, had abandoned his guests—among them, Culbert Olson, the governor of the state of California—and was holding one of the camera operators by the shoulders and leading him about. With a hand-held camera, the operator was attempting to pick up detail of falling debris and sudden flare-ups.

During a break, the chief cameraman, Ernie Haller, asked him, "How you makin' out, Buzz?"

"Fine, Ernie. Fine," he replied. "I don't think Mr. Selznick's ruining *too* much of my stuff."

The shooting went on. Toward the end of the evening, Myron Selznick arrived with a small party he had entertained at dinner. Among his guests were Ben and Willa Farber; David Farber and Ginger Rogers; also Laurence Olivier, who was about to star for Selznick in *Rebecca*, and Vivien Leigh, the English actress with whom Olivier was said to be romantically involved.

She was a small, ravishing beauty with a perfect face. Her innate intelligence, her breeding, her cultivation, her talent, all were apparent either overtly or subliminally. She was beautifully dressed and coifed and groomed. She moved with the grace of a prima ballerina. Her voice was thrilling, her laugh musical.

She stood between Olivier and Myron, watching with her wide green eyes.

"Good Lord!" said Olivier. "Look at David. I've never *seen* anyone so excited."

"Don't forget," said Myron. "He *started* this fire."

Vivien Leigh's laugh rang through the night air. People turned to look at her.

Half an hour later, David came over to greet Olivier. He was grimy again and out of breath. He turned to his brother and said casually, "Hi, Myron."

"David," said Myron. "I want you to meet Scarlett O'Hara."

Vivien smiled. Myron took her elbow and propelled her gently forward.

David stared at her. She extended her lovely hand.

"Hello," she said. "Thank you *so* much for letting me come. It's

301

all perfectly breathtaking. I'm afraid I've always been something of a firebug."

David said nothing. The assistant director appeared and said, "Ready, Mr. Selznick." David did not hear him. He continued to stare at Vivien Leigh. Embarrassed, she made a moue, then giggled.

David walked around her, examining her, studying her as though she were a great work of art on the floor of a museum.

Having circled her, he faced her again. The noisy evening fell silent. He saw her now made up, wigged, and dressed in one of Scarlett's costumes. Another. And still another. He saw her with Clark Gable, as they embraced, kissed.

He saw her again as herself.

As David was regarding Vivien Leigh, he was being observed by Ben Farber.

Finally, David smiled. A soft, slow smile that soon turned into his most winning grin.

"May I have a word with you, Miss Leigh?" he asked.

"By all means."

He took her arm and began walking with her toward the fire.

Myron and Laurence Olivier exchanged a look. Olivier's eyebrows went up, questioningly. Myron winked broadly.

Ben watched David walking away with his newest quarry.

"The war," said Ben to Willa, "—the great 'Scarlett O'Hara' War—is *over!*"

"Thank God," said Willa.

"Thank God," added Ben, "and Myron Selznick."

David, engrossed in talking to Vivien Leigh, walked her past the safety lines and virtually into the fire before three assistant directors piled in and pulled them away. A moment later, a wall collapsed, landing precisely where they had been heading.

Olivier's eyes were closed. He opened them, looked off, and crossed himself.

David, oblivious to the near disaster, continued to walk with Vivien, talking, talking, talking.

Despite the noise, the shouting, the heat, the smoke, the hundreds of visitors, all that David O. Selznick could see at this moment was the dazzling, transcendent, at long last face of Scarlett O'Hara.

302

IX

THEY ASSEMBLED at Paulette's as friends often do following the death of one of their number.

Tallulah arrived first.

"I don't know why," she said. "To make sure, I suppose. I figured you and the little chap would know for sure, if anyone would. This whole God damn town is built on the biggest pile of bullshit in the world, so how can anyone know anything for sure, ever?"

"It's for sure," said Paulette, who had been drinking steadily since the news had been officially announced that morning. "Jeez, you should have heard Charlie talking to him. I don't think they can ever speak again. I swear I wouldn't repeat, even to *you*, what he called him."

"Do you sell gin here?" asked Tallulah.

Paulette went to the bar of her boudoir. "Gin and what?" she asked.

"Gin and gin," said Tallulah.

They said nothing for a time, drinking quietly and thinking noisily.

Tallulah spoke. "Let me tell you what burns my gorgeous ass more than anything."

"Tell me."

"All right, I will. What burns my gorgeous ass more than anything is that this son-of-a-bitch told me—*told* me—it was *me* and to sit tight and not to listen to anything. I've rented my goddam house in New York, for Christ's sake! Where am I going to live?"

"Tallulah, he told *me* the same thing."

"What?"

"I swear to God. He told me, he told Charlie, they shook hands. He told me more than once that it was me."

"And thayat's exactly what he tol' *me!*" said a voice in a Southern accent.

303

They looked up and saw Joan Crawford standing in the doorway, wearing a raincoat and no makeup.

Tallulah howled.

"What so amusin'?" demanded Joan.

"Amusin'? You forgot to drop that terrific Southern accent, you silly bitch. You don't need it anymore, so stop straining."

"Jesus, you're right," said Joan and got herself a drink.

"In fact," said Tallulah, joining Joan at the bar, "I'm thinkin' of gettin' rid of *mine!*"

An hour later they were still together, sprawled variously about the room.

"There's only one good thing about it all," said Paulette. "Only *one good thing.*"

"About it all," said Joan.

"And what's that, may I ask?" asked Tallulah.

Paulette said, "This cockeyed asshole's made the blunder biggest of his whole life!"

"Biggest blunder," said Joan.

"An English broad as Scarlett!" yelled Paulette.

"Not only English," said Joan, "but *British!*"

They all laughed for two minutes.

Tallulah rose. "Do you ladies think there's a Chinaman's chance they're ever gonna even *show* this turkey in the South? Why mah daddy's the Speaker of the God damn House, for Christ's sake! He'll pass a *law.*"

"South, Shmouth," said Joan. "The rest of the country's American, too, isn't it? You think *they're* gonna stand for it?"

"Sit for it?" said Paulette.

"Hell, no," said Tallulah. She looked at Paulette tenderly. "You know, Paulette, you'd have been great in it."

"Not as great as *you,* honey. You'd have been the best."

"I don't think so," said Tallulah. "I'm no good in movies. It should've been you, Joan."

"You said *me,*" said Paulette.

"Either one of you."

"No," said Paulette stubbornly. "It was your start from the part."

"Part from the start," said Joan.

She began to cry, soon joined by Paulette and Tallulah.

304

They assembled, comforting each other.

"Anyway," said Paulette, "let's not forget that he's about to lay the biggest egg in the history of poultry." She raised her glass.

"To a bomb," said Joan, raising hers.

"To a bust," said Tallulah. "To a bust that'll make Mae West's look like two pimples."

They clinked glasses as they said simultaneously, "Bust! Egg! Bomb!"

They drank and flung their glasses into the fireplace, shattering them.

Six weeks later on Stage 5 at Selznick International, the porch at Tara had been erected, and dressed in lush magnolia. Scarlett (Vivien Leigh) sat flanked by the Tarleton twins (George Reeves and Fred Crane) in Confederate army uniforms. The cameras had not yet turned, but already Scarlett was flirting shamelessly with the young stalwarts.

Bells began to ring insistently.

The assistant director's voice rang out, "Hold it down! Quiet please! . . . I said *quiet,* fellas!"

And there was quiet.

George Cukor nodded to Ernest Haller, the cameraman. Haller signaled the assistant director.

"Roll 'em!" said the assistant.

The slate read:

GONE WITH THE WIND
Dir: Cukor   Cam: Haller
Scene 1—Take 1
(Vivien Leigh)
26 January 1939

"Speed," said the operator.

"Scene one! Take one," said the slate man and clicked the board.

"Godspeed," said George Cukor, softly, before shouting, "*Action!*"

PART VI

FARBER FILMS, INC.

I

In the middle of the following week, Hareem Adani arrived just in time to damn near louse up the deal.

I had done one hell of a job. Mr. Farber was beginning to like me; Mrs. Farber was beginning to love me.

(A Goldwyn joke: He tells the story of a film he is considering making to René Clair, the eminent French director. When he reaches the end, there is silence. Clair is thinking it over. Finally, Goldwyn, impatient, blurts out—"Well, how do you love it?")

Adani arrived in Beverly Hills at 4:00 A.M. (no airline scheduling problems for him). He came directly to Bungalow 12 and knocked on the door in the manner of the Gestapo. Scared the bejesus out of me. He walked right past me into the sitting room.

"What you got to drink?"

He headed straight for the bureau, where a tray held not much. I entertained infrequently here.

"Jesus!" he complained. "This all?"

"I didn't know you were coming."

"I *told* you. I didn't?"

He poured a shot of rye and knocked it back, neat.

309

Then he went into the bathroom and, leaving the door open, undressed, took a bath *and* a shower. He came back into the sitting room drying his hirsute body. Another drink.

He fell into the large armchair and sprawled wearily. "Chris-sake, what a flight! I'm dead. Someday I don' wanna have to do every God damn thing myself!"

"You don't."

"Looks to me like. You're here a whole week—so where are we?"

"On the verge."

"For what figure?"

"We're not there yet."

"You're not there *yet,* you're *no* place! *No* place! I *knew* it!"

"Adani, will you listen a minute? I don't mind a little coaching —when I need it—but on *this* one—"

"You haven't even got a *figure* yet, f'Chrissake!"

"As I told you—that's not the main thing involved. The guy's making a life decision—"

"Life? The ol' bastard's ninety-two years of age!"

"That's just it. It's a *final* life decision. If you let me handle it— I'll get you a deal in a week."

"Maybe. Just the same—I wanna have a look at this Sphinx. Set it up for morning. Not too early. I'm beat. Call the desk, ask 'em what suite am I. Reba checked me in."

Against every instinct within me, I did as I was told.

So at 3:15 the following afternoon, there we were, the three of us, in the parlorlike section of Ben's office. A few minutes later, we were joined by Willa. A good sign? I wondered. I rose and introduced her to Adani, who kept his seat.

To my amazement, Ben showed massive respect for Adani, and behaved with deference to him. I could think of no reason for this except that men with a great deal of money generally defer to men with even *more* money.

Adani, similarly, seemed awed by the venerable and celebrated figure he was facing. They pursued a back-and-forth exchange as powerful as champion tennis, as delicate as Ping-Pong. The language they used was new to me, incomprehensible. I took it to be Fiduciary Shorthand (not taught at Berlitz). The game slowed down and turned into something resembling chess, with the moves articulated rather than made.

"There is no way, Mr. Adani—no way that anybody can assess Farber Films. I mean, accurately."

"I got a pretty good idea," said Adani mysteriously.

"You have?"

"I have."

"I wish you'd tell *me*."

"You want *I* should tell *you* what's your business worth?"

"Your idea," Ben countered. "Your pretty good idea."

"When I offer you two hundred thousand shares of Omni Universal, you got to have some idea of my idea."

Willa asked, "What is Omni selling for today?"

"Look in the paper, lady," he said.

I could have slugged him. Instead, I answered Willa's question. "Five ten," I said.

"Thank you." She smiled at me. Whatever else came or not out of all this, I thought, at least I got to know Willa Farber. Willa Love. Willa.

"Stock I'm not interested in," said Ben. "I already told this to Guy many times."

"You crazy?" asked Adani, flabbergasted.

Ben nodded gravely. "There are many people think so. I don't."

"Nor do I," said Willa.

I held my tongue.

"You talking cash?" asked Adani. "Money cash? You nuts? The taxes. They'll kill you."

"No, no. Don't you worry. Let me worry."

"Nobody's gonna come up with that kind of cash. For *no* studio."

"Mr. Adani, you got any idea what was my original investment in Farber Films?"

"Sure. You incorporated for a hundred and twenty-five thousand."

Willa and Ben exchanged a long and searching look. How could Adani possibly know this?

Ben said, "Well, there you see what a capital gain we have here."

Adani got out a handkerchief and wiped his face.

"Lemme get something here straight. You people are saying to me you don't want Omni Universal stock?"

"I don't want *any* stock. Not AT and T, not IBM, not Standard Oil. I got plenty stock."

311

Adani turned to Willa and asked, "You think your husband understands this deal?"

"I don't know about *him*," she said. "I know *I* do."

"And what do *you* think?"

"Do you want the truth?"

"Sure."

"I don't think he wants to sell at all."

"Don't say that, darling. I'm still thinking it over."

"No," she said. "You're thinking it *under*."

When I laughed at this sally, Adani burned me with a look, then put his attention back on Ben.

It was clear now that they loathed one another.

Adani, normally voluble and loud, fell silent.

Ben ignored him, more or less, and turned to me.

"I told you already, didn't I? How Farber Films got started in the first place?"

"I'm not sure."

"Then I didn't. It's some story. If I told it to you, you would remember."

He settled back, happily, delighted to be reminiscing again.

"Up there on the hill," he said, "we used to run a picture every single night. . . ."

Adani put his face in his hands. Willa got up and left quietly.

II

THE PROJECTION room was the epicenter of the home of Mr. and Mrs. Benjamin J. Farber, high up in the Beverly Hills. John Barrymore was their Tower Road neighbor, Greta Garbo lived a short distance beyond.

The Farbers and their dinner guests were still in the dining room; two maids and a butler were preparing the projection room for the evening. The projectionist was adjusting the screen at the far end of the room. The maids put out nuts and mints and candies, mineral waters, brandies.

They heard the company coming and disappeared swiftly. The

doors opened. First to enter was Ben, with his son Abraham, aged ten; he was followed by Tessa with their younger son, Gilbert, aged eight. They led their guests into the projection room. Among this evening's visitors were Vilma Banky and her husband, Rod LaRoque; Joan Crawford and young Douglas Fairbanks, Jr.; the Marquis and Marquise de la Falaise de Coudray— she was only a short time ago Gloria Swanson. Charles Chaplin with Willa Love, his current leading lady; Mary Pickford and Douglas Fairbanks.

The guests were soon seated. The mood was one of satiated senses and pleasurable anticipation. A few lighted cigarettes. Tessa was busily attending to her duties as a hostess. She pressed her little sons into service, charmingly. They passed out nuts and mints and bonbons. Ben stood up and faced his guests. He held up a palm and spoke.

"Dear friends. Tonight Tessa and I have a very special treat for you and I'm sure you're going to enjoy it. King Vidor has most kindly lent us a print of a rough cut of his new picture. It's called . . . it's called . . . the name of it is—"

Tessa helped him out. "*The Patsy,* dear. *The Patsy.*"

"*The Patsy,*" said Ben. "He's got in it Marion Davies and that wonderful Marie Dressler and I'm sure we're all going to enjoy it."

An enormous lady pianist entered the room carrying a sheaf of music and made her way to the piano at the left of the screen. Ben noticed her.

"Oh, yes, King asked us to apologize for the no-music track yet because this picture hasn't yet been scored yet, but he most kindly sent over his piano player to help us out."

There was a smattering of applause. The overweight pianist acknowledged her reception with a stern nod. Ben started for his seat but was interrupted by Tessa.

"The tests, dear. Remember? The tests?"

"The tests?" asked Ben querulously, adjusting his hearing aid.

"You promised," said Tessa. "They have to have them back in the morning."

"Oh, yeah," said Ben. "The tests." He assumed his lecturing position again. "Dear friends. I hope you don't mind, but we have to run a couple of tests before. They have to have them back in the morning. I hope you don't mind."

313

He took his place and signaled the projectionist. The lights dimmed, the gentle whirring of the projection machine was heard. The pianist rose quietly and left the room.

There followed a showing of three or four tests. Extremely pretty girls, some of them from the Ziegfeld Follies. Extraordinarily handsome, wooden men. A precocious child dancer. All at once, the screen became a repository of astonishing beauty and magnetism. The black and white shadow of Ethel Barrymore was seen. The test camera moved toward her and held, finally, a close-up of that fabulous face. Meanwhile, she spoke Portia's "Quality of mercy" speech from *The Merchant of Venice*.

"My God!" said Chaplin as she came on. "It's Ethel Barrymore!"

"It certainly is," cried Gloria Swanson.

"What the hell is *she* making a screen test for?" asked Douglas Fairbanks, Jr., with astonishing logic.

"It's for the talkies," explained Ben. "Anybody can *talk*, they want them for the talkies now."

"Well, she can *talk* all right," said Charlie.

Joan Crawford was agog. She had never seen Ethel Barrymore. "Why, she's *beautiful!*" said Joan.

The test ended to vociferous applause.

Ben spoke to the projectionist on his intercom.

"Thanks very much, Sandy, those go back to the studio tonight. You can start the picture now."

Sandy's voice, on the intercom: "There's one more, Mr. Farber."

"One more?"

"Yes, sir."

"All right," said Farber, with a weary sigh. "*Start* it anyway. Who is it?"

"Wait a second," said Sandy. "I think it's—hold it. Oh, yeah. It's from Howard Hughes. The name is . . . on it is . . . here it is—Jean Har-low." He pronounced it so that the second syllable rhymed with "cow."

"Is that a man or a woman?" asked Ben.

"I guess a woman, Mr. Farber, because the spelling is J-e-a-n. And it's silent."

"All right."

The projector whirred again.

On the screen there appeared the overpainted yet piquant face of Jean Harlow. She was, perhaps, the first platinum blonde ever photographed, and at first blush appeared to be a pretty little white-haired old lady. She turned and moved away from the camera, displaying extraordinary equipment. She reached full-length position, turned back to the camera, and, apparently at the director's order, began to move back *toward* the camera into a waist shot. There was whistling and foot-stamping from the small audience.

"Well, there's the reason they tested her," said Doug, Jr.

"The *two* reasons," said Chaplin.

Laughter.

"Take the children out, Tessa, would you?" said Ben.

"No!" shouted Abe.

"I don' *wanna!*" said Gilbert, hanging on to the arms of his chair.

More laughter.

"Leave 'em alone, Ben," said Chaplin. "You're never too young to learn."

The test ended abruptly. The screen went black.

"I don't think so," was Ben's immediate verdict. "Blondes like that, they're a dime a dozen."

"Here's a dime," said Charlie. "Get me a dozen, will you?"

"That Howard Hughes!" said Gloria Swanson. "He signs them up and then tries to sell them off. What sort of business is that?"

"I can't tell you in front of the kids," said Chaplin.

On the screen, the test suddenly continued. Jean Harlow was joined by a partner who was, possibly the handsomest young man extant. However, he seemed to own but a single fixed expression, as though it were painted on his face. He played a love scene with Jean Harlow which led them to a sofa and into a reclining position, locked in an embrace. Suddenly both looked toward the camera and into its lens. Jean seemed to be hard of hearing, as she frowned and strained to hear what was being said to her. The boy repeated the director's instructions. They looked at each other for an embarrassed length, then Jean shrugged. Now she went to work in earnest, and did what she knew how to do. They kissed. They kissed in a remarkably undulating way, using their bodies as well as their heads and lips. The camera bumped forward and ended on a double close-up. The kiss over, the boy was

315

dripping with sweat, and he now had more of Jean Harlow's lipstick on his face than she had left on hers.

"Why on earth do you suppose they didn't make a *talking* test?" asked Tessa.

"Looks to me," said Doug, Jr., "like those two *can't* talk."

"She doesn't *have* to," said Mary Pickford.

"And *he's* not so bad either," said Gloria. "What's his name?"

Ben spoke to the intercom: "Has this man got a name, Sandy?"

"Wait a second . . . yes—Alan Bolt."

"Alan Bolt," echoed Tessa softly.

The test continued. Alan Bolt and Jean Harlow were dancing, now, extremely well, but all at once, Ben shouted into the intercom. "All right, Sandy, that's enough! Thanks." The screen went black. The fat pianist returned and took her place. The film began. She played the music for the main titles.

METRO-GOLDWYN-MAYER PICTURES

PRESENTS

MARION DAVIES   MARIE DRESSLER   DELL HENDERSON

in

T H E   P A T S Y

with Lawrence Gray and Jane Winton

Scenario: Agnes Christine Johnstone
Titles: Ralph Spence
Cinematographer: John Seitz
Set Design: Cedric Gibbons

Directed by King Vidor

It turned out to be, as Ben had promised, a treat.

Later, in the Farbers' elaborate and ornately furnished bedroom suite, Ben and Tessa were preparing for bed. She had a dressing room to the right of the bedroom, his dressing room was to the left. They moved in and out of the bedroom, chatting.

"Wonderful dinner, Tessa, wonderful. Everybody was remarking."

"I think I'd enjoy it more if it didn't cost so damn much."

"Well, you know how they say, you get what you pay for."

Tessa, at her dressing table, brushed her hair, vigorously, counting a hundred strokes. Her action released her pent-up anger.

"You made another stupid mistake tonight, Ben. I didn't want to tell you in front of everyone, but you did."

"What mistake was that? *Stupid* mistake."

"That test. That test that Hughes sent over?"

"What're you talking about? That blonde? We've got thirty blondes like that. Better than that. Than those."

"I *know* that. I didn't *mean* the blonde. That kid who made the test with her. Just because it wasn't *his* test, you didn't even look at him."

"Who?"

"See? You didn't."

"There was somebody else in the test with her?" he asked.

"A boy. The handsomest boy I ever saw. Don't you remember? They were lying on the sofa, practically doing it."

"I can't believe it. *That* I would have noticed."

"You must have dozed off the way you usually do."

"Never during a picture," said Ben. "Sometimes during a test, yes."

"Well, you missed it."

"All right, so I'll get it back and run it again."

"No, you won't. You forget such things."

"I'll write it down. See, I'm writing it down."

He wrote it down.

Tessa said, "You just missed, maybe, one of the biggest stars of the next ten years."

Ben replied defensively. "The biggest stars of the next ten years, Tessa, are all going to have to be actors. Not dummies no more. Not just clotheshorses. Look what's happening to them all. All of them. To Gilbert. And to Valentino. And you know what Ronnie Colman told me the other day? He told me that he told Goldwyn he wouldn't make a talking picture for all the money in the world. And lots of 'em feel like that. So what does that mean? That we got to bring in actors, actors who know how to speak. And how to talk. Maybe from England, even. Or from the stage in New York."

"How do you know that this young man *isn't* a talking actor?"

317

"I'll find out."

"No, you won't."

"All right, I'll tell you what. You're so interested, why don't *you* find out?"

Tessa looked at him, her eyes alive. "I will," she said. They went to bed.

Tessa took charge and indeed did follow through. She located Alan Bolt through his agent, Mike Levee, and invited them both to lunch with her at the Ambassador Hotel.

Alan considered it the break of his life. He had done the test only as a favor to his friend, Jean Harlow, who had got him a few bit parts at United Artists. He was astonished to hear that Farber was not interested in Jean, but his disappointment was greatly mitigated by the fact that Tessa Farber indicated she was going to recommend *him* to her husband.

Alan was not much of a communicator, but he was a faultless receiver and he read the various looks in Tessa's eyes perfectly. He interpreted the slight pressure of her fingers on his forearm clearly, as though she were sending expert Morse code. By the time lunch was over, he had a scenario pretty well worked out.

At this point in his life, Ben was as completely occupied with his business as a man can be. In addition, his continuing relationship with Pempy required time and effort and interest. His marriage to Tessa had always been a marriage of convenience—*his* convenience—and one could hardly blame *her* for developing a roving eye. Unfortunately, she had had little success. But in the past few years, she had become increasingly aggressive and predatory.

It was the opulent custom in those days at M-G-M to give a splendid formal dinner-dance once a month at which all the newly signed players were introduced. It was usually held on Stage 22. The food was superb, featuring the world-renowned Louis B. Mayer Double Chicken Soup as the inevitable first course; speeches, toasts, sometimes screenings of the tests of the newcomers; entertainment by the studio's musical talents: Charles King, Anita Page, Lawrence Tibbett or the Duncan Sisters. It was generally a democratic affair, a one-big-happy-family theme prevailing. Its origin had something to do with building company morale

318

and loyalty and *esprit de corps*. Strangely, it almost always succeeded.

Irving Thalberg, for one, was critical of the scheme.

"We're a *producing* organization," he said, "not a country club. And, in any case, when you talk to these people about loyalty to M-G-M, what's M-G-M? Three letters in the alphabet and two of them the same. And what do they stand for? Metro-Goldwyn-Mayer. What's Metro? Even I don't know. Of course, we all know Mayer. But Goldwyn isn't here and never has been. So what's loyalty to M-G-M? To the sound stages? To the equipment? To the backlot? How can anyone be loyal to *that*? To the stockholders? Good God! Even *I* don't know who *they* are. No. People aren't loyal to companies. People are loyal to other people. I expect mine to be loyal to me, and God knows, I try to be loyal to them and not let them down. So all this hullaballoo about building up studio loyalty, at this obscene expense, is nothing more than a waste of money. Well, that doesn't matter, we've got plenty of that, but it's a waste of *time,* and *no* one has too much of *that!*"

He spoke prophetically, since his own life would end at thirty-seven.

But the dinner-dances went on, always on a Sunday evening.

The one that was held on November 25, 1928, was memorable and was to cause a shattering upheaval in a number of lives.

Despite the fact of Prohibition, the finest French wines had been served during dinner. Now with the Île Flottante, Veuve Cliquot champagne was being poured.

At the head table, Thalberg turned to his wife, Norma Shearer, laughed, and said, "One of these Sundays, you know, we're going to be raided and carted off in paddy wagons. What a splendid story *that'll* make for the stockholders."

Mayer overheard the remark. "What're you talking about?" he bellowed. "Would *I* break a *law?* This is a private party. Like as if I would be giving it in my own home. In fact, this *is* my own home. This is my own home more than my own home—is how I feel about the M-G-M Studios. And are we charging? Are we selling?"

Thalberg regarded him pityingly and raised his glass in salute. "You're never wrong, L.B. That *would* be against the law."

Alan Bolt was among the guests of honor. Over the rim of the most delicate champagne glass he had ever seen, that pair of eyes was whispering to him again. The eyes were blue-black and larger than most. They belonged to Tessa Seligman Farber. Alan was, in a sense, her protégé. He wanted to make good, not only for himself, but for her. He was sitting on her right and doing his best. It was difficult to guess her age. Somewhere in the middle, he guessed, but she had erased the idea from her consciousness, pumping vitality into her days and nights with ideas and acts of the young. She kept herself trim in body, spent hours each day buying the ministrations of experts in skin and hair, makeup and hairdress. The fact that she spent $300,000 a year on her wardrobe did no harm either. She had learned to make herself magnetic by being inviting and forbidding at one and the same time. She was letting Alan know that she was interested. There was nothing coy about Tessa.

Later, they danced together for the first time. She was one of those talkative dancers.

"I might have known it," she said. "You are what I call a *dancer*, mister. If you can act as well as you do this, you're in. I suppose I should've got it from the test. I only saw the damn thing about twenty times. Don't blush. I didn't see it because I wanted to, but every night there for a while, he kept showing it before we ran whatever picture. *My* opinion wasn't good enough for him. He likes to get a lot of reactions, then he boils them all together, then he knows what *he* thinks. Me, I don't care for anybody's opinion. I don't even care for my own."

"You been out here long?" asked Alan.

She unpasted her front from his and regarded him as they continued to dance.

"Don't make idle conversation with me, laddie. You haven't got the time. Don't forget that the ups and downs are quickquickquick out here except in rare cases. Don't be polite. Not to me. I can't bear polite, and it's not your speed anyway, is it?"

"Hasn't been so far."

"What I thought. You're a roughneck, right?"

"O.K."

"What do you want?" she asked.

"What've you got?" he responded at once.

"We've got it all, sonny. But we give a little away once in a while. Like, say, a set of free dishes to the customers, or a name above the title to the employees. You know, whatever we have to give, we give, to get what we want to get."

"Dough was what I had in mind," said Alan, executing a spectacular spin, which she followed easily.

"Yes," she said. "We've got a lot of that. Help yourself."

They became one as they danced.

Two weeks later, he was up for a part. An important second lead that Mike Levee assured him was "in scoring position."

"They don't come up so often, but this one is built-in. It's got to be a wrapup if handled by the right guy. You may be. Who knows?"

"*I* know," said Alan, "and you *should.*"

"I stand corrected."

Alan was sitting in a shabby old portable dressing room on the set, worrying about his makeup.

"Don't fuss about how you look," said Mike. "That's in *their* hands. The acting, *that's* in yours. You know the words O.K.?"

"Good enough for the kind of words they are."

"What you should do is con yourself into thinking they're as good as Shakespeare. If you have contempt for what you do, it's bound to show."

"Beat it, Mike, will y'?"

"You want to run over them? I'll hold the script. No extra charge."

"No, I'll be all right."

Mike looked out onto the set and closed the door with his foot. "Another thing," he said, softly, "I notice Tessa Farber on the prowl out there."

"Watch yourself, Mike."

"Please. I know the action out here. She can do you good but also not so good. Play it if you want, but very very carefully, I beg you. Two verys, I hope you noticed."

"Mind your business, y'mind?"

"That's what I'm doing, Alan. This is no new gambit with her. She's a live one. I'll say it once more and that's all. Very very careful. You're up here in the horse latitudes and the air gets thin."

Alan leaped to his feet and pointed at Mike. "If I muck up this test, you dumb son-of-a-bitch, and I *may,* it'll be your fault."

"I know. It'll always be my fault, *whatever* goes wrong."

There was a knock at the door.

Mike opened it. Tessa Farber.

"Sorry," she said.

"Come in," said Alan.

She stepped into the dressing room, and asked, "Guess who sent me over?"

"Mr. Farber," said Mike.

"Not *you!*" she snapped and turned to Alan. "Guess who?"

"I give up," said Alan.

"Mr. Farber," she said.

"Think of that," said Mike.

Tessa continued. "He said for me to come over and show you the ropes a little, sort of. He likes you, but he worries you're raw. That's the word he used. Raw. He thinks I can help polish you up."

"Excuse me," said Mike, starting out.

"Where you going?" asked Alan.

"Out, if there's going to be polishing. They say diamond dust in the air is the worst thing for the nose. And me with my allergy." He stepped out of the dressing room leaving the door ajar. Alan moved to the door and touched the knob.

"Leave it open, you cluck," he heard Tessa say behind him. His hand came off the knob.

"Hand me a script and sit down," she said. "Peeking into this dressing room is the game of the day today."

He did as she said and gave her one of his practiced, serviceable looks: hunger, terror, recklessness in equal parts, served with the mouth slightly open.

"Don't give me that," she said, and laughed. "Don't waste your energy. It's all here. Just tough to get at. Take your time."

"That's the one thing I'm weak on," he said. "Patience. That and those bloody lines." He pointed to the script.

"You should worry."

"What?!" He looked at her.

"It's all set." She winked broadly.

"You kiddin' me, kid?"

"No. I took care of it over the weekend."

"Why the test, then?" asked Alan.

"Protocol. We have to give the great Clarence Brown out there

322

—also known as Nervous Nellie—we have to give him the feeling he's got something to say. So we go through the motions. Four thousand dollars' worth of motions. So that feelings won't get hurt. But he knows and we know it's all set. You're in. Say thank you."

"Thanks," said Alan. He felt light-headed.

"Now here's how we'll work it, for a start. We have to wait for His Nibs to ask you down to the Springs. He will in time. It's routine. Down there, mornings, he plays golf. I sleep. What do you do?"

"I study."

"No golf?"

"No, I study."

"Where do you study?" asked Tessa.

"Where do you sleep?" asked Alan.

The assistant director stuck his head in the doorway.

"Ready, Mr. Bolt?"

"Yes, he is," said Tessa. Three small red splotches had appeared on her face.

When Alan saw his test two days later, he remembered what Mike had said. He was photographed superbly, but his tentative approach, lack of preparation, and uncertain delivery gave his performance a negative, lifeless tone. He hoped no one else would notice.

Apparently, no one did—at least no one in a position of importance—because by the end of the week, he was called into Mr. Farber's office where he was introduced to Freddie Lavine, Mr. Farber's right-hand man, and informed with some ceremony that the part was his. He was also told, solemnly, that he was on the threshold of a great career; warningly, that he was to cooperate with everyone; gaily, that the studio had great plans for him; and tantalizingly, that it was all up to him now.

He attempted to respond to each announcement in the way he thought was expected of him, and appeared to have been successful. Then came one that gave him some difficulty.

Mr. Farber said, "Tell you what I want. You, Alan, and Freddie, you—you like that name, 'Alan'? Alan Bolt? Nothing. Let's get a name for him, somebody. Make up a list. Check it with Max. Max is good on names. A long one. That one is too short. It's over before you know it. I like long names. They look bigger on the billing. People think they're getting more for their money. Like Rudolph Valentino, now *there's* a good name. What was I saying? Oh, yes. You, Alan—or whatever we decide to call you—and you, Freddie—I like you both down to the Springs the weekend. We'll go over a whole plan for you, private. Also, I want Mrs. Farber to give a hand. She's the best in the business on creating personalities. You know what I mean? She'll find him a gimmick like a haircut or an attitude. Some piece of business to swing on. Fast cars. Athletics. I don't know. Something. Don't rush her. But she always comes up with something. O.K., fellows. Out."

On Sunday morning in Palm Springs, things went wrong.

It was an exceptionally hot day. Ben was out on the golf course. He played—as he did everything else in life—with great intensity.

He and David Selznick were partnered against Mack Sennett and Freddie.

On the tenth hole, just as he was about to tee off, Ben fainted. Mack and David carried him back to the clubhouse while Freddie ran ahead to find a doctor. No luck at the clubhouse. An ambulance was summoned. By the time it arrived, Ben had come to and refused to go to the hospital, despite the urgings of David and Mack.

"Take me home," he insisted. "That's all. Just get me home. I'll be all right."

Ben and David and Freddie and Sennett and the club nurse all got into David's car. Nothing serious had happened to Ben, but the tension and the atmosphere of crisis that was built on the journey home frightened him into fainting a second time, just as they reached the house. Had he been conscious he would have gone straight to his own room in the usual way. As it happened, David and Freddie carried him up the back stairs, missing Tessa's maid, who was posted near the *front* stairs.

In the upper hall, David and Freddie dropped him accidentally. The nurse screamed. Mack scolded her. Tessa opened the door to the bedroom suite. The whole party pressed in, excitedly. Alan, nude, made for the dressing room swiftly enough to elude all but Freddie, who followed. Freddie closed the door and as he watched the trembling Alan attempt to get his clothes on, said, "Kid, you're about as stupid as you look, and that's going some!"

Alan said nothing. He was trying to keep from throwing up.

Tessa came in and closed the door. "He'll be all right," she said.

Freddie smiled at her. "I know. But will *you* be?"

"Call your shot, baby," she replied.

"I want a lot," he said. "I come high. I want my own unit. And no supervision."

"I see," she said. "That may take a little time."

"Don't stall me, lady. I want it right away, and I want it in writing."

"You're pressing, Freddie. What you don't know is that it could boomerang. Ben knows me and how I live. And I know all about him and his. You start spouting around and he might dump *you*. He sure wouldn't dump me. He never has before."

"I'll take my chances," said Freddie, confidently. "This looks like my luck to me."

"You're wrong," she said.

She was right. Freddie lost. His revelation was met coldly by B.J. Farber, and his contract was settled. He went to Paramount as an assistant director.

Alan was less fortunate. Mr. Farber explained it to him. "I'll tell you how it is, my friend. You struck out. Mrs. Farber is a very attractive woman, and complicated, you know, like so many Hollywood wives. They feel neglected. So I don't blame her. And I can't blame you or anybody else for getting ideas. The truth is you're not good enough for me to stand for it. If you were somebody hot, what the hell, that's the price we pay. If you were, say, John Gilbert or John Barrymore, in fact, any John around here, maybe. But you're not all that good. You were a big maybe for us. Maybes are a dollar a dozen. Used to be a dime a dozen, but you know, inflation and all. So, goodbye and good luck. You can call yourself Alan Bolt now if you want, and I want you to know that in spite of everything, there's plenty of hard feelings."

Alan took one deep breath and tried. "I suppose it's no use asking for one more chance?" he said.

"No. No use. Not from me."

Alan hung around Hollywood for a while, until he became aware of being the patsy in the newest and juiciest gossip. The story of what had happened had grown in epic proportions, complete with details so accurate that when he overheard an outrageously erroneous version in the next booth at The Brown Derby, he half believed it himself.

He met secretly with Tessa several times for a series of postmortems.

He was flat broke, but she provided him with a bungalow at the Beverly Hills Hotel.

"Big, busy places like that," she said, "they're the best for a caper like ours, see? So, what if somebody sees me here? So what?"

He gathered she was no stranger to "capers like ours."

She began to turn up at odd hours—eight in the morning, middle of the night, and once, in a formal evening gown, having left a party, drunk.

On this occasion, for the first time, he refused to perform.

She berated him.

"Take it easy," he said. "I'm not your kept man, y'know."

"You're not?" she asked in astonishment. "What's the number of this bungalow, anyhow? Sorry, mister. I'll be dressed and out of your way in a minute."

The next day, she phoned him and apologized. Later, she came to him and spent the night.

Ben was in New York, attending a Metro-Goldwyn-Mayer board meeting.

Tessa had had the telephone company put in an extension of her private phone in Alan's bungalow. Thus when Ben called her from New York, she was able to take the call without leaving Alan's bed.

Tessa and Alan quarreled endlessly, mutually complained and criticized and insulted each other. It was only as sexual partners that they were utterly compatible. Each brought the other to life.

He continued to try to find a career as an actor, with no success.

In time, their bad times began to overshadow their good ones.

He complained that she was not doing as much as she might to help him find work.

She expressed sympathy and regret and said, "But it's no go for you now, Alan. They all think of you as an operator, not an actor, not even a personality. No, your best bet is to go back East and make a hit in something. If you can. Get a show. A year or two, you come back and all this'll be just a lot of who cares."

Alan had cried, not then, not in front of Tessa, but later. On a bench on Hollywood Boulevard with a sign on it advertising Groman's Mortuary.

He made a slow and miserable trip home, driving aimlessly across the wide, wide country in that sputtering secondhand Nash.

He was to return less than a year later under happier circumstances.

III

As ABE FARBER's thirteenth birthday approached, Ben began to have vagrant atavistic thoughts of a bar mitzvah. His son Haim (now Higham) had, of course, not observed the ancient ritual of the coming of manhood. In fact, he probably had no idea of its existence. But now Ben's second son could be confirmed if Ben chose.

Tessa was indifferent, but said carefully, "You better ask my father. He doesn't go to temple anymore, but he's big stuff in the B'nai B'rith, so who knows? He's such an unpredictable bastard."

"Bar mitzvah!" shouted A.L. Seligman. "What the hell are you talking about?"

"My son, Abe," said Ben, flustered. "Abe, thirteen."

"He's an American, for Chrissake! Americans don't get bar mitzvahed. He's no greenhorn, like you. You know what 'A.L.' stands for, don't you? Abraham Lincoln."

"I was never bar mitzvahed myself," said Ben.

"Why not?"

"There was nobody around. I was alone."

"Bar mitzvah," A.L. jeered. "Ridiculous. Why?"

Ben, inwardly relieved, said, "Well, A.L., it's like the fella said, a friend met him in the street and he said, 'Where you going?' So the fella said, 'To the synagogue. It's Yom Kippur.' So the friend said, 'But you never go to the synagogue, so why today?' And the fella said, 'Well, in case of a tie.' "

A.L. laughed hard. "Say," he chortled, "that's a good one. I want to remember that one."

327

"By the way," said Ben, "did you see those new unemployment figures, A.L.? Twelve million, they say."

A.L. waved the news away with both arms. "I never believe that stuff."

"Hoover says so himself."

"He's a great man, Hoover," said A.L. "But *he* has to play politics, too." He lit a cigar thoughtfully. "Speaking of unemployment —that gives me a good idea."

"Is that so?"

"Yes. Instead of bar mitzvah, he should do some work of some kind. That'll do more to make him a man than a big banquet and a little speech. He should get himself a job, your son. Your Abe."

"At the studio, you mean? Like a messenger?"

"No, no," said A.L., impatiently. "Away from you. Far away. A job like other boys do. Like a paper route, or after school—in a grocery, or a garage. Or like that. A job. Not a goddamn sinecure."

Ben hesitated. "The only thing is—"

"Yes?"

"—I don't know if Tessa—"

"Never mind if Tessa. I'll tell her what to do, and she'll do it."

Tessa did it. She called her friend, Bill Hearst, Jr., at *The Los Angeles Examiner.* Within a week's time, his circulation department had assigned a Beverly Hills delivery route to Abe. His bicycle was fitted with a large basket, and after school every day, he made his way to the distribution headquarters on Rodeo Drive, picked up 120 copies of *The Los Angeles Examiner,* delivered them door to door to subscribers. It took him about an hour and a half, and he earned one cent a copy each weekday ($1.20), and two cents a copy on Sundays ($2.40). The bulk of the Sunday edition made two trips necessary and took three hours. Still, it brought his weekly earnings to $9.60. Ben thought it not bad for part-time work in the midst of a deep depression.

A.L. Seligman was delighted; Ben proud; Tessa worried; and Abe miserable. He loathed the job. Even when he had learned to toss the papers efficiently from his moving bike, cutting the time down to an hour, he thought it all a pointless charade, a punishment for having done nothing.

One afternoon, at the corner of Camden and Lomitas, he saw

a small Chevrolet from Texas moving slowly, looking for movie star homes. As it slowed in front of the home of Ruth Chatterton, Abe contrived to maneuver his bike in front of the barely moving vehicle and to be knocked down.

The enormous myopic woman at the wheel went into instant hysteria and began blowing her horn frantically in alarm. Her undersized husband, sitting beside her, map in hand, fainted dead away.

Abe, meanwhile, was able to crawl under the car.

George Brent, Ruth Chatterton's husband, came running out of the house and took charge.

The police arrived just before the ambulance.

Abe, feigning unconsciousness, was taken to the Beverly Hills Hospital for examination and observation.

George Brent, meanwhile, had found Abe's identification and had phoned Ben, who called Tessa.

The family, including Gilbert and the Seligmans, converged on the hospital to be told that Abe was perfectly all right.

"I don't believe it!" Tessa shouted. "How can they tell? What about internal injuries?"

"They looked," said Ben. "They looked."

"She's right," said A.L. He turned to the doctor. "Keep him here a few days."

Abe looked up and said weakly, "But what about my route? I've got to deliver my papers. I've *got to.*"

"I'll do it," said Gilbert bravely.

Tessa burst into tears.

A.L. held his back.

"Don't worry son. We'll take care of everything," he said.

"Let *me* do it," said Gilbert.

Ben regarded Abe with mounting suspicion. "Sure," he said. "We'll find somebody to take over until you're better."

"Why can't *I?*" asked Gilbert petulantly.

Tessa turned to Ben and said, "What's the matter with you? He's never going to do it again, you hear. It's too dangerous."

"He doesn't have to do it on a bike," said Ben. "He can walk."

"Walk!" yelled Abe, sitting up. "Walk! Jesus, it takes an hour now. That'll take *two!* More. How can—"

He caught himself suddenly and fell back feebly. "My back," he said in a frail voice. "Pain."

329

As the doctor moved toward him, A.L. said, "Don't worry, we'll find a way. *I'll* find a way."

Thus it was that the daily routine at the Farber home was revised.

At 3:30 every afternoon, Abe, having returned from school and having had his cake and milk, was driven by Hans in the Packard limousine to the distribution center. There Hans picked up Abe's papers, loaded them into the back seat, and drove the route, stopping for Abe to make the deliveries. In time, Abe learned to throw the papers from the car window, and with the help of Hans, was able to complete his route in just over thirty minutes.

The sight of the chauffeur-driven Packard limousine delivering papers became a minor tourist attraction for a time, and the subject of a tongue-in-cheek human interest story in *The Los Angeles Times*. But Abe was held to it until Gilbert turned thirteen, whereupon *he* took over the route and Abe went to work as a film messenger at M-G-M, even though his father, having divorced his mother, was no longer there.

IV

TESSA AND Ben decided between themselves, as amicably as these things can be decided, to end their marriage. The marriage fatigue had deteriorated into marriage failure. There was little sustenance in their partnership. Not for her, not for him. Tessa no longer wanted to be married to Ben. Ben no longer wanted to be married to Tessa.

But A.L. Seligman wanted them to remain married to each other.

He sent for them and told them in no uncertain terms that he would have none of it. He took their decision as a personal affront. What about the children? Were they thinking of *them*? What would people, especially people in the industry of which he was so important a part, have to say? It was a disgrace.

Living his insular life, he had no idea that the story was already stale.

"Who decided?" he thundered. "Who was the one decided?"

"We *both* decided, Papa," said Tessa.

"Ridiculous! Two people don't decide at the same time. Who decided first? Who wanted out?"

There was a silence.

"*I* did," said Ben. "It was a matter of principle. I'm not such a religious man, but maybe it's in the blood. In the Talmudic laws, an unfaithful wife is ostracized."

"Well, I'm certainly glad I'm not Jewish," said Tessa, with a wicked smile.

Her father pointed a finger at her. "You're Jewish *enough!*" he cried. He turned to Ben. "You and your goddam Talmudic law. What does your Talmudic law say about a son-of-a-bitch keeps an *English* woman—for years?"

Ben, startled and speechless, turned to Tessa. She laughed.

"Oh, for God's *sake!*" she said. "Did you really think you were getting away with it all this time? You don't know that Hollywood is the smallest small town there is? That everybody knows everything about everybody else? You didn't *know* that?"

"But that's nothing," Ben spluttered. "That's an old . . . that's the past . . . a friend . . . an old friend."

"An old *whore!*" shouted Seligman.

Ben was on his feet. "Don't say that, Abe. Don't you *dare* say that!"

"In my own house I dare say anything."

"You don't *know* this person. You got no right—"

"Don't talk to *me* about rights! You tell me what you intend to do, and I advise you right here and now, you better damn well do what I tell you do." He looked at his daughter. "All right with you, Tessa? To go on like before?"

"Yes, Papa. If you want."

He turned to Ben, and waited.

"No," said Ben. "Never. Under no circumstances."

Seligman regarded him seriously. "Very well," he said. "You've proved you're not a *gentle*man," he said. "But I know you are a *business*man. So let's talk business a little. You know I'm in a position to make them squeeze you out of M-G-M, don't you?"

Ben turned pale. Seligman went on.

"Mayer doesn't like you. He never has. He thinks you're a Thalberg man. If you are, you're foolish, because Thalberg's a sick

331

boy, and that's no kind of a weak sister to hitch up your wagon to. You're on the wrong team over there. Also, with the money situation right now, they're soon going to be in a bind. And you're going to be out!"

Tessa came to him and touched his arm. "Don't do this, Papa. It's—it's not his whole fault. He's worked hard. I *know* how hard. I don't care about his business. If we want to be apart, let us be. But please—don't *do* this."

Seligman turned to her slowly and said, "Get the hell out of here, you *bum* you!"

Tessa left the room.

After a time, with nothing further said, Seligman went to the bar and poured two drinks. He handed one to Ben. They drank. Seligman then went to his desk and picked up a silver humidor. He offered Ben a cigar. Ben took it. Seligman lit the cigar for Ben, lit his own. They were excellent cigars, long ones, especially made for him. It took them more than half an hour to reach the end of their cigars. During all that time, not a word was spoken. Ben was thinking out the situation carefully, considering alternatives, imagining possibilities. Seligman was doing the same. It was akin to a game of backgammon, but played without a board, without dice.

Finally, Ben rose, as did Seligman. They shook hands, silently. Ben left.

He neither saw nor spoke to Seligman ever again. A.L. Seligman died eight years later, unforgiving to the end.

About three months after the explosive scene with Ben and her father, Tessa went to New York for her customary semiannual visit to see the shows, to buy some clothes. In one of the plays she went to see, she recognized, under a crepe hair beard, the face of Alan Bolt. She looked in her program attempting to identify him, but found no Alan Bolt. She listened more carefully to the words in the play and eventually figured out the name of the character he was playing. Back to the program. That character was played by Alistair Burlingame.

She went backstage to see him. The reunion proved to be exhilarating, euphoric. They went out to supper at the Ritz-Carlton, on a tour of the Fifty-second Street speakeasies, made the traditional trip to Harlem and the Savoy Ballroom, returned to the

Waldorf-Astoria, and were never separated again. He became Alan Bolt again, at Tessa's command. A few months later, in Paris, she became Mrs. Alan Bolt.

They returned to California, where Alan decided, at the age of twenty-seven, to retire. The Bolts traveled extensively, entertained lavishly, produced four children, all boys, and—contrary to the apprehensions of their friends—succeeded in marriage.

Ben Farber fared less well following the divorce. At M-G-M, he was systematically stripped, first, of responsibility, then of authority. Finally, he found himself in the humiliating position of occupying a closet-sized office, without a secretary, in which to sit out his contract. Since he was unable to function in the movie business there, and contractually prohibited from doing so elsewhere, he had to find something to do with his time. His busy, restless, imaginative mind could do no less. So it was that for the first time in his life he became interested in stocks and bonds and speculation. He spent part of every day at Bache and Company's Los Angeles headquarters. It did not take him long to learn the game and its rules and its lingo. His prowess was amazing, and impressed even the most seasoned speculators. There came a time when his brokers were asking *him* for advice. He had a ticker tape installed in his office and spent hours on the telephone with his brokers, both in Los Angeles and in New York. He was doing astonishingly well.

"Who needs the movie business?" he asked his friend Buster Keaton one day.

"*You* do," said Buster.

His contract with M-G-M ended in July 1929. He established offices in the same building that housed the offices of Bache and Company. Two months later, he was wiped out, along with thousands of others who had believed not only in their own invincibility but in the Gibraltarlike structure of the American financial system.

He took a job as studio manager for Mascot Pictures, one of the schlock firms on Poverty Row. Here, full-length feature pictures were shot in four or five days and peddled individually to fleabag theatres everywhere in the country.

One morning, looking aimlessly through his dull mail, he

opened a formal envelope and took out a wedding announcement. He read it four times before he became aware of the fact that the bride-to-be was Pempy. He had lost touch with Pempy, and in fact, had expelled her from his thoughts in this time of travail. He would go, of course. There was no question about it. Where? Glendale. When? June twenty-second. He read it again and again, trying to piece together the cracked time schedule of his life. How was it possible that the invitation could have been delivered some four months late? He looked at the envelope again. It had been sent to M-G-M. The following Sunday, using the at-home address on the invitation, he found a telephone number for her.

She came on the phone coldly, and it took him some time to explain.

"Not on the phone, Ben," she said. "It's dreadful on the phone. Do come out and see us."

"When?" he asked.

"Well, what are you doing right now?"

"Right now," he said, "I'm doing nothing, which is what I do all the time practically."

She laughed, and gave him the best route to her house.

Later that day, he drove up the driveway of a white-frame house in the San Fernando Valley, surrounded by green acres and an apple orchard. A white picket fence, reminiscent of New England, surrounded part of the property.

Pempy introduced him to her husband, Carl Larner, a sound engineer at Warner Brothers.

Larner was a tall, blond, rugged football-player type, who might easily have wound up on the other side of the camera, but for his reluctance to risk it. Instead, he had become a sound engineer and was now in charge of dubbing and recording at Warner's.

Ben liked him at once, and Carl was impressed at meeting Ben. Pempy insisted that Ben stay to dinner, which was, of course, a barbecue.

While Carl was doing the cooking, Pempy said, "I want to come and see you tomorrow."

"What about?"

"Something important."

"You can't tell me now?"

He was thinking of Mascot Pictures, that tumbledown building

334

in which his ratty little office was located. He could hardly bear the idea of Pempy visiting him there. She had been so often in his splendid offices at Metro.

"You know, I'm not doing so well right now, Pempy," he said. "I had some bad luck with the market."

"Yes, I know," said Pempy. "So many did. But what about M-G-M?"

"I'm not there anymore."

"For goodness' sake! Why not?"

"Oh, it's too long to tell. And too boring."

Carl sang out, "Come and get it!"

The next afternoon, late, Pempy turned up. She tried to hide her dismay at Ben's situation. After a time, they were able to talk, easily, in their old way.

"I was in an absolute *snit*," she said, "when I didn't hear from you after the invitation."

"They held it up," he said. "They held it up maybe on purpose, those bastards."

"Oh, I can't believe that," she said.

"You can't believe it because you don't know them the way I do. They're monsters."

"Well, all's well that ends well."

"I like your man," he said. "He looks to me like a good man."

"He *is* a good man," said Pempy.

"Does he know about me?" asked Ben. "About us?"

"Of course."

"Warner Brothers," mused Ben. "They're way ahead of everybody in the sound game. He's got himself a fine spot there."

"Yes," said Pempy. "Isn't it all too fascinating, what's happening? The sound and the talk and the music. It's perfectly lovely. And Carl says movies are going to be all in color quite soon now."

"Oh, I doubt it," said Ben. "Mind you, I'm not saying never. But *soon*, I don't know. Look how long it took for the pictures and the talking to get together. You realize that twenty years ago, when I first met Mr. Thomas Edison, that's what he was trying to do. He was trying to put together his talking machine with his moving picture machine. And look at how long it took. Twenty years. And in the end, did he do it? No. Somebody else."

While he spoke, Pempy reached into her capacious handbag and brought forth a burlap package. She unwrapped it carefully.

Inside the burlap there was a large manila envelope. It had the logo of the Bank of America stamped in the upper-right-hand corner, and her name in handwriting on the face of the envelope.

Ben stared at it for a long time. It seemed vaguely familiar. A scene from the past appeared before him, as though it were an old film being rerun.

There was Pempy, fourteen years younger, looking stunned and startled, angry and proud.

"I wouldn't *think* of it," she said. "How could you ever—?"

"What's right is right, Pempy. Please, for God's sake, don't punish me more than I'm punishing myself."

"I can't be *bought!* I *won't* be!"

"Pempy, it's not that. I've tried to explain it to you. You have to trust me. You have to believe in me. What I did, what happened, it was something I couldn't help. It was the kind of opportunity a man could wait all his life. But you and I, it shouldn't make all that difference. This isn't forever, this is temporary. Just till I get on my feet, and then—"

"And then, *what?*" she asked.

"And then, us."

"And in the meantime—?"

"In the meantime, we'll be together."

"Very well," she said, in tears. "Very well. I don't know what else to do just now. But what has that to do with a packet of money?"

"Pempy, listen, in life, anything can happen. Please understand. Try and put yourself in my place. I love you. I have a responsibility towards you. What if something should happen to me? If you don't take this, Pempy, I'll never have a day's peace, a night's peace. Please, I beg you. Whenever you decide it's no good, all you have to do is say so, but don't take our happiness away from us. You're a modern girl. You're intelligent. Please."

He was persuasive; moreover, she could not imagine a life with anyone else.

So when he came to her and put the bulky envelope in her lap, kneeled before her and took her in his arms, embraced her tightly, and kissed her, there was nothing she could do but accede to his wish.

His reverie ended, he returned to the present, and considered the envelope again. She handed it to him.

"This belongs to you," she said.

He looked at it and at her again. "No, it doesn't," he said. "To you."

"I've often thought, through the years, that I ought to return it. I knew I would one day. There's even a little codicil in my will about it. But now, what with my marriage and all, you do see how awkward it would be."

"But you said he *knew* about me—Carl."

"About you, yes. But not about this. I don't think I could explain *this* to him. Or to anyone. I don't think I could explain it to *myself.*"

He was turning the envelope around in his hands, around and around. Suddenly, he was struck with a new thought.

"Jesus Christ!" he said. "You mean to say you never even *opened* it?"

"Why, no," said Pempy simply.

"Jesus Christ!" he said. "Do you know what's *in* it—what's *in* here?"

"No."

"What's in here, you nitwit, is two hundred and fifty-thousand dollars!"

Pempy laughed merrily and said, "Oh, well, in that case—give it back."

"Two hundred and fifty-thousand dollars you keep in an envelope for fifteen years? In an *envelope?*"

"In a safety deposit box," said Pempy. "Quite safe, really. At my bank."

"Two hundred and fifty-thousand dollars," he said, agape. "A quarter of a million you keep in a *safety deposit box?* For God's sake, woman, you realize what you've done? This two hundred and fifty-thousand dollars, if you'd kept it *upstairs* in the bank instead of *downstairs* in the bank, it would now be—oh, my God, it would now be—wait a second." He turned to the automatic calculator on his desk, and played with it for five minutes, with increasing agitation. He turned back to her. "It would now be four hundred and sixty-five thousand dollars—a little more."

"What of it?" asked Pempy. "It's been safe all this time."

"Jesus Christ!" he said. "Some people and money."

337

"You make it sound," said Pempy, "as if I *owe* you two hundred thousand dollars more."

"You do," he said. "In a way you do, you nut." She began to laugh and so contagious was its sound, so insane and unchangeable the situation, that he began to laugh with her. In the end, they embraced and for a short minute, shared an echo of the ecstasy they had once known.

He took her out to her car.

"Next Sunday?" she asked.

"What time?"

That evening, he went to see his old friend, Buster Keaton. Buster was free-lancing now, making one picture at a time, autonomously. It was the way he liked to work.

They sat and talked through the night.

Ben told him the complete truth, then said, "So now, Buster, I'm in a position to make you an offer. Any story you want to do is all right with me."

"How about the story you just told me," said Buster. "The only trouble is, who'd believe it?"

"Listen," said Ben, "you heard about Knickerbocker, didn't you?"

"About them going broke?"

"Yes."

"Sure. But what's that to us?"

"Their studio. Their little studio. Out there on Sunset. It's a fine little studio."

"Well, it isn't just the real estate, Ben. What about equipment?"

"They got equipment. It's all there. It can be picked up for a song." Buster began to sing loudly. "And as far as a crew, don't worry. I've got a friend, Carl Larner, a technician, he's with Warner's, and if I ask him, he'll help me. We'll put together a crew, it'll be the best, and we'll do it *our* way."

"No, no," said Buster, "we'll do it *my* way."

A handshake sealed the bargain.

Six months later, a discreet sign over the entry of the former Knickerbocker Studios read FARBER FILMS, and on this particular Monday, a celebration in honor of the opening of the studio was under way. The ramshackle building was festooned with red, white, and blue bunting. There were floral wreaths and a poster announcing:

NOW IN PRODUCTION
BUSTER KEATON IN "THE BALLOONIST"
WRITTEN AND DIRECTED BY BUSTER KEATON
PRODUCED BY BENJAMIN J. FARBER
TO BE COMPLETED AUGUST 1930
BOOKING NOW

Inside the single sound stage at Farber Films, shooting was in progress. Buster was playing a comic love scene with his enchanting leading lady, Willa Love, who had done impressive work with Chaplin. Buster, after literally hundreds of films, was tremendously adept at leaping from the camera to the set and back again, at directing every other player in the scene while playing his own part. The sound and talk worried him tremendously, and it was apparent. He would never again be completely free or happy.

The park bench scene ended.

"How was it for you, Sam?" he asked.

"Perfect," replied the cameraman.

He turned to the soundman. "And what about you, you pain-in-the-ass, you pest, you useless appendage, you scourge of my life?"

"Beautiful!" said the soundman.

"All right, Sam, let's get Willa's close-up here."

"How close?" asked Willa.

"T-two," said Buster, indicating his chest.

"Well, I'd better touch up a bit, then," said Willa, and went off to her dressing room.

Ben watched her go. He had been unable to take his eyes off her all day. Of all the leading ladies he had ever seen or known, and there had been a great number, not one possessed the ineffable charm of Willa Love. He had been trying to isolate it, to pin it down. What was it? What was it that made her so utterly enchanting and desirable and adorable? It began to strike him that, unlike some of the others, Willa Love was absolutely real. Most of the other great leading ladies were idealizations, dreams, figments of someone's superior imagination. Willa Love, even when seen on the screen, seemed to be made of flesh and blood.

Sam was lining up the shot. Keaton was acting as Willa's stand-in, to save a little money.

Sam said, "Holy smoke, do you think she knows what a T-two means?"

"God, I *hope* not," said Buster. "Everybody doesn't know everything. How many people know that MOS means 'Midout sound'? Just because that's how Karl Freund always said it. And everybody doesn't know that T-one, T-two, T-three, T-four stands for—" He demonstrated, pantomiming each area: "throat, tit, twat, toe."

"Give me a profile, Buster, willya?"

Buster turned profile to the camera and executed a comic stance.

"Great," said Sam, "you look just like Mickey Mouse."

He had hit a nerve. Buster straightened up and spoke seriously. "That son-of-a-bitch. That dirty little rat son-of-a-bitch."

"He's not a rat, he's a mouse," said Sam.

"He's a rat as far as I'm concerned. He's putting us all out of business." His eyes took on a faraway look. "God, I'll never forget the day I saw that shot where the cat's chasing him, and he runs right off the cliff, and he stops in midair, and looks down, and what does he do? He turns around and runs right back onto the cliff again. Goddam, when I saw that, I remember going home, going to bed and just lying there all night. And in the morning, I said to Susie, I said, 'Susie, we're finished, all of us. Harold and Harry and Charlie and all of us.' And she said, 'What're you talking about? You fellas are real *people*. That's just a goddam cartoon.' And I said, 'Susie, that's just where you're wrong. To those customers sitting out front, we're all the same. He's just as real to them as we are, and the little son-of-a-bitch can do things we couldn't even *dream* of. I tell y', we're all washed up. From here on in, we'll have to be funny with words.' "

"Oh, I don't know," said Sam, "it's a big world. There's room for everything."

"Don't you believe it," said Buster, gloomily. "Don't you believe it."

Willa returned and they began to shoot her close-up.

Behind the camera, at a discreet distance, stood Ben, watching and falling in love.

The day's work was over. The party was in progress.

The fat lady who had played the piano at Ben's house was

340

providing some of the music, assisted by one of the electricians, an expert clarinetist, and Stan Laurel, who was playing the drums. They were performing "Tip-Toe Through the Tulips."

The party was as enjoyable as it was tacky. It had not been catered by anyone. Ben and Buster, Willa and a few members of the crew did the pouring and the serving. There were peanuts and potato chips, olives and pretzels. There was a barrel of beer and a few bottles of California wine. Everything was served on paper plates and the drinks in paper cups. No matter, the spirit was there. Almost everyone in the industry wished Ben and Buster well. Pempy turned up and was helping. Carl Larner, her husband, was discussing the equipment with some of the members of the crew, all friends of his.

Ben was proudly introducing his eldest son, Higham, who was twenty-one and a Harvard student. The two younger boys were there, too. Abraham and Gilbert. Douglas Fairbanks and Mary Pickford made a grand entrance. Royalty, of course. They behaved like royalty, consequently, everyone treated them as such. Charlie Chaplin turned up, and was the life of the party. What he did brilliantly was to imitate Buster Keaton. There came a moment when, not to be outdone, the Marquise de la Falaise de Coudray came on and did her celebrated imitation of Charlie Chaplin. Oliver Hardy and Roscoe Arbuckle standing beside each other looked like a group of four. Mack Sennett was there giving advice. Harold Lloyd and Mildred Harris, recently married, were there. Sam Goldwyn was congratulating Ben and wishing him well. And the two Johns—Gilbert and Barrymore—turned up, stewed to the gills, and made a considerable nuisance of themselves.

The music was now "Sweet Georgia Brown."

There were a few toasts, and three short speeches: one from Sennett, one from Goldwyn, one from Chaplin.

Then, as part of the entertainment, Roscoe Arbuckle went on and sang, beautifully. His song was Victor Herbert's, "Ah, Sweet Mystery of Life." He brought the party to rapt attention with his superb high tenor voice. Everyone listened with all sorts of vagrant thoughts. The song ended.

Sennett said to Goldwyn, "There's a personality for you, for sound pictures."

Goldwyn nodded gravely. "Yes, yes, if only—"

The party went on. Farber Films was well and truly launched. The music became "I'm Just Wild About Harry."

V

IN THE present, Guy, Adani, and Ben were still in the parlor section of Ben's office.

"And that was the beginning," said Ben. "One little stage, one camera, one crew, but the luck of it was that Buster made a smash hit. So in the next year, two, three, we were making five, six a year and built a new stage. Then Buster and I had the fight and we broke up. It wasn't my fault, and I don't think it was his. It was just what they call progress, if that's what it is, but it came to a point where I couldn't sell his pictures. They wanted talking, more and more talking. Singing, dancing. They wanted things Buster couldn't do. But Farber Films went on. What *people!* What *personalities!* Marlene Dietrich, Carole Lombard, Chevalier. And what *actors!* Paul Muni and Eddie Robinson. Everybody was turning out a product you could be proud of. *The Informer* and King Vidor and Hepburn came. What days!"

"They're *still* good days, Mr. Farber," said Adani. "It's a good business. For the right people."

Ben looked at him, blinked once, and said, "Yes, but to us, it was more than a business. Today, everybody's so serious in business—like you, Mr. Adani—it's all life or death. With us, we used to make it a rule to make sure and mix pleasure with business. There used to be a place—the Trocadero . . ."

VI

THE TROCADERO. It was located on the Sunset Strip, and it had class, in a vulgar way. Upstairs, an elegant dining room, set around the best dance floor in town. Downstairs, a less formal bar and grill and booths. Both rooms boasted the finest view of the city, far and wide below. It was more impressive by night than by day. Every newcomer was brought here in the course of his or her first week. It was *de rigueur.* The routine explained; the maître d' introduced; the step out onto the patio to observe one of the very few local sights to see—that impressive blanket of multicolored lights. On a clear night you can see as far as . . .

On the night Phil Silvers first saw it, he looked for a long time, awed. Suddenly, he made a fist, shook it at the scene, and said, dramatically, "Hollywood, I'll *lick you yet!*" Then he ducked, dove back into the room, and hid under a table. Everyone laughed because his gag had articulated perfectly what everyone felt.

On the dance floor, a jolly crowd, smartly attired, was dancing. Tommy Dorsey and his orchestra were playing. A starved-looking Italian band singer was doing his chorus of "Thanks for the Memory." Frank Sinatra. Nobody much was listening.

On the floor, a number of familiar faces and bodies floated by. Mae West was dancing with the weight-lifting champion of Brazil. George Raft, with a Paramount stock girl who had arrived from New York that morning. Barbara Stanwyck, with her husband, Frank Fay. Ben and Willa Farber.

There were also a number of less recognizable figures to whom the recognizable ones paid great deference. They were the *real* Hollywood biggies: the producers and directors, the executives, the agents.

One of the most important of the important—Johnny Hyde— was dancing expertly with a statuesque, breathtakingly beautiful blonde, precisely one head taller than himself. He had learned, after fifty-four years, not only to live with his short stature but to revel in it.

"Never mind where *her* head is," he once responded to a tease, "just look where *mine* is!"

Johnny Hyde, five foot three, a full partner in the prestigious, respected, and burgeoning William Morris Agency (Est. 1897), was an uncommonly happy man. He was married to a wise woman (not a tall blonde) who knew that she was married to a non-monogamous man, and was resigned to the fact. Other than this, he was an ideal, caring husband and a peerless provider.

Another couple danced up. Insiders would have recognized Jack Warner, the dynamo brother of the Warner Brothers and their studio. His partner was an aggressive redhead.

"Hi, Johnny," she called out.

"Baby!" responded Johnny.

"Don't talk to *him*," said Jack. "You're dancing with *me*."

"You call this dancing?" she asked.

"One more crack," said Jack, "and I drop your option."

"I wish you would," she said.

"Watch it, now!"

She went on. "You know what my boyfriend said to me when I told him I'd signed a seven-year contract with Warner Brothers? He said, 'What did you do, break a mirror?' "

Johnny howled. His partner laughed. (She didn't get it.)

Now Jack Warner laughed—so hard, in fact, that he sank to his knees. Not for long. He got up and said, "Listen, Johnny. On Bogart. Let's split the difference, O.K.?"

"No."

"It's *better* for him, four pictures a year. He'll get a public."

"He's got a public," said Johnny. "Two a year, and that's it— unless *he* wants to make a third."

"He?! He's running the studio all of a sudden? *I'm* running the studio. Who does he think he is?"

"He thinks he's Humphrey Bogart," said Johnny, dancing away.

The music changed. "Over the Rainbow."

They met again. Warner and Hyde both had new partners. Johnny's was another blonde.

"Tell you what," said Warner, dancing hard. "Make it three pictures a year and he can have *approval* on the third."

"How?" asked Johnny, dancing, mystified.

"Easy," said Warner. "We'll submit six properties, and he can choose one."

"What if he hates them all?"

"Then he ought to see a doctor, a *head* doctor."

"Yours, maybe?" Johnny asked, as he laughed and danced away.

New music. A rumba this time. "La Cucaracha." Another meeting on the dance floor. Warner had changed girls and was rumbaing expertly. So was Johnny, with still another blonde.

"All right," said Johnny. "I'll make it three pictures."

"Good."

"Wait."

"What?"

"But for the third, he gets a bonus."

"How much?"

"A hundred thousand."

"Ridiculous!"

"Goodbye."

"Hold it!" said Warner.

"For what?"

"Give me that blonde of yours," says Warner, "and it's a deal."

Johnny looked up at her. "O.K. with *you?*"

"Yes," she said. "Not because he's Jack Warner, you understand. But because he's such a great rumba nut."

"Deal!" shouted Johnny.

"Deal!" echoed Warner.

They changed partners and danced away from each other.

"They were great days," said Ben, bathed in nostalgia.

"Let me ask you a question, Mr. Farber," said Adani impatiently.

"Go to it."

"I have to go to Caracas tomorrow."

"You have my permission," said Ben.

"No, no, that's not the question," said Adani. "The question is, tell me truthfully, you think there's any use this man of mine hangin' around here talkin'? I mean, I don't mind a few more days if you're serious, but if we're just bullshittin' around here, I got other things for him to do."

Farber looked at Adani and in all innocence inquired, "You don't enjoy bullshittin'?"

"Who's got time for talk? That's the whole trouble with business in America. Talk. Everything is talk. Everything is lunch. Everything is let's have a drink. Jesus Christ, now they even want to have *breakfast* with you. I like to have breakfast by myself. I don't even like to have breakfast with my wife."

"I *like* to have breakfast with my wife," said Ben.

Adani was on his feet. "So what do you think? Should I leave him here? Or no?"

There was a long pause before Ben replied.

"Leave him here," he said.

Adani disappeared, abruptly and rudely. Guy and Ben seemed relieved to have him gone. They looked at each other and smiled. Ben happily picked up the thread of his story:

"Willa Love. In practically every picture I had her. And I kept trying to sign her to a contract. That's what you needed in those days. You had to have actors and actresses under contract, and writers and directors, so you could build careers, and build them up. I signed quite a few. But I couldn't sign her. No matter what I did—no matter what I offered—the answer was always the same. . . ."

VII

"No," said Willa. "Really no, Ben. You ask it now almost every time we meet."

"I *mean* it every time we meet."

"No," she said. "I'm quite content to go on this way doing one at a time. You know I'll always do it for you, if I like it. I like working for you, but I can't commit myself. I *won't!* I've been under contract, and one feels enslaved, somehow. I'm terribly keen on freedom."

And so it continued for five years. Ben was relentless.

Finally, one day, it came close to turning into a quarrel.

"It's not right," said Ben. "It's not fair. Suppose I give you this great part and you make a hit and then you go somewhere else and they get the benefit of it."

"That's the way it's going to be, Ben."

"I want to look for stories for you. I want to get you the right directors. I want to build you into the biggest star. But how can I do that if I don't know I have you permanently? What can I do to have you permanently? I've offered you more money than you've ever gotten. Any kind of conditions. I'll build you your own dressing room. What can I do to have you permanently?" He looked at her and looked at her and looked at her. His anger subsided. She was looking back at him, answering his question with her eyes. After a stare that lasted for five minutes, he heard himself say, "Would you?"

"Of course," she said. "I thought you'd never get round to it. Where do I sign?"

Willa and Ben were married in April 1935.

Ernst Lubitsch was now Ben's partner and was making *The Marriage Circle* with Willa, Lew Cody, and Jack Holt.

One day on the set, when Willa was wearing a particularly revealing Fortuny gown, Lubitsch noticed an unseemly bulge around her middle. For the next few days it became an obsessive fascination and seemed to be growing before his eyes. He sought out Ben.

"Your wife?" he asked. "She's pregnant?"

"Yes," said Ben. "We were hoping you wouldn't notice it, not for a while yet."

"Why, you Goddamn double-crossing bastard, you do that to me? I've got nine weeks yet to shoot and you do that to me? How am I going to shoot? How am I going to make my picture?"

"Maybe close-ups?" suggested Ben.

"Close-ups?" screamed Lubitsch. "Close-ups? That's for the Russians. Me, I *hate* close-ups. I hate *faces*. Especially right now I hate *yours!*"

What was there to do? The picture had begun, and had to go on. Lubitsch used all his ingenuity and more to achieve the result. He shot her from behind. He shot her lying down. He shot her in flowing peignoirs. He used doubles to run up and down stairs. He came in close, closer than he was accustomed to doing. He found new ways of using close-ups. At length, the picture was finished. An enormous success, mainly because of the visual style it had achieved.

They sat in Ben's office one afternoon, reading the reviews. Lubitsch began to laugh as the public relations man read, " 'And in his artful use of the close-up Lubitsch brings a new dimension to the screen art.' "

Not long after, Willa and Ben's first son was born and named Ernst.

At the boy's brith, which was solemn, the male guests wore

yarmulkes, a rabbi officiated. Familiar faces stood about, the ceremonial wine was passed around, the baby screamed.

Twenty-three years later, the baby, now aged twenty-three, was still screaming:

"Because I don't *want* to, Pa. That's why not. I don't *like* the movie business. Right now I'm not sure I even like movies. Good God, you've got to remember that in all my years there was hardly a day that I didn't see a movie. That means I've seen over seven thousand movies. Eight. That's enough. Enough for a while anyway. I love pictures that don't move. Pictures I can stand and look at and study."

"You want to break my heart," said Ben. "Go ahead. Break it."

"Why me?" asked Ernst. "Why not Gilbert? Or Abe?"

"Abe?" said Ben. "You know Abe. He's only interested in his cars and in his starlets and skiing and golf, and the biggest favor he can do me is to stay *away* from the studio."

Later, there was a talk with Gilbert, who explained patiently and carefully that he had to find his own identity, he wanted to be in business for himself.

Ben understood and watched his son's rise with pride.

VIII

"AND NOW," said Ben to Guy, "he's one of the biggest men in TV. You don't think that's funny? It's like he's going to be responsible for eating us up. He comes in and we do business. He leases some of my old pictures. He tries to convince me that TV is not competition to movies. I let him think he's convincing me. It makes him feel better. But it's all different.

"Listen, the business part—that I think you should better talk over with Willa. You may think I don't know that sometimes I'm not all there. But I *do* know it. And it would be unfortunate if we happened to get down to serious matters and I had one of those peculiar times, you understand?"

"Of course, Ben," said Guy. "Of course."

348

A few days later, Guy was out at the Farbers' spectacular beach house at Trancas. Ben sat on the open deck, watching the sea. At dusk, a little while before dinner, Willa and Guy were walking slowly on the beach.

"I'm sure," said Willa, "that Dean Johnson can bring in satisfactory appraisers—that is to say, satisfactory to both—who'll compute an inventory. There's been, of course, a great difference of opinion with regard to the estimated value of the older films."

"I don't want to talk business with you right now."

"Really? Why not?"

"I don't know," said Guy. "I just don't feel like it."

"Shall we go in, then?"

"God, no. Please, no."

They stopped walking.

"What is it, Guy?"

"I don't know. But please let's not talk business. Maybe not talk at all. Maybe just walk or stand or sit or nothing. Let's just occupy the same space for a while. Would you mind that terribly?"

"I don't think so."

"Thank you, Willa."

"What a curious young man you are!"

They continued to walk. He took her hand and held it. They went on. As they passed the house, they saw Ben give them a single wave of his hand. A kind of blessing? They waved back, walked, and said nothing more until the sun set. Then they went back to the house and to Ben.

PART VII

THIS YEAR'S BLONDE

"You never heard of Li'l Abner?"

Ben shook his head sadly. "I see it again, Abe. Your whole trouble—you're not a serious man."

"Thank God for that."

"That's why you're not married, why you're not in here with me, why you think you're an Abner when you know you're an Abe."

"Look, Pop. You have simply got to let go. Let me do my business and you do yours. Once in a while, maybe we can do business together and do each other some good."

Ben sighed, defeated. "All right, Abe, have it your way."

"*Abner!*"

"What?"

"My name is *Abner. Abner L. Farber.* Got it?"

Ben smiled gently. "After Abner Lincoln?" he asked.

His son laughed.

"Exactly," he said. "How did you know?"

"I'll try to remember," said Ben.

"You'd better," said Abner forcefully. "Because if you don't, you won't ever see me."

"All right, Abe, I'll do my best."

"*Abner,* God damn it! *Abner.*" He was on his feet. He took a step toward his father and pointed a finger at him. "Say it! Come on, Pop, *say* it!"

Ben studied him for ten seconds, then said, "I can't, Abe. I just can't. It's like you're somebody else, not you."

"That's just it," Abner shouted, and slapped the desk. "I'm not who you think I am. I never was and I never will be—because I don't want to be. What's more—" He stopped.

"Yes?"

"Oh, the hell with it." He started out. On his way, he said, "G'bye, Pop."

"Goodbye, Abe."

Abner kicked open the door and left.

She picked up the trade papers to see if she could find the cause of this morning's crisis. It did not take her long.

On page 3 of *The Hollywood Reporter,* she read:

FARBER, LEE FORM
NEW AGENCY

Shirley Lee and Abner Farber announce the—

She stopped reading as it struck her—Abner. *Abner?*

In Ben's office, he and his second son glared at each other across Ben's massive desk.

"Your name," Ben was saying, evenly, as he tried to stay in control, "your name is Abraham."

"My name," said his son, "is any goddamn thing I choose it to be! Like Archie Leach wants to be Cary Grant, so that's it! I'm thirty-seven years old, f'Chrissake! Don't mother me."

"You were named for a distinguished man who—"

"Mom says he was a dirty bastard."

Ben took a deep breath and said, "Tessa is not always right. Your grandfather was a remarkable man. Even his enemies admired A.L. Seligman."

"Pop, I just got sick of people calling me Abe. And sometimes, even Abie."

" 'A.L.' stands for 'Abraham Lincoln.' "

"So what? So that's even more embarrassing. What's a name, anyway? A handle, that's all. A business convenience. Isn't 'Tony Curtis' more practical for an actor than 'Bernie Schwartz'?"

"Actors," said Ben, "that's different."

"Wrong again, Pop."

"You didn't think to discuss it with me?"

"Of course not. Why should I? Did Haim discuss it with you when he changed it to Higham?"

Ben was instantly angered. "Don't talk to me about *that* stuffed shirt," he said. "He doesn't live in the real world. A man of forty-six and he thinks he's still in Harvard!"

"Isn't he?"

"Abner," said Ben, testing it and rejecting it. "What kind of a name is Abner?"

"You never heard of Li'l Abner?"

Ben shook his head sadly. "I see it again, Abe. Your whole trouble—you're not a serious man."

"Thank God for that."

"That's why you're not married, why you're not in here with me, why you think you're an Abner when you know you're an Abe."

"Look, Pop. You have simply got to let go. Let me do my business and you do yours. Once in a while, maybe we can do business together and do each other some good."

Ben sighed, defeated. "All right, Abe, have it your way."

"*Abner!*"

"What?"

"My name is *Abner. Abner L. Farber.* Got it?"

Ben smiled gently. "After Abner Lincoln?" he asked.

His son laughed.

"Exactly," he said. "How did you know?"

"I'll try to remember," said Ben.

"You'd better," said Abner forcefully. "Because if you don't, you won't ever see me."

"All right, Abe, I'll do my best."

"*Abner,* God damn it! *Abner.*" He was on his feet. He took a step toward his father and pointed a finger at him. "Say it! Come on, Pop, *say* it!"

Ben studied him for ten seconds, then said, "I can't, Abe. I just can't. It's like you're somebody else, not you."

"That's just it," Abner shouted, and slapped the desk. "I'm not who you think I am. I never was and I never will be—because I don't want to be. What's more—" He stopped.

"Yes?"

"Oh, the hell with it." He started out. On his way, he said, "G'bye, Pop."

"Goodbye, Abe."

Abner kicked open the door and left.

II

In Bungalow 12, Guy continued to receive Jack Heller, who brought him new information and updates. It was becoming increasingly clear, as he studied the material, that Farber Films was a dying company. Only the rental of the exceptional library to the television networks was keeping it alive.

"There's a new twist," said Jack.

"Like what?"

"The old lady."

"Don't call her 'the old lady,' you jerk!"

"Well, you know who I mean," said Jack, flustered. "Mrs. Farber. She's setting up a whole slew of family confabs. She's even getting the professor coming down from Stanford. You know. The son. Ernst. She's trying to get them all on the same side—on her side. Fat chance with that bunch."

"You're not making any sense, fella," said Guy testily. "Lay it out."

"I told you, didn't I, that *she's against* the deal?"

"You said maybe. You said she keeps changing her mind."

"Well, can I help that? Right now—the last few days—she's dead set *against*."

"Shit!"

"In fact, one of the things she may take up is getting herself appointed conservator."

"How can she do that?"

"If she can prove he's incompetent or incapable, it's automatic in this state. The complication is she wants to do it without his knowing. She wants him to go on thinking he's in charge."

"What's her angle?"

"God knows."

"Well, find out," said Guy sharply. "Damn!"

He went into the bathroom. When he came back, he asked, "Could it be she's going to try to get one of the sons to take over?"

Jack laughed. "Hell, no. She's been to *that* fire before. There's

356

the oldest one—Higham, in the East. He married rich and social and he's the one hasn't spoken to the old boy in I don't know *how* many years."

"Twenty," said Guy glumly.

"The professor? He thinks this whole business is a crock. He lives up there in the horse latitudes. In the seventeenth century. I don't think he's seen a picture—I mean one that *moves*—in thirty years."

"What about the agent?"

"Abner?"

"Yes. Isn't that the pattern right now? Agents taking over studios?"

"Sure, but not him."

"Why not?"

"He swings. He's got a neat business where he comes in maybe two hours a day—when he's *here*, that is. The rest of the time he enjoys—and that's all. He had a taste of working at the studio once—years ago—and found it too hard."

"So who's left?"

"The daughter—nothing. She lives in Italy and couldn't care less. So that leaves Gilbert—the TV hotshot. He doesn't like the picture business—thinks it's old-fashioned."

"So what's all the conferring about?"

"She's crazy."

"What?"

"She's *always* been crazy. She's got this nutty idea that the only thing keeping the old man alive is his business. She's convinced that if that's pulled out from under him it'll be the end of him in no time."

"She may be right," said Guy.

"Willa," said Gilbert, "it pains me to say this, but that's the most *neurotic* notion I've ever heard!"

"I'm in a position to know," said Willa tightly. "I *live* with the man!"

"You live with him and you forget he's ninety-two," said Abner. "You look at him and you see hair on his head—but he's *bald*, Willa! He's bald-headed!"

Ernst spoke. "Look, Mother—just tell us what you want us to do and we'll do it. At least, I will."

357

"I want you—all of you—to convince him not to sell. You must believe me when I tell you it's life or death."

"O.K., Willa, O.K.," said Abner. "But how about a little practical, a little sensible? He's an old, old man. So how long has he got anyway?"

Willa regarded him and said, "You've always been the callous one, Abner, haven't you?"

"The no-baloney one," he replied.

"As one grows older, Abner, each day becomes more valuable, more rare—don't you see that? What is *one day* of life worth to you? To your father, to me—a *very great deal!*"

"Sorry, Willa," said Abner. "I didn't mean to upset you."

Beth, who had been sitting quietly in a corner of the room, now moved silently to her great-grandmother's side, sat beside her, and embraced her.

"Hey, Beth!" said Abner. "What the hell are you doin' here? Why aren't you out makin' money for *me?*"

Beth regarded him, with a hot, pitying look.

Gilbert rose, paced about for a time, exchanged a look with Abner, then said, "Willa, listen. It's time to face a few tough facts."

"Such as?"

"Such as the fact that if Farber Films doesn't get unloaded, it's only a matter of time before it'll be wiped out—it'll be nothing!"

"Don't be ridiculous," said Willa.

"Don't *you* be. I know more about it than you do. Pop knows—he keeps it from you, naturally—but it's going down the tubes, Willa. The company hasn't had a real hit in four years."

Willa was outraged. "What are you talking about? What about the—?"

"I know, I know—but those two were so costly that even the big grosses couldn't move them into the black. And the points he had to give up to get Redford and Fonda left damned little for him, for the company."

"I don't believe it."

"So don't. What's the difference? *He* knows. Pop knows. There's never been anyone in the picture business shrewder."

"Answer me this, then," said Willa, blazing. "If what you say is true, why is he hesitating? Why is he—?"

"Stubborn, Willa," said Abner. "He wants to hang in there until the last minute. Hell, I can see that. It's his life—whole damn life

358

—but he *knows*. He doesn't even understand the lingo around here anymore. He looks at *Grease* and *Close Encounters* and *Star Wars* and *Superman*. Willa! He had a shot at every one of them— and turned them down! It's another time. God Almighty—he still won't stand for a nude shot or somebody saying 'son-of-a-bitch.' He's out of it, Willa!"

"There's room in the world," said Willa, "for all sorts of things. Pictures. Books. There's room," she repeated weakly.

The family meeting ended on this sad and inconclusive note.

Within ten minutes, Guy, having eavesdropped, was on the phone to Adani from the gas station down the road.

"We're in!" he said.

"For how much?"

"Good God! It seems to me I've heard those two words lately more than any others in the language. I don't *know* how much, Adani, but believe me, I've come to know this business and the product, and *whatever* you pay for it, you're getting a bargain!"

"You want me to send Tessler out? And the other lawyers?"

"No, no. Not yet. No lawyers yet. The next moves are with Mrs. Farber. I'll let you know."

"Hurry up," said Adani. "I have to go to Switzerland Friday."

III

THEY WERE back at Trancas. Beth had come out for the day and had changed Ben's disposition from gloomy to sunny. Ben, an inveterate walker, walked less here. The sand caused his steps to become unstable, and he was afraid of falling. But he loved the feel of the undulating tide and frequently sat near the edge of the water, allowing its movement to play over the lower part of his body. Guy had joined him.

Ben said, "I'll tell you what's happening, Guy, over these last few days. What's been happening I didn't tell you because it wasn't time, but I think now it *is* the time. What's been happening is that I've been talking to all the members of my family. All the ones who still talk to me, that is. Willa and me, we've considered the whole thing, every angle. I had a long talk on the long distance with my son Higham, who doesn't speak to me, but in a case like this—so important—I called him. To tell you the truth, he's not too interested. He's a very independent type in every way. He said to me, 'Do what you want, Dad. Anything that'll make you happy.' In my whole life, he's the only one ever called me that. Dad. It don't sound right. I don't look like a dad, do I? And I talked to Ernst, a fine boy. And to Leonora. Long distance to Italy. Imagine it! It was like she was in the next room. She was very interested. Especially in how much for her." He winked. "And to Abe and Gilbert. Even a few of the grandchildren. And even two of the great-grandchildren. Beth. Isn't she a choice girl —even though she's an agent! How did she get to be an agent? Who knows? I'll tell you a secret—even she don't know it. She's my favorite. You know why?"

"No."

"Because she reminds me of Alice—my first wife. A lovely girl —so long dead. Alice Bohl . . . I don't think I'm going to sell, after all. How can I sell all those years of my life—and other people's, too? You see?"

Guy stripped and stood under a cold shower for ten minutes.

He came downstairs just as Beth was leaving.

"Don't go," Ben was saying to her. "Stay and have dinner. Squab. Strawberry shortcake."

"Cut it out," she said, putting her hands over her ears.

"Please," said Ben.

"I can't, darling. I've got a date. With a movie."

"What movie?"

"*Flesh and the Devil.* The silent. With Garbo and John Gilbert."

"For God's sake," said Ben. "Where do they show a thing like that?"

"At the Farber Studios. My private movie palace."

Ben was about to importune her, when a bearded young blade in jeans appeared.

Ben studied him for a moment, and said, "I give up. One thing I know. I know when I'm licked."

"Tony Salta," she said, "meet everybody."

"Hi," he said. "Ready?"

"You bet."

Swift, perfunctory kisses and Beth was gone.

"Some girl," said Ben, looking after her.

The Farbers and Guy were having drinks before dinner in the spacious sitting room. The Farbers sat with their backs to the sea. They habitually gave their guests the ocean view.

"I can remember so well," said Willa, "the first time we drove out here. It seemed to hell and gone, but each year it's plainly closer and closer to Beverly Hills."

She went on, talking animatedly about the details of designing and building this beach house, but Guy's attention wandered and fell upon the wide array of framed photographs behind the Farbers on the refectory table. This particular display, he noted, contained no pictures of the stars or writers or directors with whom Farber had been associated, and whose pictures were all around his study back in Beverly Hills, in his offices in Hollywood and even out at the pool house. Celebrities, Presidents: Roosevelt, Truman, Eisenhower, Carter. A signed photograph of George Bernard Shaw, and one of Eugene O'Neill. Guy had been duly impressed, but he noted that here in this informal casual atmosphere, all the pictures were of the Farber family. The sons in various stages of their growth. The daughter, the grandchildren. Crowded family cookouts on the beach. The boys surfing. The children growing. A fascinating panorama. All at once, his eyes fell upon a photograph that seemed remarkably incongruous in this collection. It was a head shot of the scrubbed and innocent and lovely, haunted and haunting face of Marilyn Monroe.

After dinner, Willa asked to be excused. She explained that she had to make a prearranged call to Italy to her daughter Leonora.

Ben and Guy settled down to talk.

"Marilyn Monroe," said Guy.

Ben's eyes popped. "What did you say?" he asked.

"I can't help wondering what she's doing on your family table, Ben. She's not related, surely."

"I don't know what you call related," said Ben.

"Well, I mean, is she part of your family?"

"Legally, no," said Ben. He got up, walked across the room, took the picture of Marilyn Monroe from the table, brought it back, sat and looked at it reverently. "She was my friend," he said, "and I was her friend. For a long time. Well, I say 'a long time'— that's in terms of her life. It was not such a long time in years. But I knew her for most of her life. I was always interested in her— and I'll tell you why. Because she was interesting. There was a time, I can tell it to you now, what does it matter? There was a time I used to play around a little like everybody else. Not so much, but carefully and always where it wouldn't be noticed too much. Nice people. Friendly. Never—I swear to you—never with anybody who ever worked for me. Never. And there was this wonderful fellow I knew—Johnny Hyde. He was one of the own- ers of the William Morris office. A fine agent. A little guy, and his main worry was not having enough fun out of life. We used to go out on crazy dates together and ... Just getting together with people to have some enjoyment with each other if we felt like it. You follow? And we knew all kinds of people. Never with any- body who worked for me. I made that as a rule. But studio people. Script girls or hairdressers or cutters or negative cutters. Negative cutters were always women—they still are, I think; never men— because the work is so delicate, so dainty that it turns out only women can do it. Anyways, I called him up one day, Johnny—" He laughed.

"Johnny, you're never going to believe this, but guess what I got lined up for tonight?"

"What?"

"*Two* negative cutters." Johnny laughed. "How about it? Early dinner at Lucey's, and away we go."

Johnny hesitated. "I don't know," he said. "I think I have to—"

"Johnny, listen. I *know* these two. A-one. This is no blind date. The only thing wrong with them is they're not blond, neither one of them."

"I can handle that," said Johnny.

"So, O.K.?"

"Sure," said Johnny.

It had been a rough day. Columbia had suddenly called off a picture in which he had five clients, including the director, Frank Capra.

Johnny drove over to Lucey's, swung into the parking lot and parked. On these little excursions, he always drove himself in his own car.

As he walked toward the restaurant, he looked across Melrose Avenue and noted that the gate to the Paramount Studios had been painted since he saw it last. He wondered if the Morris office could not use a coat of paint.

Lucey's was crowded, as usual, but its arrangement of private booths was such that it was perfect for assignations or business conferences.

He approached Ben's customary table with some difficulty because the room was dimly lit, mainly by the candles on every table.

Ben's voice: "Here we are."

Johnny approached the table and saw that Ben was sitting with two attractive young women, one a dark-skinned brunette; the other a small vibrant redhead with green eyes.

"This one's yours," said Ben, indicating the latter.

As Johnny slid into the booth, he saw a child. On closer inspection, he saw that it was a little girl, twelve or thirteen years old, blond, sullen, a few pimples, dirty fingernails.

The waiter brought him his drink, J&B on the rocks. Johnny never needed to order here. He noticed that there was a glass in front of everyone except the child.

"Wouldn't you like something to drink?" he asked. "What do they call it? A Shirley Temple?"

The girl's eyes burned him with a look. "I *hate* Shirley Temple!" she said.

"How about a Coke?"

"No."

"Tomato juice?"

"No."

"Ginger ale?"

"No."

"Lemonade?"

"No."

"Doctor Pepper?"

"No."

"Well," said Johnny, "I guess that does it. I guess you don't want anything to drink."

"No," she said, "I want something to *eat*."

"Well, for God's sake, why didn't you say so? Waiter!"

The moment the waiter appeared, the little girl said, "Antipasto lasagna garlic salad."

When the food arrived, they all watched her eat, swiftly, ravenously, animal-like.

Johnny spoke to her mother. "What'll you take," he asked, "for the movie rights of this kid eating?"

"Her name is Norma," said the woman. "Norma Jean."

"Well, she's a very nice little girl," said Johnny, "and certainly talented. I mean, with that knife and fork."

There were jokes, movie gossip, talk about some of the new pictures in release: *Mr. Smith Goes to Washington, Ninotchka,* and the blockbusting *Gone With the Wind.*

Later, they stood about the parking lot, and as they parted, Johnny could not help saying to his erstwhile chum, "Thanks a lot, Ben."

Ben, embarrassed, shrugged. He leaned over and mumbled, "Tell her to get rid of the kid. She will."

"It doesn't matter," said Johnny.

Mrs. Baker and Norma—Norma Jean—drove off in a rusty Chevy.

Johnny went up to Ciro's, on the Strip, where a chance encounter led to a long night.

"Crazy days," said Ben to Guy. "But that particular date had a fantastic ending. Wait till I tell you.

"It must've been about like maybe ten years later. . . ."

Palm Springs. 1949. The Racquet Club.

Johnny sat by the pool, beautifully dressed in white. Charlie Farrell, the owner of the club, the mayor of Palm Springs, came up to him.

"Hey, Johnny! When'd y' get in?"

"Last night."

"Good trip?"

"Two hours and twenty minutes."

"Holy smoke! Who drove you? Eddie Rickenbacker?"

"Not exactly. That."

He pointed out an Amazonian beauty, blond, of course, and athletic.

"She's a swimming champion."

"Looks it," said Charlie.

"From Norway."

"They swim there?"

"She's Sonja Henie's cousin."

"Honest?"

"Swear to God."

The beauty executed a prize-winning swan dive. Charlie and Johnny applauded.

"But God!" said Charlie. "Look at the size of her. She could probably pick you up in her teeth by the scruff of the neck and drag you around the room like a mother cat."

"Could?" said Johnny. "She *does!*"

"Say, how'd you like it? The picture. I saw you at the preview."

"Sunset Boulevard?"

"Yeah."

"Sensational," said Johnny.

"I thought ol' Gloria was double great, but what a chance he missed, that chucklehead Wilder."

"How do you mean?" asked Johnny.

"Me," said Charlie Farrell. "He should've had *me*. Not that De Mille. *Me*. How come he—?"

"Help!" cried a unique, husky voice. "Help!"

Both men jumped up and made their way to the edge of the pool.

A darling head, encased in a red bathing cap, its face contorted with pain, appeared. Its owner's hands grasped the ledge.

"Cramp!" she cried. "Leg cramp! Ow!"

The men assisted her, carefully, out of the pool.

She lay down on her back. She was wearing a fairly daring red one-piece bathing suit.

Johnny looked down and experienced considerable difficulty in getting his next breath.

"Which leg?" asked Charlie.

"Right," she moaned, writhing in pain.

Charlie began to kneel to it, but Johnny, although a head shorter, muscled him out of the way.

"I'll do it," he said. "I know about leg cramps. I get them all the time."

"Go ahead, then," said Charlie, with an understanding grin.

Johnny knelt, took a deep breath, touched her right leg. He shivered.

"Let me know if I hurt you," he said. "I don't want to hurt you."

"That makes two of us," she said breathily.

Johnny began to massage her leg, carefully and expertly. His face was suffused with the expression of a man who had just entered heaven.

"Better?" he managed to ask finally.

"I think so," she replied. "Oh, gosh!"

"What?"

"You're going to get those beautiful pants all dirty."

"Would you believe it, missy," he asked seriously, "that I've got another pair of pants?"

"Hey!"

"What?"

"It really *is* better."

She sat up and ripped off her bathing cap, releasing a mass of beautiful, natural blond hair.

Charlie laughed. Johnny shook his head in wonder.

"Figures," he said. "Figures."

Later. In the bar. Johnny and the little blonde were having a drink. Champagne, the best in the house, from a cooler at their side. From time to time, the waiter replenished their glasses, and when the bottle was empty, he replaced it with another, automatically. Johnny was known here.

"You want a laugh?" asked Johnny.

"Sure thing," she said. "I don't get to laugh much."

"Well, here we are, old friends—for two hours already—and I don't even know your name."

"My name is now Marilyn Monroe. What's yours?"

He got out his wallet and handed her his card.

She examined it, looked up.

"You're Johnny Hyde?" she said delightedly.

"That's what it says, doesn't it?"

"But I've heard of you. You're *important.*"

He looked at her for a long time and said, "What's more important is that I know *you're going* to be."

"What makes you think so?"

"I didn't say think, I said *know.*"

She giggled.

"I mean it," he said. "I get hunches. They're almost never wrong."

366

"Almost," she whispered.

"What did you mean before?" he asked.

"When?"

"When you said your name is *now* Marilyn Monroe?"

"Well, it was *Mona* Monroe."

"I see."

"And before that, Norma Jean Mortenson."

"Uh-huh."

"And before that, Norma Jean Dougherty."

"Wait a second."

"And before that, Norma Jean Baker."

Johnny laughed.

"And did I say Bolender?" she asked.

"No."

"Well, that too. But my father's name is Gifford."

"What are you, anyhow?" asked Johnny. "Some kind of a bank robber?"

"Never," she said. "Not even once."

"What do you do?" asked Johnny. "May I ask?"

"Of course. Guess."

He looked at her long and hard.

"I would guess—at least you look like, to *me,* that is—an airplane engine mechanic."

"Wrong."

"Wait. Don't tell me. Anesthetist."

She frowned. "I don't even know what that is."

"Wait! . . . Brain surgeon," guessed Johnny confidently.

"Right!" she said.

They shared a laugh. She turned his card over in her hands.

"But I haven't got my card with me," she said.

"I'll come and get it," said Johnny. "Any time, any place you say."

"No use. I haven't got a card."

Johnny took a deep breath and plunged ahead.

"Are you down here alone?" he asked.

"No. I'm with Mr. Schenck's party."

Johnny's eyebrows moved upward. "Joseph Schenck?"

"Yes," she said. "He's my friend."

"He's a fine man, Joe."

"He's been very nice to *me*. Except—"

"Yes?"

"He doesn't think I'm an actress."

"Are you?"

"I want to be."

Johnny eyed her expertly.

"How *much* do you want to be?"

"More than anything in the world," she said passionately, tears coming to her eyes.

"What have you done up to now?" he asked professionally.

She recited her meager credits like a litany.

"Well, I've done some modeling and some posing, and I had a bit in *Ladies in the Chorus* at Columbia. I was in *Love Happy* at U.A. with the Marx brothers. I had a scene with Groucho, and—"

"Hey! Wait a second. I remember you," said Johnny. "He's a detective, Groucho, right? And you did that wavy walk of yours into his office, and you said, 'I think some men are following me.' You're that blonde did that bit?"

"No!" she shouted. "You've got it wrong. I said—"

She jumped up, walked away, and returned, using her wavy walk, then said in her supercharged sex voice, "I believe a man is following me."

She sat down.

"A *man,* not *men.*"

"Yeah, that's right."

"It got a very good laugh."

"I remember."

"And then at Twentieth, I was in *A Ticket to Tomahawk,* but most of me got cut out."

"Well, that happens."

"So now I'm just scrounging around again."

"Who's your agent, honey?"

"Abner Farber. Farber-Lee."

"Oh, sure."

"But I think *he's* getting pretty discouraged, too."

Johnny leaned over and took her hand.

"Listen, Marilyn, never get discouraged. Not in this business. Every career's got ups and downs, and believe me, it's better to have the downs earlier instead of later. You've got it, believe me. I'm an expert. You've got youth and looks and appeal, and you're unique. And most of all—the one thing that's indispensable for a movie career—personality."

"I have?"

"Yes. That cramp in your leg may turn out to be one of the luckiest things ever happened to you."

She looked glum, embarrassed.

"What's a matter?" he asked.

"I didn't have any cramp in any leg. I just wanted to meet *you.*"

Johnny jumped up.

"My God!"

"What?"

"And you can *act,* too!" He sat down, hard. "A shoo-in. You're a goddam shoo-in."

"What is it—a shoo-in?" asked the swimming champion of Norway, as she joined them.

Johnny rose and seated her.

Marilyn was impressed. She did not get around much with gentlemen.

"Miss Monroe, Miss Seedorf," said Johnny formally.

The waiter poured a glass for Miss Seedorf.

"I was watching you dive," said Marilyn. "My God!"

"It's my business. What's yours?"

"She's an actress," said Johnny. "And she's going to be a great star."

"Oh, really? That's nice."

They all drank.

Johnny asked Marilyn, "How long are you going to—?"

A sleek young man interrupted him and said to Marilyn, "Mr. Schenck wants you."

"O.K.," she replied.

"Right now," he insisted. "Bungalow A."

"I *know!*" she said testily. She finished her drink and said, "I won't be long. I'll be back."

"No," said Johnny, tightly. "Don't. We have to leave."

"We do?" asked Miss Seedorf.

"Yes."

"Oh," said Marilyn, disappointed.

"But you'll hear from me," said Johnny.

"Oh, I hope so," she said, and went off with the messenger.

Miss Seedorf touched Johnny's face. "You tell a lie, huh? We don't leave, no."

Johnny looked at his wristwatch and said, "Look, it's just five o'clock. We leave now, we can have a terrific dinner at Romanoff's. There's nobody here. Nobody. It's a cemetery."

He rose and looked off in the direction of Marilyn's exit.

"I want to finish this," said Miss Seedorf.

"In the car," said Johnny. "Let's go."

He took the bottle from the cooler, handed it to her, pulled her to her feet, and they left. But not before one more look back.

The following afternoon, Johnny was in Abner Farber's office on Sunset Boulevard. The Farber-Lee Agency was a smart, chic operation housed in an impressive Colonial structure that resembled, in miniature, the house in which Abner had been raised.

He had been listening to Johnny's proposal, searching without success for the hidden motivation which he suspected.

"I understand, Johnny," he said. "But look. I have to level with you. I don't want any bad feelings later. I respect you and the William Morris Agency."

"You should, Abby. We never raid, never steal or go after a client of anybody's. It's a standing principle. It's something Mr. Morris would never do, even though it was done to him many times."

"I can believe it. What I'm saying is, I've had this kid around. Interviews, tests. We've invested. Pictures, glossies, even some film. Publicity. And nothing. Sure, everybody wants to use her, but in the wrong way."

"How much?" asked Johnny.

"How much what?"

"Have you invested?"

"I don't know. I could look it up. A few thou."

"We'll pay it."

"You will?" asked Abner, astonished.

"Yes. Plus which we'll give you a third of the commission."

"You will?"

"And not only for the term of your deal. For as long as we represent her."

Abner shook his head in disbelief. He got up, went to an Adams cabinet, took out two glasses, a bottle of thirty-year-old bourbon, and a siphon.

"Bourbon O.K.?" he asked.

"Sure, anything."

"To seal the deal."

He poured. They drank. Abner laughed, rather hysterically.

"What is it?" asked Johnny.

"I just thought of that story they're telling around. You know, about the little agent . . . on his ass . . . every client gone. He's waiting for the phone company to come and take out his phone. It rings. A guy says, 'You Gus Miller?' 'Yes.' 'Good. This is Cary Grant calling.' The agent's heart almost stops. Is it a joke? No. It really *does* sound like Cary Grant. He pulls himself together. He says, 'What can I do for you, Mr. Grant?' 'Well, I'd like you to represent me.' 'You would?' 'Yes, I've had it with these big offices, and I've just broken up with my old agent, and I hear you're young and clever and aggressive.' 'I sure am, Mr. Grant.' 'Fine, then. I'll want you to handle everything: pictures, radio, TV, personals. Come right over here to my house and we'll draw up an agreement. A straight ten percent satisfactory?' 'Certainly, Mr. Grant.' 'All right, then, nine-oh-one Tower Road. I'll wait for you.' 'I'll be right there, Mr. Grant.' 'Oh, just one question, Mr. Miller . . . are you *Jewish?*' There's a long pause. Then he answers, *'Not necessarily!'* "

Johnny laughed. "What's that got to do with us?" he asked.

"I don't know, just it's been such a crazy week for us, and something tells me we've just made a good deal."

Johnny Hyde's partner did not agree with Abner. He did *not* think Johnny had made a good deal.

"This splitting commissions, it's no good, Johnny, and you know it. It puts people in our business in a way we don't want them in our business."

"This girl is great," said Johnny stubbornly.

"And another thing. You yourself are always saying how mixing personal life with business is not healthy."

"This is different," mumbled Johnny.

"Well, if it's done, it's done, but God knows I wish it wasn't."

Johnny Hyde was to live with this disaffection for the rest of his life. He tried to keep it from Marilyn, and thought he did, but she knew. Her instincts were sound. It all served to add to her appreciation of and love for this remarkable, different, new man in her life: Johnny Hyde. He would become not only her agent and

371

sponsor, her adviser and lover—but in a curious, kindred way, the father she had never had.

"*I'm* taking *you* out to dinner tonight," Marilyn said, as they finished a drink in the new apartment Johnny had provided for her. "I could make it here. I'm a sensational cook. Is that a kick? And sometimes I will. But tonight, we're going out. I'm going to pay, and everything."

"Fine," said Johnny. "Where?"

"You'll see."

She drove, very badly, straight out on Melrose Avenue, to Lucey's.

Johnny had not been there in years. It had fallen off badly, but still retained a homelike and charming exotic atmosphere.

They went to a booth she had reserved. They ordered drinks.

"You're not going to ask me why?" she asked.

"Why what?"

"Why I'm taking you."

"You *owe* it to me, that's why."

"No."

"What, then?"

"This place doesn't seem special?"

"Well, I used to come here all the time. No more. I don't know why."

"This booth?"

He frowned. "Come on, honey, you're gonna give me a migraine."

"O.K. O.K.," she said quickly. "I'm buying you dinner in this place—in this booth—because *you* once bought *me* a dinner in this place. In this booth."

Johnny looked about, considered the booth, and said, "No. Mistake. I wouldn't forget a thing like that."

"It was some time ago," she said. "Like about nineteen thirty-eight, nine."

"Are you sure?" he asked.

"Sure I'm sure. With my mother."

At this word, memory exploded in his head, and Johnny saw —in this transcendently beautiful creature before him—the revolting child she had been. He went pale, but smiled, leaned over, and kissed her tenderly.

372

"A brandy, please," he said to a passing waiter.

When he had finished it, he said, "Marilyn, honey, don't—if you can help it—ever pull jolts like that on me, huh? I've got a little heart condition—it's nothing much—but I'm not supposed to get shocks. O.K.?"

She burst into tears.

"Oh, come on, don't," he said.

Weeping, she said, "I thought it was going to be sort of a funny . . . I mean, romantic . . . no, I mean both—"

"It is, it is," he said, comforting her.

"And instead of it, I give you a heart attack—"

"Who said anything about a—? Come on, honey, let's eat."

She stopped crying suddenly, looked up at the waiting waiter, said, "Antipasto lasagna garlic salad," and laughed.

Johnny wondered why.

IV

THUS BEGAN for Marilyn Monroe the most important and significant relationship she was ever to know. And for Johnny Hyde, a lovely and loving coda to his life.

He had been recently divorced and had bought a comfortable home on the Beverly Hills "flats." The real estate agent had described it as "an ultraluxurious Cape Cod cottage."

Johnny had Billy Haines, the silent star turned interior decorator, redo the house with special emphasis on a wing for Marilyn: bedroom, dressing room, wardrobe, sitting room, and kitchenette.

Marilyn wondered when she was going to be asked to move in. Johnny wondered why she did not ask. Both were shy.

Meanwhile, he took her on a week-long shopping spree for a four-season wardrobe (they would be going to New York from time to time, of course); coats and hats and shoes and accessories and jewelry.

"I don't feel right about it, Johnny," she complained one evening. "It makes me feel like a—you know—some kind of a—"

"Some kind of a *nothing!*" he snapped. "We're building a star, and this is how it starts."

But with all his generosity, he was practical as well.

Marilyn came in from Rheingold's one afternoon, and showed Johnny two pairs of earrings she had bought.

"*Two* pair!" he exclaimed. "How many ears have you *got?*"

"The usual," she said. "It was just I couldn't make up my mind between the two—"

"So you bought them both?"

"Right. Did I do wrong?"

"For God's sake, no. Listen, maybe once in a while you'll let *me* wear a pair."

Johnny called for her early one evening. They were on their way to the premiere of *The Heiress*.

He found her sitting at her dressing table, in one of her newest evening gowns, a knockout in pink by James Galanos, and wearing one of each pair of the earrings (a joke). The makeup man and hairdresser that Johnny had engaged had been and gone. She was a perfect vision. Why then was she sitting there looking so miserable?

He came up to her from behind and kissed the nape of her neck.

"Did you ever see this bump on my nose?" she asked.

"What bump?"

"This one."

"Of course not. What're you talking about?"

"This *bump* on my *nose!*" she cried.

"Don't keep saying that, honey. People'll say I gave it to you."

"Ah-hah!"

"What 'ah-hah'?"

"Then there *is* a bump."

"No, of course not."

"Mel says—"

"Who's Mel?"

"The makeup man. And you yourself said he's the best in the business."

"He's nuts."

"No, he's not. Look. Right here."

They both leaned in to the mirror. She indicated a spot on her nose without touching it. Johnny peered and peered, finally put on his reading glasses, squinted.

"I can't see it," he said seriously.

"Of course not," she said, "because Mel's got it made up so you can't."

"So what's the problem?"

"The problem is it's there. I can't have Mel Berns move in with me, can I?"

Johnny smiled.

"I wouldn't recommend it," he said.

Marilyn stared at her image glumly.

"God," she said, "I look like W.C. Fields."

"Not exactly," said Johnny. "He *never* wears pink."

It was a nervous evening. Johnny observed that his date was much admired. All through dinner at The Brown Derby, and later at the Pantages Theatre, and still later at the studio party at the Beverly Wilshire Hotel. But he also noted that whenever anyone came up to them to be introduced, Marilyn did something to cover her nose—with her handkerchief or bag or napkin.

Back at her apartment, it led to their first quarrel.

"It looked ridiculous," he said, "that covering your face all the time."

"Just my nose," she grumbled.

"People thought—God knows what—that you were snubbing them, or having a nosebleed, or sniffing cocaine."

"How do *you* know what they thought?"

"I don't."

"So?"

"Maybe worse."

"I'm not going to do that Paramount test. Not unless Mel makes me up."

"He can't."

"Why not?"

"Because he's RKO, and the test is Paramount."

"So why don't I do the test at RKO?"

Johnny took a deep breath and put his hand on his chest. Marilyn was instantly contrite.

"Oh, Johnny! Johnny, sit down." He did so. "Drink? Brandy? What?"

"Nothing, honey, don't get excited. O.K., water."

As she ran off to get the water, he took a gold pillbox out of his vest pocket, selected a small white pellet, and placed it under his tongue.

Marilyn returned and knelt beside him. "I'm sorry, Johnny. Please forgive me. I'm so sorry."

He kissed her forehead.

"Nothing to be sorry. Tomorrow we'll go see about a nose job. They're very expensive, good ones. I know a man." He looked at her tenderly. "Thank God, you've only got one nose." He kissed it. She embraced him.

"Johnny, I'll try. You'll see how hard I'll try. And if I don't make you proud of me someday, I'll kill myself."

Johnny laughed. "But, baby, that wouldn't solve one damn thing, now would it?"

She put her lips to his ear and whispered, "Let's make love, Johnny. Please?"

She did not see the tense and anxious look pass over his face, because by the time she came away from his ear, and gave him her eyes, he was smiling.

"Very well," he said. "Very well. Girls with bumps on their noses kind of get me."

"Close your eyes," she said, and he did. She kissed him.

The next morning, they sat in the plush offices of Dr. Myron Berkowitz, the most celebrated plastic surgeon in California. He had completed his examination and was now delivering his verdict.

"You are a very beautiful girl, Miss Monroe," he said. "Do you really think *I* could make you *more* beautiful?"

Marilyn turned to Johnny and said, in a panic, "He's not going to *do* it!"

"Wait a second, honey," said Johnny, taking her hand. "Go ahead, Doctor."

"There are plastic surgeons," said the doctor, "—many—who do aesthetic work. I do not. I had to make a decision long ago in life. Would I use my time and training to help people who have been hurt or disfigured by accidents or by nature, or use it to feed vanities?" He put his attention on Marilyn. "So you have a tiny bump on your little nose, what of it? Maybe it adds to your personality, maybe it *is* your personality. Also, remember, it's possible

376

to perfect the nose and ruin the face. My advice to you, young lady—"

Marilyn was on her feet. She barely managed to say, "Thank you, Doctor," and bolt from the room before bursting into tears. The men could hear her sobbing in the outer office and being comforted by Miss Schuller, the doctor's nurse.

"I'm sorry," said the doctor. "I certainly didn't mean to upset the young lady."

Johnny rose and moved closer to him. He drew together all of his considerable forces of salesmanship and began. "Doctor," he said, "I understand what you're saying perfectly, and I agree. I'm afraid the young lady does not. Please remember she is very, very young."

"Oh, yes."

"But, Doctor, this is not a case of some rich society woman who has a big nose and wants a small one, or a man getting old and wants a facelift. This girl is an actress—"

"I know."

"—who has to be photographed at close range. Sometimes the camera like right here." He put his palms together and pushed them close to the doctor's face. "And if she's conscious, self-conscious, about an imperfection, no matter how small, it could ruin her performance and the picture and maybe even her entire *career!*"

"But my dear man—"

"Wait a minute, Doctor. And in this case you have someone whose career is her entire life—so whether *you* think she needs it or not, *she* does. I can't see how you can call this vanity or a matter of aesthetics. This is a matter of life and death for this girl." He sat down, out of breath.

After a long pause, Dr. Berkowitz said, "I see. By the way— aside from the little nose business—you know her right jaw is not symmetrical and could be corrected with a small cartilage implant."

"Will you do it, Doctor?"

"Yes, Mr. Hyde, I'll do it."

"Thank you."

They shook hands.

"And by the way, Mr. Hyde," said the doctor, "I wish *you* were *my* agent."

377

Marilyn spent four days and five nights at the Cedars of Lebanon Hospital. When the bandages were removed, her face was swollen and bruised. She had promised the doctor and Johnny that she would not use a mirror until told to do so—but she had broken her promise and kept looking at her image every half hour and saying, "Oh, my God!"

When she was able to leave the hospital, Johnny moved her into his house—"Our house," he insisted—for the two or three weeks of further recuperation.

The doctor had been mistaken. The result of the surgery was near miraculous. The pretty girl had become a great beauty. Part of this metamorphosis came as a direct result of the surgery; the rest from her own inner powerful conviction that she could now face the world unblemished.

In the three weeks of her recovery, Johnny went nowhere other than to his office when it was necessary. The evenings were spent at home, talking, talking, talking.

He learned far more about her horrendous childhood than he wanted to know; about the accident of her birth, an unwanted embarrassment to her working mother and the married-man father, a film laboratory executive. The various foster parents, cruelties, molestations. She felt compelled to tell him all, and, carried away at times, *more* than all.

"Very interesting," he said one evening after she had told him the circumstances of her marriage to Jim Dougherty, a police officer. "So it didn't work out, so what? So now try with me. Maybe it *will* work out."

"Please, Johnny, not again. I'll be with you as long as you want me, but I don't want to get married. I can't."

"Why not?"

"I can't tell you, but I can't."

"That's no answer."

"Anyway, what does a man like you—a somebody—want with a—"

"Don't say it," said Johnny. "You're going to be the biggest star in this business."

"Oh, Johnny," she said impatiently.

"I *know* it."

"How can I?"

"Well, first of all, you've got to stop saying, 'Oh, Johnny,' when I tell you. You've got to believe in yourself—the way I do."

"You believe in me because you love me."

"That's right," he said. "And you've got to love you, too."

"What? How can I?"

"Do it," said Johnny hypnotically. "Do it. Like yourself and your talent. Be nice to yourself. Believe. Just picture it all happening out there in the future. Yes. And love yourself."

She shook her head sadly. "I'd rather love *you*, Johnny. You're some guy."

For the next two weeks Johnny concentrated on building up a portfolio of stills with which he hoped to prime an important test.

At length he had what he considered a superlative set of photographs—Marilyn in every conceivable mood, in various costumes and makeups. Finally, some classy cheesecake and bikini shots. He decided to begin with his friend Ben Farber.

He went in to see Ben, lugging the great portfolio.

"How are you, Ben?"

"I've got a headache," Ben replied. "Since nine thirty this morning already."

"Don't worry about it, Ben, I've got something here to show you that'll take your mind off all your troubles. A real painkiller."

"What's that?"

"I'm bringing you a star. A real star. A *big* star."

"Oh, my God," said Ben gloomily. "You've already got your this year's blonde."

"One more crack like that," said Johnny, "and I'll take her to Paramount."

"Paramount needs her," said Ben.

Johnny got out an 11 x 14 color head shot of Marilyn. He handed it across the desk to Ben in the manner of someone bestowing a valuable and impressive gift.

Ben looked at it with mild interest. A beautiful girl, all right, no question. But he had played this scene with Johnny many times before. Almost every year Johnny came around touting a beautiful young actress, usually blond and generally without talent.

Johnny presented another picture. A waist shot, featuring what was to become one of the most celebrated bosoms in all the world.

Another and another and another.

379

It was clear that there was nothing haphazard in this presentation. The order of the photographs Johnny was showing had been carefully calculated for maximum effect. The pictures had more and more girl, less and less clothing, creating a vicarious striptease.

Finally, he was down to the bikini shots; Marilyn standing, dancing, jumping, lying in the sand. Ben's desk was covered with photographs by the time Johnny was done. Now he brought forth the climactic picture. An extremely large color shot of a girl in full figure lying on pink satin sheets.

"Don't tell me," said Johnny, "that this isn't the most important find of the last five years, maybe six, possibly seven."

Ben was staring at the final picture. "I think I know this girl," he said.

"You couldn't."

"Very familiar."

"She's only done a few bits around, Ben. You couldn't possibly have noticed her."

"Not in bits, no, but I think I've met her."

"If she'd met *you* she would've told me."

Ben rose and started out of the room. "Come with me," he said.

Ben walked with long, long strides. Johnny could barely keep up with him.

Ten minutes later, they reached the property department of Farber Films. Without knocking, Ben walked into the office. The walls seemed to be papered with pinups. There, over the desk, was a three-sheet-size calendar. The famous and infamous nude shot of the girl who was later to become Marilyn Monroe.

Ben and Johnny looked at it carefully. Johnny had never seen it. In fact, he had no idea of its existence.

"That's not her," he said. "That's some different girl."

"Same girl," said Ben stubbornly.

"I'll bet you a thousand dollars," said Johnny.

"I wouldn't take your bet," said Ben, "because I know that's the girl."

"Come on, Ben. Don't be a mule. Girls can look alike. Why wouldn't they? But this girl on the calendar is much taller than Marilyn. Much."

"Same girl," said Ben. They started walking back to Ben's office. "Johnny, you know I like you," he said. "We're pals. But this kind of thing has got to stop. It's not right for you. Every year the same thing."

"This one is different."

"They're *always* different."

"This girl is going to be a star, a big star. She's got everything it takes. She's beautiful, and a figure, a distinctive voice—you've never heard a voice like it—and she can act. She's funny, and she's absolutely adorable. And what's more—" His voice caught and he was unable to go on.

In Ben's office he collected all the photographs, grimly put them back into the portfolio, and left without a word.

Johnny asked, "But, Marilyn, why didn't you ever *tell* me about it?"

"I was ashamed to," she said. "I thought it would just get lost."

"What did you do it for anyhow?"

"For fifty dollars," she said, and made Johnny laugh.

"Well," he said, "we'll ride it out the best we can, but, oh, baby, when you get to be a big star—"

"If."

"When! It's going to be trouble."

"Why? When I'm a big star those calendars'll be worth a fortune."

"Not to us, baby. Not to us."

Johnny Hyde, who was in the habit of visiting every major studio every single day, made his presentation on twenty or thirty desks without success.

"All right, so don't sign her," he pleaded with Dore Schary at M-G-M. "So don't give her a part, not even a bit, make a test. Shoot a test."

But Dore Schary pointed out that the studio had a plethora of pretty blondes and was not at present in the market for any more.

"Not until some of the ones we've got wear out," said Schary.

Johnny realized that one of the chief difficulties he was having in placing Marilyn was the fact that there was—in the parlance of the business—"no film on her." The few bits she had done were not representative and, in any case, did not, in Johnny's opinion,

381

show her full potential. Marilyn insisted that they showed only the former bump on her nose.

Johnny began to attempt to persuade the various studio heads with whom he was in daily contact to test her with a view toward a term contract, even a stock contract. No luck.

"Cute blondes," said Jack L. Warner, "they're thirty-five cents a dozen this week at Farmer's Market."

"This is *not* a cute blonde," said Johnny heatedly.

"Well, if she's not," said Jack, "what's she doing around with *you?*"

"If a suitable part comes up, Johnny, I promise you I'll keep her in mind," said Buddy DeSylva at Paramount. "What's her name again?"

Darryl F. Zanuck was more outspoken. "I glommed her when she was on the lot here. Nothing. Furthermore, I've got Betty Grable and Alice Faye and if I want I can get Betty Hutton or Lana Turner, so what do I need *her?*"

At length, Johnny, in desperation, decided to produce a test of Marilyn himself. In the case of almost any other promising William Morris Agency client the agency would have financed such a project, but the fact that Johnny Hyde was personally involved with this girl made the situation sticky. Johnny went ahead anyhow. He engaged space at the General Service Studios and an art director, a hairdresser, Mel Berns for makeup, Joe Ruttenberg of M-G-M as cameraman and got the superlative King Vidor to direct it as a favor.

Marilyn did a dramatic scene from *Rain,* a comedy scene from *Gentlemen Prefer Blondes,* then sang and danced a verse and two choruses of "My Heart Belongs to Daddy."

The test took three weeks to rehearse and prepare, four days to shoot, ten days to edit. It was received politely but without enthusiasm at the agency.

Even Marilyn worried. "I don't know," she said to Johnny. "It doesn't even seem to be me I'm looking at. Is that me? It's like a whole nother person, and I'm not even sure I *like* that person. It's like I was showing off my body, which I never do, or is that just the way it was photographed?"

"You don't know what you're talking about, sweetie. It's a terrific test."

It may have been, but Johnny found it difficult to get the right people to see it. Some of those who did, underlings, were impressed, but to get it to the attention of the studio heads, who were the only ones capable of making a commitment, was not easy.

Johnny continued to carry the single can of film under his arm wherever he went. It was as though he had a delicious pie in it that he was anxious to share with others. No one was hungry.

He took it to the Warner Brothers Studios, to Jack Warner's office. He went into Warner's private projection room and gave it to the projectionist, then he went in to see Jack and asked him to look at the test.

"Will you stop it, Johnny? You've been on this with me already. I'm a busy man, I've got problems. I've got these two goddam gangsters, Brown and Bioff, on my hands. They're around picking up payoff money from everybody. They claim they're going to pull the projectionists out of every theatre in America, these two mugs, hoodlums, a couple of gangsters. If they come in here, I swear to Christ, I'll throw 'em out on their ass. I'm begging the other guys to do the same, but they won't. You know what they're doing? They're all paying off."

"I know, I know," said Johnny. "It's a bad situation, but couldn't you give me ten minutes of your time to look at a star?"

"I've got plenty of stars," said Jack. "I've got too many stars. The more stars you have, the more trouble you have. I'm going to drop a few."

"Nobody in the history of pictures ever had too many stars, Jack."

"Material. That's what I need. Material. Why don't you bring me some stories, some plays or some books I can make a buck with? Not just one blonde after another."

"How do you know this one's a blonde, Jack?" asked Johnny.

Jack regarded him evenly. "If *you're* bringing her around, she's a blonde."

Discouraged, Johnny Hyde went out to the projection room, picked up his film and went his way.

One morning he had a call from Harry Cohn, the powerful boor who was the head of Columbia Pictures. Cohn had a favor to ask.

The all-star cast he was assembling for *Born Yesterday* was having scheduling problems. Two of the stars, Judy Holliday and William Holden, were William Morris clients, as was the director, George Cukor. Would he consider, in the interest of the picture, a two-week postponement?

Johnny agreed.

"Thanks, Johnny, you're a prince."

Thirty minutes later Johnny Hyde was back. He stood in front of Harry Cohn's desk, the now battered can of film under his arm.

"Please, Johnny," said Cohn. "Not now. You've hit me at a busy time."

"When is it *not* a busy time for you, Harry?"

"Look, leave it here, leave it with me. I'll run it first chance I get. I give you my word."

"Your word is *shit,* Harry! And you know it. So don't give me that."

"I don't have to take insults from you, Johnny."

"Of course not, only favors."

"They're no favors if I have to pay back double."

"*What!* Listen, you creep, let me ask you this. How far is that door on your right from you?"

"What're you—?"

"How far? Six steps? Seven?"

"Maybe eight," said Cohn.

"And when you go through it, what's there?"

"My projection room—you know all that. What the hell's the matter? What *is* this?"

"So I'm asking you to take eight steps and watch a fourteen-minute test of somebody I believe can be a great star—and you won't do it?"

"No, I won't. What do you know about that? Great star, my ass. Another one of your cuties. I'm getting sick of 'em."

Johnny dropped the can of film to the floor and began to remove his jacket.

Cohn clicked on his Dictograph and yelled, "Get in here! Everybody! I've got a *lunatic* on my hands!" The swift entrance of two secretaries and a security guard was all that prevented a nasty scene.

Cohn shook his finger at Johnny and said, "You know you're nuts? Flying off like that. You and your heart. You know you've got a heart condition, you little muzzler." Johnny, in control, was putting on his jacket. "You want me to be responsible for a keel over?" He looked at his staff members who had come rushing in and said, "O.K., everybody out. Out!"

Now he was alone with Johnny. "Let's have a drink, O.K.?" he asked.

"O.K."

As he poured the drinks he said, "A test. What's a test f'Chrissake? Listen. You believe in this broad—I mean this girl —that's good enough for me. I'll give her a standard stock contract. Seven years. Starts two hundred goes to two thousand if she's still here."

"Nothing doing," said Johnny. "One year at a time and she starts at *three* hundred."

"All right."

They clicked glasses and drank.

Cohn asked, "What's her name again?"

Marilyn was overjoyed when she heard that Johnny had achieved a contract for her at Columbia. With the number of pictures they made there, and Johnny to help, she was certain she could and would break through.

She was wrong. The deal that had been made in rage and haste proved to be meaningless.

She reported to the studio daily, was cast in a few nothing bits, tested with several young hopefuls, averaged two propositions a day, and became more and more discouraged.

She and Johnny were lying out by the pool one summer evening, having had a skinny dip and made love in the pool.

"Oh, Johnny," she sighed.

"What, baby?"

"I know you say I'm not supposed to get discouraged. But how can I help it? Look, it's almost six months I've been in that hellhole and I feel I'm going backwards, not forwards."

"It was a mistake, darling. My fault."

"—not that, but—"

"I'll get you out of there. Tomorrow."

385

"And then what? After all, who *am* I?"

He rolled over to be closer to her, looked down at her and said, "Listen, you know who *I* am?"

"Of course."

"No, you don't. You *think* you do, but you don't."

"I don't?"

"No. Did you ever hear of Ivan Haidabura?"

"No."

"That's me."

"It is?"

"I swear."

"Say it again."

"Ivan Haidabura."

"Ivan Haidabura," she repeated. "How do you spell it?"

"H-a-i-d-a-b-u-r-a. Haidabura."

"Why, that's *beautiful!*" she said. "How come you changed it?"

"Nobody could *say* it. Not in this country, anyway. In Russia, everybody."

Marilyn sat up. "You're a Russian?" she asked, astounded.

"Yes. Is it all over, then?"

"Oh, Johnny."

With a faraway look he said, "The Nicholas Haidabura Imperial Russian Troupe."

"Nicholas?"

"My father."

"What did it do?"

"What did what do?"

"The troupe. You said troupe."

"Oh, we were acrobats."

"Acrobats?" she screamed, and began to laugh.

"Sure," said Johnny. "Our whole family. When I was about five, maybe four. I can still do some of the act." He stood up. "You want to see?"

"No. Please, don't."

"Thanks," said Johnny, and sat down. "We played all over Europe and finally—the big break, America. The Hippodrome. We got to be a standard act. And we all started to learn English. And all of a sudden I was no more Ivan, I was John. Then Johnny. Johnny Haidabura. Then I got too big for the tricks, too heavy to catch with one hand, and, of course, the big thing was to have a

386

little kid to throw around. So my father got me a job in his agent's office and here I am."

"No wonder we make such a good pair," said Marilyn. "You spent your childhood getting thrown around and I spent mine getting *kicked* around."

"What do we care?" he said. "That's probably what makes us so strong."

"Are we, Johnny? Strong?"

"Damn right. We don't take no for an answer. Listen, sometimes I don't even take *yes* for an answer."

They laughed. It was another thing they did well together.

Harry Cohn was glad to release her, at Johnny's request.

"She's nothing, Johnny," Cohn informed him. "You're wasting your time. She's for one-line telephone operators or walk-away-funny waitresses."

"You've been wrong before, Harry."

"Who not?" said Cohn.

Marilyn could have told Johnny the real reason she had been dropped, but thought it best not to. Cohn had made a fierce pass at her and had taken the rejection badly. He was not accustomed to turndowns. Not from stock girls, at any rate.

V

THE TROCADERO again. The dance floor is more crowded than ever. It is a swinging Saturday night. Benny Goodman and his orchestra are playing "Stompin' at the Savoy."

Johnny Hyde is dancing with Marilyn Monroe. He has always been an exceptionally good dancer, but with Marilyn, he rivals Astaire.

Eleanor Powell's partner is Louis B. Mayer. He does *not* rival Astaire. He is a serious dancer, unsmiling, careful, correct.

Johnny and Marilyn greet Ben and Willa Farber.

A stir on one part of the dance floor, then an uproar of laughter. Groucho Marx, in a sudden switch of partners, is dancing with his brother Harpo.

Elsewhere, John Huston is dancing cheek-to-cheek with a stately New York society girl-cum-actress, Whitney Bourne.

Glimpses of Loretta Young and Errol Flynn and Bette Davis and Jimmy Cagney and Abner Farber with Lana Turner. It is one of those nights at the Troc.

When Johnny spots Huston, it takes him no more than ten seconds to spin his way over.

"Hello, John," he says, looking up.

"Hi, John," says Huston. He glances at Marilyn and continues. "Who's your friend?"

"John Monroe," says Marilyn.

Huston laughs. Johnny introduces them formally. "Marilyn Monroe, John Huston."

"And this is Whitney Bourne," says Huston.

There is a chorus of acknowledgments.

Marilyn says, "I think your father is *just great,* Mr. Huston."

"Thank you," he says. "So do I."

Johnny, still dancing, produces a loud stage whisper and says, "Now tell him *he's* great, too."

"*You're* great, too," says Marilyn.

Johnny to Huston: "See how she takes direction?"

"Oh," says Marilyn, "are you a director?"

"Oh, my God!" says Johnny as he whirls his partner away briefly.

Huston and Whitney laugh. They think Marilyn is kidding.

Johnny dances back and says, "I hear that thing you're going to do at Metro is sensational, John."

"Yes, it is."

"What's the name of it?"

"*The Asphalt Jungle.*"

"Oh, what a wonderful title!" says Marilyn.

"That's better," Johnny says. "Now you're getting the idea." He looks up at Huston again. "Anything in it for this terrific girl? She's a marvelous actress."

Huston looks her over and says, "With her equipment, she doesn't *have* to be."

"Well, *is* there?" asks Johnny, persisting.

Huston is studying Marilyn as they dance, then says, "As a matter of fact, I think there just might be. Yes."

Marilyn, in her excitement, throws her arms about Johnny and kisses him. Huston laughs and says, "Say, aren't we a little out of sync here?"

"What time do you want me to bring her in Monday?" asks Johnny.

"No time."

"What?"

"We *start* Monday." He speaks to Marilyn. "Be on the set at nine A.M. Don't be late."

Marilyn is beside herself as she shouts, "I'm *never* late!"

Huston begins to dance away. Johnny calls after him. "Wait a second, John. What's the deal?"

"I don't make deals, Johnny. I make pictures. Talk to the brass. Didn't I see L.B. tripping the heavy fantastic around here somewhere?" He dances away.

Johnny glides Marilyn all over the floor looking for L.B. Mayer, at length finds him.

"L.B.?"

"Hello," says a surly Mayer.

"This is Marilyn Monroe."

"Hi," says Marilyn.

"Pleased to meet you," says Mayer glumly, as he tries to dance away. Johnny follows and says, "John Huston wants her—"

"I wouldn't be surprised," Mayer interrupts.

"— for *The Asphalt Jungle*," says Johnny.

"Congratulations," says Mayer to Marilyn.

"When can we talk deal, L.B.?"

"Never."

"What?"

"I don't make deals for bit players, Johnny. You know that. Talk to Mannix or somebody over there."

He dances away clumsily, irritated. Dancing is difficult enough for him without conversations.

Ten minutes later the music is "Buttons and Bows." Johnny, still dancing with Marilyn, is haggling with Eddie Mannix.

Johnny, improvising, says, "He figures it's like six, seven days, so why not make it a two-weeker?"

"No, no," Mannix responds. "We'll give her a day-player contract. Two hundred a day. O.K.?"

"O.K.!" yells Marilyn.

"Shut up, sweetheart," says Johnny. He turns back to Mannix. "Take her for two weeks at five hundred."

"You drunk, or what?" asks Mannix. "Seven days, two hundred is fourteen hundred. *Your* way she gets only a thousand."

"I know," says Johnny, "but I don't want her to be a day player."

"Why not?" asks Marilyn. "Fourteen hundred is more."

"Don't talk." Then to Mannix. "What d' y' say?"

Mannix shrugs and shakes his head. "All right. Have it your way."

"You want an option?" asks Johnny. "In case she hits?"

"No, thanks," Mannix answers.

"Cost you nothing," says Johnny.

"What's the point?" asks Mannix.

Johnny replies, "It looks nice on paper."

"Sometimes, Johnny, I don't understand you."

"That's O.K., Eddie, as long as *I* understand me. See you Monday morning."

Johnny and Marilyn dance off on a cloud as the music switches to "Baby, It's Cold Outside."

Johnny and Marilyn return home in an increased state of excitement. They go directly to the bar, where Johnny begins to open a bottle of champagne.

"It was luck!" he exults.

"It was not, Johnny. It was you."

"Luck, baby. We're lucky for each other."

"I'm not going to be able to sleep for two weeks."

"You better. You're gonna need the cream of your energy, sweetheart."

Marilyn says thoughtfully, "Johnny, it really is the big time, isn't it?"

"Bigger than big time. It's an A-picture. It's John Huston. It's M-G-M."

"I just hope I don't drop dead."

"No, don't. I'm sure they want you alive."

As they drink the champagne, they discuss details. Who will coach her? Should she take off a few pounds? Ask Huston? No. Do it. How?

By the time they finish the champagne, they are both talking at once, happily, ecstatically.

They move about putting out lights, preparatory to going upstairs and to bed.

They start up.

Halfway up the stairs, Johnny suddenly clutches the rail and sinks to his knees.

Marilyn panics. "Johnny!" She yells, "Johnny, what is it?"

He shakes his head and sits down on a stair. He looks up at her and smiles wanly.

"Excitement," he whispers. "Maybe too much."

"Take your medicine," she says.

"What? Oh, yes."

He gets out his pillbox and takes his digitalis.

"Doctor?" she asks.

"No, no."

"Just to be sure?"

"I'll be O.K."

"Do it for me, Johnny. Please."

"All right," he says.

"Stay where you are till he gets here. Promise?"

"Promise."

When Dr. Engelberg arrives, he and Marilyn help Johnny up to bed. Johnny keeps telling the doctor about Marilyn's great break, until the doctor knocks him out with a shot.

Marilyn and the doctor are finishing the champagne.

The doctor says, "He's simply got to avoid overexcitement. Although frankly, Marilyn, I don't see how that's possible with you around."

Marilyn eyes him carefully.

"Do you mean what I think you mean?" she asks.

"Yes," says the doctor.

"But he's the one in control, not me. He's the man, after all."

"That's the whole trouble," says the doctor. "Well, just do what you can . . . or should I say, *don't* do what you can—any more than you have to."

"I'll try my best, Hy. I really love this little guy. He's the best man I ever knew in my whole life."

"And I'll bet," says the doctor, "that you're the best *he's* ever known."

He steps over and checks Johnny, who is sleeping peacefully.

Marilyn asks, "You want to see something adorable?"

"Sure."

"Come with me."

She leads him into her bedroom, adjoining, as she speaks. "He was telling me about when he was a little kid, and I was so fascinated. And then a few weeks later, I came home and I found this over my mantelpiece. Where he ever got it—or how—I can't imagine—but look. It's my favorite thing in the whole world."

Over the mantelpiece, in a modest frame, is a colorful turn-of-the-century circus poster. It proclaims The Nicholas Haidabura Imperial Russian Troupe. All around the lithograph are illustrations of the various stunts performed by the troupe.

In the center, an odd family portrait—two women (in acrobat costumes), six men (in more elaborate dress), and one tiny boy, standing on his father's outstretched hand.

The doctor is charmed.

"Marvelous!" he exclaims.

"Can you tell which one is Johnny?" she asks.

"Of course. Right there." He points out the little boy, smiling proudly and triumphantly. "Couldn't be anyone else."

"He says they were really a great troupe." She laughs. "And he says his father had a wonderful line. He used to come forward and say to the audience—" She tries to imitate Johnny's imitation of his father, with a heavy Russian accent—" 'Our next treeck, ladies and gentlemens, eess *eempawssible!*' "

She looks up at her poster again.

As they move away, the doctor says, "Well, let's hope your little man still has a few tricks up his sleeve."

They exchange a long look.

"What else?" she asks.

"Are you, by any chance, a religious girl, Marilyn?"

"I used to be. No more. Why?"

"Well, if you were, I'd ask you to pray for him."

"Oh."

They go downstairs.

As she shows the doctor out, she says, "Hy?"

"Yes?"

"I think I'll pray anyway."

The doctor kisses her cheek, and leaves.

During breakfast the next morning, Johnny in bed, Marilyn at his side, he asked Marilyn for the seventh time to marry him.

After a long tearful pause, she said, "No, Johnny. I don't think we should. Not the way things are."

"You mean because I'm sick? But that's just the *point!* My divorce is final now. My wife got a good settlement. My boys are taken care of. And I want you to have the rest of it. You deserve it. You've earned it."

"Don't put it like that, Johnny," she said. "It sounds—"

"You know what I mean, darling. You've been great with me. And I love you. And it would be perfect. And listen, who knows, I may *not* check out. But if I do, I want to feel that you're taken care of, that you're not going to have any worries or troubles, that you won't have to do things you don't really want to do."

"Johnny, I can't. I'd just feel cheap. I'm going to stay with you, but I can't take anything from you. My God, you've already given me practically a career."

"You've still got a long way to go, honey," he said. "But I never believed in anything in my life as much as I believe in you and in your future. All it's going to take is that you keep your head and never lose your innocence."

Marilyn laughed. "Oh, my God!" she said. "I lost that way back."

"Not the kind of innocence I mean. The kind I mean, sweetheart, is loving your work, loving your friends, even loving yourself. It bothered me, it bothered me terribly, that you didn't like that great test you made. You've got to learn to appreciate yourself and value yourself. And most important, always consider your price high. Promise me."

"O.K., Johnny, I promise."

He asked her again. And again. And again. But he was unable to shake her. In fact, as time went by and he did not seem to be recovering, she was less and less inclined to accept. It seemed ghoulish to her somehow, although she had no words with which to express this feeling.

Johnny was put on a diet, nine hundred calories a day. He grew thin and pale, but always came to life brilliantly when he talked about Marilyn Monroe and her future.

It is the night of the premiere of *The Asphalt Jungle,* which is to take place at Grauman's Chinese. Ben and Willa Farber are to be Johnny's guests.

Johnny's house is a hotbed of excitement.

Marilyn is being prepared for this important public appearance by a team of experts, including Mel Berns and a hairdresser and two wardrobe mistresses. In addition, the press agent for the film, Speed McGraw, is also hovering about.

"What time is it?" asks Marilyn.

"Take it easy, missy," Mel says. "I've been in this business twenty-two years, and I never saw a pre*meer* start on time."

"But I want to *be* there."

"If you get there too early, dumbbell, nobody'll see you."

"I don't want anybody to see me. I want to see them."

"Let me handle it, O.K.?" says Speed.

"How's Johnny?" asks Marilyn.

"He's in there with the doctor," says Speed.

"What doing?"

"Oh, the doctor's giving him a little pep talk and a couple of calmer-downers, I think."

In Johnny's room, he is talking to Dr. Engelberg.

"Hy, listen to me. I don't claim to be brilliant, only practical. And here's my feeling about the whole gismo, about life. You've got to live, or else. I don't want to live the life of an invalid, or even a semi. I want to live my life—for as long as I can, and that's all."

"You're very foolish, Johnny."

"Fine. So foolish."

"I'm saying that there are all kinds of lives. What's so great about yours that it can't change a little? All I'm asking is . . . that, number one, you don't go more than those nine hundred calories a day—"

"That I can do. That I'm *doing,* for Christ's sake!"

"All right, calm down," says the doctor.

"O.K. I'm calmed down."

The doctor continues, "Number two, that you get your proper rest. Like remember, you promised me you'll go to the premiere, but not to the party after."

"No, no. The Farbers are going to take her. Willa and Ben."

"Number three, that you don't overdo—*anything.*"

Johnny smiles wickedly and asks, "You mean like not too much golf?"

"Exactly," says the doctor.

Johnny gets up, goes to the connecting door, opens it and looks into Marilyn's room. He sees that Mel Berns has finished with her.

"Mel! Hey, Mel!"

"Yeah, Johnny?"

"Got a minute?"

"For you, sure."

Mel goes into his room.

Johnny closes the door.

"Listen, Mel. Can you help me out a little?"

"How do you mean, Johnny?"

Johnny looks at himself in the mirror.

"Jesus Christ!" he says. "Look at me. I look like I've joined the majority already."

"Sit down, Johnny. I've made up many's the corpse, an' when I got through you couldn't tell the difference!" Johnny and the doctor exchange a look. The doctor winces. Johnny smiles and sits down. Mel begins to make him up, skillfully, discreetly.

"Do me a favor, Mel. And you, too, Hy. Don't mention this to anybody? Not to her, not to anybody. Holy smoke, I'd never hear the last of it at Hillcrest!"

"Don't worry about it, Johnny," says Mel. "My lips are sealed."

Hy says, "Mel, you happen to have Louella Parsons' number on you?"

Marilyn's first appearance on the screen in *The Asphalt Jungle* was greeted with a few appreciative wolf whistles. She wondered if this was the right reaction, looked over at Johnny and at the Farbers, saw everyone smiling, and knew that all was well.

Her first exit got a neat round of applause. The tough premiere crowd was welcoming a fresh face, a unique and original personality.

Marilyn thought she might faint.

She and Johnny were sitting at the rear of the house, holding hands. When that applause came, she turned to him, her mouth wide open, her eyes shining. She smiled. Johnny was looking at her, tears streaming down his cheeks. She stopped smiling. Ben reached over, shook Johnny's hand, and patted Marilyn's cheek. Willa blew each of them a kiss.

In the lobby afterward, a crush and a confusion of faces—familiar and strange. Compliments. Was that Harry Cohn? L.B. Mayer is standing at her side, acting like her proud father. Zanuck rushes up and embraces her.

Someone asks her for her autograph, the first time ever. Terrified, she shakes her head. What if she spells her name wrong? What if she writes "Norma Jean Baker"?

At last, the safety of the limousine.

"Marilyn," says Ben, "you were a wonder. I swear."

"You're on your way, dear," says Willa. "Godspeed."

They drop Johnny at the house.

At the last moment, Marilyn decides she wants to stay with him and skip the party. Johnny will not have it.

"Nothing doing," he says, "The party's part of it. Willa and Ben'll look after you. I'll wait up."

"Should you?"

"I've got a script to read. Or if I'm asleep, wake me."

"Fat chance," she says.

"Good night, darling. Have a good time. There's only one thing to do with success—enjoy it."

"All right."

"In my whole life," says Johnny, "and it's gone on for weeks now, I never was so proud of anybody as I was of you tonight."

"Johnny," she says, holding him close, "you saying that—and meaning it—makes this the top of *my* life. Johnny. Oh, Johnny."

She had a spectacularly good time at the party. A few people she knew and many whom she did not know offered congratulations, some sincere, some fulsome, but what did it matter? She could hear the faint sounds of the Overture to Success.

She was the darling of the photographers that night and was photographed over a thousand times.

Elia Kazan sought her out to praise her, as did Frank Capra, Norma Shearer, Billy Wilder and Barbara Stanwyck and Dashiell Hammett.

It was 2:00 A.M. when Ben and Willa brought her home. She was surprised to see all the lights on.

396

The Farbers came in with her to find the two maids, in their nightclothes, sitting in the front hall.

"What is it?" asked Marilyn.

"The hospital," said Ellen. "They came and took him to the hospital."

Lena began to cry. "He looked so bad, Miss Monroe. Oh, so bad. But he told us you were wonderful," added Lena. "He said you was the whole hit."

"That you stole the whole picture," said Ellen.

"What hospital?" asked Ben.

"Cedars," Lena replied.

The Farbers and Marilyn got back into the car immediately and drove to Cedars.

When they arrived, they were told that the doctors had left, that Mr. Hyde was in the intensive care unit and was doing well. His condition, in hospital language, was stable.

"Well, then, I suppose we ought to go," said Ben.

"No," said Marilyn. "I'm going to wait."

"How do you mean? How long?"

"Till I can see him," she said simply.

"You want us to wait with you?"

"No, no. I'll be all right, Ben."

"No, we'll wait with you," said Willa.

"All right."

They sat in the visitors' waiting room.

At 4:30, Willa fell asleep, awoke, fell asleep again, and finally agreed to go home with Ben.

"I'll be back," he said.

"Sure."

Marilyn waited, trying to put the two crazily disparate elements of her existence into place. Tonight. What had happened tonight? On the one hand, her greatest happiness, the realization of a ridiculously unattainable aspiration. For the first time in her life, she believed there *was* a future for her that was worth living.

At the same time, somewhere in the dimness above her, lay her friend who had been responsible for it all, in grave danger.

She fell asleep.

At 8:00 in the morning, when the doctors arrived, she was permitted to see Johnny.

397

She found him sitting up in bed, laughing cheerfully. They embraced.

"You can't kid me," he said. "Look at you. You've been out all night. Where've you been?"

"Oh, Johnny," she said. "Johnny, Johnny, I was so worried."

"Well, stop worrying. I'll be out of here in time for lunch. Where would you like to go? Romanoff's?"

"Please, Johnny, you have to be careful."

"Certainly, I'll be careful. Tell you what. I'll have the whole nine hundred calories for lunch. Then we won't have to eat again."

"Oh, God," she said. "Wasn't last night wonderful? Wasn't it the greatest? Did you ever think there would be such a night?"

"She's talking, doctor," said Johnny modestly, "about the premiere of her picture, not about anything else."

"I think I better go," said Marilyn. "I think I better go change, and then I'll come back. Would that be all right, Hy?"

"Certainly," said Dr. Engelberg.

"Don't worry about a thing," said Johnny. "It was nothing. Just excitement. I'll be fine."

"Please be, Johnny. *Please.*"

"Hy," said Johnny, "would you excuse us for two minutes, please?"

"Why not?" said the doctor, and stepped out into the hall.

Marilyn and Johnny kissed.

Then he said, "Now look, sweetheart, when I tell you I'm going to be all right, I mean it. That's what I *think*. But on the other hand, things like this are always little signals, you know what I mean? You wouldn't reconsider?"

"Listen, Johnny, you get better—all better—and we'll talk about it seriously."

"My God!" cried Johnny. "I'm making progress. I'm up to 'maybe.' "

"When you get better," she reminded him.

They kissed again, sealing their bargain.

The doctor returned with two assistants.

"And now would *you* excuse *us,* Marilyn? We've got to do a little work on your boy."

"Boy, hell!" said Johnny. "*Fiancé!* Almost."

Marilyn wandered about the halls for a time, went downstairs, and all at once was aware of hunger. She went into the coffee shop, ordered a club sandwich and a Coke. She bought the trade papers and read them aimlessly, not even seeing the excellent reviews for *The Asphalt Jungle* and the special notice paid to her.

Halfway through the sandwich, a sickening feeling came over her. She got up, dropped a five-dollar bill on the table, forgot her coat, and went back upstairs.

The first thing she saw was a red light over a door. Whose? His.

She ran to it, losing a shoe. She tried to open it. It was locked. She banged on it. It opened.

A nurse said, "Not now, dear."

"Is Doctor—?"

The door closed.

She moved down the hall and waited.

Activity in the area of the room. Doctors, interns, nurses, in and out. Equipment rolled in, rolled out. Everything and everyone moving at breakneck speed, like a crazy, undercranked movie. Or did it only seem so?

Time. Ten minutes? Ten hours?

Hy Engelberg at her side. He puts his arm around her shoulders.

"No!" she screams. "Don't say anything. Don't!"

He holds her tightly. She covers her ears.

He signals a nurse, who brings a pill and a Lily cup full of water. He makes Marilyn take the pill.

"No!" she says.

"He's gone, Marilyn."

The red light goes out.

She tears herself away from the doctor's grip and rushes into the room, freezing the routine activity. Johnny lies peacefully, as she has seen him so many times. There must be some mistake.

She goes to him, takes him in her arms, and cries, "Wake up! Please wake up! Oh, my God, Johnny! Johnny!"

She faints and falls to the floor before anyone can get to her.

She wakes to find herself at home, in her own room. She sees Lena puttering about. Dr. Engelberg sits under a lamp, reading the evening paper.

"Hy?" she asks tentatively.

He comes to her.

"How do you feel?"

"Hy, was it a nightmare—or true?"

"Not a nightmare, no."

She starts to get out of bed.

"I want to move around," she says.

"Careful, though, huh? You've had quite a lot of sedation."

She puts on a beautiful pink marabou-trimmed dressing gown.

Dr. Engelberg looks at his watch and asks, "Will you be all right, Marilyn? I've got a very sick patient back there at Cedars."

"I'll be all right," she says.

"Lena's here. And Ellen."

"Yes," she says.

He comes to her, embraces her.

"You know how sorry I am."

"Yes," she says. "Me, too."

"Just remember him with love."

"No," she says. "He *was* love."

The doctor is gone. Marilyn moves about the house. Lena and Ellen observe her, but keep carefully out of her way.

In the dining room, she hears the sounds of a merry dinner party. It recedes, and Johnny's voice is saying: "She's a marvelous actress. She's a terrific actress. Marilyn Monroe. Marilyn Monroe. She's a wonderful actress."

In the sitting room, the sound of a piano playing "It's Magic." Johnny's voice: "Darling, if I didn't believe with all my heart that it would work, I wouldn't ask you. Please. You'll see. I'll make you so happy."

In Johnny's room, she hears him on the phone: "Listen, L.B., it only runs fourteen minutes. And if you don't agree with me that it's the best test anybody ever made—well, call me when you *do* have time. No, never mind, I'll call you again."

In her own room, there is a sudden burst of loud circus music. She looks up and sees the poster of The Nicholas Haidabura Imperial Russian Troupe. Johnny's voice goes deep and affects a Russian accent as he imitates his father: "Ladies and gentlemens, our next treeck eess—*eempawssible!*" Laughter. In his own voice: "And you know what my father used to say, sweetheart? It was a Russian saying, I think, like a toast. 'May you live every day of your life.' "

400

And all at once, the room is still. Time has stopped. The world waits.

Marilyn moves closer and closer still to the poster, until all she can see of it is the tiny boy perched on his father's hand.

"Good night, little Mr. Haidabura," she says. "Goodbye Ivan. John. Johnny."

She kisses the tip of her forefinger and gently covers the face of the small smiling boy.

Within twenty-four hours, his family had ordered her to leave the rented house and take her belongings with her. They attempted to bar her from attending his funeral, but failed.

Bereft, she turned to Ben for help. Ben became her friend, her adviser, her confidant. Even Johnny had never occupied this indispensable position. Johnny was, after all, her lover.

Ben was touched by her loneliness and by her confusion. She came to the Farbers' often.

At one time, she had a brief fling with Abner Farber.

Ben discouraged it.

"It's not good, Marilyn, not for you. Abe's my son, but he's no damn good. Maybe my fault, maybe Tessa's, maybe God's, but he's not for you. He's not a serious person. You're a serious person."

VI

THE WORLD WAR II years had been difficult for Ben and for Farber Films. So much of the talent was otherwise occupied. Raw stock film was difficult to get. Gas rationing had battered the drive-in business. There were endless problems to solve. But somehow, Hollywood had survived.

Ben lay stretched out on the sofa in his office, his shoes off, his jacket removed, his tie loosened, listening to Pempy Larner tell him a story.

She had been with him now for five years at this job, and she did it superbly. She covered forty or fifty properties a week and called to his personal attention the six or seven worthy of note. It saved his eyes, his time, his attention. Moreover, there was something marvelously soothing and pleasant in the sound of her voice and in her British accent that he found unendingly charming.

"And then *The Queen of Nevada,*" she said, "which will be an enormous success, is trash nevertheless. I suppose *Moses* will make a fine film, but I'm certain that that particular project would prove to be far too expensive for us."

"Everything's too expensive for us lately," mumbled Ben.

"I enjoyed *Gentleman's Agreement* greatly, but I'm sure you'd find that too controversial."

"Why controversial?"

"Well, it has to do with anti-Semitism and this young gentile journalist posing as a Jew in order to get a story and then—"

"Anybody poses as a Jew," said Ben, "has got to be a half-wit!"

"The one I liked," said Pempy, "out of this whole batch is *The Snake Pit.* It's really a horrific story. But extremely entertaining. And a marvelous Academy Award part for a woman."

"*The Snake Pit*? What does that mean, *The Snake Pit*?"

"It means an insane asylum. A hospital for mentally deranged women—"

Ben sat bolt upright. "Jesus Christ, Pempy!" he said. "You want me to make a picture about deranged women? About nut houses? Pempy, I'm sorry to say, I think you're slipping. Maybe you and Carl should go somewhere for a vacation." He stood up.

"Sit down," she said. "I'm going to tell you the story."

"I don't want to hear it," said Ben. He rose again.

"Sit down, Ben," she said. "I know what I'm talking about."

He sat down and stretched out on his back, determined not to listen.

Pempy began, reciting the story from notes on a pad in her lap.

"It all begins," she said, "with a picture of the most normal possible, the most average and attractive young girl, who lives in this—"

He did not, indeed, hear the first five or six minutes of her storytelling, but as time went by, the excitement and urgency in her voice proved to be contagious and he began to listen. Then he began to hear and, presently, to understand.

When she had finished, he rose solemnly, moved to her and kissed her. He went to the phone. "Who's the agent?" he asked.

"Leland Hayward," she said.

He buzzed his secretary. "Get me Leland Hayward."

Alas, he was too late. *The Snake Pit* had been bought two days earlier by Twentieth Century-Fox.

He was bitterly disappointed. He looked accusingly at Pempy. "You should have told it to me last week," he said.

"Ben," she countered gently, "I've been waiting two weeks for this appointment."

"I've been busy," he explained.

"You've also been remiss," she said. "This material comes in at a great rate, as you know, and we have to cover it as swiftly as possible. Remember, the majors usually get the first crack. They have people planted in all the publishing houses photostating manuscripts and bribing secretaries. The trouble with us is that we're legitimate."

"That's always the trouble," said Ben.

"Well, better luck next time," she said.

He poured a glass of water from the carafe on his desk and drank it thoughtfully. "Tell me a little bit about *Moses*. Make it short, like two, three paragraphs."

Pempy laughed. "It's an epic, Ben. A great Biblical epic in the manner of *Quo Vadis, Ben Hur, King of Kings*."

"So what?" said Ben. "I could tell you any of those in *one* paragraph."

"Very well, if you insist, let me try." She took a moment to collect her thoughts, and began. "Well, as I have said, the period is—" The buzzer on Ben's desk went off. Ben clicked the switch of his Dictograph. His secretary's voice: "Abner is here."

"Oh, sure, send him right in." He clicked off. "I'm sorry, Pempy, we'll do this later."

"Of course," she said, gathering her materials. "I understand. Good night, Ben."

"Good night," said Ben.

She started out.

"Oh, Pempy," he called after her. She stopped and turned back. "Yes?"

"I'm sorry for what I said before. I apologize."

"No matter," said Pempy. "After all—"

The door opened and Abner Farber entered. "Hey, Pempy!" he said. "How are you? Where are you? Swing it in here." He embraced her and kissed her neck.

"Mister Abner!" she said as she left, blushing.

"Come here, Abe," said Ben. "Come in and sit down and cool off."

"Never," said Abner. "Never, I hope."

He sat down, slipped off his shoes and put his feet up on Ben's desk.

"Well, Pop, how's the movie business?" he asked.

"It depends who you ask."

"I'm asking you."

"Me?" said Ben. "I'm worried. I think this television thing is going to eat us up. Why should they go out for entertainment and pay if they can stay home for entertainment and get it free? How can you sell something to people that somebody else is giving them for nothing?"

"Ah, come on, Pop," said Abner. "*You're* smarter than that. There're plenty of things you can give them that TV won't be able to touch."

"For instance?" asked Ben.

"Well, for instance, mature subjects. Adult themes. They can't do that."

"*We* can't do that either," said Ben. "Not with this goddam Breen Office on our neck all the time."

"Well, they're gonna have to loosen up, but TV is never going to be able to show anything but family entertainment."

Ben thought hard for a moment. "You mean, Abe, we start in making dirty pictures now?"

"Not dirty. Mature. Language they can't do on television, so if people want to hear the real stuff, they'll have to come out."

"I don't know," said Ben. "I'm still worried."

"Don't. Something new every day. Like Skouras is high on—

"You mean that cinema-screen, or whatever the hell he calls it?"

"Cinemascope," said Abner. "This tremendous screen. *Three* times the size of what we've got now. They won't be able to do *that* on television. Big stuff. Spectacle. *Tremendous* screens."

"Yes," said Ben. "I've seen it. I don't like it."

"I'm not so crazy about it either," said Abner. "It hurts my eyes, and I'm not used to that long, long shape." He laughed. "Did you hear what Harry Kurnitz said about it the other day?"

"No, what?" asked Ben.

"Harry said, 'The only love scene you can do on Cinemascope is one with two dachshunds.' "

404

Ben frowned. He failed to see the joke.

"Stop lookin' so worried, Pop," said Abner. "There's another thing. People are always going to want to go out."

"Sure," said Ben. "But they can go out to lots of things. They can go out bowling, and dancing, and my God, don't you remember what happened to us with that goddam miniature golf! For a year there, it practically had us on the ropes."

"That's exactly what I'm saying," argued Abner. "What happened to miniature golf and what happened to you guys?"

"There's more to it than that," said Ben. "Gilbert was telling me they're starting in now to buy up *movies!* Old movies to show on the TV. So if people are going to get movies free, why are they going to come out and pay?"

"*Old* movies," said Abner. "*Old* movies. Who wants to see old movies? That's not gonna mean a thing. Anyway, movies on television don't look right. Only the close-ups look good. The minute you're in a long shot, the characters look like there's a fly crawling around on your screen. Stop worrying, Pop. You're making *me* nervous. So. What is it, Pop? What'd you want to see me about? Business, I hope. What can I sell you? Who?"

"Today nothing."

"If you're going to start in on me about coming back into the company—save your breath. There's no room here for me and you know it. Anyway, I hate this company."

"Save your breath, Abe. I don't want you in the company. I used to. But no more."

"So what is it?"

"It's Marilyn."

Abner's feet came off the desk with a bang.

"What?!"

"Marilyn Monroe."

Abner began putting his shoes back on.

"What about her?" he asked.

"What are your intentions?"

Abner laughed. "You kill me, Pop. People don't ask things like that anymore."

"*I* do."

"What're you? Her father?"

"No. I'm *your* father."

"And that gives you a right to stick your nose in my affairs—I mean my *life?*"

405

"Abe, this is a very insecure, a vulnerable girl. Her whole life almost, she's been treated bad. It's time it should stop."

"God damn it, Pop! You got me all the way over here to give me a lecture on none of your fucking business?"

"I'm asking a favor because this girl—"

"Listen," said Abner. "There are a hell of a lot of people who can pass moral judgments on me. But you don't happen to be one of them."

"I wasn't passing—"

"Telling me how to treat women. I treat them a damn sight better than you treated Pempy!"

Ben rose swiftly, glared at his son, sat down and poured himself a glass of water from the silver carafe on his desk.

"Goodbye, Abe."

Ben need not have been concerned. Like most of Abner's involvements, this one ended abruptly, as soon as his conquest was complete.

In time to come, Ben learned of Marilyn's too active sex life, mainly with characters from the various front offices.

"You're doing it the wrong way, honey," he said. "There used to be a nice actress from the stage, Ina Claire, and somebody once said to her, 'Do you really have to sleep with all the producers and the directors to make good?' And Ina Claire said, 'Of course you do—if you haven't got any *talent*.' But you, Marilyn, you've got talent. In fact, you've got better than talent. For the *stage*, people need talent, For the opera. For the movies, not so much. For the movies, what they need is personality. Sometimes the great actors don't become great movie stars, but the great personalities—they never fail. And that's *you*. You've got a great personality. That isn't going to do you any good, that knocking around with Joe Schenck and Darryl Zanuck and Errol Flynn and all those other ones. You're better than that."

As she continued her swift journey, higher and higher, to take her place among the stars in the Hollywood constellation, she constantly sought Ben's advice and opinion.

She would often come to him and read him a script that had been submitted. Frequently, she would discuss the way in which she planned to play a certain part.

406

Ben appreciated this and, indeed, it stimulated him to be in touch with this young actress on the rise. What he found less entertaining was Marilyn's predilection for discussing her love life with him.

Then, in a burst, came stardom and celebrity far beyond the wildest dreams she had ever dreamed as she had wandered about the courtyard of Grauman's Chinese as a child, fitting her little feet into the footprints in the cement.

One morning she phoned Ben.

"Ben," she asked, "would you consider this? If I came and got you in my car and took you someplace for a picnic lunch? I'll bring the picnic. It's very important. I'm in trouble."

"What trouble?" asked Ben. "I see in the trades they're offering you everything from *Little Annie Rooney* to *Apple Annie*. So what's trouble?"

"I don't mean business trouble," she said. "It's personal."

He laughed.

"I'm glad the language has changed. A girl used to say, 'I'm in trouble,' used to mean she was pregnant."

"Oh, no. It's not that with me," she said. "I wouldn't call *that* trouble. I'd call that the greatest. But what about it, Ben, can you come?"

"You don't mean today, I hope?"

"Yes, I do."

"No, honey. Today is impossible. We've got a big Motion Picture Producers Association meeting. Some New York brain is coming in to advise us on the television matter."

"Well, what about tomorrow then? Or the next day, or the next?"

Ben could tell from the sound of her voice that she was desperate.

"All right, all right," he said soothingly. "Calm down. Tomorrow."

She drove badly, her mind elsewhere, terrifying Ben all the way out to the deserted Zuma Beach. In her aimless wanderings she had discovered this lovely stretch. It was a place she went often to be alone, to read, to think, to cry.

She parked her car in a familiar spot, spread a blanket on the

407

sand and prepared the picnic. She had had it catered at the Vendôme and it was complete: pâté, jellied Madrilene, cold chicken, potato salad, sliced tomatoes, fresh fruit, bread and rolls, and chilled wine. Hot coffee.

Ben was delighted.

"For God's sake," he said, "how does a dish like you know how to do dishes like this?"

"My mother," she said. "She wasn't very good in the kitchen, but she loved picnics and she got me to love them, too. For me, this is better than the best banquet, even in those New York restaurants."

They sat on the beach and ate with their fingers.

After a time, Ben said, "Tell me the trouble."

She drank a full glass of wine slowly before replying.

"It's a man," she said.

"That I knew in advance," said Ben. "What kind of a man?"

"Well, not really a man," she said. "More like a boy. A young boy."

"And the trouble?"

"I think I'm crazy about him, but I don't want to be."

"Why not?"

"Well, you know. Johnny and all. What's the *matter* with me?"

"So far as I can see, Marilyn, there's *nothing* the matter with you. You're a young girl, you're alive, you have certain needs, and a man, or even a boy, is one of them. What're you beating on yourself for?"

"I didn't want you to think I was the same kind of tramp I used to be."

"Tell me about this boy."

She leaped to the subject eagerly.

"He's young. I think he may be a little younger than me, but I haven't asked him. And he's a writer."

Ben nodded gravely. "Writers can be all right."

"He's published a novel already, and it's only wonderful, and then he got the job of turning it into a screenplay, but they fired him because they said he was sticking to the book too much, but he's not even bitter about that, he says that's their business, so now he's writing another movie and I think he wants it to be for me. He's a *fantastic* writer, Ben. And he's so smart. He knows *everything*."

"*Everything* is good," said Ben. "It's *good* to know everything."

"Now, this next part, I don't think you're going to believe. I don't think I believe it myself."

"Go ahead."

"We've been going around together for two months. I see him every day or every night and we've talked and talked. Sometimes all night. I know everything about him and I've told him quite a lot about myself. Not everything, but a lot. And a few nights ago he kissed me and that's as far as anything has gone, because I didn't feel right about it. And I didn't think *you'd* think it was right."

"Oh, for God's sake!" said Ben angrily. "What kind of a tyrant are you making me out to be? You have to live your life now. Do what you need to do. I think you loved Johnny, I *know* you did, but he's gone. Now, you'll love somebody else. By the way, this picture your boyfriend is writing, let me have a look at it, huh?—before he sells it to somebody else."

"Of course," she said. "Sure."

In due course, the screenplay was delivered.

Ben gave it to Pempy, who reported on it most enthusiastically.

He gave it to Willa, who asked, "Who is this writer? How can it be I've never heard of him?"

All the reports and the reactions were so enthusiastic that Ben did something he rarely did: he sat down and read the script himself. He, too, was overwhelmingly impressed. He sent for Jock MacPherson, his chief executive assistant, and told him to make an offer for the screenplay.

"How far do you want to go?" asked Jock.

"What do you think? Fifty? Sixty?"

"Let me find out what he got from Fox."

"I can tell you. He got fifty for the book and fifty for the screenplay."

"Does that mean you'll go a hundred?"

"Well, I wouldn't like to if I didn't have to. Let's try seventy-five."

"Right. I'll let you know."

Two days later, MacPherson asked for a meeting, saying it was urgent.

"On this deal with Goodman," he said, "we're in a little trouble."

"All right," said Ben. "So give him the hundred, what's the difference?"

"It isn't that," said MacPherson. "You could have had it for fifty. That's what I offered and his agent said yes."

"So?"

MacPherson looked at Ben mysteriously and handed over a bound portfolio. He opened it, ran his finger down the page and pointed to a name. "Thomas Goodman," he said. "See it there?"

"Jesus Christ!" said Ben. "Oh, my God! Do you think she knows this?"

"I don't see how she could," said MacPherson. "Not unless *he* does, and that's unlikely."

"So where does it stand?"

"Well, it's a little rough on me, boss, because I made the offer and Swannie accepted it. So now it's a question of reneging."

"Is there somebody I could talk to?" asked Ben. "Maybe we could make an exception." There was a worried pause. "I don't know what to tell you, Jock, you'll have to get out of it one way or another. How *I'm* going to get out of it, I still don't know."

To make matters worse, that very evening Marilyn brought Tom to dinner at the Farbers'.

Willa was full of praise for Tom's work. It was a distinctly up-beat occasion.

On the way home, Marilyn and Tom were bubbling with plans for production, casting the other parts, arguing about the right director. They discussed it in bed through most of the night. The following morning, Ben phoned Marilyn.

"Oh, what a wonderful evening!" she cried. "I wish I could look forward to something like that every single night of my life."

"Same here," said Ben wearily. "Same here."

"What's the matter? You sound slugged."

"I'm depressed, darling."

"What about?"

"Well, I've just this minute come out from a meeting with my staff and—what can I tell you?—we can't go forward with Tom's picture."

"You can't go—what do you mean? What're you *talking* about? You told him how much you liked it, *loved* it, even. And Willa. What *is* all this?"

"It don't fit into our schedule. We went way over our budgets on some pictures lately, and we have to cut down. This is not the only one we're dropping. We're dropping six or seven."

"But this one is great. Even *you* said so."

"Marilyn, what can I tell you? I'm not alone. I have partners, backers, the bank people, the exchanges, the distributors, and exhibitors. If it was up to me it would be a different decision. It's everybody."

"All right, Ben," she said.

It was hard to explain to Tom. He had been built up out of all proportion, and the letdown was a toboggan of despair.

His script went the rounds, was enthusiastically received at every studio, but no action. A meeting with his agent, H.N. Swanson, was not satisfactory. Swannie could only shake his head and wonder.

Toward the end of the meeting he asked, "You've got to tell me something, truthfully, Tom. I'm promising you that I'm going to keep this in the strictest confidence. But is there anything of a political nature in your life?"

Tom was stunned.

"Me?" he asked. "Holy Moses! My father's a *Republican*. He always has been and—I don't know—without thinking, I guess I became a Republican, too. That's how I'm registered at home. In Muncie."

"That doesn't answer the question completely, Tom. I'm sorry to sound like one of these son-of-a-bitchin' witchhunters that're getting to be so fashionable around here these days, but I'm trying to make sense out of this senseless situation. There's *got* to be some reason why everybody's crazy about *Hoopla* and nobody'll buy it, and this is the only thing I can come up with."

"But it *couldn't* be that. What about my picture at Warners'? From my novel." Swanson was silent. "I mean, what about it! They're going ahead with that, aren't they? That should prove *something*."

After a long pause, Swannie said, "No, Tom, that's just it. They're *not* going ahead with it. It's been called off."

"Holy shit!" said Tom. "Is this a nightmare or what?"

"Let's start from the beginning, Tom. A lot of times young people get involved with things or clubs or committees, with demonstrations or actions. I'm not saying what they're doing is wrong, because they mean well most of the time, maybe they do it without realizing what they're doing. But look back—say high school, college, any time like that? Were you ever on the debating team? What did you debate? What clubs did you belong to? Who were your friends?"

"No clubs. One fraternity, Phi Beta Kappa. I wasn't very active, though. ROTC, believe it or not. Captain. No, honestly, Swannie, I can't think of a thing."

"None of my business, Tom," said Swanson, "but do I understand that your people are—well—well-off?"

"Enough. Why?"

"I think your only chance is to dig into this, to find out, privately, to get a good lawyer, get the best, and fight it out."

"But how would one do that? I mean, I haven't been accused of anything by anyone, so what's there to deny? They can all say the way Ben Farber did, there's just no room on their program, and there's an end to it."

"Well," said Swannie, "more than one way to skin a cat. God damn! This certainly is a poser."

"I'll call my father tonight," said Tom. "And by the way, Everett Dirksen's a great friend of his, Senator Dirksen, they went to college together. Do you think that might help?"

"Dirksen could help, yes," said Swannie. "If he wanted to."

The affair cost Tom's father over $30,000 in money and cost his son four months of time. In the course of the four months, Tom's health deteriorated steadily. He found that he could not sleep. Sleeping pills were prescribed. He could not write. There seemed to be little point in it. He stopped eating almost entirely.

Early on in the adventure, Marilyn went to see Ben.

"Ben," she said, "you wouldn't lie to me, would you? If I asked you something?"

"No, I wouldn't, but I would rather you didn't ask me."

"I have to know, Ben."

"Marilyn, leave it alone. There are some things have to be left alone."

"But could you tell me just one thing?"

"What?"

"What's a black *list?*"

Ben looked at her long and hard. "A what?"

"A black *list.*"

412

"It means a list of people who can't get into a certain club, for instance."

"Or into a certain business?"

"Sometimes."

"What I want to know," she asked, "is this. Once your name is on a black *list*, how can you get it off?"

"I don't know, Marilyn," he said. "I don't know."

"Is there one in the movie business right now?"

He looked her in the eye and said, "No. Of course not. What ever gave you such an idea?"

"Isn't it against the law?"

"Of course it's against the law."

"Ben, something's happening to Tom and we don't know what to do."

Ben shook his head. "Something's happening to me, too," he said, "and *I* don't know what to do."

Six weeks after Tom Goodman's death, at the age of twenty-eight, the mystery was solved. There had, indeed, been a leading member of a Communist Party cell in Chicago, Illinois, whose name was Thomas A. Goodman. This Thomas Goodman was also no longer alive. He had joined the Lincoln Brigade and had been killed in the Spanish Civil War. Had he lived, he would now have been forty-two years old.

The Goodman case was one of the principal points of contention in the course of the secret meeting of the ad hoc committee of the Motion Picture Producers Association that was held in New York in the spring of the following year. Ben Farber and Dore Schary and William Goetz made a point of hammering at it. Joe Schenck was being swayed in their direction.

"But how many times do people die because of something like this?" asked Darryl Zanuck. "All right, there's that one, but name me another one. And anyway, how do we know the little son-of-a-bitch didn't knock himself off?"

"We have a doctor's report," said Schary.

"Oh, come on, his old man's loaded. I can buy you doctors' reports by the dozen—on anything. I'll get one certifies you've got the clap!"

"It's taken us this long to get things organized," said Jack Warner. "I don't think we can walk away from it now. It's working

413

damn well. We've got everybody satisfied. The Legion, the DAR, even the goddam WCTU."

"Maybe nobody else died because of this," said Ben, "but are we sure that every name on the list is correct? Shouldn't this prove to us that maybe there could be some more mistakes?"

"What list are you talking about, Ben?" asked Warner.

"For God's sake, Ben!" said Mayer. "You know better than to use that word."

"There's a story around," said Schary, "that one guy, an actor, I don't want to mention his name, *bought* his way off the list for twenty-five grand."

"Who got the twenty-five?" asked Warner.

"You know who, Jack."

"All right, so what? So maybe he shouldn't have been on the list in the first place."

"*You* just said the word, Jack."

"Listen," said Zanuck. "This is a war. Nobody who looks at it any other way has got any brains. It's a war and in a war people get killed. Sometimes innocent people. You can't have a war without people getting killed. So it's just too goddam bad, it was a mistake, it was a blunder, and as far as I'm concerned, I have no regrets at all. You gotta look at the big picture. You gotta look at it overall. You've got to take the long view."

"You know, Darryl," said Billy Goetz, "if you had another brain, you'd have one."

The meeting went on far into the night. Dinner had been sent in from Le Pavillon. At two o'clock, supper was brought in from "21."

At four o'clock in the morning, a unanimous agreement was reached. The blacklist would continue to be enforced.

The meeting for the following morning was put off until eleven. Only matters relating to the onslaught of television were discussed. The political situation was not mentioned.

Some months later, Ben was horrified when Marilyn told him she was about to marry Joe DiMaggio. Much as he admired the legendary baseball star, he saw it clearly as a misalliance. When that marriage ended in ruins, Marilyn again saw the value of Ben's counsel.

"It's Gilbert on the phone," said Ben's secretary.

"Oh, good. Put him right on . . . Gilbert, how are you?"

"Fine, Pop, fine. Never better."

"How's the television business? Terrible, I hope?"

"Could be better."

"I'm glad to hear it. How's Agnes?"

"Oh, the same. You know. Busy."

"And the kids?"

"Great . . . Listen, Pop. How are you fixed for lunches this week?"

"I think fine. You know I told you, lately I don't have business lunches anymore. Dr. Sellers says I shouldn't. So I eat mostly alone. Sometimes your mother comes. Sometimes with somebody around here, somebody calm. What's on your mind?"

"Well, I was at a dinner party the other night at Willie Wyler's, and René Clair was there. You know who he is?"

"What are you talking about, for Chrissake? I knew about him before you were *born*."

"Well, there was a lot of talk about film and television and Mr. Clair had some things to say that I thought were absolutely fascinating. And frankly, I think you ought to hear them."

"Why not? Call up Martin here and make a date. Any time is all right with me."

"Good. I'll clear it with him and we'll do it."

"Fine."

"Have you ever met him?"

"I think maybe once in France, years ago. A handsome fellow?"

"That's the one."

"Well, fine. I'll wait to hear."

The next afternoon at one o'clock sharp Gilbert Farber came into Ben's private dining room at the studio with René Clair. There were cordial handshakes all around, exchanges of, *"You're looking very well"*—a certain indication of advancing age.

They sat down to an appropriate French lunch that had been carefully ordered by Willa.

After a time, Gilbert led Clair skillfully into a repetition of the ideas which had so impressed the guests at Willie Wyler's.

"My father, Mr. Clair, still thinks that television and movies are competitors, deadly enemies."

"For the business, yes," said Clair. "Maybe for the present. For tomorrow, who can know?" He shrugged a French shrug.

"Goddam right," said Ben, "I could show you some grosses. They would make you sick. Some nights when that Milton Berle goes on all over the country we feel the dip."

Clair said, "Yes, but Mr. Farber, can you think *so?* Suppose always we have had such a thing—tele*vision*—from the time of children. Every home would have such a box, always, n'est-ce pas? And suppose now, in this year, comes a brilliant inventor, somewhere, and he invents this such a thing as *film.*"

Ben was listening with interest, trying hard to follow the convolutions of this most original mind. Clair went on. "Very well. Suppose we, you and I, we have never heard the word *film.* We are not sure what is celluloid. But he invents it. So now it becomes possible to put all things onto this film, the film onto reels, and this can be put onto machines and comes out on the television, n'est-ce pas?"

"N'est-ce pas," said Ben.

"Imagine. This film can even be sent from place to place. It can be stored, put away. Now here is my question. Would not the invention of film be the most profound, the most greatest thing, that has ever happened in the history of television?"

"Yes," said Ben gravely, "I see what you mean."

"And not such a bad thing for this new film idea, also. And if we could be—any of us—in one business or the other, in the television or the film business, which would we choose?"

"Damned if I know," said Gilbert.

"I do," said Clair, "I would prefer the *film* business."

"Why?" asked Ben.

"Because the film is, do you see, the *product.* And the television, the box, is only the means of the distribution."

"You know this son-of-a-bitch has got a point!" Ben shouted.

"What did I tell you?" said Gilbert.

Encouraged, Clair went on. "If we can think of the whole matter in the historic terms, then we can see that the invention of television is not the enemy to film making but maybe—in the end —the best friend."

Ben smiled, and said, "Have some more wine, Mr. Clair. It's the best."

Marilyn was not given to drinking much. She hated the smell of liquor. Childhood memories of early seductions were somehow permeated with boozy breath. Similarly, she lived in fear that perhaps she might have inherited abnormal tendencies along these lines from her mother.

Whenever she blocked a word or had the tiniest lapse of memory or forgot where she had put her hairbrush, she panicked.

Moreover, she had begun to realize that her physical equipment, and that meant all of it, inside and out—her hair, her eyes, her skin, her stomach, her intestines, and buttocks and legs and toenails—was, in the strictest sense of the word, her estate. This was what she had. This was what she owned. This was what she had to sell. Therefore, convinced of her value, she was in the habit of taking great pains to look after herself. Dr. Engelberg had discussed with her the matter of skin tone and the effect of alcohol upon it. He had convinced her that she would do well to avoid it as much as possible.

"Oh, sure," said Dr. Engelberg, "by the time you get to be fifty or sixty—by the way, it's hard to imagine *you* at sixty—but by that time, sure, I suppose a couple of drinks now and then wouldn't do you any harm. In fact, it might do you some good. Osler said. 'Whiskey is the milk of old age.' Who knows? Maybe he was right. But I've noticed something about Frenchwomen. They, of course, start drinking wine when they're four, five years old. And they do pretty well, and then all of a sudden, there comes one day when they reach the age of forty and crash. They fall apart. All French-women fall apart at forty, and we've figured out that that's how long it takes for the liver to reject any more work. I think, on the whole, booze may be the most aging thing there is. So if it's important to you in your job and in your work to look young and fresh—lay off!"

"You're asking a lot, my boy. But I'll try. You ought to lay off, too. You look pretty old to me."

He patted her behind playfully, and saw her out.

VII

"I'M GOING to New York, Ben," she announced one evening.

"Really? That's nice. For how long?"

"I don't know. Maybe forever. I'm going to stay there till I learn to act."

"You're a star, Marilyn. You're a great star."

"I'm a great star, but I don't know what I'm doing."

"Just do what they tell you, and you'll be all right."

"Oh, Ben, you're so *wrong!* You've been so right for a long time, and now you're so *wrong.* You can't just put yourself into some-one's hands like a piece of putty, like a piece of clay, because then everything depends on those hands. What if they squeeze you out of shape? What if they make you into something ridiculous? Sure, with some of the writers and some of the directors it works, but there's a lot of incompetence around, Ben. It's no good saying just do what they tell you. I've got to know more on my own. I've got to learn to be more self-reliant, self-supportive."

Her vocabulary, he noted, was beginning to be studded with odd intellectual references. Where were they coming from?

He noticed the book under her arm. *The Autobiography of Lincoln Steffens.* What the hell was that?

She went to New York and enrolled at the Actors Studio. What could be more strange than the presence of a Hollywood super-star sitting in slacks and blouse, spectacles perched on her nose, among the beginners, the tyros, the hopefuls? But it was another world for her, and a meaningful one.

When Ben came to New York she visited him and even per-suaded him to come to the Actors Studio, where she was to per-form two scenes. He went and was duly impressed. She intro-duced him to Lee Strasberg and to Paula Strasberg.

She was delighted when she was told that she would be playing the lead in a new play called *Across the River* by Norman Rosten, which was to be a workshop project at the studio.

Ben gathered that it must be serious when she broke three consecutive engagements with him because of rehearsals.

On his last night in New York, they had dinner together.

"Guess who I met?" she asked.

"I give up."

"You'll never believe it. I went over to Brooklyn Heights to the Rostens' because Norman wanted to talk to me about the play and you won't believe this, but you know who else was there?"

"Who?"

"Arthur Miller. Arthur Miller was there with his wife. They must be, I guess, the nicest people I ever met. And isn't he the greatest playwright who ever lived?"

"Well, one of the."

"Boy, you sure don't meet people like that at Jack's-at-the-Beach."

Ben noted that she was changing before his eyes. For the better? He wondered.

As the first public performance of Rosten's play grew near, a series of previews were given for audiences numbering ten or twelve. Arthur Miller, a close friend of Rosten's, attended the last of these. Afterward, he went back and congratulated Marilyn on her performance.

"I'll tell you the truth," he said in his refreshing Brooklynese. "You surprised me. No, no kidding. I didn't expect anything like the depth. I figured, a Hollywood blonde. So what? But you're really good, Marilyn. You've really got a lot of stuff. Someday I'd like to write a play with a part in it for you."

Marilyn thought she might pass out.

"Oh, please," she said breathily, "do that. I'd love it. I'll do any part, in any play, by you, any time, anywhere."

Miller laughed.

"Well, read it first!"

"Write it first," advised Rosten.

They all went out to supper. Not to "21," not even to Sardi's, but to Joe Downey's, where the working actors and actresses went. Not the stars. Norman and his wife left. Miller talked to Marilyn for another hour, then said, "Let me drop you."

"Oh, would you? You don't have to."

He smiled. "I know I don't have to. If I had to, I wouldn't want to."

She was living in an apartment at 55 West Fifty-fourth. As the taxi stopped in front of the apartment house, she said, "Would you like to come up a minute, or is it too late?"

"It's not too late," said Arthur. "It's never too late."

That was the beginning.

The situation was difficult and complicated by the fact that Arthur Miller was devoted to his wife and to his teenage children, but in a short time it was clear that he was in love with Marilyn and that Marilyn was in love with him.

She returned to California to make *Bus Stop* and went almost at once to see Ben and tell him of this new complication in her life.

"I'll tell you, Marilyn, after what you went through with Tom Goodman, and what this whole *business* has gone through, I think you should be very careful about your next association. I'm not saying anything against Miller. I don't even know him. I know his work a little, but you know, people aren't only what they are. They're a little bit what their reputations are. And this is not too good an idea for you. In this world, you've got to stay as much in the middle as possible. Not too right. Not too left. You have to remember, you're a public figure now. You're not just a struggling actress, even though sometimes, there in New York, when you were sitting with all those people, maybe you felt like you were just a little girl beginning. But you're not. You're already there. Now the trick is to see if you can stay there. And that is some trick, believe me. Stars most often don't last too long. Six, seven, eight years and it's all over unless they develop something special, some kind of staying power. That's what I want you to do. . . . I don't know why you're so interested all the time in goddam men!"

Marilyn looked at him, in all innocence, and said, "Maybe it's because I'm a goddam woman!"

Ben's counsel notwithstanding, Marilyn married Arthur and for the first time in her life felt herself to be part of a family. Arthur Miller's Jewish mother was delighted with her beautiful new daughter-in-law and all at once Marilyn had sisters-in-law and brothers-in-law, nieces and nephews. The bosom of the Miller family was capacious and soft and warm.

And yet, the pressures of her life, her anxieties, her insecurities, her unfounded feelings of inferiority in the circles in which she was now traveling, conspired to make her depend, more and more, on artificial relaxants and stimulants.

She drank a little more than was good for her. She was beginning to use sleeping pills indiscriminately.

Because he had known her for so long, Ben was keenly aware of her deterioration. It was beginning to have a deleterious effect, not only on her body but on that part of her mind responsible for taste and judgment.

How else is it possible to explain her thoroughly reprehensible behavior during the making of *The Prince and the Showgirl* with the distinguished Laurence Olivier acting as both costar and director? She insisted, in this instance, upon bringing along Paula Strasberg as her coach and looking over at Paula at the end of every take, waiting for the rare nod and the frequent shake of the head. Certainly she had been a professional actress long enough to know that there was not a single reputable director in the business who would countenance such an arrangement. Instead of learning from Olivier, she fought him. Instead of being inspired by him, she insulted him. In the end, the picture emerged as a lifeless failure.

She and Arthur returned to America but remained in New York. When the picture opened there, they went to call on Ben at the Pierre. He had seen the opening of the picture and thought it poor, indeed.

"I don't know what happened," he said. "*You* tell *me*. Or you, Arthur. Something. Olivier is a great man. The teaming was perfect. Good chemistry. What happened? Why didn't it work?"

"I was miserable," said Marilyn. "I was miserable the whole time."

"I think it was the coaching," said Arthur. "Too much coaching. I know, around a play, I try to stay away from the actors because I might tell them one thing and the director tells them the opposite and then where are we? You can only have one captain running a ship."

"It was *not* the coaching," said Marilyn solemnly. "I *need* the coaching. Listen, he knows how to act. He should. He's been acting all his life. He's an experienced actor. If I hadn't had the coaching, he'd have walked off with the picture."

"He did anyway," said Arthur.

"He did *not!*" said Marilyn. "We were both *lousy.*"

"That's the whole thing," said Ben. "You have to remember, people start to make a movie together, they're all on the same side. After all, this was Marilyn Monroe *and* Laurence Olivier in. It wasn't Marilyn Monroe *versus* Laurence Olivier in. And, by the way, that billing," said Ben. "That didn't embarrass you?"

"No, why should it?" asked Marilyn. "I'm a bigger movie star than he is."

"Well, I suppose now you're married to Arthur, you'll understand what I'm going to tell you. For you to let yourself be billed ahead of Laurence Olivier, Marilyn, that was real *chutzpa.* Think how elegant it would have been if you had let it go the other way."

"Don't think the question didn't come up," said Marilyn. "I fixed that!"

Arthur and Ben exchanged a knowing look.

There they were, the four of them. Mr. and Mrs. Yves Montand (Simone Signoret) and Mr. and Mrs. Arthur Miller (Marilyn Monroe). Chums. Friends. Compatible in every sense of the word.

Simone and Yves had done Arthur's play *The Crucible* in Paris. Thus, it was through him, by way of Marilyn, that Yves Montand was cast as the leading man opposite her in *Let's Make Love.* They all admired and respected the director, George Cukor.

Arthur felt close to Simone and Yves on many levels, professional and political. Marilyn, goggle-eyed, went along with the whole idea. During the pre-production phase of the picture and, indeed, during most of the shooting, they all lived at The Beverly Hills Hotel in adjoining duplex bungalows. Many evenings, they did their own cooking. Yves was an especially accomplished chef. Simone provided wonders from the tiny kitchen. Life was enchanting for them all. Arthur even helped with the script, rewriting gratis and uncredited.

Ben dropped by to visit Marilyn in her dressing room at Twentieth Century-Fox early one morning. "I'm hearing some bad words about you, Marilyn," he said.

"You don't say."

"I do say. How can you be so foolish? It's not like you."

"I don't know what you're talking about, Ben."

"I think you do. The talk is, the gossip, that you and your leading man, the Frenchman—"

Marilyn laughed merrily. "Oh, my God!" she said. "I think *he* probably *started* it—or she did—to get a little billing around here. A little publicity. God knows they could use it. The two of them."

"What kind of talk is that?" asked Ben. "I thought you were all such friends, all four of you."

"What gave you *that* idea?"

"You *told* me. That's what gave me that idea."

"Oh, well, it's all over now. I can't wait for this bloody turkey to be over."

"Is it true?" asked Ben.

"I really don't know what you're talking about," she said in a new, haughty way.

"Marilyn, I've been your friend a long time and I'm trying to stay that way and I'm asking you. You don't have to tell me, but I'm asking you."

She looked him straight in the eye and said, "You're asking me if I'm having an affair with Yves Montand, is that what you're asking me?"

"Yes."

"O.K. The answer to that question, Mr. District Attorney, is no. No, I am *not* having an affair with Yves Montand. I am not having an affair with anyone. Does that answer your question?"

They exchanged a long look.

"I think you're lying, Marilyn."

"Oh, I know," she said. "That's something you've never done in your life, have you? You've *never* lied. I remember asking you once about the blacklist and I remember the look you gave me and the way *you* said no. And I believed you. God, I was dumb in those days. I remember calling it a black *list*. Can you imagine that? And you said no. Because that was the answer that suited your convenience just then. Well, this is the answer that suits my convenience right now. Would you like to hear it again? No, I am not having an affair with Yves Montand or with anyone. So now may I go?"

"Oh, Marilyn," said Ben. He looked away from her and added, "I'm so disappointed in you."

When he turned back to observe her reaction, she was gone.

In a massive attempt at reconciliation, Miller wrote *The Misfits* for her. All through its preparation, they sought Ben's advice on the production. He gave it freely. He saw in this venture a chance to salvage her marriage and, at the same time, advance her career. All agreed upon John Huston, with whom she had found such compatibility years earlier in the making of *The Asphalt Jungle*. Clark Gable, although approaching his middle years, was still possessed of the most powerful charisma on the American screen.

423

Montgomery Clift, always astonishing, was in the supporting company, as were Eli Wallach and Thelma Ritter. How could it fail? It did.

Again, the reasons were the same.

VIII

"YOU SEE," said Ben, "to make a movie it's like you have to put together a team, and everybody has to pull in the same direction. It's an engineering job, a movie. It's like as if you want to build the Empire State Building or the Golden Gate Bridge. Everybody has to follow the plan and the pattern. If you got one man who's not doing what he's supposed to, it leads right away to trouble. That picture of theirs—it was a tragedy, not a movie. It ruined their marriage, it killed Gable, it lost its whole investment. And the reason? No discipline. No accepting the responsibility of what it is to be a star. The great ones, so many of them I've been in business with. They were always like partners. I'll never forget one of them. Carole Lombard. When she was in a picture, she used to come to the studio *every day* when it was shooting. Even on the days when she wasn't called. When she didn't have a single shot to make, she would drive in all the way from the Encino valley, where she lived on a ranch, and she would turn up in the morning. She would sit on the set. She would watch. She would go to the hairdressing department, she would watch the rushes. I once asked her why she did that. 'Because I'm in the picture,' she said to me. 'I'm in the picture even when I'm not in it.' But that was some girl. And there have been others, too. Many. Not so many now. Now a kid makes one hit, he wants to be his own producer, his own director, writer, cameraman. He wants to make his own raw stock film in his cellar. What is it? Power. They don't see that the greatest power is to use their talent to the fullest? To the potential? . . . And what's all this now with the dope and the grass and cocaine? What can be a bigger high than a hit? And they think it's all so new and modern and daring. Jesus! They never heard of Wallace Reid or Alma Rubens or Mabel Normand or—oh, what the hell! Where was I? Oh, yes—Marilyn. It was something tragic. She was a star before she became an actress. She was a wife before she became a woman, and she was dead before she had a chance to grow up. Even so, she stays in my memory. She's a part of my life. I think of Johnny Hyde and his enthusiasm and his belief in her. His faith. Maybe if he would have stayed alive, maybe if he would've been around to keep her in line, to advise her in the right way, maybe it all could have turned out different. Who knows? She would maybe be alive today. But that's what they call the luck of the game, I suppose. And it's still, by the way, a great game—one of the best. Keep that in your mind."

"You've certainly taught me *that,* Ben, if nothing else."

"Let me tell you something. At the peak of our business here, we were making seven hundred and fifty—eight hundred features a year. Think of it! Now they say, Oh, well, Hollywood is shot. They only make two hundred and fifty—three hundred features a year. But what they forget, what they don't know is the *footage.* That's where they go wrong. We are shooting here more film by the foot than ever before in the whole history of the place, and I was here from the beginning. Right now, today, more footage. All right, so some of it is for tele*vision.* So what's the difference? It's still the movie business and it'll still be a movie business if you show the pictures in theatres or by cassettes or televised or if you sell them in supermarkets, in A & P's wrapped up in cellophane. Maybe they'll be selling movies by the pound someday! What's the difference? It's still movies! It's still the movie business. It's still dreams in a can. That's what we've been selling here all these years, and that's what we'll go on selling. So don't you let that Adani get any idea he's coming in here to bail anybody out. If he buys in here, he's buying into one of the greatest businesses in the world. The most exciting. The most thrilling. The most different every day. You'll see. We're running a picture tonight. I hear it's a masterpiece. I hear it could gross maybe a hundred million, a hundred and fifty million. Think of these numbers I'm saying. Why, at the top of our business in the old days—even what they call the Golden Days—a big picture went out, did four, five million. So you see how things are changing. . . . What was I saying?"

"I don't know," said Guy.

"Sure you do. You were sitting right there. I went off rambling. We were talking about somebody." He closed his eyes tightly. "Somebody beautiful and good; somebody I love very much." He opened his eyes and demanded crossly, "Who *was* it?"

"Marilyn Monroe," suggested Guy.

Ben relaxed and said softly, "Yes. Yes, that's it. Marilyn." Then, picking up the thread of memory, he said, "I'll never forget toward the end . . ."

His chauffeur drove him out to Marilyn's home. He found her in bed, her face a smear of makeup and tears.

"Johnny!" she cried. "—I mean, *Ben!*"

He came over and sat beside her on the bedside. She wept bitterly.

"What is it?" he asked.

"I can't say it—I can't say the words."

"Go ahead."

"I thought it could never happen, not to me. It never happened to me in my *whole life!* Even when I was starting, even when I was *lousy* it never happened."

"What happened?"

"They . . . they . . . fired me?" She softened the blow by turning it into a question.

"Why?" asked Ben.

"I don't know. Nothing was smooth but I didn't think—"

"Did you miss days?"

"Yes."

"Did you come late a lot?"

"Yes."

"Did you know your part?"

"Yes."

"*Did* you?"

"No."

"Then why are you surprised?"

"They could've gotten mad. They could've yelled. I'd've changed. But they *fired* me, and they didn't say it was because of late or being sick and all. They said what they were getting on the screen was no good. Could that be?"

"It could be."

"I'm going to get my lawyers," said Marilyn. "I'm going to *sue*

426

them! I'm going to make them show me the stuff. I want to see it. I want to see *myself* how no good I am. I did everything they told me to do. . . . Ben, what am I going to do now? What can I do?"

Ben stood up and looked down at her. "You can change, Marilyn, and that's what you should do. If you don't, then there's no hope. Everybody can change if they want to. The main thing is, you have to want to."

"I do," she sobbed. "I'm going to. I'm either going to change or I'm going to die."

"Don't die," he said. "Change. It's much easier. Get well. Make yourself well. You're not healthy right now."

"Why not?"

"You don't *look* healthy—and look at this room. Everywhere I look. Pills! Pills and pills! Believe me, Marilyn, hardly anything that ever came out of a bottle was good for anybody." All at once he was angry. "And look at this goddam room. A few years ago that little writer . . . that little fat writer . . . what was his name? A friend of yours with glasses. Yes. Truman something. Truman *what?*"

"Capote. Truman Capote."

"That's it, Truman Capote. Remember what he said? He said he loved you because you were such a nice slob. That was the word he used, slob."

"I slapped his face for that," said Marilyn. "I slapped his face and poured a whole bottle of champagne on his dumb head."

"At that time, Marilyn, I'd have done the same thing. You *are* a slob. Look at this room you're living in. You've got resources. You can hire maids to keep things clean and orderly. Look how your clothes are thrown all over the place. Look at the dirty dishes—in a *bedroom!* What kind of a way is this for you to live? And that's what happens in the rest of your life and in the rest of your work. It starts here. It starts in your own bedroom. You're a slob here and you turn out to be a slob in the world."

She covered her ears with her hands and screamed, "Don't keep saying that *word! Stop* it!"

"I'll stop it," said Ben, "when you stop being a slob. I'll come and see you tomorrow."

He started out.

"*Don't* come see me tomorrow!" she screamed. "Don't *ever* come see me. I hate you! Who needs you? You were supposed to be my friend. You're just another goddam pest, hammering at me. Leave me *alone*."

They were words in the dead air. Ben was gone.

"I never saw her again after that," said Ben. "And a few weeks later, she was dead. Did she kill herself? I don't think so. That wasn't her way. Probably a mistake. She wanted to block things out. She wanted to sleep. But she couldn't. So she did what a lot of people do. She took a sleeping pill—and who knows what happened then? Maybe a glass of champagne. Maybe she forgets she's taken sleeping pills, so she takes another one, maybe two because the first one didn't work. Who knows? Who was there except her and her devils? What are you asking *me* for?"

"I didn't ask you, Ben," said Guy.

"You didn't? I thought you did. I thought you asked me. Lots of people ask me. For years they ask me. How should I know? I wasn't there. But I can't believe Marilyn killed herself. She knew she was in a business full of ups and downs. One minute you're a star, the next minute you're a has-been, and all of a sudden you're a star again. It's happened over and over. I've seen it. She must have known she could still make it. She could still make it fine. It was an accident. And listen. One thing I can't stand. That's when I hear some of the highbrows talking about it and they say, 'Oh yes. Hollywood killed her. Hollywood ruined her. It was all Hollywood's fault.' That's a lot of poppycock. How is it Hollywood *doesn't* kill so many people? . . . No, it was just a case of bad luck, mismanagement. She met the wrong people, she got bad advice. Look at me. Look at my luck. I met the right people and got good advice. Where would I be if not for Fred Barovick and Sennett? Even *Edison* when he helped me. And Griffith—he didn't even *like* me and he helped me. And if not for Buster Keaton and Arbuckle—who knows? And what about Pempy? Pempy. I did everything wrong to her and she paid me back by doing everything right for me. That was *my* luck. And finally—Willa. Imagine it—a woman like that stayed with me for over forty years."

"It isn't all luck, Ben."

"It's a lot. But I look back on the whole thing. My life. It's like a long, long movie. Long, long. Too long. What I would like to do with it would be to put the whole thing on a Moviola and cut it; and cut it down to some sensible size. There's so much I would like to take out, and a few things I'd like to put in. Except I don't think there's time anymore now for any retakes. No—a few big cuts and let's send it to the lab. Don't you think so? Anyhow, I had a good time. No complaints. And I'm finished with it. So the next couple days . . . you'll start getting together with my people and with Willa—she'll speak for me and . . . We were talking about somebody. God damn it! Gone *again!* Wait a second, don't tell me. Please. *Tell* me. No, *don't!* I got it. Her. Marilyn." He smiled. "You know, somebody was talking against her not long ago. Who was it? When? Doesn't matter. Somebody said, 'All the dumb blondes like that. There're dozens every year in show business. Dozens just like her.' Well, in a way he was right. Sure. Every year, dozens just like her. Blonde and beautiful and sexy and a little dumb, or if they're not dumb, they play dumb because it makes them a little more attractive. Dozens, sure. Maybe hundreds. Maybe thousands. And Marilyn was exactly like the rest of them, except for one little difference. That's all. *One little difference.*"

"And what was that?" asked Guy.

"What was that?" Ben repeated. "She was *wonderful!* That was the difference."

PART VIII

COMING ATTRACTIONS

I

In Room D, the smallest of the projection rooms at the Farber Studios, *Flesh and the Devil* was flickering to a close. The soft hum of the projector added to the dreamlike quality of the event.

Beth was leaning forward in her seat, bound to the shadows before her.

Tony occupied the next seat but one. Earlier, he had taken her hand, only to be told, "Later!" Unaccustomed to rejection, he had moved away. Beth did not notice.

On the screen, Garbo was racing across the frozen lake to the island where the boyhood friends were about to engage in a duel to the death.

"Oh, my God!" moaned Beth.

Crack! The ice gave way and such was the magic of the silents that the noise was deafening. Beth's hands flew to cover her ears. Garbo fell through the ice and into the swirling, fatal waters.

Beth was on her feet. She took a step toward the screen, inadvertently—her fist in her mouth. She remained fixed in this position until the end title faded on and off.

She sat down. The lights came on.

"Terrific," said Tony, who had been asleep for about ten minutes.

"That it?" asked the projectionist on the intercom.

"No," said Beth. "Would you run the last reel once more, please?"

"Sure thing. Be a minute. I gotta rewind."

"All right."

Beth moved to Tony, sat in his lap and kissed him. He feigned impassiveness, but not for long. They slid to the floor and exchanged excitement until the lights went out and the final reel of *Flesh and the Devil* came on again. They sat up and watched it from the floor, providing a pantomimic subplot of their own.

At length, Garbo drowned again, Beth wept again, the film ended.

"That it?" asked the projectionist.

"Thank you, Red," said Beth.

"Terrific flick," said Tony.

"The *feeling*," said Beth. "Jesus! That's what you don't see much of in the new stuff—feeling. Everything's clever and talented and smartness and slick—but where's the *feeling*?"

"C'mere and I'll show you."

"I mean it, Tony. Take TV. I'll bet you could sit all day in front of the tube and not get *ten seconds* of feeling."

"I don't know. There's a deodorant commercial gets me every time—*right here.*"

"And aside from that—did you notice something else? The photography? Good God, that picture's fifty years old—more— and the photography's every bit as good as what we're doing now —maybe *better!*"

"Not better than Lucy's. Have you seen the stuff from last Saturday night?"

"Beautiful. Exciting. But it's a different kind. This is mood stuff. Hers is—what's the word?—impressionistic. That's it."

"Let's go, O.K.?"

"Sure."

They walked slowly and circuitously to Tony's car, all around the lot, in and out of the cavernous, echoing sound stages. The studio and its invisible patina of astonishing achievement and faraway memories held an ever-growing fascination for Beth, one that invariably communicated itself to whoever happened to be her companion.

"God Almighty," she said. "The talent that lived here and worked here! I can smell it!"

"No kiddin'? What does talent smell like?"

"Lubitsch made pictures right here—right where we're standing. Gary Cooper. Marlene Dietrich. Jean Harlow. Jimmy Cagney. Spencer Tracy. Hepburn. Gods and Goddesses."

"I'm hungry," said Tony.

"I've got cold cuts up at my place," said Beth. "What've you?"

"No, no, the kind of hungry *I* am, let's hit The Palm or The Diner or—"

"O.K. Whichever."

"Whichever's nearer."

They headed in the direction of the Executive Building, where they had left the car. All at once, Tony found himself walking alone. He stopped, looked back, and saw Beth standing, transfixed, looking up. He joined her.

"What's up?" he asked.

She put a silencing hand on his arm and spoke softly. "Something odd," she said.

"Where?"

"B.J.'s office. The light's on and the blinds are down."

"Cleaning women," said Tony. "Come on."

"No," she said. "His cleaning women work six to eight A.M."

"How do you know?"

"I know because I know," she said. "Never at night—because there's often been work up there at night. That's the routine—six to eight—it's always been, as long as I can remember."

"Want me to call Security?"

"No. Come on."

"Where?"

"Stick with me."

"You sure, Beth? I don't think it's anything—but if it *is* anything—"

She had disappeared into the surrounding shadows. Tony followed her. She made her way up the fire escape of an adjoining building and tried to see into B.J.'s offices. No luck. She climbed down and went up the fire escape of the Executive Building, motioning Tony to stay below. The drawn venetian blinds blocked her view, but by putting her eyes directly on the half inch between the blinds and the sill she was able to peer in.

She saw Jack Heller and smiled with relief. Nothing. B.J.'s sec-

435

retary working late. So what? But wait. Why behind drawn blinds? Why not? She watched as he carefully sorted through a sheaf of papers on B.J.'s desk. She watched him as he made his way to the outer office and beyond. Changing her position, she saw him in B.J.'s private mail room running the IBM copier. What sort of night work was this?

She took off her shoes, climbed down, and found Tony. Imploring silence, she led him away.

In the car, Beth said, "Listen, Tony. Have you ever tailed anyone?"

"Do I look like Bogart?" he asked.

"Cut it out, Tony. This is important."

"Do me a favor, huh? If you want to play Beth Farber, Girl Detective—get yourself another Sancho Panza. Like I told you, I'm hungry."

Beth began to cry. "Please," she said, "help me. I've got a feeling something terrible's going on!"

"All right, then, God damn it! Call Security. Or the police. Or somebody! Don't be such a fucking *take*-charge."

She stopped crying as abruptly as she had begun and said, "Don't disappoint me, Tony! I need your help. Security, police—that's hopeless. Whatever's going on, we don't want to *stop* it—we want to *understand* it."

"Who's *we*?"

"We is me," she said, then suddenly: "*Down!*"

She ducked down and pulled Tony out of sight. Three minutes went by before a car nearby started and drove off. As it did, Beth sat up, punched Tony's shoulder, and said, "Let's go!"

"Christ Almighty," said Tony. "I'm mixed up with a fruitcake!"

"There he is!" said Beth as they left the lot. "That white Mercedes. Thank God for white! Not too close. I'll watch him. Try to keep at least one car between us and him."

"Okay, Chief," said Tony. "And what do we do when the guy riding shotgun starts firing?"

"Left," she said, "*left!* He's turning left. Oh, shit!"

"Don't talk like that, Beth. It's unbecoming." He giggled.

"Sorry—but, oh God. I hope not the freeway. That'll make it harder."

"And dangerous, baby. I'm no Mario Andretti, y'know."

"Damn!" she said.

"Freeway?"

"Freeway," she said.

"You can say shit *now* if you want to," he said.

They trailed the white Mercedes past five exits. At the sixth, a van moved off, following it. They followed the van.

"Luck," said Beth.

A right turn. The van hesitated. The light changed to red.

"Go!" shouted Beth. "Go!"

"I can't."

"Back up! Pass!"

Panicked, Tony threw his station wagon into reverse, and backed with a crash into the tiny Volkswagen behind him.

The evening ended in a morass of two cars and police officers and accident reports and insurance papers. It was well after midnight before they were on their way again.

"Palm?" asked Beth. "Or Diner?"

"Nothing," Tony replied. "I'll take you home. I'm not hungry."

"I am."

"So you've got cold cuts."

No more was said, not even good night.

II

AFTER A night of deeply troubled sleep, Beth decided to take Willa into her confidence.

They went out to Trancas and walked on the beach while Beth related in careful detail the events of the previous night.

Willa was confounded. "What on earth do you suppose it can be? What's the worst?"

"Blackmail?" suggested Beth.

"Oh, no, dear! Ben's way beyond that—what on earth could he have to hide? That he's keeping in his office, I mean."

"I don't know."

They walked in silence for a long time, perplexed. Finally Willa said, "I think it's time the professionals took over."

437

They went back to the house. Willa moved straight to the telephone and picked it up.

"Wait," said Beth. "Who are you calling?"

"Matty. Our lawyer."

"Don't. Please."

"Why on earth not?"

"Grandma, listen, the worst about a situation like this is that you don't know who you can trust."

"But Matty, dear, is—"

"I don't care!" Beth shouted. "Before today wouldn't you have trusted Jack?"

Willa thought for a moment and said, "Implicitly," and put down the phone.

Beth referred to the Yellow Pages, found three investigative agencies and phoned them.

She and Willa paid a call on each of the three and finally decided on one—the largest and the oldest: Kelly Security.

One of their men was put to work on the night crew at the Farber Studios and three days later was able to report that Jack Heller made regular trips from B.J.'s office to bungalow 12 at the Beverly Hills Hotel. Bungalow 12 was at present occupied by a Mr. Guy Barrere.

"I'm shocked," said Willa, "but not surprised."

"Are we going to tell Grandpa?" asked Beth.

"What do you think?"

"Yes."

III

To THEIR astonishment, Ben laughed. "Say, listen," he said, "it's the way of the day, a sign of the times. Crookery and lying and bugging telephones. In the highest places even, so it becomes the fashion. Everybody says I ain't up-to-date, but *now* I am, wouldn't you say?"

"Never mind all that, Ben," said Willa. "What are you going to do about it? I mean after you get rid of that damned rascal—"

"What do you mean, get rid of? What's the sense of that?"

"But surely you're not going to keep him?"

"Not only keep him," said Ben, "but use him. What's the matter with you?"

Four nights later, Guy, looking aimlessly through the newest material that had just been delivered by Jack, suddenly rose and asked, "What the hell is this?"

"Is what?"

"This cable. You haven't read it?"

"No," said Jack. "I don't stop to read the stuff. I try to make time."

Guy handed him the copy of a cable from London. It read:

UNDERSTAND YOU ARE NEGOTIATING SALE OF FARBER FILMS TO
OMNI STOP BELIEVE I CAN OFFER INFINITELY BETTER DEAL AND
ONE WHICH WILL GUARANTEE CONTINUITY BY MEANS OF MERGER
WITH MY SUPERLATIVE ORGANIZATION STOP PLEASE PHONE ME
TO DISCUSS POSSIBILITY EARLY CONFERENCE HERE OR THERE
STOP SHALOM

LORD GRADE
LONDON
TELEX 23762

"Holy Christ!" said Jack.

"When did that goddam thing arrive?"

"Tonight. Six, seven."

"You mean he hasn't seen it?"

"I guess not. Not yet."

"You *guess*, you asshole! Get your dumb ass back there and bring me the original, God damn it—and fast!"

Jack disappeared as though he were part of a magician's act.

For the first time, the detective from Kelly Security had difficulty following him and barely kept him in sight as he returned to the studio and an hour later back to Bungalow 12.

IV

THE NEXT morning in Ben's office, Guy took a hard line.

"I think we've Ping-Ponged this thing long enough, B.J. Adani's men are all out here and we're ready to close. So how about you?"

"Me, too," said Ben. "I'm ready, too."

"Good."

"But not at the old figure."

"No? What's the new figure?"

"Double," said Ben.

Guy was speechless, thrown, nonplussed. Finally he said, "What?"

"Double," Ben repeated. "By double I mean twice as much."

Guy stared at him. "You really have gone up the wall, haven't you?"

"Yes," said Ben, smiling. "But in a nice way."

Guy rose. "Well, you know where to reach us when you come to your senses."

"Goodbye, Mr. Barrere. It's been very interesting knowing you."

They exchanged a long, suspicious look.

Guy left.

Ben was sure he would hear from him or from Adani in a day or two—but when a full week passed in silence, he began to grow restive. He would wait one more day—two?—and then contact Adani directly.

Three days passed. Call? No, he would hang on. His vast experience in negotiation told him that he was engaged in a delicate, desperate waiting game.

A buzz. Would that be it?

"Yes?"

"Beth," said Jack.

"Send her in."

A moment later, Beth, flushed and excited, came into the office. She went to Ben at once and kissed him.

"We're all set, Grandpa."

"What?"

"Our date. The screening." He looked blank. "God! Don't tell me you forgot! I told you. Today's the day. It's the most important thing in my whole life!"

He looked at her and saw Alice. What was she so mad about? Of course, he had forgotten their date. Why hadn't someone told him, reminded him? He hated it when Alice got mad. Beth.

"Tell me again," he said. "Please."

"The movie! *I* put it all together. The whole package—the whole *picture*. We thought we could bring it in but—well, you know—trouble, weather, and we went over."

"What is it?"

"*Disco*—that's the name of it and it's only super great! It's like six different stories all going on at the same time—some funny, some sad. And then night after night these people—the ones in the stories—there they are at the disco and they express themselves in the way they dance and behave. It's—I can't describe it but—"

"You're doing very well, my darling. *Very* well."

"—but you've got to *see* it!"

"All right. When?"

"Right *now!*"

"What do you mean right now?"

"Our *date!* This was it! Today! They're all here—waiting—in your projection room."

"Who?"

Beth took a deep, tense breath and said, "The director, and the two writers, and the camerawoman—"

"Camera*woman?*" asked Ben, amazed.

Beth laughed. "Come on! You look as if I just said 'camera*flea*'!"

The young filmmakers rose as Ben came into the room. Beth introduced them without delay.

"This is Benjamin J. Farber," she said, unable to keep the pride out of her voice. "Aram Zinesian, the director . . ."

"I'm honored, Mr. Farber."

Ben nodded as they shook hands. What a grip, he thought.

"And the writers—Nancy Goodman and Tim Connor."

"You're too pretty to be a writer," said Ben to Nancy. Then, to Tim: "But *you're* not!"

Laughter cracked the tension in the room.

441

"And finally, our wonderful cinematographer, Lucy Olson."

A happily overweight young woman came forward.

"My grandfather worked for you for a long time, Mr. Farber," she said.

Ben looked at her and said, "Olson. Olson. Richie Olson, the property man?"

"Yes."

"The best. Thank God you don't look like him! How is he?"

"He's dead," said Lucy.

"I'm sorry to hear it," said Ben. "Good property men are hard to find. Well, shall we begin?"

"Yes," said Beth.

They all took seats, with the exception of Beth, who said to Aram, "Do you want to do the introduction or shall I?"

"I'll do it," said Aram, as he got up.

"What introduction?" asked Ben.

"Just a sort of orientation," Beth explained. "This is unfinished, you know."

"Yes, I know," said Ben. "I also know that a picture has to speak for itself. If you have to explain it—it's already no good."

"He's right," said Aram.

"He is *not*," said Beth. "Come on, now. Let's not blow this. It could be our last chance. *I'll* do it."

"Sit down, Beth," said Ben.

He buzzed the projectionist and the room dimmed to darkness.

The work print was rough from too many screenings, and in some parts badly scratched from its countless trips through the Moviola. No matter. The vitality of the work was unmistakable.

As Ben watched the unusual, original camerawork, he was aware of the fact that the film had been shot entirely on natural locations in San Francisco and probably with available light. The way we used to do it, he thought.

Now, strangely superimposed, he began to see flashes of scenes from the films he had worked on in the early days, also on real locations, and with no light other than what was there. Black and white. An odd effect as it blended with the color.

What was happening to his eyes, to his head? Crazily intercut with the remarkable film he was seeing, came sudden shots of Mabel Normand and Buster Keaton and Willa Love and Fatty Arbuckle. San Francisco. As it is, and as it was, commingled crazily.

442

He closed his eyes tight, shook his head, opened his eyes and forced his attention back onto the half-finished *Disco*.

His heart was pounding. He was in the present: color, sound. He was in the past: black and white, silent. He was young again, young in every way. *Disco* returned. The heightened eroticism of the dance scenes began to affect him. The undulating, desirable, and desiring girls moved invitingly, sensuously. He became aware of a throbbing erection in his middle. On the screen, he saw Sennett and Griffith; then, in a crazy Slavko Vorkapich-like montage, clips of key scenes from his own past: Pempy, Tessa, his sons, Leonora, Garbo, John Gilbert. A huge, smiling, triumphant close-up of Hareem Adani. *Disco* again. A spectacular traveling shot. Then a "Scene Missing" slug. Dancers. "Scene Missing." A wild, spinning shot. Black. Another slug: "End Titles to Come."

The film spluttered out. The lights in the projection room came on. Everyone looked at Ben. His eyes were still fixed on the empty screen.

After what seemed to Beth too long a time, Ben rose and started out of the room. He was gone. The group exchanged worried, confused looks. What was going on?

"Beth?" asked Aram.

"What?"

"What do you think?"

She exploded. "How the fuck do *I* know what I think? And what's the *difference* what I think? Why don't you all just ?"

Ben returned.

"Don't go away," he said. "None of you. Beth—"

"Yes?"

"You come with me. Now."

She followed him down the hall, aware that something momentous was happening.

But what? He was walking differently, his posture had undergone a dramatic change.

He paused in his outer office and spoke to Jack.

"Get me Mr. Adani on the phone."

"Yes, sir."

"Right away."

"Yes, sir."

"And monitor the call, please."

Inside his office, Ben looked about, seeing it for the first and

443

last time. He went to his desk and sat in the thronelike chair. He motioned Beth into the visitor's chair.

"It's my San Francisco package," she said slowly and patiently. "Don't you remember?"

"No. And don't use that word."

"What word?"

"Package," he said. "I don't like it. A package is a parcel post, not the motion picture business."

"O.K., O.K.," she said placatingly. "Motion picture. Film. Fillum. Cinema. Flick. These kids of mine—they're halfway through a classic."

"A half can't be a classic," said Ben glumly.

She proceeded as though she had not heard him. "But they're stuck—for dough. Hell, they only need maybe three hundred and fifty, four hundred thousand to finish. Put it up, Grandpa, and I'll get you the distribution and everything."

He smiled. It irritated her. "What's so funny?"

"Nothing, nothing. You sound like *I* used to sound. But what's it all about?"

"I *told* you all this. I swear."

"And *I* don't remember. *I* swear."

"So what about it?"

"They've got no completion bond?"

"No."

"Then they're in trouble."

"I know I am. What about it, Grandpa—*Disco?*"

"Yes," he said. "Whatever you want."

Beth gulped. "Really?"

"Really. It's a splendid piece of work. Just see that the last part doesn't let down."

"Oh, my God!" She got up and started out.

"No, no," said Ben. "Not yet. I'm not finished. There's more."

"Like what?"

Jack Heller's voice: "Mr. Adani on three."

"Thank you." He clicked on the Speakerphone and said, "Here I am."

Adani's voice: "Good."

"What do you mean, good?"

"I mean I'm glad to see we're back in business. You an' me."

"What makes you think that?"

"Well—you called me, didn't you?"

"Yes, I did."

"Well—what about?" asked Adani uncertainly.

"To tell you," said Ben, in a strong, clear voice, "that there is no deal! And that there will *be* no deal."

A pause. Then, Adani: "I think, mister, all the time I spent . . . you got no right . . . I mean—what the hell? Why? Hey!" he said heartily. "How's about one more meeting? What do you say?"

"Not even a *half* of one more meeting," said Ben wildly. "Listen, can you hear me good? We got a good connection?"

"Sure."

"All right, then, listen. Farber Films is going to *stay* Farber Films! For as long as I live. And even after. What do you know about *that?*"

The responding sound was a hollow laugh, then Adani said, "I think it's going to go right down the toilet, Mr. Farber."

"It *was!*" said Ben. "It *was* going. But no more."

"What gives you that idea, you old man?"

"Read the papers the next few days," said Ben. "And oh, yes. By the way. Take your stinking Goddamn little spy out of here. He's in the way."

As Ben continued, Beth went to the connecting door and opened it. Jack Heller was already gone. His extension phone dangled from its stand.

"It was interesting meeting you, Mr. Adani. But what is a mystery to me is how such an intelligent, creative man can be such a no-good crooked bastard."

"It's easy, you old fart. Easy. When you're soon dead, *then* I buy you."

"No way!" shouted Beth into the Speakerphone. "No way!" She clicked off.

Ben got out of his chair slowly, and with great ceremony. His eyes moistened as he looked across the room and said, "Come, Beth. Come." He pointed to the chair. *"You sit here now."*

Beth, in a daze, followed his direction. She moved to his great chair. He took her shoulders and sat her into it, gently, firmly, permanently.

"What's happening?" she whispered.

He kissed her, in the way of movie kisses from the beginning of

445

movies. He became all the leading men; she, all the leading ladies; and together, all the happy (at least temporarily) endings.

"Fade out," he said. "The End."

He kissed her again.

V

Two DAYS later, I was back in New York. Three days later, Adani fired me. Four days later, I was on my way back to California. Why? I had no idea and was too exhausted to attempt to figure it out. Let the wind blow.

The news of Benjamin J. Farber's death six weeks later was not on the Six O'Clock News, but did make the Eleven O'Clock. (Is *that* what brought me back out here?)

I phoned Willa at once and she asked me to come over. Beth was there, in her nightclothes. Gilbert was on the phone to Leonora in Milan. Betty Shapian, the head of Farber Films' Public Relations Department, was in Ben's study with three secretaries: phoning, wiring, and cabling.

Food was being served, and wine.

Ernst was on his way down from San Francisco.

Abner had not yet been located. His housekeeper thought he might be in Acapulco but was not certain.

Willa sat serenely through the impossible hours, with dignity and nobility. She had never been—to me—more beautiful.

I did what little I could do to help and left at about 6:15 A.M.

I drove back to The Beverly Hills Hotel slowly, thinking clearly for the first time in months.

I have decided that after an appropriate interval, I am going to ask Willa to marry me. I have reason to believe that she will accept. I love her—and the memory of Ben.

And then? Well, what I would like best of all is a job in the new administration of Farber Films, Inc. I am willing to take *any* job. The point is, I would like to learn the business.

446